ANNA MAXTED is the author of the international bestsellers *Getting Over It, Running in Heels, Behaving Like Adults,* and the novel *Being Committed.* She lives in London with her husband, author Phil Robinson, and their children.

Praise for *A Tale of Two Sisters*

"Lovely." —*Jane*

"Anna Maxted has always succeeded in writing thoughtfully on assorted knotty issues without ever losing her sense of humor."
—*Daily Mail*

"Maxted finds unexpected depths."
—*Entertainment Weekly*

"An incredibly moving story of terrific loss, acceptance, betrayal, and reconciliation."
—*Austin Chronicle*

"Maxted hits a home run with another delicious story about relationships. If you have a sister, you'll want to share this book with her."
—*Library Journal*

"This is a hilarious, funny tale, which also manages to be wonderfully touching."
—*OK!* Magazine

"With good humor [and] genuine emotion . . . Maxted amiably delivers."
—*Kirkus Reviews*

Select Praise for Anna Maxted

"Maxted smoothly meshes life's grim realities with youthful optimism and determination. Entertaining . . . Marvelous."
—*Chicago Sun-Times* on *Behaving Like Adults*

"A deft, on-target balance act of humor and heart."
—*Entertainment Weekly* on *Getting Over It*

"Charming, intelligent, and often hilarious."
—*The Washington Post Book World* on *Running in Heels*

ANNA MAXTED

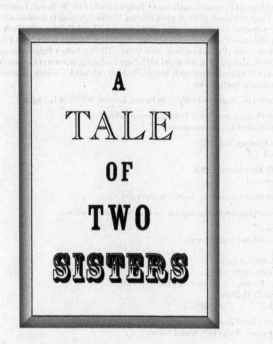

A
TALE
OF
TWO
SISTERS

A PLUME BOOK

PLUME
Published by Penguin Group
Penguin Group (USA) Inc., 375 Hudson Street, New York, New York 10014, U.S.A. • Penguin
Group (Canada), 90 Eglinton Avenue East, Suite 700, Toronto, Ontario, Canada M4P 2Y3
(a division of Pearson Penguin Canada Inc.) • Penguin Books Ltd., 80 Strand, London WC2R 0RL,
England. • Penguin Ireland, 25 St. Stephen's Green, Dublin 2, Ireland (a division of Penguin
Books Ltd.) • Penguin Group (Australia), 250 Camberwell Road, Camberwell, Victoria 3124,
Australia (a division of Pearson Australia Group Pty. Ltd.) • Penguin Books India Pvt. Ltd.,
11 Community Centre, Panchsheel Park, New Delhi – 110 017, India • Penguin Group (NZ),
67 Apollo Drive, Mairangi Bay, Auckland 1311, New Zealand (a division of Pearson New
Zealand Ltd.) • Penguin Books (South Africa) (Pty.) Ltd., 24 Sturdee Avenue, Rosebank,
Johannesburg 2196, South Africa

Penguin Books Ltd., Registered Offices: 80 Strand, London WC2R 0RL, England

Published by Plume, a member of Penguin Group (USA) Inc.
Previously published in a Dutton edition.

First Plume Printing, May 2007
10 9 8 7 6 5 4 3 2

Ⓟ REGISTERED TRADEMARK—MARCA REGISTRADA

The Library of Congress has catalogued the Dutton edition as follows:

Maxted, Anna.
A tale of two sisters / Anna Maxted.
    p.   cm.
ISBN 0-525-94973-9 (hc.)
ISBN 978-0-452-28851-5 (pbk.)
    1. Sisters—Fiction. 2. Spouses—Fiction.   I. Title.
PR6063 .A8665T35 2006
823'.914—dc22   2006015123

Printed in the United States of America
Original hardcover design by Leonard Telesca

To Mary Maxted, with love

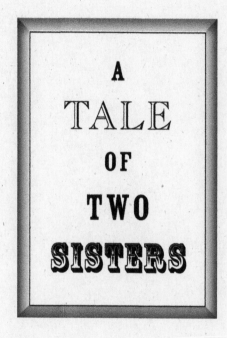

A TALE OF TWO SISTERS

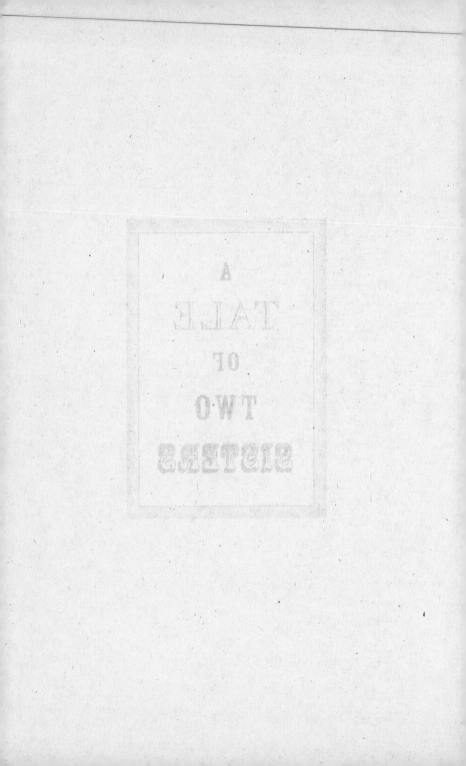

A
TALE
OF
TWO
SISTERS

CHAPTER 1

Lizbet

When my sister left her jungle villa after two weeks at the Datai, on the tropical island of Langkawi, she wrote a little note for the manager.

> Dear Sir,
>   Nearly everything was perfect. However, I think one of the monkeys has a cough.
>
>   Sincerely,
>   Ms. Cassandra Montgomery

When she returned home a fortnight later (she and George had gone on to stay at the Regent, in Chiang Mai), a thick cream envelope was waiting on the mat. Cassie tore it open.

> Dear Ms. Montgomery,
>   I am delighted that you and your husband enjoyed your stay.

*Thank you for pointing out that one of the monkeys has a cough.
We have informed our vet.*

Sincerely . . .

When Tim and I left our bed and breakfast accommodation on the Isle of Wight, I wrote a little note to the owners.

Dear Martyn and Tanya,

Sorry to leave early without saying good-bye. I hope the Garlic Festival was fun. It's just that the rain and the viral gastroenteritis have reduced our previously great wealth of activities to watching daytime television and hanging over your khaki green toilet bowl. Also, Tomas's cold is getting worse—he claims that the "horrid smell"—the pleasant Forest Blast air freshener!—makes his head hurt. And, it's quite hard to cater for an irate two-year-old's extraordinary dietary demands when you don't have a kitchen.

Best,

Elizabeth M.

I never got a reply, which made me feel less guilty when Tim confessed that *his* parting message had been to piss against their wall.

The holiday might have been less of a strain were we not looking after our godson while his parents were in Japan for a funeral. We weren't bad, as godparents go, so I thought. Most people are pleased at the honor, counting it as evidence of what fine human beings they are. Their conceit wanes as fast as it takes for the child to open its mouth and say "WAAAH." Then they realize: This isn't a compliment, it's a contract. Your friends croak, the kid's yours. Even if they do manage to stay alive, the constant outlay on gifts is on a financial par with keeping a string of racehorses.

Though it was tempting, I didn't think that Jeremy and Tabitha had asked us because we were fabulous. Tim immediately suspected that they didn't have any gay friends. I also felt it was because they presumed that we were too childish ourselves to have children. I'd never *said*, but people assume. If you ever dared to inquire, you'd be appalled at the poor impression you make on even your closest acquaintances. "Oh!"—on seeing your ramshackle cutlery collection mainly assembled from airlines—"I'd have thought you'd have everything in matching silver!"

Tabitha and Jeremy lived next door, and from the day we moved in and Tabitha knocked with champagne, they were determined to love us. I'm not complaining. It was only a problem in that I felt anxious about living up to their kind expectations. The house was a deal tidier than it would have been, thanks to Tabitha's habit of popping in for a coffee most days. (I'd had to ban Nescafé Instant from the premises after a near fistfight, "Oh, I'll just have the cheap stuff, Elizabeth!"—"Absolutely not, I'll make filter!"—"No! I won't hear of it! Please don't go to any trouble!"—"Tabitha, I insist, don't you dare, give me that jar," etc!—"Well, if you feel that strongly!")

Tabitha had been there when Tim's German aunt had invited herself round to show off quite the plainest baby I'd ever seen. "Hah!" she'd said, as I tried to resist the hypnotic lure of her enormous bosom. "Elizabett is getting broody!"

I had met Tim's German aunt twice, and the assumption I'd made of *her* was that she could never understand why another person might oppose her opinion.

"No, I'm not!" I heard myself say in a loud, cross voice. "I'm not getting broody at all!" Then, so as not to appear petulant, I added, "I like babies. They're very . . . small. I just don't want one, *personally*."

Tim's German aunt pulled the baby closer, and zoned me out of her eyeline. Tabitha darted me a sharp look, and purred, "All babies are beautiful, aren't they? And what a nice size. Is he feeding well?"

I hurried into the kitchen to make a great big *cafetière* of Italian coffee with every last scrap of caffeine processed out of it, which I hoped would please everyone.

I felt like a wet cat for a long time afterward. Till at least ten forty-five. I didn't like having to defend myself for what wasn't even a *decision*, yet. I was thirty at the time, and it didn't seem that long ago that I'd had to defend myself, aged fifteen, to Aunt Edith for not having a boyfriend. Not content with assuming that you were prim about cutlery, people assumed that you wanted children and were jealous of theirs. And commented openly! I couldn't decide which was ruder.

I had caught Tabitha's sharp look, and wondered what it meant. Six months later, when she and Jeremy invited us round for dinner, Tabitha grown to the fine shape of a ripening squash, it *sort of* made sense.

"We'd love to be godparents! What a lovely, lovely, er, thing!" I croaked, before Tim said something inappropriate, like "It's still half-fish; aren't you supposed to wait till it's born?" I loved Tim with all my heart, but in social situations he trod a fine line. Dinner parties were rare these days, what with everyone around us procreating, but when we were invited out, I'd spend the night with my hand hovering over his—less because we couldn't bear not to be touching than because the arrangement enabled me to gently suffocate any faux pas at its inception.

(Now I sound like a Tory wife, but the last time the pleasure of our company was requested, Tim announced to a rather smug guest who had moved to St. Albans—a small town half an hour from civilization—"If I moved to St. Albans, I'd feel like I'd failed.")

St. Albans was a sore point. Tim was a designer. He'd designed a TV remote holder, a dartboard, an ergonomic footrest, all of which, despite painstaking computer-enhanced imagery, failed to sell to a manufacturer. Then, three years back, he'd designed a potty in the shape of a train. I have no idea why, as he had no knowledge of young children, beyond that gathered incidentally in supermarkets. He then borrowed thirty thousand pounds to pay for an injection mold. (The TRAINing Seat™ required a "particularly complex mold," said the guy from Plastik Magnifik.) The prototype was featured in *Best for Baby* magazine, billed as "The Pot They Actually Want to Sit On!" This secured Tim a meeting with Woolworths, which led to an order for five thousand Trains. (And when Tim mentioned his vision for a pink Fairy Throne, they went for that too.)

While Woolworths wasn't the Conran Shop in style or kudos, it *was* a national chain, and Tim and I felt queasy with the promise of endless wealth. We all know that money doesn't buy happiness, but it buys lots of other nice things, which go a long way to compensate. He secured himself an agent, who brokered the deal—which was impressive enough to get Tim featured in the *Times* business section. The headline: *Sitting Pretty, The Potty Prince*.

This did little, as you might imagine, for Tim's credibility or, indeed, his popularity. (Only his mother, who bought twenty copies of the paper, couldn't find fault.) But not only had reports of his wealth been greatly exaggerated—tax, agent fees, etc.—eighteen months later, barely long enough for the royalties to kick in, a rival store released a blue potty in the shape of a *racing car* (what dastardly genius, etc?). And—woe upon woe—a pink potty in the shape of a princess's pony.

It was a bit bloody inconvenient, to tell the truth, as we'd taken the agent at his word—"This is new house money!"—and moved next door to Jeremy and Tabitha. It was also a trifle annoying in that all who knew us were convinced we were millionaires, and not for any glamorous reason either. (Though, *were* we millionaires, I think, in time, with intensive electroshock therapy, we might have come to terms with the stinky-bottom foundations of our fantastic jet-setting multi-mansion lifestyle.)

My point is that—after finally opening our last bank statement—Tim and I had made the drive of shame to St. Albans. Tim was entirely disagreeable about the whole exercise.

"Where *is* this place?" he said, as we tried to get out of it. And then, "It's, like, *nowhere*." And, finally, "It feels like *death*." And, soon after, "The people are *different* outside London." And, as we sped down the motorway, "I'd be spending all my time wanting to escape from it." And, as we approached our road, "We're *bigger* than St. Albans." And, as we pulled into our drive, "I'd rather move to *Australia*."

This excursion wasn't mentioned to Tabitha and Jeremy—who were forever having work done on their beauteous house and, we feared, had little affinity with poor people. Particularly poor people who were godparents to their firstborn. I exaggerate. Not that my job as assistant to the deputy editor at *Ladz Mag* was pulling in a hefty wage, but if you can afford to donate seventy-eight pounds a month to a health club, just to help it along with its profits, when you haven't set foot in the place for seven months, because you can't bear the fat girl finality of canceling your membership, you're not, strictly speaking, poor.

We weren't, however, able to afford our lifestyle. Our neighbors were doctors and lawyers and bankers—people with serious jobs and serious pay packets. Tim and I had no business living alongside them—all we did was prat about with words and potties!

Hence the decision to spend this year's summer holiday in England. We booked late, which reduced our choices to the Isle of Wight. Everyone reacted like we were off to French Polynesia. Wonderful ... marvelous ... amazing beaches. It never occurred that these people were the same liars who'd assured me that I looked great in culottes. Then Tabitha came round, with sad news of the demise of a university colleague's father. They *had* to attend the funeral, in Tokyo. No point going all that way and staying less than a week. They were between nannies. (Tabitha went through nannies like a tractor through muck.) Would we mind Tomas? I hadn't understood at first. Would we mind him doing what?

Then I got it.

"Would it be okay to take him to the Isle of Wight?"

Tabitha looked confused. I don't think she really believed in money worries; she must have thought I was being ironic.

"Of *course*!"

So Tomas came with us to the Isle of Wight. His luggage alone was worthy of Ivana Trump. The list of instructions on his welfare, daily routine, habits, likes, dislikes, favored topics of conversation, preferred pastimes, allergies was as long as the New Testament. It was unfortunate that Tim left it in our hallway. It was also unfortunate that even before we left London, Tomas found and ate an unidentified object off the floor that he would only describe as "blue."

Prior to the "holiday," I had considered myself to have a fine relationship with my godson. I babysat at least twice a month, and Tomas loved coming to our house, primarily to play with the cat litter ("sand!"). We had conversations *easily* as advanced as the ones I had with Tim. I mentioned to Tomas, for instance, that in four months' time, his mother was going to have a baby.

His response: "I hit baby, with stick. I sit on his head. I push him. I smack his bot."

My response to his response: "Oh! Really? I'm sure you wouldn't. I'm sure you're very gentle with babies."

His response: "I wear pink dress."

En route to the Isle of Wight, our relationship deteriorated. I was frantic about his consumption of the blue object. Tim refused to be alarmed, but this was just laziness. Actually, no ill effects from the blue object ever presented. Except that Tomas, despite being dressed like a lunar explorer, caught a cold. And Tim and I found that, even with a three-decade advantage, wit-wise, we were no match for a two-year-old. There was no organic food on the Isle of Wight, only chips. Tabitha had said, "He won't eat junk. He *loves* avocado."

Not on our watch. The kid ate Cocoa Pops for breakfast, a jam sandwich (white bread) for lunch, chips or pizza for dinner. Offer anything nutritious and he'd scream until his lips turned blue. He *made* us play his Bob the Builder video ("No more than twenty minutes of Bob a day") at least four times, morning and afternoon. He refused to go to bed till midnight. If it weren't that he got up at six thirty—"I awake now!"—you'd have thought he was a teenager.

We might have coped, were it not for the viral gastroenteritis (which bypassed Tomas, but zeroed in on the runts of the litter, Tim and me, with ferocity). And did I mention the flies in our living room? And our cold bedroom. And the mean weather. And the fact that no restaurant opened until seven ("Tomas eats dinner at five thirty, certainly no later"). We got to the beach once, where Tomas fell in the sea three times in ten minutes, soaking every item of clothing I'd packed for him.

After three days of retching in a green bathroom, and little sleep—less thanks to Tomas than Tabitha, who phoned on the hour (we lied a lot)—we admitted defeat, and left early. Two days later, we handed an only slightly snot-nosed Tomas back to his rightful owners, and crawled into bed to recover. We were no longer those naïve optimists who'd set off so carefree only five days before. Now we knew. That we would never holiday in England again. That we were not happy being poor. That we were *awful*, absolutely, *awful* with children—they didn't like us, we didn't like them, and please God let Jeremy and Tabitha live forever.

I discovered I was pregnant two weeks later.

CHAPTER 2

I told Tim I was pregnant and he replied, "No you're not."

"No, I am," I said, and showed him the stick.

"Do another one."

"I have."

"Fuck," he said.

"We must have."

I'd had a bad feeling when I'd cried at an advert in which a small boy knocks on a door and presents a box of inferior candy to an old woman. I think she gave him his ball back instead of spearing it on the end of her stick. I considered myself intelligent, but I was as easily turned as a doorknob. Pry open my soul, and you'd be splatted with a sticky green gloop of materialism and gullibility. I'd see a product on the screen—say, Corn Flakes ("Have you forgotten how good they taste?")—and think, Have I? Maybe I have. Better check, and send Tim to the grocery store to buy a packet. But the weeping was suspect.

I felt sick, and it was nothing to do with hormones. I was an idiot, a disappointment to myself, and there's no worse feeling. I didn't like babies. They frightened me. It was like a fear of spiders, except rational. At the magazine company, women swelled up routinely, disappeared for three months, returned in triumph as if from a heroic venture, portly figure half-deflated, bearing a small screeching bundle, and everyone would crowd round—as if there was something *new* to see, when truly, all babies look alike and are thus given wrist tags in hospital. I'd hover at the back, a tight smile on my face, hoping I wouldn't be forced to touch.

I didn't *want* one.

It was my sister's fault. Cassie. She was five years younger. I remembered trudging up the hill with the Canadian nanny, Cassie roaring away in her stroller.

"I don't want babies," I said to the Canadian nanny. "I prefer dogs."

The nanny—she had hair that frizzed at the tiniest speck of moisture and so hated England—replied, "*Well*. All the other ladies will be pushing their babies in prams, and *you'll* have a dog on a lead."

Fine by me.

Cassie bit. You could muzzle a dog. She also required endless entertaining. There was no peace. It was like living with Henry VIII—a voracious eater, short-tempered, easily bored, scarily powerful. I became her substitute caregiver after the Canadian nanny was sacked by our mother for shutting Cassie in the walk-in larder while she watched episodes of *The Professionals* on the video cassette recorder. (We were the first family I knew to own a VCR. It was battleship gray and the size of a suitcase.) Cassie passed her time in the larder roaring, and eating raisins that gave her severe diarrhea.

The diarrhea, in which an alarming number of unchewed

raisins were clearly visible, plus a neighbor's casual remark to our mother, "I always hear her screaming," raised our mother's suspicions. She crept home early from the office, and caught the nanny in flagrante with Bodie and Doyle. Our mother was physically sick at the thought of Cassie being mistreated, but there was no question of her giving up work. She adored work. She was editor of a magazine entitled *Mother & Home*.

Dad was a concierge in a central London hotel—he liked his job, would have left it for us, but didn't. I think he knew our mother would not have been comfortable with a house husband. Was there even a word for it then? So Kristina, the Danish au pair, was employed. Blond and beautiful, within days of her arrival she was snapped up by an Englishman with a sports car. Despite the zircon engagement ring, she remained in our house. She treated Cassie like a prize doll. I noticed that our mother was irritable around Kristina—who had a vague dreaminess and a smug aura—but she couldn't fault her child care. I saw Kristina as a goddess. Our mother was glamorous, in a brittle way, but Kristina was *exotic*, even in track pants. Our mother murmured the word *dumpy*, but I didn't understand it, any more than I understood the box of individual white-paper-wrapped tubes in Kristina's bedroom drawer. ("Are they *cigarettes*?")

Every day Kristina would collect me from school, present me with a Curly Wurly or a Flake, and talk to me as if I were an adult. Her boyfriend was a businessman. He had a house in Scotland. They'd marry in Denmark. She would wear a "massive" dress like a princess. In return for these jewels of knowledge, I'd play with Cassie in the playroom while Kristina sat on the pink carpet and watched, a faraway look on her fairy-tale face. I didn't *like* Cassie; I just wanted to be near Kristina.

Cassie and I developed a relationship similar to that of two prisoners sharing a cell. Cassie was probably the drugs baron; I was the dodgy accountant. I devised a series of games that bored me comatose but enthralled Cassie. For instance, "Magic Chick." I'd hurl Cassie's toy chick across the room like a cricket ball. Da na, Chick had disappeared. I'd order Cassie to close her eyes and decide whether Chick should appear from the ceiling or the floor. Depending on Cassie's choice, Chick would drop on her head or nudge her bottom. It was a compliment, I feel, to my powers of deception and authority, that Cassie continued to believe in Magic Chick a good three years after she'd publicly scorned our mother for referring to Father Christmas and snubbed our dad for alluding to the Tooth Fairy.

Long after Kristina moved in with her Porsche-driving prince, I remained Cassie's chief of staff, ents. Without liking a single minute of it, I performed one-woman plays alongside a cast of bears, told long, rambling tales about favorite toys, recreated *Dallas* inside Cassie's Pippa dollhouse, read from her big fat Walt Disney book—"Snow White," I recall was my favorite, as I'd force Cassie to stare at the picture of the wicked witch with a wart on her nose until she cried. I also invented a game called the Bravery Test, which entailed Cassie sitting on hot radiators for as long as she could bear (max points for max pain).

I had no illusion that having a child was fun. I'd discovered the truth aged five. Kids ruined your life. And at least back then I'd had the benefit of backup. Our parents were not a constant presence, but they did their bit. Rather like our cat, Sphinx, who daily offered Tim and me withered leaves harboring insects, or, if she was feeling flush, a frog, our parents were always bringing home small gifts that they hoped might appeal.

Our father was given a surfeit of flamenco dancer dolls—the hotel had a lot of Spanish guests—and Cassie built up a fine collection of gorgeous swirling ladies in scarlet lace, holding black fans up to their coy faces. He also received many key rings, and it became legend (it wasn't true) that I was obsessed with amassing these rather dull objects I had no need of. Our mother bought me a corkboard with a picture of a bee on it and a box of colored pins which, hobby-wise, sealed my fate. Aged twelve, I was the mortified owner of a hundred and thirty-two key rings—one of which was the shape of a fried egg—and no keys.

Vivica and Dad weren't intuitive parents, but they did pay the electricity bills and the mortgage and provide food. Every weekend, we ate at the Harvester. Our father liked it, because you could refill your plate at the salad bar unto infinity. (Now I think about it, while you *could* refill your plate at the salad bar unto infinity, I'm not sure you were *meant* to.) Our mother sat there with a pinchy face, picking at a bowl of warm cottage cheese. Cassie and I ate fish nuggets—soon-to-be-eclipsed precursor of the poultry version—and chips.

It wasn't haute cuisine but it was better than dining on anything our mother had prepared. She was a dreadful cook. She tried, but every dish tasted foul. Even her porridge had lumps in it, when all she had to do was add milk and *stir*. Also, she rarely bothered to read labels, which meant she frequently added turmeric to our oats instead of cinnamon.

She and our father flailed about when it came to what one does to entertain children. Over the course of years, Cassie and I were hauled around all the stately homes in Britain—armor, tapestries, moats, the same every time—and on Sundays I'd humor our father by helping him to wash his Volvo. It would take an hour, turn my hands chapped and raw, and—as our water source was always a bucket not a hose—the car would remain dirty. Meanwhile, Cassie would be trapped in the kitchen helping our mother make a disgusting cake.

One thing man and wife were agreed on: fresh air. We spent a lot of time out of the house while our parents remained inside it. There was a sandpit in our garden, full of orange sand, which every local fox and feline assumed was a litter tray, and Cassie and I passed many a winter afternoon crouched on our haunches at its edge (we didn't dare sit on the wooden corner seats because nests of spiders lurked beneath), cracking through its frost coating, scraping away purple worms and squirls of poo, digging through the orange sand to the brown mud underneath.

Our mother and father had a religious belief in itineraries. The Museum of Mankind, Whipsnade Zoo, the London Transport Museum—if Cassie and I had a fixed destination to stare at something hairy or engine-driven, they felt they had fulfilled their parental duty. Actually, Cassie and I preferred the unscheduled time we spent squashing red berries at the back of the house, or climbing over the white fence at our garden's end to the daisy- and buttercup-filled lawns of the mental home beyond. Their grass was better than ours, because no one ever cut it, and I could make daisy chains the length of my sister. We only saw a mental patient once. ("Look," said Cassie. "You've got that jumper.")

I'm not sure that our parents trusted the imagination. They felt safer if we were formally occupied. Twenty years ahead of every supermodel, my favorite pastime was knitting. Aunt Edith had started me off—I couldn't start or finish, I could only do the middle bit—with ten little balls of brightly colored wool. I embarked on the longest scarf in history. If you rolled it onto itself, it had the span of a wagon wheel. (Not the chocolate sort, a real one.) Aunt Edith gave me her cast-off wool, and I might have kept going forever, except that one day the scarf was donated to a children's home, and the next day, our mother announced that I was going to have tennis lessons.

We weren't a sporty family, although our mother was good at kaluki. It didn't help that my tennis racket weighed about as much as a Le Creuset frying pan. Cassie got out of tennis by breaking the neck of every tennis racket our parents bought her, on the same day. Hand her a Dunlop, she turned into a cat with a sparrow. It was swiftly decided that she was better suited to ballet. She wasn't. At one fairly desperate point—the Junior Arts and Crafts and Miss Prickett, the neighborhood piano teacher, were oversubscribed—our parents decided that I should learn Hebrew. (Prayer books are literally sacred in Judaism, and after the tennis rackets, I don't think they dared risk it with Cassie.)

I was sent to the local synogogue on Sunday mornings, where an ancient Polish woman with sparse hair forced us to read from the Torah. For the life of me, I couldn't master the Hebrew alphabet, nor did I engage with the subject matter, God, God, God. It never occurred to those in charge that a Hebrew translation of, say, *The Lion, the Witch, and the Wardrobe* might have more appeal to a gaggle of twelve-year-olds, and while in retrospect I admire the staunchness of their principles, I do feel they ultimately scored an own goal.

I spent those interminable three hours at Hebrew classes marveling at perspective—squinting, measuring between finger and thumb how tiny the blackboard duster appeared from where I was sitting (a centimeter, if that), when I knew for a fact it was the size of a brick. It made the minutes pass and invoked the wrath of the old crone, who screeched at me, "All you do ees peck peck peck!"—here, she mimicked the shape of my finger and thumb, like a bird's beak, opening and shutting.

Funnily enough, it was Cassie who came to my rescue. She

agreed to consider pony riding, but only if I came too. The stables' timetable clashed with the synogogue's, but so eager were our parents to please their younger daughter—or, indeed, to be guaranteed rid of her for a morning—that I was freed of that stale, airless classroom the same week. Instead, I spent my Sunday mornings shifting horseshit in an enclosed space, while our parents paid handsomely for the privilege.

I didn't blame our mother and father for not understanding us. I didn't understand *them*. But I knew from experience that parenthood was a thankless task, one long concerted effort to get your ungrateful offspring to leave you in peace. And my parents were lucky. God help you if you didn't have money to throw at the problem (which Tim and I didn't). Not that it was any use in my current predicament, but—despite the shaky start and a few mild radiator burns—one good thing had emerged from my less than perfect childhood.

Cassie and I were great friends.

CHAPTER 3

When I was younger, the fact that abortion existed was like the fact that our parents' car existed—it was available as a convenience should I require it. A few times I'd stared at a small white stick, until it deigned to reveal my future like a Roman emperor: thumb up, thumb down. "You can always get rid of it" were the words hammering in my terrified heart, as I waited for the thin blue line to appear. Back then, it was always an *it*. Fear made me callous; I couldn't think beyond myself.

But now I was in a settled relationship (I'd love to chance upon a description of a long-term love affair that doesn't weld slippers to the feet of those involved). I was also thirty-two. Not only were the policemen younger than me, the sports heroes, the singers, the actors, the artists were too—I had no excuse anymore. I had got to the point where you look back on the skittering trail of your life so far, and think, "Phew, bypassed *that* dilemma by the skin of my teeth."

Getting rid of it was no longer an option. Tim and I couldn't even consider it.

That said, nor could we think of what would happen in nine months' time. Tim *said* he was happy. He communicated this by spending all day out of the house. He'd return, eventually, shaky and pale.

After a week of this curious behavior, I decided to crash the party. The mystery was solved in minutes. We lived in a child-infested area, and everywhere Tim looked, fat fathers with thin hair and shocked expressions trudged along pushing buggies—their deportment was a disgrace (as Tim's mother might say), they were schlemiels (as my aunt Edith might say), and the clothes they wore! Did they even care that they were men? Saggy, baggy material shorts; shapeless, faded sweatshirts; white socks; unfashionable sneakers—clothes for a life that was one long treadmill.

Tim had been spending each day slumped in the window of Starbucks, downing cappuccinos in half pints and watching his own future—and it looked a lot different to dreams he'd pinned on his wall aged fourteen. There comes a day when a man realizes that he will never be asked to play for Man U, that he is never going to win a Grand Prix, or be a millionaire by the time he's thirty—and, sitting in Starbucks, aged thirty-one, that day had come for Tim, with a scythe and a black hood and unfashionable sneakers.

Meanwhile, *I* had thought vaguely of taking a small child to the ballet one day and everyone going "Ahhh!" but this was the first time I had thought of the real consequences—or rather, had the consequences paraded before me—and I had no sympathy. Had Tim seen the *women*? I thought of them as mothers-who-don't-give-a-shit. Now that I was forced to face reality, I recalled a prime example living on the corner of our street. She was forty years old. I knew this, because I'd heard her shouting it to Tabitha at seven o'clock one Saturday morning—"I'm forty today! Harold's making a barbecue! Do come! Bring John! And, er, Toby!"

She looked fifty and I never *ever* saw her wear anything but an old gray tracksuit. Maybe she'd iron it for the barbecue. She might have been pretty, but she never wore a scrap of makeup and her skin was dry and lined. Her black hair was streaked with gray, and it seemed like she never brushed it. What killed me was, she had a boy who must have been Tomas's age, and she only ever dressed *him* in an old navy tracksuit. "I Don't Care" might have been written on her forehead. I worried that she was setting up the kid to be bullied.

"We won't be able to do *this* anymore," said Tim, as we sat in our preferred local restaurant one Thursday night. He said it like he was joking, but I saw the naked fear. We won't be able to do *this* anymore. . . . He said it about fifty times a day. If we went to the cinema, "We won't be able to do *this* anymore."

"Good," I said, after sitting through a particularly vacuous film about five unpleasant teenagers who are murdered one by one in a wood by a monster. "I don't care about these people. They're nasty and they deserved to be eaten. I'm from a different generation."

"You know *why* every other film is about teenagers? Because everyone older is stuck at home with their *kids*."

This was undeniable. But as I pointed out, we happily lived in the age of the DVD, and if it emerged that he missed the cinema experience unbearably, I'd willingly shift an armchair to directly in front of the sofa, in order that Tim could enjoy the perimeters of each scene of our rented film around the silhouette of my head.

I shared his fear of change—of course I did. But there was a thrilling edge to my terror. Everyone makes such a *fuss* over pregnant women. I hadn't done anything that anyone had thought was worth making a fuss over. There was no "since" in that sentence.

I had pretended to myself that I could afford to see a private obstetrician. (I often did this. I had a builder in, giving me quotes to convert our garage into a study. I had a decorator in, giving me quotes to paint our hallway, landing, and two bedrooms. I ordered the *Elegant Resorts* brochures for Europe and the Caribbean. I ordered the new Audi catalog for Tim. I made inquiries as to what it might cost—should Tim ever ask me—to get married at Skibo Castle. [It cost Madonna £120,000 to book all forty-seven rooms. Not *bad*, considering.] We received many respectful letters from people hoping to take our money, and then we did precisely nothing, until they gave up and left us alone. But the interim was fun.)

I'd called the obstetrician's secretary. She had the same surname as he did, so I presumed she was his wife. "How far gone are you? Seven weeks? You've left it too late. He's all booked up," she said. Then she added, "But you never know. Someone might have a miscarriage."

I put the phone down on her and called my local doctor's office. I felt her bad taste and put a hand on my stomach before I realized. "I'm sorry," I murmured. "I hope you didn't hear that."

Then I ate a mango.

I became sullen with Tim, because I thought he was against us, even if he didn't realize it. Then one night he got a video out. Nothing remarkable. But there was one scene in which a gangster discovers his girlfriend is pregnant and beats her and she loses the baby. She runs away. Later, he goes through her stuff and finds two red sweaters she'd knitted. One is man-sized, and the other is so tiny. I tried not to cry but the tears ran down my cheeks. Then I looked at Tim and his eyes were as red as the sweaters.

He said, "I feel I've let him down already," and put his face in his hands and sobbed.

I pressed *pause*, put my arms around Tim, and kissed his hair. There was a muffled "Fucking St. Albans!"

"That's mad," I said. "It's love they want, I promise. It's their relationship with you."

He cheered up, and we managed a cute chat about a tiny person who looked like us.

But there was a cold, scared part of me that agreed with Tim. I wanted the best for this baby. It was not a "fetus" as the doctor had said, it was a baby, okay? I wanted this baby to have everything it needed. A BMX. A big house, *not* in St. Albans. Babies were like dogs. They needed space to run around. I didn't want this kid to be born and despise us for everything we couldn't give it.

I wanted to tell people. But—already, a whole new world—I learned that it was not etiquette to brag about your news until the baby was "twelve weeks." With a new sense of gravitas and self-importance, *we* decided to wait until sixteen weeks. We needed the extra quiet time to acclimatize.

I imagined Cassie's and my parents would be pleased—I know they generally were about that sort of thing, but you couldn't legislate for *our* mother and father. Vivica (I stopped calling her "Mummy" aged two) was more at ease with me, now that I was five foot seven and less likely to wipe my nose on her trousers. But I wasn't sure she'd look kindly on the daughter who booted her into grannyhood.

At least Cassie would be pleased. Curiously, she loved children. Part of it, perhaps, was that they loved her. I had read that babies were biased toward any face with even features. Fair enough—why should a kid like a monster peering into their cot? It's not as if this bias ever changes. Ugly people aren't exactly prized in our society. Cassie had the same effect on adults she had on children. Men and women wanted to please her. She could be charming, or rude, it made no difference.

She was on the phone to me recently, while in a cheese shop— "No, that's too big. Yes. That. No. I've changed my mind. That. Yes. What? I'm on the phone. I've got a twenty. That's it."—and all the while I can hear the cheese man—"That do you, love? No problem! Not to worry. There you go. Pop it in your bag, shall I?" The last time *I* had been in a deli, I'd wanted a precise measurement of crumbly white cheese for a recipe and the guy behind the counter had just about chased me out of the shop. I know now that ricotta is unmeasurable because it falls apart if you cut it.

I wouldn't say Cassie was beautiful. She has huge dark blue eyes and thick brown hair, and she is always tanned, with a fine bosom, which helps. But it wasn't just the way she looked. She's a barrister, who occasionally bangs off a feature on family law for the *Telegraph Weekend*—and while she *might* call herself a writer, it isn't as if she reviews anything.

And yet. She was always calling this or that press office and being given free tickets—to the theater, to premieres, to Wimbledon, to gigs. (I rarely got a free ticket and I worked on a bloody men's magazine!) She had a husky voice and no one could resist. It wasn't as if she needed the free stuff—she lived in a tall, tapering house in Primrose Hill with George, who worked in radio—she just liked getting it. She'd been upgraded seven times. Me? Never. I always ended up in economy class with some bozo knocking coffee over my best suit.

I'm not an eyesore, but I don't have her magic ingredient. My hair is what I call yuck brown, thin and flyaway, and my eyes are the exact same black as a squirrel's. (A squirrel's eyes are not his best feature. But at least a squirrel has a nice fluffy tail.) "Hey. You really look *nothing* like your sister," a boyfriend of Cassie had once said, when introduced. He'd then added, "Sorry."

I was used to it, by now. Her *allure*. Cassie must have been thirteen when Duran Duran kicked off, and I swear to God, she ended up in Simon Le Bon's kitchen, "interviewing" his mum for her school magazine. Meanwhile, the teenybopper no-hopers languished outside the gate. She'd always had a thing for Boris Becker (I couldn't see it myself), and—despite her checkered history with tennis rackets—got herself a job as a ball girl and had several chats with him just before he won Wimbledon. "He was quite taken with me," she'd said, and I had no doubt. Her every male boss nurtured an unrequited crush. Flirtation was her natural state, but she rarely took it further. Just knowing was enough. I wondered if George knew how lucky he was to be married to her.

Their life was ordered, busy. If you were a fly on the wall of Cassie's home (impossible, as you'd be squashed and dead before your filthy little legs soiled the paintwork), you wouldn't have thought that kids would be welcome here. The massive mother-of-pearl chandelier that hung imperious as a stalactite above the polished 1930s Italian dining table in their lounge, the white Japanese silk blinds that gently filtered the sunlight, the dark American walnut and leather "Astoria" chair and matching side table—allegedly the work of some guy called Franco Bizzozzero for some other guy called Bonacina Pierantonio—none of it suggested that brats were part of the grand plan.

But no. We'd meet to eat, and Cassie would talk about her friends' kids and how cute they were. Really, there was no need. She didn't have to. It wasn't like she had to impress me. It wasn't like this sort of talk *did* impress me. I could only conclude that the subject matter was of genuine interest to her. One conversation I recall. Some ex-bulimic didn't want to pass on any hang-ups to her little girl, so, explained Cassie, "She offers her fruit *and* chocolate on a tray, and some days Delilah picks the chocolate and some days Delilah picks the fruit."

Oh really. I'd seen children in the presence of chocolate, and fruit could take a running jump. It was Tomas's second birthday party. Tabitha had spoken at length with her therapist and the local vicar before commissioning Harrods to create a massive additive-ridden Bob the Builder cake, smeared in chocolate ganache, spattered in Smarties, a paean to the gods of sugar, caffeine, fat, and chemicals. She brought it into the conservatory, and it was like a scene out of *Lord of the Flies*. It was a good five minutes before Tabitha surfaced from a crazed swarm of toddlers cramming great chunks of blue cake into their mouths—I was surprised she didn't lose an arm.

But it wasn't mere talk. Cassie asked to hold babies—rogue babies who'd vomit in your face as soon as look at you—she had a two-hour conversation with Tim's German aunt about the complications of breastfeeding, and even when those rogue babies quietly deposited a great white gobbet of half-digested milk on the shoulder of her Karen Millen demin jacket, Cassie just wiped it off with a tissue and said, "It needed a wash." She didn't blink at changing diapers. (I had an inbuilt fear of human waste; I didn't even trust myself to *see* it. Tim had changed every one of Tomas's diapers on the Isle of Wight—how's that for a real man?).

My sister was going to make a fabulous aunt. She would *dote* on this baby. I felt happier, knowing that the child would have one competent close relative, a person who might actively ensure its survival. I bit my tongue until our self-imposed sixteen-week embargo was lifted. It had been hard—we'd wanted to call her the second we got home from the three-month scan, so dazed were we with the euphoria of witnessing our own private miracle. But we'd held out.

Now, however, the wriggler was sixteen weeks along and the size of a grapefruit. I picked up the phone to call the Montgomery-Hershlag household.

"Cass? Hi!"

"Hello, lovely! How *are* you? I'll pick you up at eight for dinner tomorrow, okay? I've booked St. John's. Oh, you *must* have heard of it! 'Nose to Tail Eating'? Pig's trotters, bull's testicles, belly of rat—it'll be a gastronomic adventure, you'll love it!"

I was having trouble keeping down water.

"Well . . . ," I said. "I'm still on for going out. But we might have to change the booking to something a little less fabulous . . . say, Pasta Bella."

"Lizbet. Don't be square! It's my treat, okay? Come *on*. You have to try these things. And don't tell me it's against your religion. I've seen you eat squid."

"Cass. It's not that. Blimey, what do you take me for?" (No one likes to be told they're not a rebel, even if they're not.)

"Why not then? Entrails aren't fattening." She was really selling it to me.

"We-e-e-ll, madam. I'll tell you exactly why not. Guess what?" I could feel the big dopey grin on my face. "I'm pregnant!"

I expected a shriek of joy. Or a gasp of delight. Or a scream of "Fantastic news!"

What I didn't expect was what I got. A few slow seconds of stunned silence. And a distinctly frosty "Oh."

CHAPTER 4

Tim liked Cassie. George was more an acquired taste—a human olive—but Tim liked George too. He'd made an effort with George, ever since they first came round to us for dinner and George perched on my extendable beech table from Habitat and broke it. It was quite a spectacular break—splintered wood, mangled metal, and George sprawled on our floor with his big toenail almost split in half. George was almost crying with pain and embarrassment (Cassie laughed but I don't think she meant it), and I didn't know *what* to say to make the situation better.

Tim said, in an admiring tone, "Not even Jackie Chan could break a table with his arse!"

And then we really did laugh—if more from relief than amusement. If he chose, Tim was good at making people feel comfortable, even if they didn't deserve to. I was a little peeved with George for sitting his arse on my table in the first place—what, did he leave his manners in a box?—and although Cassie wrote a check, I think she was a little peeved with him too. Cassie was charming, as I've said, but a lot of that charm depended on things going her way. She didn't react well to unscripted events.

However, one of the first things she said to Tim that evening was "You know, Lizbet's cheated on every boyfriend she's ever had," so it wasn't as if she didn't appreciate the glee of an awkward situation. The difference was, Cassie liked to *create* the awkward situation. Then she could bring it down, with the control and showmanship of a stunt plane pilot. At the time, though, I didn't feel in a position to appreciate how terribly clever she was. I froze where I stood, almost snapping the stem of my glass of red. I felt sick and silly and, staring into my drink, remembered the time Cassie invited me to dinner and (to show the other guests how close we sisters were) I casually placed my bottle of Syrah in the fridge. Cassie removed it, smiling. Her guests looked at their feet, not catching my eye. Really, it was like I'd put a *baby* in the fridge.

The cheating comment was only Cassie's way, throwing down the gauntlet to see if Tim would cope—and there was probably an element of flirting too. If you made bold, controversial statements, people noticed you. It was the verbal equivalent of a low-cut top.

Tim just laughed and said, "Oh, I'll tame her—*ker-cher*!" and cracked an invisible whip.

Cassie smiled and lit a cigarette. Out of fright, I ate a whole bowl of chili peanuts (even though they were disgusting: the precise reason I'd bought them—so there would be *no question whatsoever* of me being tempted to eat them). Tim went to check on the pasta, and I glared at Cassie. "Thanks for that," I said. At that moment I saw her as a cute toddler with the heart of a devil, her hair pulled into dinky little bunches (which she'd cut off, leaving stumps—I'd handed her the scissors).

"Come on, Lizbet, that man adores you, he worships your body with his eyes."

I pshawed (I've always wanted to say I did that, what a great word!), but already the anger was bursting to nothing, like bubbles in a bath, and I was grateful to her. Worships my body!

"No he doesn't," I mumbled, but she winked at me, and I blushed. Tim *did* adore me, and Cassie was just ensuring that this was the case.

I had felt a flutter of anxiety, just before they were due to meet. I'd built her up into an approximation of Angelina Jolie—surely the worst woman in the world to be your love rival (gorgeous but nuts, men can't resist that fatal combination)—because it was the only way to ensure that Tim would clap eyes on her and feel slight disappointment. I trusted *him*. I knew he was crazy about me. And I trusted her; she and George were a secure unit. Cassie only required men to display their admiration, like a peacock displaying his tail, then she was satisfied—she had no interest in any man who tried to take anything further. I didn't trust *myself*, my ability to keep a man like Tim.

I know that sounds weak. I mean, before "Jolene" was a way of bleaching your black mustache yellow, it was a song, and frankly, I despised the singer. Her happiness depended on Jolene! "Whatever you decide for me, Jolene!" So if Jolene decides to pinch her man, he's off! Plainly, the singer had no self-respect if she didn't dump this dithering fool immediately. What woman tolerates being second best?

I knew I wasn't second best for Tim (just as I knew that in real life, Jolene's flaming locks and eyes of emerald green stood no chance against the ace of spades that was Dolly Parton's chest), but it took some believing, because I'd been second best to my sister for most of my life. That shakes your faith in yourself. I'll bet Angelina didn't grow up with a Cassie. (In fact, I know she didn't; she has one brother, and they are *worryingly* close. I sometimes dismay myself with just how much I know about celebrities' lives. More than I know about my own.)

After they'd gone, I said, testing him, "I can't believe she said that, about me cheating on all my boyfriends!"

He replied, "I think that was more about me than about you. She's very protective of you. It's like *you're* the younger sister."

I loved Tim more than ever then, because he understood Cassie and me, he understood *us*. Cassie might present as mean as a snake, but in fact, she loved me in a fierce way. She just didn't like to appear soft.

So when she said, "Oh" about the baby, Tim was able to reassure me.

"It's the initial shock," he said. "Look at our reaction. *We* were shocked. She has to readjust her image of you. She *is* happy about it, but you're *her* sister, and she's possessive. Her gut reaction is 'This kid's going to steal my sister off me.' Give her time to work it all through. I promise you—she'll turn up tomorrow with booties."

She didn't.

The phone rang at 8:49. "I'm in the car."

Ah, yes. The Car. The black Mercedes CL65 two-door Auto bi-turbo Coupe that cost more than my first flat. (Apparently, George's mother winced every time she saw The Car—The *German Car*—although, as I'd begged Cassie not to point out, Mrs. Hershlag had no problem with her Bosch dishwasher, Neff stove, and Miele dryer.)

I ran outside, opened the door, and stuck my head inside. The Car smelled of new leather. Normally, I'd breathe it in deep, but today it made me feel slightly sick.

"Helloooo!" I said.

She sat there, on the cream upholstery, staring straight ahead. "Take off your shoes," she replied.

I didn't want to take off my shoes, but Cassie was fanatical about keeping The Car showroom-clean.

"All right if I bag them?" I said, my bum on the seat, my feet still midair.

She nodded, and I retrieved two Sainsbury's bags from my coat pocket (purloined for this exact purpose) and stuck my feet inside them. The arrangement wasn't exactly elegant, and the bags rustled every time I shifted position, but I really hated being out in my socks. You can't outrun a predator in socks. Actually, if I could, I'd sleep wearing shoes.

I sat back, grinning, waiting to be congratulated. I couldn't help it. From the second I saw that little kidney bean squirming around inside me, I'd become another person. I mean, *it* was another person—another person, for godsake! If that isn't a life-changing moment, tell me what is! I had this marvelous secret; I was never alone. I talked to the baby, silently, and aloud. She—I felt it was a she—heard everything, understood, and agreed with me.

"So, where are we going?" said Cassie.

I heard her dull, flat tone and it was as if a stone plummeted to the pit of my stomach. The whole family dreaded Cassie in a bad mood. Some people sulk and you breeze through it until they're bored into feeling sheepish and try to make friends again. But if Cassie decided on a silent fury, it was as if Siberia had slunk into the room and was whipping its chill winds around you. You felt cold fear. You didn't dare move or speak, and your heart thumped in your chest.

Not that evening, though.

Being stabbed feels just like a punch, apparently. You don't feel the knife going in; you just get a vague sense of the pain. You see the blood, and *then* you realize just how seriously you've been hurt. It took me a good few minutes to realize, "She's had time to think about the baby and she *isn't happy for me*."

I didn't feel cold fear, I felt confused, and then I felt another emotion altogether.

"Well," I said. "I can't eat anything spicy. Thai is out, because I'd want the pad thai and they put peanuts in it—I can't risk increasing the chances of the baby having a peanut allergy. And I can't eat meat, obviously, just in case it's not thoroughly cooked. Toxoplasmosis. We *could* go to Pizza Express, but I wouldn't be able to have the Fiorentina—I'm not allowed to eat soft-boiled egg—so that kind of defeats the object. I suppose I could have the quadro—the quarto—the four-cheese one. Although I'd have to ask them if all four cheeses were pasteurized."

I heard my voice, unfamiliar with its hard edge, and I thought, "Look at this, *me* being the difficult one for a change." Then I glanced at Cassie. Her face was like flint and a wave of cowardice swept over me. I'm brilliant at facing down the supermarket if a chicken's off, or haranguing Barclaycard if they've charged me twenty quid for a letter—but I'd rather cut off my own toe than pick a fight with my sister.

"Let's go to Pasta Bella," I said, in a chirpier tone.

We went, and it was like trying to make conversation with a Trappist monk. "I think I'll just have spaghetti with tomato sauce," I said. I considered adding, "Although, pasta is just flour and water, empty calories, as George once informed me. Ideally, I'd prefer a potato, you know, something nutritious for the baby."

But I had the curious feeling that if I did she might actually rise from her seat and hit me. So I didn't.

"What are you having?" I said.

She shrugged. "This really isn't my sort of thing."

"What," I said briskly. "*Pasta* isn't?" Wasn't that like saying "*Food* isn't my sort of thing"?

"Yes," she said, equally briskly. "Pasta isn't my sort of thing. It's just flour and water. Empty calories."

I stared at her. Maybe *she* was pregnant too! That would explain the huff. She did not like to share the limelight. (I once showed her a photo of these girls we'd been at school with, in the local paper. They were twins marrying twins, on the same day. Cassie had looked at the picture and said, "I really cannot think of anything worse than a double wedding. Thank Christ we're not Mormons.") I held my breath—was she going to announce it?

"What I actually feel like is . . ."

I leaned forward in my chair, with an encouraging smile.

"Cervella Alla Caprese."

"Oh. Oh, well, that sounds nice.

Cassie leaned forward in her chair and said, "Calves' brains."

"What!"

"Calves' brains in butter, capers, and garlic."

"I hate capers."

"Calves' brains—"

"Stop saying calves' brains," I whispered.

"Calves' brains are *real* food!" said Cassie, snapping the Pasta Bella menu shut and groping for her cigarettes. "Food that tastes interesting. Food for grown-ups. Some days you wake up, and you think, I'm in an offal mood."

"I agree, you're in a horrible mood, but why would that make you want to eat something revolting?"

Cassie gave me a death look.

"Poor little calf," I added. "It's only a *baby*. A poor little baby with rickety legs. You want to eat the brains of a poor little *baby*." I gulped. There was a lump in my throat, and if I didn't watch out, I was going to burst out crying in Pasta Bella.

Cassie took a drag on her cigarette and exhaled the smoke through clenched teeth. Flick to "Steaming with rage" in the illustrated dictionary, and there was my sister.

"Elizabeth," she said, taking my hand and squeezing it.

I smiled, uncertain. Maybe I was wrong. It was a loving gesture, except the cigarette was now bang in front of my face. I fanned the smoke with my free hand. She gave me a pitying look, and raised her forearm in a quick, sharp gesture so the cigarette was level with her left ear, and for a second I thought she was giving me a Nazi salute.

"Elizabeth," she said again. "You go through life being so *afraid*. You should extend your gastronomic experience. I've had chicken hearts cooked on a skewer in a Japanese restaurant, and I swear it was one of the best meals I've ever had."

I swallowed hard. "I—"

"But calves' brains are *divine*. Beefy tasting with a soft creamy texture . . ."

As I ran to the toilet to throw up my own innards, I could hear Cassie making her order, her voice as clear and pure as a church bell: "Yes, I *have* made a decision. The cheese and spinach tortellini, with tomato sauce. As long as it's not too spicy. It isn't, is it?"

CHAPTER 5

Everyone else, though, was lovely. Even the boys at work made a fuss.

"Ah, Baby, that's so sweet!" said my boss, Fletch, the deputy editor. "You clever girl! I'd *love* a baby! I'm *so* broody!"

"Really?" I said. Fletch was "dating" a porn star (C-list). His previous girlfriend was a lesbian. And the one before that, a very nice girl from the home counties. And her husband.

Toby, the editor, had his PA order me a bouquet of white roses. Toby was professionally charming. He didn't care one jot. All wit and warmth was activated in view of a higher purpose: management. I compared a chat with Toby to eating cheap sweets—nice with a nasty aftertaste. (Tim did a fine impression of what he imagined Toby was like in a features meeting: "I want ya to think of sports ya can do wearin' ya suit!")

Even the rest of the staff—a group of men who at some point every day converged on the light box to squint at a thousand pictures of naked breasts—dredged up shreds of memory from their long-discarded middle class upbringings and politely declared, "We *thought* your tits had grown!"

I accepted the compliment. I was one of three women in an office of twelve men, and sometimes you fought the urge to gun down the lot of them for the sake of civilization. It was the honesty made you wish you were deaf. They were brutal. Mariella, the fashion director, had, in error, slept with a freelance writer, Bill Marks, and the boys were so vile about it, no one was surprised when she fled to a job in the more refined surrounds of *Nutz*. As Fletch said, "It wasn't enough that she suffered the experience once; she had to relive it every day."

While as individuals they were delightful, as a group they were savages. As Toby schmoozed advertisers in expensive restaurants, his staff set each other's hair on fire, read porn in the toilets on company time, and relieved themselves down the back of Toby's suede sofa (he'd refused them pay raises). I did dream of suing for distress, discrimination, *everything*, and retiring to a five-bedroom villa in Sandy Lane, but I was fond of them. Once, a reader wrote in from jail complaining he'd spotted a pubic hair on the bikini line of a model, and they printed his letter and ridiculed it. "Women do have pubic hair, you mutt."

I felt grateful, which was, I suppose, wrong.

I saw my job as an education. I was like an early explorer, treading uncharted territories. As assistant to the deputy editor I arranged interviews with "stars." (One pouty little soap star bypassed her agent to insist that we pay her:

FLETCH: "How about we pay you what we paid Robert De Niro?"

HER: "Yes, okay."

FLETCH: "Great! I'll make out a check for zero pence!")

I also researched orgy etiquette, sports watches, interesting wounds, and strange facts. Toby urged us to "Think aspirational!"

although the back pages told a different story: *Combat Hair Loss, Fast Fone Fun!, Karen's Escorts* . . .

I frequently amused myself by watching the staff's breathless efforts to sleep with the models. As Fletch said, "If a model agrees to sleep with you—it's like God giving you a present!" And I spent a lot of time saying "No," when anyone but Fletch asked me to nip out for coffee, biscuits, or hemorrhoid cream. Now, of course, I had an effective weapon with which to discourage impertinent requests: gynecological detail. "I went for tests, and the speculum was . . . ," I'd begin, and they'd shrink away like slugs from salt. Those men could stare all day at vaginas on a porn site. Show them one in a medical textbook and they'd be gagging over the bin.

I learned that men will joke about anything—they live to offend, they see it as proof of masculinity (as opposed to stupidity). Once, hunters mounted moose heads as trophies. In our office, furious letters from Christian groups were pinned on the walls. My coworkers talked endlessly about how *tiny* their penises were (I think they preferred to mock themselves than be mocked). They were casually violent, yet dreadful at fighting. Even though they loved to throw things—balls, darts, computers—they couldn't throw a punch.

But what I liked about men? While they were dirty, lazy, shallow, spoiled, vain, selfish, rude, unreasonable, demanding, and piggish— I'm speaking of the intelligent ones here—if a bloke was angry with another bloke, there was no *mystery* about it.

The day after Cassie spent two hours in my company without congratulating me on the baby—even a mention would have been nice—I felt the frustration of someone who is being manipulated. If she was angry, why didn't she *say*?

Normally, I let the bad behaviors of relatives pass through me like ghosts. Unless you're from one of those dysfunctional families where the father steals the son's girlfriend and everyone's only slightly surprised, my attitude is: These people love you, and where there's love there's always a bit of hate. You accept the bad with the good.

I couldn't. It felt like a betrayal of the baby.

"Speak to her," said Tim, like it was the simplest thing.

I considered this option and rejected it. I didn't want to speak to her. I wanted to punish her.

I waited till Friday Night.

The Jewish Sabbath lasts from sunset to sunset, Friday to Saturday. "Work" is forbidden, although, interestingly, driving is considered work, so religious Jews walk everywhere. (Personally, I'd have it the other way round.) Traditionally, families attend synagogue, then return home for further prayers and the Friday Night meal. They light candles, break bread, drink wine. That said, every family has its own variation on tradition, and our family variation was to dispense with the religious bits and cut to the food.

"Shabbat shalom!" said my father with relief, after struggling through the Hebrew prayers for the sake of George's parents, who were more correct about these things.

"Shabbat shalom!" cried Tim's parents, who were also more correct about these things, despite being Church of England.

The whole scenario was my mother's worst nightmare, as she was expected to cook. Also, George's mother was a fabulous cook. (The poor woman—she loved to see you eat, and yet George was maintaining the charade of being vegan, an insult comparable to roasting a pig on a spit in the front room. Ever hopeful that it was a fad, his mother would prepare fish fried in matzo meal whenever he and Cassie visited. George would sniff the air, unzip his coolbag, and extract a jar of blackstrap molasses, a bottle of almond milk, a plastic bag of organic porridge oats, and a box of three dried apricots and seven raspberries, all of which he'd assemble into a meal and eat at the table, daring anyone to comment. Mrs. Hershlag would beg him at least to cook the oats. "Who eats raw porridge?" George would ignore her. I tried to see what Cassie saw in this man, but I just couldn't. He was clever, amusing, yes, but like the Joker, he didn't use his intellect for the greater good. Hey, even the lesser good would have been *something*. And Cassie became more abrasive in his presence.

Tim's mother wasn't such a direct threat, as whatever she thought of Vivica's cooking, she knew her place and was programmed to murmur, "This is wonderful, Vivica." I don't think our mother considered that the men might have an opinion on her food, but if they did, she didn't care to hear it. Year in, year out, our father never uttered a word—I think, on the principle, if you can't say anything nice, say nothing at all.

I thought I detected a small element of resentment in the way our mother crashed the soup bowls onto the table. However, the big element of resentment turned out to be contained in the soup itself, an enterprising mixture of vegetable soup and Campbell's Cream of Chicken.

I saw George's mother glance at George's father and put down her spoon. Our father stood up, and removed their bowls in a quick, quiet movement.

"Can I cut you some more *chhhallah*?" he said, sounding like radio static. He was really trying. Usually he pronounced it "holler." Actually, I lie. Usually he pronounced it "bread."

I squeezed my knees together in embarrassment. Even half-arsed Jews like us didn't tend to eat meat and dairy produce in the same meal. Even our parents' neighbor, Letty Jackson, who kept a kosher home but ate bacon sandwiches in her car (it was a Saab—I think she thought it neutral territory, like Sweden), drew the line at adding butter. For my mother to serve cream of chicken soup to the Hershlags—who, if not observant, were fairly traditional—she might as well have spat in their faces.

Normally, Cassie and I would have exchanged complicit glances: "Look what she's done now." That evening, we avoided eye contact. I willed our father to apologize. He never reprimanded Vivica; he knew it would be like starting a fight with America. I observed our mother, and saw that her thoughts were concentrated solely on her next cigarette. There was no trace of regret on her face, just a faint aura of irritation. She smoked Vogue Super Slim Menthol 100's, nasty thin cigarettes. When I first moved out, she gave me a box of linen she wanted to get rid of. As I pulled out a green and blue bedsheet, a Vogue stub fell to the floor, and I noticed a brown singe hole in the center of the material.

It was Cassie who spoke.

"Mummy."

Cassie went to Cambridge University (she studied law at Magdalene, I mean, she didn't just *go* there on a day trip), and we all noticed that her voice was a great deal smarter upon her return. Only posh people call their mother "Mummy" beyond the age of ten, and I think Cassie presumed we all knew this.

Our mother jumped and refocused.

"Ivan and Sheila can't eat this, Mummy. It's milk and meat." I noticed that she didn't bother to maintain the pretense that *we* couldn't eat it. I supposed the Hershlags already knew that we were Jews Lite. They did now. I held my breath for our mother's reaction. Cassie's tone held a frisson of annoyance, enough to suggest to our mother that it was just possible she might have made a huge, grotesque, and offensive error, but that everyone was prepared to be friendly and forgiving about it.

I didn't think our mother had done this on purpose. The mistake was a consequence of her complete disinterest in serving a Friday Night meal to relatives. She was egocentric. Other people bored her. Her internal narrative would be something like "It's boring, why can't *they* do it?" She was like a three-year-old in her inability to convincingly perform a task that she didn't enjoy. She was also like a three-year-old in her extreme and violent dislike of being told off.

Our mother's look of shock changed to one of displeasure. "It can't be," she said. "The tin says, 'cream *of* chicken.' It all comes from the chicken!"

"What—*cream*?" said George—a trifle rudely, I thought.

Yes, *his* parents had borne the brunt of the insult, but he was a hypocrite. Whenever George took Tim to the David Lloyd Club (George's way of trying to make Tim more Jewish—a Lloyd membership was pretty much the equivalent to converting), they'd play tennis for five minutes then George would beeline to the nearest McDonald's and order a hamburger with extra cheese. He practiced the Letty Jackson form of veganism.

"George, it doesn't matter!" said his mother.

"What are you talking about, it doesn't matter—it matters!" said Mr. Hershlag. He dabbed his face with his napkin. He was breathing heavily, and his *kippah*—"kipper" as our father would say—attached to his thinning hair with a girl's pink hairslide, had slipped and was flapping off the side of his head.

"I thought the soup was lovely," whispered Tim's mother.

"Yes, dear, but it was *traife*," said Tim's father. "Not kosher," he added, for my mother's benefit.

"I'll serve the main," said our mother, with a face like slate. She did. No one spoke. You could cut the tension with a knife (the same could not be said for the lentil bake, which had chunks of carrot in it the size of bolts). My heart began to race, and not in a good way. I cleared my throat. My announcement was no longer to punish Cassie. I didn't want to hurt her, I wanted to make things right. I grasped Tim's hand under the table.

"Hey," I said. "Would anyone here—er, except you, Mr. and Mrs. Hershlag—like to be grandparents?"

CHAPTER 6

All of a sudden, I knew how it felt to be David Hasselhoff (who, by his own admission, once brought a child out of a coma). I had no idea—luckily, or I'd have got pregnant aged fourteen. There was a sparkle in people's eyes when they looked at me. A reverence.

"Oh, Elizabeth!" said Tim's mother. "To have a *baby* in the family again!" and she held my hand with the lightest touch, as if it were the hand of God. Our mother leaped to her feet and cried, "I'm going to be a grandmother! Oh, what fun! I can take him to the opera! We can go to the Ritz for tea! He'll be my little friend! This is *so* exciting, and Ralph does *such* cute baby clothes!"

The baby's diary all worked out, I glanced at our father, and I saw with a jolt that he looked close to tears. He walked around the table, shook Tim's hand, and pecked me on the temple. Then he said into my hair, "Well done. Your mother and I are very proud."

The words rang in my ear. I'd never heard them before. I was also aware that our father was congratulating me for having had sex. I felt bad for the Hershlags—being left out—but they seemed as crazed with delight as the real grandparents.

"Maz-*al*tov," said Mr. Hershlag, blowing his nose. "This is wonderful news. Wonderful news! How are you feeling? Even if you're sick, you must eat! You gotta force yourself!"

"I knew it," said Mrs. Hershlag, smiling. "I knew it the minute I saw you! You looked different. There was this look about you, a *magnificence*. Now, my dear, you will be a mother until the day you die."

I nodded. There was a lump in my throat.

"Marvelous. Marvelous!" said Tim's father. "We thought we'd be waiting for years yet, didn't we, dear?" He beamed around the table. "So, Cassie. An auntie! Congratulations!"

"Thank you," said Cassie. She said it like her mouth was full of ash.

Everyone looked at her, each face aglow with joy.

She sipped her water, and said, with a little laugh, "When are you dropping this sprog then?"

"Where will you have the baby?" said George, the one person I knew who ever spoke over Cassie. "Will you go private? You should go to the St. John and St. Elizabeth. They let you do everything as naturally as possible. It's where Gwyneth Paltrow had Apple."

"She had what?" said Mr. Hershlag. "An apple? A woman gives birth—that's all they give her? What's the matter with them?"

Mrs. Hershlag put her hand on his arm. "*Apple!* It's the name of her daughter!"

"Why?" said Mr. Hershlag.

I giggled, and shook my head at Tim. He shook his head too, and smiled. He didn't say a word. I guessed that, for the moment, he couldn't, and I wasn't surprised. It was like stepping out of your house into a force ten gale.

"Hello, Baby," said Tim later, to my stomach. "Everyone's expecting you. You are a *very* important person."

"Yes," I said. "Everyone's expecting you except Cassie. Sorry you had to hear that, Baby. She's jealous because everyone's making a fuss of you, not her."

"Yeah," said Tim. "This baby's going to be born, and Cassie's going to regress. She'll start wetting the bed and asking to have her bedtime milk in a bottle!"

"Hah-HAR," I said, and tried not to mind.

"Hey," said Tim, and he winked at me. "It's a new idea. She'll get over it."

Because of Cassie, there was a small gray pebble of gloom amid the happiness. Still, I didn't obsess about it, as my head was filled with a thousand thoughts and opinions and recommendations that belonged to everyone else. Tabitha Next Door had given birth to Baby Celestia two weeks before, and was milk white with exhaustion. She was also sporting five scratches on her face, courtesy of Tomas, who was less than pleased with the interloper.

"You'll love being a mummy!" she cried, summoning a shred of energy to raise her voice. "And *one* is a piece of cake! Where will you go for your equipment? *We* went to the Baby List. So did Liz Hurley. But I don't recommend it. So pricey! I suggest you go to John Lewis; you can't go wrong with John Lewis. And what schools have you put him down for? Well, if you hurry you might just be in time. They'll squeeze him on the end of the waiting list. Ideally, he'd go to St. Michael's, but you need a letter from the pope, and also you're *just* out of the catchment area. It would be so much easier if schools had their own estate agents. You could try the Catholic school, but you'd have to become a regular churchgoer. I know you're Jewish, Elizabeth, but people will do anything for their kids. Shoshana Goldberg made her husband, David, get a 'JESUS' tattoo. They also claimed they'd attended St. Ethelrede's every Sunday for two years but 'sat at the back.' They're appealing. Oh, but I do know, there's a house for rent two doors along, you could always move in for six months. They could hardly refuse him a place then. You'd have to get *everything* changed, though—the address on your bank statements, everything. They will check. They'll knock on your door one morning at seven, to ensure you really *do* live there. Well, how far gone are you? Thirteen weeks? Oh, you've got a bit of time. I wouldn't trust the other local primary. Do you know they only have two computers in a class of over thirty children! And dreadful sports facilities. And they're *still* turning down kids left, right, and center. Yes, thirty mothers are fighting the council; they've been forced to send their children on a two-bus journey to a school in the next borough—did you see it on the news? There was a fatal stabbing in the infant class. The hamster bought it. But don't forget. John Lewis for the baby gear. I bit the bullet and bought a double buggy last week, but it was so *ugly* I couldn't bear to see it standing there in the hall. They took it back—*not* a problem, madam. They're not cheap, but you pay for the service. . . ."

Tim's mother disagreed. *She* thought Mothercare. I wasn't used to Tim's mother pressing her opinions on me. But, here she was, *telling* me, on the phone at 8:32 A.M. on a Sunday, what the baby needed.

"A Moses basket, on a stand, so the cat won't get him. And a car seat. Will you choose a cheap and cheerful car seat that you can carry indoors, or a sturdy well-made one that stays fixed? I wouldn't go for convenience over safety, that's the only thing. Are you going to change your car, love? The Renault Megane does well in all the safety tests. And you can't fault a Volvo. You can't take risks with a baby. All it takes is one careless driver. You don't get a second chance. Will you get a rain cover for the pram? What about a footmuff? The slightest chill—pneumonia! And a head hugger? You want Baby to be snug and secure in there, you don't want someone to be able to lean in and pinch him, there was that woman in the shopping center in Australia. What pram will you buy? The Bugaboo seems to be what everyone is going for these days. A newborn needs to lie flat, I think they worry about curvature of the spine. You'll need a changing bag. And a sterilizer. One whiff of dodgy bacteria in the bottle, you're looking at intensive care. But they're ever so clever these days, you can sterilize in the microwave. Will you be feeding with bottle or breast? Don't they say now that formula destroys the immune system, gives the baby asthma, and all sorts? Although if you choose breast and the milk doesn't come through, Lord, I've heard of newborns starving to death because the mother didn't realize. Best to buy bottles, and powdered milk in case. Although these days, they do ready-prepared milk in cartons, it's the cleverest thing! There are some beautiful cots on the market, I think you have to buy the mattress separately, and new—you don't want Baby to suffocate. It's the dust mites, they're *everywhere*. You'll need quite a few changes of sheets. And a changing unit, but *do* get one with sides; we can't have Baby rolling off and hitting his head on the floor, God forbid. A sling is nice—it's nice for the *man*, I think—and you don't always want to be carting the pram around. Although there was that poor, poor woman who tripped on a paving stone, her poor, dear baby—fractured skull. You'll have to buy a cat net. Or will you be getting rid of Sphinx? One scratch, and Baby's blinded, there's no going back. You'll need at least three cellular cot blankets, a fleece blanket, a waffle blanket, swaddling sheets—will you want to swaddle? It's *so* easy for Baby to overheat, they get a rash of little ones dying every time the temperature goes up, their poor delicate systems can't cope. They say that eighteen degrees is the perfect room temperature for a little one to sleep in, even as low as fifteen, but I mean, that's ridiculous! You might as well leave Baby in the garden! It's fashion, that's all it is! In *my* day, we kept our babies as warm as toast! Mind you, I say that, but in my mother's day, well, she'd leave Tim's poor uncle Rupert outside in the drizzle for hours, and when she remembered, shout at me to go and brush the rain off the pram's hood! You should get a digital room thermometer, though, just in case—you don't want to find Baby blue in the morning. And a baby alarm, one that monitors their heart rate. You can even install a little camera, I think Martin knows someone. Muslin squares, they're always vomiting—lay them on their side, heaven forbid they choke on their own vomit, it's always a worry. I'd invest in a V-shaped pillow, for nursing. A nursing chair, even. You have to be comfortable. A good bouncy chair is important, they spend a lot of time in their bouncy chairs. But always on the floor, yes? Or we're looking at brain damage. What do you feel about pacifiers? They *maintain* they're not a choking hazard. I'm not so sure. But of course you'll make up your own mind. You'll need nail scissors, an ear thermometer, a play mat, and a baby bath, and some soft towels, we don't want to irritate Baby's soft skin. Now if you need me to wash Baby's clothes, I'll be happy to do that. Oh, yes, you have to wash *everything*. It's the starch, and they are so sensitive. If Baby takes after Tim, he'll be covered head to foot in baby eczema, but don't worry, love, he'll grow out of it, poor little mite. But you'll need nonbiological detergent and no fabric softener. Baby will need booties. And vests, and Babygros, and scratch mitts, they have nails like razors, given half a chance they scratch themselves to bits, bless them! Bibs!—don't forget bibs—and hats, and you'll have to get the house safe for

Baby. Will you be getting an air purifier for Baby's bedroom? These pollutants do goodness knows what damage. Will you be phasing out the use of household cleaning products? They're full of cancer-causing chemicals, and lemon juice and vinegar is as effective, and at least you have peace of mind—God forbid Baby is poisoned by the atmosphere, they're so susceptible at that age. Or will Baby be sleeping in with you? Not in your bed, of course, you could roll over and crush him, here, let me pass you over to Martin. . . ."

"Hello, there, my dear, looking forward to the new arrival? I've blocked off the next five weekends to help you and Tim on the house. You'll want to strip off the wallpaper in the Little One's room before you repaint. As it happens I've looked on the Internet, and there's a nontoxic paint available. I'd give it a few extra coats, myself, because your average paint contains all this poisonous stuff for ease of application, so I'd imagine this *organic* stuff is a little thin. And you'll need to replaster here and there, it's inevitable if you strip a wall. And rip up the old carpet. And sand the floor. And varnish it. You'll need a stair gate for the basement door. And at the base of the stairs. And at the top. How do you feel about the steps at the front of the house? It's going to be tricky, maneuvering a stroller up and down those steps. It wouldn't take much to turn those steps into a ramp. It's no trouble to hire a cement mixer, I've already checked it out. . . ."

Eventually I put down the phone to see Tim standing in the doorway with a funny look on his face. "Hi!" he said.

"Hello!" cried my mother, popping out from behind him.

"Vivica's been shopping," added Tim. "She's brought round . . . stuff."

I stared at her. Vivica never came round unannounced.

"A few bits for my first grandchild!" said my mother. "We don't know if it's a boy or a girl yet, do we, so everything's in yellow!"

My mother started to rip open bag after bag, flapping tiny trousers and tops in my face until they became a blur. I was reminded of Gatsby, pulling shirts out of his wardrobe for Daisy. I picked up a doll-sized undershirt. It was the color of full-cream milk and there was a small red butterfly embroidered over the heart.

"Baby Dior!" said my mother. "You can't beat the French!"

I tried to imagine the little person who would fit inside it, but I couldn't. My mother departed seven minutes later for a hair appointment, leaving the kitchen in a cloud of tissue paper.

"Tim," I said. "This baby is going to cost us twenty thousand pounds before it's even born. We don't *have* that money. It's *all* essential," I added. "All of it." I paused. I could hear my voice, and it was high and hysterical. "There's the Symphony-in-Motion 3-D Developmental Mobile, for instance. It plays Mozart, Bach, and Beethoven. It's designed by a team of baby development experts, including psychologists and musicologists, it's based on the latest research into infant hearing and sight and the influence of classical music on infant mental and emotional development, and it costs forty quid, *forty quid,* one of a million items we *have* to buy, we have to, we need it, the baby needs it, and if we don't, the baby will be . . ."

"Retarded?" said Tim. "Christ! How do women in Africa manage?"

Happily for him, there was a ring at the door. I opened it to find a man dwarfed by a tall bouquet of deep red roses. I knew immediately that they were from my father, because I recognized them as Grand Prix roses. He *always* sent Grand Prix roses to my mother, because he said, "You should never send a woman any other rose." I supposed you couldn't work for a smart hotel for thirty years without some patina of romance (or snobbery) rubbing off on you.

"With love, Dad," said the note, in handwriting that wasn't his. I touched my fingers to the dark velvet petals and breathed in their heavy scent. It was fitting that he sent me red roses—the color of sex and death, the color of the blood that gushed from me when I miscarried my baby girl three days later.

CHAPTER 7

_____ *Cassie*

When Mummy and Daddy came into my bedroom the day I turned thirteen, I presumed it was to give me tickets for the a-ha concert. (I always provided a typed short list of acceptable gifts—unlike Lizbet, who expected our parents to know what she wanted, even though she had a roomful of junk as proof that they didn't. For *her* thirteenth birthday, Mummy bought her a tape, *Noel Edmonds' Prank Phone Calls,* and a china ornament of a collie dog. Daddy bought her jeans from Marks & Spencer and a key ring with a small fork hanging off it.)

Instead, they told me I was adopted.

It took a minute or two, to adjust.

I said, *"We're* adopted?"

"Not Lizbet," they said. "Just you, Cassie." I pursed my lips. And *then* they gave me the a-ha tickets.

"Six months after we had Lizbet, there were . . . complications," said Mummy. Suddenly, she looked as though she might cry. "It was . . . horrible."

I narrowed my eyes. There were tales in family lore of Mummy sitting on a rubber ring after Lizbet. But my mind was already soaring away from our semidetached house with its double glazing and crazy paving, far, far away to a sunshine land of yellow sands and blue skies and ripe peaches the size of beach balls (Torremolinos?) where my mother was young, beautiful, barefoot, fatally attractive to men, a bit like Ursula Andress in *Dr. No*, and my father was Mick Jagger.

"Lizbet . . . monster baby . . . swelled up . . . ankles to forehead . . . loose stomach skin . . . vibrating machine . . . tone up . . . easy . . . mini-treadmill . . . thick elastic band . . . plug it in . . . shook you into shape . . . so violent . . . must be doing wonders. . . . Two hours . . . reading *Vogue* . . . bumper issue . . . agonizing pain . . . bleeding . . . beige shag-pile . . . only had the carpet four weeks . . . your father . . . 999 . . . emergency operation . . . nice turn-of-the-century, red brick mansion a block off Harley Street . . . ectopic pregnancy . . . hadn't realized . . . entire womb . . . whipped away . . . practically hollow . . . terrible."

"What?" I said.

"It was *terrible*," said Mummy. There was a defensive edge to her voice. Daddy patted her knee and looked grave. They were sitting side by side on my white bedspread like two bad children. I sat stiffly behind my white vanity desk, and lined up my lipsticks like toy soldiers. My mind bulged gray and thick with the new information, and I felt that if I moved my head so much as an inch, it might distort, like a pumpkin mutating into a butternut squash.

"We thought it was the right time to tell you," said Daddy. He paused. "Now that you're a *woman*."

I rolled my eyes. Our parents were all gnarled up because Nina Sara, the fat daughter of Mummy's best friend and arch rival, Evelyn Toberman, had recently had a bat-mitzvah—where she'd stood up in synagogue in a dreadful purple frock and sung Hebrew prayers at the pitch of a mosquito to mark her spiritual journey into *womanhood*—and I'd refused. Frankly, our parents would have been hard-pressed to tell the difference between a bat mitzvah and a vampire bat. But they resented Evelyn Toberman sucking up the glory, and being invited to lunch by The Rabbi's Wife. (The only dealings Mummy had had with The Rabbi's Wife were about *Sukkot*, the Jewish harvest festival, where you do a lot of sitting outside, and she'd blown it by saying, "Well, the weather looks as if it will hold—touch wood!")

"So, can I stay out till one in the morning?"

"Certainly not!" said Mummy. "You're barely out of diapers!"

"Right." I pursed my lips again. They unpursed of their own accord and re-formed in a grin. "*You're* not my parents," I said. "You can't tell me what to do!"

Technically, this could be fantastic.

I added, "And if I'm not Jewish, Passover is nothing to do with me. So from now on, I'll be skipping Seder Night prayers and just be joining everyone for the food."

Daddy frowned. "Cassie. You *are* Jewish. Your biological parents were Jewish. So you'll be sitting through the entire length of the Haggadah each year, just like the rest of us. And we *are* your parents. Not in the genetic sense, but in every other real sense. Including the telling-you-what-to-do sense. But maybe," he hesitated, "you can stay up till one in the morning tonight, *inside* the house. I hope it's not been too much of a shock. If you want to ask us anything," he added, backing out of the room, "don't feel that you can't or that you'd be hurting our feelings."

"You seem fine anyway," said Mummy, in a voice that brooked no argument. "Are you pleased with the O-Ho! tickets?"

I gazed at the tickets. They were front row, which I'd expected.

Daddy was renowned for being able to secure the best tickets to any event, and was not satisfied unless the hotel clients reported back with comments along the lines of "We were sitting in front of the prime minister!"

"Yes," I said.

I hoped they weren't expecting thanks. I glanced at their faces and saw that they weren't. They looked as if they were being eaten alive by ants. Possibly, they feared that I was devastated at their news and was going to exhibit some extreme form of reaction, which they would be required to address. Luckily for them, as parents they were distinctly average, and it was a relief—actually gratifying—to realize that we weren't related. Now I had a chance of being born again. To a superior sort of parent. The only part of the drama that I didn't like was that as a baby—*me*, precious *me*!—I'd been passed about like a handful of beans. I didn't like that. I didn't like it to the point that I decided not to think about it. If a thought was not going to lead anywhere good, I would block it.

"Does Lizbet know?" I said.

They shook their heads. Daddy took a small step back into the room and said, "We thought that *you* should be the one to tell her. That is, if you want to."

My chest felt hot and tight. I was thirteen and cast-iron selfish, but even I could see that the news would be a loss to Lizbet. It would make her feel alone. They had no idea. They didn't understand her. They hadn't taken the trouble to get to know their own child. Instead, they'd spent all these years kissing up to me, because I was the one who was *meant* not to feel special. They didn't understand me either. Now I knew they weren't my real parents, I felt very special indeed.

And yet. What did it mean for me and Lizbet? For a second it felt like we were forcibly being torn apart, and I was drowning in rage, before I realized that for *me*, nothing would change how I felt about her. But it was *other* people—with their prying ways and their pathetic need for concrete definition—that you had to worry about. I could imagine it. "Oh, so you're not actually *sisters* . . . so what is she . . . your . . . step? No . . . your adopted . . . ah, she's their *real* child . . . yes, that's right, I *do* have the emotional intellect of a gnat. . . ." I couldn't give a toss what other people said, but Lizbet would.

"I'm not going to say a word," I said. "I want it to stay a secret."

Daddy cleared his throat. "Cassie. If you want to trace your original parents, we will support you. I have a number of documents in my possession. Or rather, in the bank's possession. I can retrieve them at any time."

Mummy assumed a sad face.

I looked at my new pink Casio digital. "It's four oh six, and seventeen seconds. The bank shuts at four thirty. So, if you break the speed limit, you should make it."

"Right," said Daddy. "Right then. Absolutely. Okeydoke."

He got the box and gave it to me. I snatched it from his trembling hands without a word, raced upstairs, and placed it on my bedspread. I stared at it, my heart beating fast. And then, in a fast, fierce movement, I shoved it under the bed, pushing it far away from me, into the farthest, darkest corner, until you wouldn't know it was there. Perhaps I thought about that box every day. But I didn't touch it again for years and years. Because what you don't know can't hurt you. Or the people you love. I could comfort myself with my secret when Daddy or Mummy was infuriating and then, when the moment passed, brush it off as if it were a dream. As long as my origin remained a glorious figment of my imagination, *I* was in charge. I had the power. But once I let the facts into my head, they would control me. It was impossible for this to be otherwise, as they pertained to the body, the soul, the very start of me. The details in that box might rip out my heart. Curiosity was a mild irritant, but nothing in the face of fear like this. By doing nothing, I determined that nothing would change, and it didn't. People moan about "being in limbo," but actually, I found limbo the safest place to be.

I might have kept the past at bay forever, but eight years later, I met George. Well, not George *himself*—George's parents. Then I began to wonder what I'd been deprived of. Ivan Hershlag had a thick Russian accent despite living nearly all his life in the East End, and remained at odds with the modern world when it suited him. Sheila Hershlag ran the house around him. She was a refined version of the Jewish mother cliché. She was desperate for you to eat, but this wasn't necessarily a bother, because her food was delicious. (I'm not saying I ate it. I can eat a whole ball of mozzarella, same as the next woman, but I can't always eat under *pressure*.)

They idolized George.

"Isn't he so *handsome*!" Mrs. Hershlag would cry, cupping his face in her hands. "This is my *baby*!"

"Mm," I'd say. And then, because it wasn't enough for her, "Yes, he is handsome."

Not that I wasn't one of George's biggest fans. He was difficult, with a high intellect, an even higher self-opinion and a nasty sense of humor. I loved that. He reminded me of myself. And he was tall, with an artistic frame, and dashing eyebrows. The role of the eyebrow in a man's general attraction has been severely underrated. So Mrs. Hershlag was right, her son *was* handsome. I just don't like to have my emotions choked out of me.

Out of thin air, Mrs. Hershlag could recall the time of day that George took his first step (after lunch, at eleven and a half months), the first thing he ate (pureed rusk and milk "with a *dot* of sugar," in his blue spotted bowl), the age at which he caught chicken pox (three weeks after his first birthday, leaving him with two scars, one on his right ankle and one above left of his belly button), his favorite toy (his Soo Panda puppet, from *Sooty & Sweep*, the nose fell off and he sewed on a new one, in green), his first word (addressed to a yellow rose in the garden—"fower"), the midwife's comment when he popped out ("What a lovely round head!").

Mr. Hershlag might not have his wife's Terminator-like instant recall for events of over thirty years ago, but he was an expert on the minutiae of George's daily life. George worked at the BBC Radio Four Drama Department as a broadcast assistant (another term for "secretary"). To hear Mr. Hershlag talk, you'd have thought George was in fact the director general. You'd have also thought that Mr. Hershlag worked on the next desk.

Actually, Mr. Hershlag was a tailor. I could never step in the house in my vintage Donna Karan raw silk evening coat without him crying, "Why are you wearing a *schmutter*! Let me make you up a proper coat!" George would shout, "Dad! She doesn't want you to make her a coat!" and Mrs. Hershlag would echo, "Leave her alone, she doesn't want a coat!" The conversation would persist for quite a while before Mr. Hershlag sadly pocketed his tape measure and left the room. Thirty seconds later he'd bounce back in with "Your jacket's no good, let me make you a jacket!"

When he wasn't threatening heavy linings, he was discussing office politics with George. No detail was too mundane for his attention.

"So *I'm* the one who has to stand on the street to welcome Sir Ian out of the taxi. . . ."

"What was he wearing, on top, like?"

"A bomber jacket."

"He doesn't trust their security? . . . Did you get a feel of the lining?"

Mr. Hershlag had an intimate knowledge of the eating habits of George's colleagues. ("Josie had a Twix? Since when does she eat a Twix? She has a Galaxy bar, every day she has a Galaxy bar, what's with the Twix all of a sudden?")

He knew every link in the creative process, from the writers, the lazy good-for-nothing freelance writers—"This is the fourth, fifth draft! What's wrong with her? Why doesn't she listen? *You* should write the play, yes, you could write a very good play, you have a great imagination, ah, so Josie doesn't think you can write, what does she know? You give her the play, you say it's by someone else, she says she loves it, you surprise her, I'm the writer, so there, bang!"

- to listener preferences—"He suggested a *murder*, for the afternoon play? There was *swearing*? What is he, mad? This is Radio Four! He doesn't know a thing!"
- to the flighty nature of actors—"He dropped out the day before recording? Bloody chutzpah. Don't tell me! He got the movie offer! These actors, they want to do the wireless, the radio, they can't wait to do radio, they kill to do radio—but the minute they get the movie offer or the TV—radio? who cares about radio? They disappear, you don't see them again!"
- to the tricks of the trade—"It was too long? So you put it through the time scratch! You lose two minutes, who knows the difference!"

Meanwhile, Mrs. Hershlag noticed if George was *going* to be ill, up to two days in advance. "He gets a touch of redness around his mouth. I think it's lack of iron." Then, in a hushed voice, "You could always put fresh chicken stock in a pilaf."

If George *was* ill, it was DEFCON 1. "When he's poorly, he

likes to lie on the sofa, underneath a nice thick duvet, watch anything starring Mel Gibson or Bruce Willis, drink Ribena, and eat plain crisps. Walkers are fine. He won't eat homemade."

It was like she was in a time warp and George was still twelve. However, although she was giving me this information for a reason, I think she knew that I wasn't going to follow up on any of it. And yet, she hoped. It irritated me, at first. The way they adored him, and how he took it as a given. *My* reaction, when George was malingering on the sofa, was to say, "You wouldn't cut it in the SAS."

"I might not ring every day," said Mrs. Hershlag to me, once. "I don't want to be a nuisance. But George, and you, are always"—tapping her head—"in *here*."

They were the most warmhearted, generous people I knew, and it took my breath away. While the fiercest rays fell on George, I felt myself thaw in the sunshine of their love—they weren't mean with their affection. It was a revelation that parents could be this wonderful. Lizbet and I were absurdly fond of Mummy and Daddy. If pressed, we might even admit to the L word. But it was a frustrating, disgruntled, rolly-eyed sort of affection because—apart from once living in the same house—we had little in common with our parents; we didn't always respect their *choices*. Time spent with them felt like a duty.

But Sheila and Ivan astounded me with the selflessness of their love. With George and me, they deferred their needs instinctively. If their son behaved toward them in a way that was less than ideal, they bore their disappointment in a truly adult way. No sulks, no anger, no petty retribution, they merely *absorbed* it. It made me realize how much of a child Vivica was in her parenting. *She* had been the baby of her family, cloyingly close to her mother (dead, of cancer, six months before Lizbet was born). I now saw Mummy's unconscious wish to remain a daughter forever.

Sheila and George were parental prototypes, and their pure, un-filtered love made me realize how much, as a child, I had missed. Now I better understood Vivica, but I wasn't sure I forgave her. I didn't really care about her pathological desires. *My* feeling was, You have a kid, you become a parent: You put your babies first. I'd bet that *Sheila* had needs—she just ignored them, because she felt that George was more important. I know that's not ideal from a feminist perspective, but—fuck it, I'm speaking as the *child* here.

I worshipped Mrs. Hershlag, as the ideal mother. Her love was addictive. The more I got, the more I wanted. It made me wonder. It made me hope. I was twenty-six and a half years old. I had gradu-ated from Oxbridge with a first in Law. I was making tracks as a family barrister at a prestigious chambers. I was a married woman approaching her *fifth* anniversary. And for the first time in my life, the truth hit me: Inside I was still a child and I wanted my mummy—my true and natural mother who was surely somewhere out there desperate to show that kind of love to *me*.

I dragged out the box from under the bed and opened it.

CHAPTER 8

There was a brown envelope inside the box, stuffed with old papers. I pulled them out with clumsy fingers. There was a pounding in my head, but if it was excitement, I crushed it like a king crushing a peasants' revolt. I skimmed the various headings—*National Health Service INNER LONDON EXECUTIVE COUNCIL, National Children Adoption Association,* whipping through the pages, scattering them over the kitchen counter. It was covered in buttery rye toast crumbs, where George had eaten breakfast, but it was so important that I didn't care.

A sentence typed on a manual typewriter caught my eye.

No Affiliation Order has been made against the alleged father; he cannot therefore, in law be named.

Mick Jagger! I knew it!

I recognized the spidery handwriting of my father-to-be, on the back of a white sheet: *"Mother Sarah Paula Blatt 24 Latimer Road Edgware."* Mother? *My* mother? Sarah Paula Blatt! Sarah Paula Blatt. Wow. She was from Edgware. Crazy. I squinted. The next line read *"Baked Bean."* I looked again. Ah. *"Baby Born"* and my birth date. "New name Cassandra Gabriella." I riffled through dry, yellowing papers until I found one headed NATIONAL CHIL-DREN ADOPTION ASSOCIATION.

Dear Mr. and Mrs. Montgomery

We are pleased . . . blah blah . . . two forms . . . . com-pleted . . . signed . . . consent . . . mother . . . birth certifi-cate for Jane Susan Blatt born on the . . .

Excuse me? Jane Susan? Jane Susan Blatt! Good Lord. Save yourself the bother—name me "Human Being Number One"—you might as well! Thank God I was adopted! I mean, at least *act* like you care! Jane Susan. I was Jane Susan. I tried to imagine my-self as her, going through life, quiet and dull. She was a different person entirely. I thought of Mummy and Daddy, renaming me Cassandra Gabriella, probably the most glamorous and elaborate name that Mummy could think of, probably she'd read it in *Vogue*, and I felt a flash of gratitude. She and Daddy had done their best. They really had.

I rang home before I could change my mind. Daddy picked up. This was rare, for him. He spent all day, every day, at work answer-ing the phone, and he point-blank refused to answer it at home. It was the one job our mother couldn't force him to do.

"I opened the box," I said.

"Did you indeed. Did you indeed. The time was right, was it? Well, we all need to know where we came from. I don't blame you, one bit. Quite right! Good for you, Cassie!"

My heart squished. Daddy was king of the perfect pleasantry, the gentle affirmation. It was part of why he was such a great concierge—he was courteous, kindly, without being overfamiliar.

He made the hotel guests feel comfortable, and cared for. The trouble was, the perfect pleasantry wasn't entirely appropriate for a father-daughter relationship, as it made Lizbet and me feel *un*cared for. As if he were maintaining a cautious distance. But a pleasantry is also a tactic to mask emotion, and I knew that Daddy's professionalism was furiously battling against his private sadness and regret. How did I know? Because he was a plain old human being who'd brought me up as his own, and at that moment, the most rational man in the world would have felt abandoned and betrayed.

"Jane Susan!" I said, to make a joke of my treachery. "Jane Susan? What the hell sort of name is that? Just call me Bore Bore Blatt—I don't care!"

He laughed—a valiant effort, even if he did sound like a cat coughing up a hairball. "You were probably named after someone, Cassie."

"Really." I knew I sounded petulant, but if I took the juvenile stance, they were obliged to be grown-up about it.

"One second, dear. Mummy wants to speak with you."

"Darling?"

"Bore Bore Blatt here."

"Oh, darling!" The tone was sympathetic, but I thought I detected a smile in her voice.

I tore through the rest of the papers. "Is . . . is everything here?"

Mummy coughed. "Yes. Yes, I think so. Why? Do you think that something is . . . missing?"

I paused. "If she . . . my . . . Sarah Paula had written to me . . . to the adoption agency . . . afterward—would they have passed it on?"

"Yes."

"But, there's nothing here. No . . . notes or anything."

"No."

"Right. Okay. That's fine. I just, you know, wondered."

There was an intake of breath, then Mummy spoke in a rush. "Cassie, darling. We do know that your mother was *very* young when she had you. Twelve. What? *What*, Geoffrey? Eighteen. And divorce then was a disgrace, but getting pregnant when you were unmarried . . . my golly, it was all we thought about, it was our greatest fear, I don't know how she could have been so stupid to let it happen! The shame of it, I can't tell you. You must have caused—well, not *you*—but your mother falling pregnant, it must have caused a great deal of sadness and trauma. Yes, she gave you up, but she was probably just doing as she was told. In those days, you didn't argue. Her parents probably convinced her to get on with her life." Mummy paused, sighed. Then she said, "She must look around now, at all these single mothers, and kick herself. She probably thinks of you a lot."

Mummy never spoke like this. It must have cost her. I replied, "I think of Sarah Paula aged eighteen and I want to smack her round the face."

Mummy laughed, with a slight hysterical edge. "I could never understand a woman who would give away her baby. But," she added, "her loss was our gain."

I nodded. Yikes! Any indication of a mushy emotion scared the life out of me—in a perverse way I hankered for it, but it was always a struggle to accept when it came. Once, I was washing up my favorite bone china coffee can, wearing my white Splendid top—a favorite of Teri Hatcher in *Desperate Housewives*, since you ask— and Mrs. Hershlag came up behind me and rolled up my sleeves. I stiffened, as it felt like a *criticism*. Then I realized, she was being maternal! Not patronizing, *loving*. Not invading my space, *helping*. If I was to find my real mother, I'd better get used to all that stuff.

"I'll speak to you later," I told Vivica. "Thanks."

Then I ran upstairs and hit *Google*. I typed in "Trace birth mother" and a million references jumped on-screen. I clicked on *adoptionfamilynetwork.com*. "WANT TO BE REUNITED ON TV?" I clicked back. There was a British Web site called *helpmefind*, and I called it up and saw line after line after line, page after page after page, of people looking for family members:

- "Seeking birth son, adopted Birmingham, 1978 . . ."
- "Jem: Seeks to give message to Stan, Missing . . ."
- "Nicola, Looking for daughter, Adopted, born 1979 . . ."
- "Seeking contact with Mum: Joelle, Mexbrough? . . ."
- "Adopted female, born 1981, seeks mother . . ."

I scrolled down the list with a cold heart. *You fucking careless bastards*. After two hours, I was on page forty. There was no sign of anyone named Sarah Paula and I shut the laptop with a snap.

I had case notes to read through for work, but I was consumed. And then I realized. I had an address. Sarah Paula had been eighteen; she certainly lived with her parents. And people who made you give away your illegitimate baby, despite it being their own *grandchild*, were not the adventurous sort. I bet they were still living in the same house. I called directory inquiries, gave the name and address.

"Is it B. Blatt?"

"Yes," I said smoothly, and took down the number. I stared at it, dialed.

"Hello?" said a smart voice.

"Is that the doctor's office?" I said.

"You have the wrong number," replied my grandmother, and she put the phone down.

No, I haven't. It was an intoxicating thought. I had the power to give this woman a heart attack. It would be the perfect crime. I'd ring back. I'd say, "Oh, hello. I'm calling for Sarah Paula. It's Jane Susan. Remember me?" She'd suffer a cardiac arrest and fall down dead, and even if the police traced the call, they couldn't convict me of *speaking*.

The phone rang, and I jumped.

"Cassie? It's Dad. I can't speak for long, I'm calling from work. I wanted to check you're okay."

"I'm fine," I said. He seemed to require more, so I added, "It's weird."

"Yes." He paused. "You weren't too upset by the letters?"

"What letters?"

"The letters from Sarah Paula."

"She didn't write any letters," I said.

"I think you'll find she did. She wrote to the agency, and then, somehow, she got *our* address, and wrote to us. Vivica hit the roof. Vivica . . . Cassie. I'll call you back."

Sixty seconds later, the phone rang. "Mummy will be round shortly," said my father. "She has some letters to pass on. I'm afraid she saw fit to . . . edit the documentation. We realize this is the right thing for you to do. But . . . don't be too hard on her."

When Mummy showed, she was wearing dark glasses, a head scarf, and a beige raincoat, in deference to some tragic heroine of the silver screen, possibly Audrey Hepburn. She passed over a white envelope. "I don't care what you think, she was a silly, silly girl," she said, and stamped back to her new Beetle convertible in tornado red (Daddy had called it "tomato red" by mistake one day and she'd gone mad).

"God's sake," I muttered, and shut the front door. Then I walked upstairs to my study, and pulled out the letters.

Sarah Paula's girlish handwriting, in black ink, was squat and rounded. Thick handwriting, I thought, with a sneer. The letter was addressed to the general secretary of the NCAA.

Will you kindly let me know how my little babe Jane is, I'm so anxious about her, I would have wrote to you last week but I've been ill . . . and parting with little Jane hasn't helped. I know that you will hear from Jane's new mummy from time to time but I wish you could have someone who could pop in at her new home on the spur of the moment just to see if she is being treated all right.

The next letter was dated two months later.

Dear Madam,
    You promised me that after my little girl was taken away that you would get her new mummy to send me a photo of her. Just to give me peace of mind, I will pay whatever it is as I must have a picture of her. I worry so much about her. I am hoping you will let me know all about her and how she is keeping. It would break my heart if I could not get a photo of her. Sorry to trouble you but I know you would feel the same being a mother yourself.

The third was dated two months after that.

You must forgive me for bothering you so much. There are just a few things I would like to ask about Jane. If anything should happen to her parents. If they get killed or die and little Jane is left they couldn't put her in a home if I was still alive could they? Please let me know as it keeps me awake at night and I cry myself to sleep just thinking all sorts of things. If anything was to happen and she

was left without parents you would let me know wouldn't you? I
would die if she ever got sent away to an orphanage. I would just
search the world over to find her. You say so little when you answer
my letters. I don't want to know where she is, all I want to know
is, are her new parents poor people? If I thought she wasn't getting
looked after as she should I'd kill myself as I'm so worried about
her. Maybe she's living with poor people and she never gets any
sunshine. Please let me know everything about her as she was one
year old yesterday and it just tore a hole in my heart when I
thought of her, wondering what sort of birthday she had.

I folded the letter in half and closed my eyes. I pressed my hand
over my mouth, and bent double. The noise in my ears roared so
fast and furious I felt that my head might fly off my shoulders and
explode like a red paintbomb. I fought the rising nausea and forced
my attention to the next letter.

I wrote to Mrs. Montgomery last week to see if she would do me a
favor by writing to me each year. I haven't had any reply, and no
doubt she doesn't intend to answer my letter. I wonder if you will
be good enough to write to her and explain that I won't bother her
anymore, if she will just send me one *letter a* year *and a snap of*
little Jane whenever she can spare one. I know I have no claim on
her, all I want is an assurance that she has not come to any harm.

The reply from the general secretary was also enclosed.

The adopters are very sympathetic and understanding toward you,
but they do so wish to feel that the little girl is now entirely their
own daughter, and they are prepared to give her an excellent up-
bringing. Now that the adoption has been made legal, you have no

further claim to her, and you can never reclaim her. Let me assure
you, she is a very fortunate little girl. The adopters do not desire to
receive further correspondence from you and are sorry they could
not see their way to send you photographs at intervals. The little girl
has recently been taken to a photographer and a copy of the picture
will be sent specially for you, but this copy must be the last. We hope
that you are now feeling happier, and we will post the photograph
as soon as we receive it. Little Jane is really very fortunate.

Yours sincerely,
General Secretary

A whole alternate life spread itself out before me like a red carpet unfurled before royalty. Little Jane was not fortunate, and General Secretary, a mother herself, knew it, whatever she said. Jagger
was off the hook. I didn't care. Nothing mattered, except finding
Sarah Paula, my Mr. and Mrs. Hershlag rolled into one. Of course
Mummy had hidden the letters. The ferocity of their passion was
alien to a buttoned-up person like her, but even she could sense
their power, would know that such a feral love would storm
through the years and reclaim me, that when I found her I would
fall into Sarah Paula's beautiful embrace and not look back.

CHAPTER 9

I called Greg. Greg was boss of Hound Dog Investigations. We'd met at a dinner party and hit it off. He was rude and he didn't care and I liked that in a man. He didn't blink when I said I'd like to trace my birth mother. No fuss. Greg was emotionally intelligent. Not like some people—tell them something sad about yourself, they weep, and instead of being touched you're disgusted, because you know it's nothing to do with *you*, it's all their stuff.

He listened, told me to assemble all the facts—"Nothing crap like 'she likes opera'—I need information that will help identify her. You don't know her birth date?"

"I have an address," I said, with a pang. *How could I not know my own mother's birthday?* "And a phone number. I think her parents still live there. I was hoping you'd ring and pretend to be from the council, and trick her address out of her mother."

I didn't say to him what I thought, which was, I didn't *want* this to be a long, arduous search, trying to dig out birth certificates, marriage certificates, over weeks and weeks. I wanted it to be one quick trick call, as if I hadn't gone to any trouble.

"We'll see," said Greg. "So what prompted this, girl?"

"Oh," I said, airily. "I read the letters. She wrote these letters. And *then*, two weeks after I read them, George was telling my parents that for our fifth wedding anniversary his father was giving him a family heirloom—his gold watch. And my mother—my adoptive mother—remembered something. She'd forgotten it. All this time. It was a tiny gold Star of David. We're Jewish—it's the equivalent of a crucifix. My original mother had pinned it to my Babygro. I thought of her, pinning it. And I thought, if only I'd known, if only they had told me . . . because all this time, I'd thought she didn't . . . but it showed that she . . . I might have tried to find her before."

Greg paused. Then he said, "We'll do this one for free, girl. It'll be our good deed for the century."

"Greg. You don't have to." But I wanted him to. Not because of the money, but because I was looking for anything that would make this *less* of a deal, that would squish it and squash it, until it was a tiny, tiny, inconsequential nothing.

"I will. Make me feel better about all the other terrible things we do."

"Thank you," I said.

I had lived for so long *not* tracing my birth mother that our conversation felt surreal. As if I was an imposter in someone else's life. Perhaps I was. Reading Sarah Paula's letters, it was as if time was frozen and I could only think of her as eighteen years old, nearly a decade younger than myself, my poor little mummy. Her handwriting hadn't lost its puppy fat—no adult I knew wrote like that. It was strange to think that she was now in her mid-forties. I couldn't see her as a middle-aged woman; I tried to imagine it but the image wouldn't come.

I wondered if she lived nearby. In the next street, for example. You hear about that—it happens a lot—one man commissioned

Hound Dog to track down his real dad, and it turned out that as a teenager he'd delivered papers to his own father's house. I don't think that was mere coincidence. I think, with family, *real* family, there's an unconscious pull and there's nothing you can do about it—it's like the sea is helpless to the pull of the moon. Thank God I'd had my teeth whitened. Of course, Sarah Paula wouldn't care if my teeth were black and rotten—okay, maybe she would—but only because black rotten teeth aren't really acceptable in today's society and she wouldn't want me to be shunned. My black rotten teeth wouldn't matter to *her*, is what I mean. And what would I wear? Tricky. It's no problem deciding what to wear if you want a *man* to fall in love with you. They're easy to please. Short of rolling in manure then wrapping yourself in a horse blanket, it's hard to go wrong. But your own mother? Actually, my own mother was going to be easy. The last time she saw me I was red, scrawny, screaming, and covered in blood. And yet, she *yearned* for me, there was a physical ache, it was right there, in the letters, the pain dripped off the page. But I wanted her to look at me and think, Wow. And, although I saw now that it wasn't entirely her fault, I wanted her to regret giving me up, I wanted to show her what she'd missed. So. Hair at Michaeljohn. A Pure Collagen Velvet Luxury Facial at the Dorchester Spa. My black Joseph flares. My burgundy snakeskin boots with the three-inch heels from Pied A Terre. A good quality white linen shirt, under my Nicole Farhi lilac cashmere V-neck. My Elsa Peretti letter "C" pendant in sterling silver from Tiffany. My Elsa Peretti teardrop earrings in sterling silver, also from Tiffany (a present to me, from me—George could only afford H Samuel, so I told him to save his money). Although, Sarah Paula, aged eighteen, didn't sound a very Tiffany sort of girl. I didn't want to frighten her with too *much* Tiffany. Ah, bloody hell. It wasn't as if I was planning to pin a £23,000 gold spider brooch encrusted with diamonds, rubies, emeralds, and sapphires to my chest. My Tiffany armory was *me*, and she could take it or leave it. Well, no, actually, she couldn't leave it. I very much needed her to take it.

It was the first time in my life that I worried about making a bad impression. I've always been of the opinion that other people can accommodate *me*. You get nowhere being soft. I've never gone for that girly big-eyed wheedle-you-round shit. Women who beg and cajole to get what they want are not only stupid, they are traitors— they tarnish the rest of us, make us ashamed to be female. I find it more effective to intimidate people. That way, they respect you, even if they hate you. But usually they're drawn to you, because you have faith in yourself, an irresistible trait. You see them watching, hoping that some of your shine will rub off. They want to ingratiate themselves. It means you'll probably get what you want.

But I wasn't so sure that this strategy was appropriate *now*. I was feeling . . . doubt. For once, maybe softness was the way to go. I'd never given softness the time of day. I wasn't even sure *how* to act soft. What do you do, get a feathered fringe? Lizbet had a softness to her. (I don't mean that she was feeble—when I was little she was superb at making my life a misery, a master of psychological tor-ture; in technique, at least, she would have been an asset to the KGB. But at the core, she was a gentle person. There'd always be a point in the Bravery Test—usually after she'd made me sit on a bunch of brown thistles from Mummy's dried flower display— where my eyes might water, and she'd fall on me, covering me in gloopy kisses, promising sweets. I'd claw and scratch to extract my-self from her grip and run off and she'd lumber after me, shouting, "Cassie! Please! Wait!" She needed to please people.)

I needed to please Sarah Paula. This wasn't a confrontation. I wanted to be, damn it, *mothered*. I wanted someone to call me "My Darling Little One." I wanted her to step into my house and start folding my underwear. She could even lick her finger and wipe dirt off my face with spit.

I had to soften or she wouldn't dare. Whereas Lizbet was huggable, and people wanted to protect her, they saw me as hard and unapproachable. And they saw right. I didn't expect Sarah Paula to be up to protecting anyone, let alone *me*—my nickname at work is Steel Claw—but I wanted her to feel that I was giving her the option.

It struck me that Sarah Paula and Lizbet would get on. I knew they would. In fact, I couldn't wait to introduce them. I wasn't sure where we'd meet—maybe in a royal park or a museum, somewhere casual yet of *note*—but I wished that Lizbet could be there, like an asset, alongside the shoes, the hair, the jewelry, the white teeth; see, look, this is *my* sister, I haven't done too badly, have I?

Lizbet was *not* going to be there, as I wasn't going to tell her any of this. She would crumble. Let me tell you about Lizbet. Lizbet has been happy and cozy with Tim for years. They have a fun little lifestyle, just the two of them. Amusing, low-stress jobs, no kids, no desire for kids, just meaningless sex and general frivolity. She doesn't like change. As far as family goes, she likes what she's familiar with, even if what she's familiar with isn't that fabulous. To discover that her childhood and our relationship were based on a lie would damage her. I didn't want to be the one to inflict that wound. Anyway, if she was ever to know, Mummy and Daddy should be the ones to tell her. I felt it wasn't *my* lie to confess to.

But in the grand reunion I was going to have with my real mother, I could still fantasize about Lizbet, as an appeasing presence. If there were any awkward silences, Lizbet would smooth them over, leaning forward with that smile of hers, the smile that warmed you from the inside out, like a mug of hot chocolate, the perfect question on her lips to draw Sarah Paula out of herself. I had this fear that I might perch there in dumb silence, sitting on my hands, a daft smile on my face—*me*, Cassandra Gabriella Montgomery, who was unfazed by anything and anyone; because most people were all the same in being nothing to me.

I wondered if I'd recognize her. After all, this would be our second meeting. I told George that I was tracing my mother, and all he could say was "Weird" (and then, two minutes later, "Cassie! Your sister's cat has pissed in my sports bag!").

I had expected him to understand, but he didn't, and in those few seconds, I saw the ground between us split in two. Not to make light of accidentally dropping my marriage and cracking it, but the mental landscape was like something out of *Tremors*.

"Do you *need* to?" he added, later. "I could understand it if you were eighteen."

I was shocked to the core. I knew he was selfish, but I'd always assumed he was selfish for *us*, not just for *him*. It hit me that he liked the fact that I had a ho-hum relationship with my parents. George didn't want to be knocked off the top spot. I lost all respect for him then. If he didn't understand my need to find my real mother, then he had no respect for what I, as an abandoned baby, had suffered in being given up. (Actually, I didn't think I had suffered *that* much, but George wasn't to know that. It was the principle.)

Although he did speak to Vivica, who rang allegedly "to see if we'd received the e-mail" (a photograph of a squirrel on water skis). She said to George, apropos of nothing, "So. It could all end happily for Cassie," and I knew she was frightened. The role of mother in a family does tend to be assumed by a single person. And yet—unlike George—she was trying to see it *my* way. I almost felt sorry for her, because I didn't think she could help being the mother she was.

"Ask Cassie to call me if she has a moment," she said, but I didn't.

I had tunnel vision. Sure, my life was fine, but here was a whole *new* life. And don't we all want to refresh our lives once in a while? I was like a gauche teenager dreaming of romance; the details were fuzzy but the gist was clear. Walking through rippling meadows, arms linked, laughing over coffee in a spacious white kitchen while the sun streamed in through the windows—perhaps she lived somewhere hot? I didn't doubt that she'd never forgiven her parents for forcing her to give me up, I could understand if she'd put oceans between them.

Greg would get back to me with her address, and first I'd go and spy on her, see what she looked like, watch her go about her business, and then I'd write to her. *The Adoption Reunion Handbook* listed the advantages of going through an intermediary, but I was gripped by a compulsion to reach her *myself*; yes, it was probably sensible to be cautious, and slow, but I had no patience, my rational mind was no match for my racing heart. In fact, I barely trusted myself to spy on her; I saw myself tumbling out of the car and running across the road and flinging myself on her. Or, even, walking calmly toward her and saying, "Excuse me, I'm looking for the library, can you. . . ?" but I wouldn't finish the sentence because she'd stare at me with this hunger, and we'd gaze at each other, feasting on every detail, and she would *know* it was her baby come back.

I'd composed my letter. Or rather, I'd *re*-composed my letter. My first letter, written before I'd read *her* letters wasn't . . . entirely suitable:

Sarah Paula,
    You'll remember me as Jane Susan. Excuse me writing—curiosity got the better of me. I realize we are strangers, and I have no desire to intrude on your life. However, there is an interest to

see where I came from—in a strictly biological sense—and I would like to speak with you. You may decide against this—however, I would be grateful if you would do me the small courtesy of a response either way.

Sincerely,
"JS"

I'd read it out to Mrs. Hershlag. (George had blabbed, and actually it was good to have her support. She felt for Vivica, but she felt more for me. Mrs. Hershlag was immersed in being a mother to the extent that it informed her whole world, and so to her, I would always be, in some sense, "a motherless child." *She* could hardly bear the thought of it, and was almost as keen as I was for this tragedy to be rectified.)

She'd said, "Oh, Cassie. That's a nice letter. But . . . well, dear . . . it isn't *really*, is it? I think it's healthy to get all the anger out, very positive. But I do think if I was your mother and I received that, well, I might think about putting myself under twenty-four-hour armed guard. It's just a thought, but maybe that can be your *first draft?*"

Dearest Sarah,

I hope you don't mind me writing. God, I hope you don't. My name is (or was) Jane Susan, and I think I may be your daughter. Well. In fact, I know I am. I am settled and happy [I'd got that bit from The Adoption Reunion Handbook; *I presumed it was code for "I am not a nutter."] but I would so love to see you, again. To tell you the truth, it is all I think about. I only read the letters you sent to the adoption agency recently, and saw the Star of David, which is why I haven't written before. I feel stupid for that. Just so you know, I went to Cambridge and I am a successful bar-*

rister. I think you would be proud of me. Oh! And my new name is Cassandra Gabriella Montgomery—but don't worry, I'm not too posh! I had a reasonable upbringing. My adoptive parents are fine, and I have a fabulous sister, Lizbet—one day, I'd love you two to meet. The thing is, I miss you, and I have always missed you. I hope that doesn't scare you, but from what you say in your letters, I feel confident that it won't. Actually, I don't feel confident, I feel sick, but, I can still dream. A lot—everything—rests on this, for me. I hope, for you too. I understand that you have your life—and I have mine—but I need to be with you, to see you, to touch your face. I almost crossed out that bit, as I don't want to scare you off, but if you are the same person who wrote those letters about me to the agency, I know that scaring off you would be impossible. Despite what you had to do, I want you to know that you are more of a mother than I have ever had.

> *With all my love, and hope,*
> *"Jane Susan"*

I didn't show that letter to anyone. I knew what they'd say— "Oh, tone it down, be a little more *circumspect*"—and I couldn't blame them, I'd have said the same, if I was them. But, you see, I *had* toned it down. So much. Also, they didn't know Sarah Paula, they hadn't read her letters. It might seem begging and desperate to those who didn't realize, but I knew that to my real mother it would seem, if anything, reserved.

When the doorbell rang that night, I thought it was George, forgotten his key, but it was Greg.

"Hello! This is a nice surprise!"

"Cassie," he said. "I came because I found her."

"Oh my God, I knew it, I knew you would! You didn't have to come, you could have rung! Come *in*, come in—don't just stand there—you look all serious, standing there—like a police detective with . . . bad news . . . with . . . news of . . . oh no . . . oh no, no . . . please . . . Greg, just, go . . ."

I tried to shut the door on him, but my strength left me and I sank to the floor and he edged inside and crouched beside me.

"Oh, Cassie," he said, stroking my hair. "Oh, Cassie. She died last year. She just . . . died. I . . . I'm so very, very sorry."

CHAPTER 10

There was other family but I wasn't interested. I didn't want new cousins, a grandma, and an aunt—aunts are ten a fucking penny—I wanted my mother, and I knew that if I met the others, I'd resent them for living when she was dead. I'd barely be able to meet their eyes for the disgust I felt. Greg said, "They toast you, every year, on your birthday, girl," and I felt a pang. My hands itched and I was back to wanting to give Sarah Paula a slap, a slap for having a crappy weak heart and abandoning me a second time.

Greg wanted to stay with me, but I made him go. He asked me to ring George—who was out with the cast for an end-of-recording drink—but I didn't want to see George, complacent ungrateful George with a full complement of loving parents. George would try to give me a hug, the last thing I wanted in the world. He'd *say* he was sorry, but privately, he'd be relieved. My skin felt prickly all over and I couldn't stand to be touched. I wanted to get away; I needed acres of sky, and I saw myself running across that rippling meadow, alone.

I picked up the letter that I'd written to Sarah Paula and folded it in half, and again, and again, until I couldn't make it any smaller, and then I made a gargling noise in my throat and threw it at the wall. I stood up, took a deep breath, slowly exhaled, and smoothed my hair and skirt. I washed my face, drank a glass of ice water. I retrieved the letter from the floor, and jammed it in the box containing *her* letters, and the other documents. And then I shoved the box underneath the bed, with enough force for it to go *thunk* as it hit the wall.

It was 6:37 P.M. I considered walking to the corner shop and buying ten Marlboro Lights. I needed a smoke. I'd quit about ten times; it was a habit that could be resurrected in an instant. I fantasized briefly about the taste of smoke on my tongue, filling my lungs with delicious poison. I stared out of the window; the garden looked cold and still, as if it were holding its breath. There was a small tree in the middle of the lawn with ugly yellow-green leaves, and I felt a rip in my chest. I found George's gardening axe in the shed (a present from a friend, never used) and started to hack at the tree.

Tap tap! "Darling! Darling! Lady Cassandra of Montgomery! What the fuck are you doing?"

I glanced up, to see my neighbor Peter-the-Hairdresser leaning out of his bedroom window. He looked concerned.

"Chopping—hah—down—hah—this—hah—*TREE*!"

"Er, hello—protective *goggles*, Cass?"

"Don't—hah—care—hah—don't—hah—care!"

"You will when a wood chip flies in your eye and blinds you, love. Oh, for God's sake, I can't stand it, I'm throwing you my Oliver Peoples." He paused. "And I'd lose the heels. It's just a thought." I didn't reply. He shook his head and shut the window. Then he opened it. "Okay. I'm a fag, what do I know about tree-felling? But here's a tip. Start with the smaller branches, OR THE TREE WILL FALL ON YOU!"

Chopping down a tree was harder than it looked. The axe kept sticking in the bark. I staggered about with the effort, and spat my hair out of my face. The sweat stung my eyes and tasted salty in my mouth and I wiped my forehead on the sleeve of my Karen Millen pink wool jacket. I panted as I hacked, "Fucking—hah—hate—hah—you—hah—stupid—hah—*bitch*!"

I wasn't even sure who I was referring to. Fate probably. My hands were blistering like Bubble Wrap, and my arms, shoulders, and back ached, but I couldn't stop. I wasn't making as much impact as I wanted, so I took a ferocious swing at the trunk, lost my balance, and tripped. I sprawled on the grass, and the axe went flying, slashing my palm. I crawled in the dirt, gasping, for a bit, then staggered to my feet. My hand was already slippery with blood. There was no pain, but I couldn't catch my breath; I was panting, quick and shallow, like a cat.

Peter's window flew up and he yelled, "That's it! I've had enough, I'm coming round!"

"No, don't," I whispered, but he ignored me. The tree still stood there, crooked, ragged, but upright, mocking me, and I gave a shrill scream and flung myself at it. There was a sickening crack as the trunk split, an ominous rustling, and a thud as it hit the ground.

Peter bandaged my hand, and made me a cup of tea—which I never drink, only coffee with full cream milk—but I gulped it down. When he saw me up close, he stopped joking around.

"Did George leave you?" he said, and I shook my head. "I didn't think so." He sighed. "It's something terrible, isn't it?"

If I was going to tell anyone, I would have told Peter—he was a man who had people rolling out their family secrets before he'd so much as taken a snip at their fringe—but I could barely form a sentence. I felt myself closing up small and tight like a mussel, folding away all the bad feeling deep inside. I was ashamed. I disgusted myself. That letter I'd written—*pathetic*. There was a sense of having made a ridiculous exhibition of myself—for nothing. I was like an actor, blabbing to everyone about my brilliant audition for a starring role, how I was certain the part was mine, fame and universal adoration were around the corner . . . and then I didn't get it, and *everyone* was laughing at me. Who had I told about Sarah Paula? Thank God, not Lizbet. But I had told Greg. Vivica and Daddy. George. His parents. I was a failure. I couldn't shake the sense that if Sarah Paula had loved me enough she'd have forced herself to stay alive.

Peter ran me a hot bath, and asked if there was anyone he could call. "Apart from George, obviously." (Peter disliked George, ever since Peter and his partner Scott had got drunk one New Year's Eve and showed us their teddy bear collection. They'd had mugs printed up with photographs of Red Ted on them, and George had laughed, not in a nice way. George was therefore the only person in Peter's acquaintance who didn't receive a title. If he hadn't been so bloody rude, he'd have been Lord George of Hershlag. As it was, he was plain George.)

I shook my head, even as I thought, *Lizbet*. Lizbet bumbled her way through life, hoping for the best and never getting it; she wasn't competent. And yet, she was the person you wanted when you felt like this. You didn't need her to *do*, you just needed her to *be*. But I couldn't tell Lizbet about Sarah Paula. Lizbet saw me as confident and successful, and I knew she was proud of me for that. I didn't want her to see me a mess. Her admiration was important to me; I had no wish to come across as weak. I also didn't want her to feel rejected. Because she would, if she knew the truth, in so many ways. I didn't want her to feel *less*.

Peter left me with a brimming glass of Châteauneuf du Pape, his mobile number, and the kitchen broom ("If it gets too much, bang on the wall."). I lay in the bath, in two inches of hot water—I dislike being submerged—and stared at the wall. I was alone, one small girl, alone in a big, mean world. It wasn't fair. I could have had someone who looked like me. I felt sick as I thought of all those people growing up in the bosom of their natural parents, blithely taking for granted their family resemblance. *I* grew up looking like *no one.*

I clenched my jaw. It had been my marvelous magical secret— *she's out there somewhere*—and I'd clutched the knowledge to me like an invisible shield. And now, pfft! Gone. Vanished. Forever. I sniffed. I could have had my own family, my own real family, I could . . . I sat up in the bath. I *still* could. And I wasn't talking about aunts.

When George eventually made it home—"Helena is such a laugh. We get out the lift in Bush House, a mouse runs in front of us, she doesn't blink, and you know after a few drinks she's not *that* plain though I couldn't shake the thought that if I sniffed too hard she'd smell."—I was waiting for him. In my red La Perla Frou Frou babydoll, with black Frou Frou thong, Prada heels, and a spritz of Jo Malone Verbenas of Provence cologne. The axe was back in the shed.

"Hi," I said, throwing down *Home Cinema Choice* (the UK's ultimate home entertainment magazine).

He goggled at me. "You look—sex. I mean, sexy."

I tilted my head back in the armchair and closed my eyes. I could just about feel my lashes causing a draft. My hair was piled on top of my head, Roman-empress style, and my face was caked in subtle makeup. (George believed that "Really pretty girls don't need to wear makeup," and I once overheard him tell a friend, "My wife *never* wears makeup, and if she did I wouldn't have married her." I could only presume he was bigamous and referring to his other wife. I'd thought it sweet at the time. Now, in the cold light of my new reality, I reassessed and found it offensive.)

When I opened my eyes, he was still standing there, staring.

"Well?" I said.

"Should I . . . shower?"

I fluttered my eyelashes and tried not to sound annoyed. "George," I said. "Do whatever. But *rush*." The last word came out as a hiss.

George gulped. "Let's go upstairs." He grinned, and took my hand. I smiled back, and tried to feel it. What I actually felt like was booking myself into a hotel so exclusive that it had no other guests and all dealings with staff were executed via computer. Ideally, the staff wouldn't be people, they'd be robots. But I didn't even feel up to socializing with machines. They'd probably bitch about me behind my back. ("She was so stiff and unnatural, I mean, is she even, like, *human?*")

Over the next twelve months, George and I went upstairs a lot.

Nothing happened.

Except, George lost seven pounds.

And I joined the ranks of women who, for no apparent reason, *can't*.

I'd always liked my body. It was slender, tanned easily; my legs were long, my waist was small, my bust was fabulous, and I was never going to have a problem with arm flab. Short of flying, my body had always done everything I asked it to do. Now I despised it. It felt useless and pointless, like a painting of a flower. I spent a fortune on balconette bras, and padded plunge bras, and frilly briefs and camiknickers, and lured George to the bedroom, day after day, night after night, but it felt like a sick joke. I was a prize turkey, in ridiculous frilly paper leg cuffs.

I stopped seeing other women in terms of beauty. I saw them in terms of fertility. George and I watched a film where an actress took off her top, and my first thought was Those look like they'd be good for lactating. Every person in the world had a baby except me. I read that if you spent time with a baby, it sent positive vibes to your womb, so I took a day off work to play with Justin, the five-month-old son of my boss, Sophie Hazel Hamilton. He was fat and jolly, bald as a coot, with big blue eyes, and he shrieked with laughter at the very sight of me. When I hugged him, he snuggled into my neck, breaking my heart into a thousand pieces.

Sarah Paula, you gave up *this*?

It was like trying to perform magic. I stopped drinking coffee. I wouldn't even have a glass of red. I tried hypnosis. Acupuncture. Reflexology. I ate mostly organic anyway—George insisted. (I was the perfect suburban wife: the highlight of my week was the delivery of my box of organic root vegetables.) I put on weight. I lost it. George stopped enjoying sex and became resentful of being frog-marched into the bedroom. Once he was done, I had no use for him, and he knew it. He wanted to have a baby, but in the same way that he wanted an LCD TV. He didn't *need* to have a baby, the ache of absence wasn't eating at his soul until it felt like a husk.

And then my sister announced she was pregnant.

CHAPTER 11

The possibility hadn't even occurred to me. Lizbet couldn't stand babies. She wasn't maternal. She preferred cats. She had a cat, what was it called, Sphincter? The *cat* was her baby. It ate fresh Atlantic prawns from Marks & Spencer, and like the babies of many Hollywood stars, it slept on a pink cashmere blanket from *ChicStuff.com*. It had a better standard of living than most people. How dare she get pregnant! Just buy another cat, *Lizbet*. She didn't deserve a baby. She had no idea about babies.

Even as the word formed in my head, I felt my insides ooze molten in desire. *Baby*. Ah, there's nothing in the world like a baby. The solid warm chunkiness of a baby, the absolute perfection of the *body* of a baby, the look of an angel in a dreaming baby, the magnificence of a raging baby, the awesome purity of a baby's smile, the musical coo of a social baby, the businesslike look of a baby drinking, the sly Pink Panther eyes of a baby on the edge of sleep, the hilarious toothless gums of a baby, the fabulous fatness of a baby's face viewed from below (the eternal question—when do the cheeks become chin?) . . . . All of it left her cold. She'd step over a baby in the gutter.

It made me sick. The neighbor had asked her and Tim to be godparents—that laughable potty design had them all fooled—and the first time Lizbet babysat Tomas, she begged me to be there because she was *scared*. I think she was actually proud of being useless with kids, disliking babies. It was a pose to show the world that she was far too modern to further the species. Yeah, dying out—cool. I'm not even convinced she believed her own hype. It was a defense; she saw her childbearing hips as a mark of the Devil. She was insecure, and a lot of her life was *show*.

Even now, she spoke to her godson like he was an idiot—"Ooh, Tomas, that's a nice top you're wearing, what color is it?" Quite rightly, Tomas wouldn't dignify her questions with a response. I suppose she'd got *slightly* better with him, but she reminded me of an arachnophobe who'd successfully completed a course at the zoo and was now holding a tarantula in her hand. You felt that at any minute she might throw her arms in the air, let out a bloodcurdling scream, shudder from head to foot, and run from the room.

Whereas, the cat. Jesus. She'd have put it down for Oxford if she could. I'd be standing in her kitchen and the cat would be sprawled on the *counter*, literally; it would crap in its litter tray, filling the room with the aroma of shit, then leap onto the side where food was prepared. It was disgusting. Then it would collapse, like Cleopatra on a daybed, with its poo-flecked arse touching the countertop, and Lizbet would cry, "Cassie, doesn't Sphinx look like she's on *Question Time*?"

What? No! What the hell was she talking about?

I'd say as much, and she'd say, "Oh you know, the way she's got her paws tucked in, and she's leaning to one side, she looks so serious and intelligent ... She also reminds me of the Chinese Mandarin in that old story, "The Little Shepherdess"; you know, those big sleeves, his hands clasped together but you can't see them?"

Really. I mean, what?

Every time I thought of her, smug and unknowing with a baby inside, I felt a rip of rage. *I* was the one who was supposed to breeze through life, with it all going right, and I'll tell you why—because I *worked* to ensure that it all went right. And I just couldn't believe how *wrong* it had gone for me. I hate that phrase "Nothing's certain in life except death and taxes," because actually, I feel that some things *should* be certain. For instance, if your perfect mother dies before you meet her, you are owed. In that situation, you are owed whatever you fucking want. It made me *snarl* when I thought of all the work I'd put in to trying to conceive. You work hard, you expect the payoff.

How had *she* managed it? *She* was the bumbling one. She was the older child, the girl who had to hack her way through jungle, clearing the path for *me*. That was how I thought of it—her, disheveled, dirty, exhausted, sweat running in rivulets down her face, in the wrong trousers that creased over the crotch, and me, walking neatly and swiftly after, pristine and glamorous in my Marc Jacobs mules. That was how it had always been. Lizbet made the mistakes; even though she was such a good girl, our parents never gave her credit, they had no idea of their luck.

Even now, if Lizbet spoke at the table and I even *looked* as if I had a thought in my head, Mummy would say, "Elizabeth! Let your sister speak!" Although Lizbet had never interrupted me; I was always the one who interrupted her. But Mummy never saw that; she confused size with strength. Lizbet is a great big girl, and the reason is, she's *uncontrolled*—with food, spending, everything. She feels she was deprived as a child, so as an adult, whatever she wants she must have. Her cupboards are crammed with Cappuccino Mix. No one needs Cappuccino Mix. It's not dignified. She watched *Super Size Me*, and went straight to McDonald's. She did the Atkins Diet, "but with potatoes."

And if a new chocolate bar is launched, Lizbet has to eat it that same day. She'll ring me from the shop. She and Tim refer to chocolate as "brown." She tells me how much she's eaten, like I'm a priest and can rub out her guilt. That's Lizbet; she wants someone to erase the consequences of her mistakes. *I* find it a bit retro, going on about chocolate. It's the twenty-first century—I think women can eat a bit of chocolate with impunity. But Lizbet hates being weak. "YOU ARE A BIG FATTY" is spelled in fluorescent magnetic letters on her fridge, and I once caught her taking an instant photo of herself naked from waist to knee. "I'm going to stick it on the larder door," she explained.

"Right," I said. "You're going to stick a snap of your vagina on the kitchen wall. That'll be a nice warm welcome for guests."

I'm the maternal one. It irritates me that people are always surprised by that—as if it's impossible to be more than one thing. I have a tough exterior, and interior, but a good mother *needs* that, and, by the way, I love children. They make me laugh. They're crazy, and honest, and pure undistilled emotion, and I appreciate that—in others. I understand children. For God's sake, *Lizbet* is like a child! *I* look after her. She's *always* screwing up. Even though she has the air of being sensible, she isn't. She's a liability. She pays a great deal of attention to little things that don't matter—"Hang on, no, not that cup, I can't drink out of a cup that shape, get the one that Tomas painted, the purple, yellow, and black one—no!—sorry, I've changed my mind, the bone china one with cats on the side, yes! Great, just pour in the coffee from the other cup"—and the big things that *do* matter—say, buying the house that she can afford rather than the house she *wants*—are ignored.

Children aren't called "dependents" for fun, Lizbet. You need a hundred grand a year to raise a kid in London. They'd been in that house three years and it was a wreck. Lizbet was a laughingstock in the Jewish community for marrying out to a man who was *bad at DIY*. The paintwork was flaking, the wall plaster was chipped, and *still* two sheets of blackout material hung from their bedroom curtain rail instead of curtains. And there was a large grease stain on the wall above the bed. When Lizbet saw me looking, she shrugged and said, "It's from the previous owner's head, I think. I don't lean back, or else I prop the pillow up really high."

Lizbet is so happy-go-lucky, and I don't like happy-go-lucky people—"happy-go-lucky" is a polite phrase for "too lazy to *try*." Just, happy and lucky without trying. Her optimism borders on stupidity. Every week, she doesn't win the lottery, and is surprised. And she thinks that pension planning is for other people. As for what she *does* worry about: "Cassie, can Buddhists wear fur coats?" "Cassie, is it possible for a body to fart after dying?" "Cassie, you know when you say 'it's too much aggro?' Aggro is short for aggravation, so shouldn't it be 'it's too much ag*gra*?'"

She's so . . . *distracted*. She's just wafted into pregnancy. She has no idea. My boss, Sophie, and I were gazing at baby Justin—asleep with an imperious look and fists clenched after a full hour of blue-faced screeching—and I thought, Where's your knuckle-duster reading "R U TUFF ENUF"?

Fair enough if Lizbet was neutral about babies. But she regards them as an affront to her human rights. Aunt Edith once asked Lizbet when she was going to have a baby, and Lizbet said, "It's private." Aunt Edith is *elderly*. She is also the person who spent every Friday of the seventies and eighties cooking the two of us veal escalopes, beef goulash, black cherry sundaes with fan wafers, choux swans (she fashioned the neck shapes out of pastry), and meringue gateaux—topped with pink icing, raspberries, and crushed pistachio nuts. So you make allowances. Lizbet doesn't have the wit to see that the question isn't offensive if it's borne out of love. I mean, Aunt Edith has a subscription to *Ladz Mag*.

But I forget. "Mother" has always been a dirty word to Lizbet. She finds mothers threatening, her own included. *I* hold Mummy in abject disregard, but that's her own fault—she couldn't really be bothered to do her job (and I don't mean as editor of *Mother & Home*). When we were little we only ever played with the kids in our road, because Mummy was never at the school gates to network with other mothers and get us invited to *proper* places.

I misbehaved for sixteen years to get her attention, and it only half worked. But I adored Aunt Edith; I saw how motherhood could be done. Aunt Edith focused, and nothing I did could shake her love. Lizbet says that aged four I bit her and told her to "Fuck it" (she wouldn't let me hack the "magic curling hair" off my Quick Curl Barbie with a carving knife), and Aunt Edith said, "That's unacceptable behavior, young lady. It also makes me sad because I love you, Cassie. Say sorry, let's have a hug, and we'll be friends."

I always remembered that, and reminded her of it, years later. She smiled and said, "You weren't naughty in the slightest, Cassie. You were a normal toddler—boisterous, challenging, powerful— that's the nature of the beast!"

Why wasn't *our* mother like that?

Lizbet doesn't see that being a mother is an important occupation, *the* most important occupation. No one's suggesting that's all she's good for—but if they were—it's a compliment, even if, in these skewed times, it doesn't seem to be. A good mother has to be *nails*. You have to be tireless, not like these City wimps who can only function on five unbroken hours of sleep a night. You have to be alert, patient, fun, resourceful, diplomatic, selfless, thoughtful, creative, clever, loving—for, oh, the rest of your life. But never mind all that. What would make Lizbet truly content is if she got a three-hundred-word feature on DIY sex disasters printed on page 93 of "The Filth Issue" of *Ladz Mag*.

Because she was never glamorous growing up, she needs to feel glamorous now—and while writing for *Ladz Mag* scrapes the barrel in glamour terms, she sees it as glamour of a *sort*, in that it's slightly seedy, risqué, it suggests she's a bit of a bad girl. (Nothing could be further from the truth.) Being a mother wouldn't satisfy her, because in her mind there's no glamour in it. *Duh!*

She's not qualified to be a mother. I remember how she was with *me*. Always making me sit on radiators. I'd do it to humor her. *I* looked out for Lizbet, because she couldn't even stand up for herself. She attended Hebrew classes for a year before I intervened. She hated Hebrew classes, yet she meekly trudged off to synagogue week after week, even though Mummy and Daddy were joke opponents and would have packed her off in a red bikini if she'd said, "*No* one has Hebrew classes anymore. Mrs. Schuller says we should be spending our Sunday mornings at sauna baths—she says they're springing up all over the place."

Vivica and Daddy didn't have a clue; they flapped around with their hopeless child-rearing theories: learn the trombone, see a monkey, get some fresh air. They needed direction and discipline—which I provided. I showed them a firm hand and set boundaries, and they were far happier. But Lizbet never had the confidence to *lead*. That was fine when she only had her own life to ruin, but as a parent, it's disastrous. You need to be fearless. If you're afraid of the world, you kill your kids' self-esteem. They see *you* scared, and it's like Dorothy seeing the Wizard of Oz scared. Lizbet's idea of being tough is penning the supermarket a polite note about a brown avocado.

Her child is doomed.

CHAPTER 12

I couldn't look at Lizbet. I didn't want to be in the same room as her. I didn't want to be on the same *planet*. Everyone ooo-ing and cooing, talking about booties, even George's parents. And I saw Mrs. Hershlag's eyes pass wistfully over *me*. Me, the barren career bitch. Lizbet didn't even notice I was upset—she was totally consumed with herself and the baby. I and everyone else around her were white noise. You see that in pregnant women. Unless they're looking at nursery furniture, their gaze doesn't actually lock on.

She'd told me, on the phone, before she told our parents, and for a minute, I was robbed of the ability to form words. Do you even know how significant that is, for a *barrister*? No one knew how I had been feeling, for so long. I was a good performer. I preferred to keep all mess inside. You have to be one selfish sod to let another person see you, as a grown adult, snot-nosed from crying.

But some days I had to force myself to stand upright instead of cringing, heaving my heavy self around like a human question mark, because I was sure the sky was about to fall on my head. Disaster was imminent, always. At any moment, I expected the ceiling to collapse on top of me—great rocks of concrete crashing down like a biblical hail—and smash my skull to bits of eggshell.

The feeling might have coincided with news of the death of Sarah Paula, but I couldn't tell anymore. The badness was all mixed up in one nauseating swirl. Gloom had arrived, sudden and heavy as a rain cloud, and stayed. It had been over a year now, and I was used to it being there, an oppressive, dragging presence. It was like having an inoperable hump. Nothing I could do about it, except maintain the pretense of pursuing my life as normal. But that was the problem. I was *pursuing* life—chasing after the meaning of existence—and it was eluding me.

I took it as a personal affront. Forrest Gump was wrong. "Life is like a box of chocolates—you never know what you're gonna get." What a crock; it was a flawed analogy. You *do* know what you're gonna get with a box of chocolates; you read the illustrated leaflet, usually to be found resting on the top layer, and it describes each filling and flavor *exactly*. It turned out that life was not like this at all. Every last bite was a disgusting shock.

And there was more. The truth had been creeping after me for a while and it had finally caught up. I didn't know what to do—it was a rotten situation. At first I'd thought it was a phase, but it wasn't. *I was out of love with George.*

It had always been hard for people—except George—to see what I saw in George. His mother had given him the confidence of ten men, and he expected all women to find him irresistible, even though, in a *Cosmo* quiz, he'd have scored nil points. For one, he was rude. We met at a Brazilian restaurant in West London. It was Lizbet's birthday, and a friend of hers had brought him along. He sat between us and ignored me for an hour, while he explained why *he* was a viable candidate for Mensa and Lizbet wasn't.

"How much do you weigh? Right. And you're not *that* tall.

You're a viscerotonic endomorph. I'll explain. When babies are born, they're composed of gut, muscle, and brain in equal amounts, yes? However. Things change. Some people grow up to have more muscle than gut—Schwarzenegger, for instance [all George's references were thirty years out of date]—and in others, the brain develops, so effectively, you get a person with more brain than gut. *Me,* for instance. Feel my abs. Go on. Can you pinch anything? Go on, try! Go on! See? Can't get a grip, can you? And wouldn't you say that my head was on the large side? To house the brain, see? Whereas, *your* head is medium sized. You're more . . . gut."

He made me laugh. He was so sure of himself. A lot of men wouldn't dare approach me, which I found pathetic. And if they did, they wouldn't know what to say. George *always* had something to say, even if it was rubbish. In fact, you could have fed George into a sausage machine and chances were he'd still be talking until his head disappeared down the chute and emerged the other end, a frankfurter.

When he finally got around to acknowledging my presence, he said, "I can't believe you're sisters. You look nothing like each other. Who chose this place? The wine's good, but . . . all this *meat*. Every five seconds I look up and there's a man wielding a beef joint and a large knife two centimeters from my head. It's like Friday Night at my mother's house."

George always referred to his parents' home as his "mother's house," as if his father had moved out and was now living in a tent on wasteland. George certainly didn't appreciate his father, or how much his father loved him. He once told me that his father "threatened me a lot, as a child." I was surprised, and disappointed, as I couldn't think of a gentler soul than Mr. Hershlag. *What,* exactly, had he done?

George did an impression of his father at the breakfast table, when he, George, was fifteen. "If you get a degree, I buy you a car! Only if you get a degree! No degree, no car! And don't become a junkie! All these kids I see on the street, they're all junkies! You become a junkie, see that knife? [at this point Mr. Hershlag would jab a finger at the bread knife] Take it! Take it and kill me! Kill me! [banging on his chest with the flat of both hands] Right here!"

Of *course* George got his degree—he wasn't going to miss out on a free car. He reminded me of myself, in that he had no guilt about squeezing every last penny out of his parents—they could have been homeless in the street before *he* suffered the slightest twinge. In the first term of his Media, Culture, and Society degree, he claimed that Birmingham was freezing, so Mrs. Hershlag sent him money for a winter coat. He immediately spent it on . . . a winter coat. (Me: "Weren't you tempted to spend it on beer?" Him: "*No!* I was cold!")

He was irrepressible. His old roommate at college had once described him as "like a shit in a toilet that wouldn't flush down." While this was a little harsh, the *essence* of the simile was correct. George always bounced back, despite your best efforts.

Initially, I was cool and frosty toward him, but he was so convinced of his own charms, I don't think he noticed. On our first date, ordained by George twenty minutes after we met, without my consent—"Shoulder of what? *Lamb?* Ugh! Cholesterol city! No thanks! [turning to me] *I'll* take you somewhere proper to eat"— we went to a sleek Japanese restaurant, sat on hard chairs, and ate a little raw tuna and rice. (George set the chopsticks to one side and reached for a fork, before we were served.) I found him intriguing. He was funny, in a terse sort of way. He said what he thought, not what you wanted to hear.

It all went wrong for George when the world didn't acknowledge his brilliance with the same rapture as his parents had. He had done well to get into the BBC (he'd claimed to be half-Russian on his CV—"basically, as ethnic as possible"). Oxbridge graduates were clamoring for the job he had, even though broadcast assistants were paid meanly and worked like mules—but George had always seen the BA job as a short-term position, to last him until the commissioning editor knocked on his door and begged him to become a drama producer. But there were no vacancies. George's only hope was that a colleague would die.

He'd been waiting for six years, and was tired of always being the one to run across the road to buy cake for birthdays. He was bitter. His colleagues never saw it, but I did.

I hadn't at first. But the discovery—and loss—of my real mother threw our relationship into sharp relief, and I saw a lot that previously I'd been blind to.

Especially when we failed to conceive, George acted as if his failure—*all* failure—was my fault. We had the home, car, and lifestyle to show for *my* success, and it began to dawn on me that he was jealous. He knew he wasn't a partner, he was a dependent. His resentment turned him into an old woman. He was sullen to me, curt to my friends, and anal about the house. He was forever slipping coasters under my coffee mug. If I loaded the dishwasher, he'd rearrange it. We weren't allowed to sit in the front room until he found the right sofas.

George was tall and thin, with dark hair and a slight potbelly. (Lizbet had indeed felt his abs at her birthday party all those years ago and—she was a little drunk—cried, "There's nothing there!") But gorgeous men bored me, and anyway, George's arrogance was attractive. Now he'd lost it, and the spell was broken. Everything he did annoyed me. Like, he pronounced Lemsip, "Lem*zip*." You don't zip it! You sip it!

And then came The Art Project. George decided he wasn't pretentious enough and enrolled in an art course at a London college close to "The Beeb." George studied Renaissance Art, but he couldn't paint a picture to save his life. (I'd seen him draw a house; it was a triangle on top of a square). To save face, he took refuge in modernism—a genre he would otherwise have loathed. He called his creations "bodyworks." He'd tip a vat of paint on a sheet of plastic and roll in it naked. Then he'd roll on the canvas. He was definitely protesting against something. I just wasn't sure *what*.

Once, I peered closely at a finished "piece" and said, "There are three pubic hairs on this!"

He snapped, "It's all *integral* to the *installation*, don't you *seeee?*"

His final thesis was entitled "Inhabitation of a Male Skin in the Post-Modern Era," and he spent many an evening naked and blindfolded in the living room, groping himself and painting "what he felt," while a video camera on a tripod recorded the proceedings. The college held an exhibition for all graduating students, and while George wore a suit for the occasion, the entire room saw his particulars (as Aunt Edith might say) on a large screen. I found it silly and humiliating, and I felt that in awarding George an A, the college was pandering to childish behavior. I was grateful that Mr. Hershlag was in hospital with pneumonia.

I made George's comfortable existence possible—without me, he'd be living in an East Acton squat—and yet he was so disrespectful. He was the only person who *ever* interrupted me. If we had dinner with, say, Tim and Lizbet, George would jump in and provide the last word of my every sentence. And get it *wrong*.

ME: Whenever I'm in a posh restaurant, I always order scallops. I don't even really *like* scallops, but I feel compelled to order them. It's something about the—

GEORGE: Texture?

ME: *No.* The word "scallops." It sounds delicious.

I'd look at Tim and Lizbet's relationship and I'd be envious of what they had. They were so *happy* together. They had fun. They were best friends. Even with no money. How did they do that? I wouldn't know how to have fun without money. They were like kids together—they had their own private words, like "jel-jel" for "jealous." They laughed together about little things.

"Tim," Lizbet had said, the last time I'd visited. "Show Cassie that flyer." Tim rustled around the desk by their front door and handed me a poorly typed photocopied leaflet. It read, "TIRED OF CLEANING YOURSELF? LET SOMEONE ELSE DO IT!"

I'd smiled and handed it back. I knew that if this leaflet had dropped through *my* mail slot, I'd have considered showing it to George. And then I wouldn't have bothered. But Tim and Lizbet shared, and so their days were scattered with lovely moments. They were a team, and—I noticed—they touched each other a lot.

When Tim had secured his potty deal, they'd gone to Amsterdam to celebrate, and "had a bit of a sesh" in a hotel. Only after had they noticed a guy in the building opposite, binoculars in one hand, penis in the other. Presuming they were putting on a show, the man had put down his binoculars, or penis (Tim didn't specify), to wave at them. I laughed as Tim and Lizbet recounted, but secretly I was *stunned*. Imagine that! Tim and Lizbet still had sex for fun! And it wasn't five minutes of doglike humping under the duvet! It was fancy enough to be *entertaining*!

Seeing those two together left me with a dollop of gloom in the pit of my stomach. George and I bickered *more* in their company, and I think it was because the warm cohesion of their relationship threw ours—jarred and damaged—into sharp relief.

Also, I couldn't help thinking that Tim was the better man.

So you see, I was caught. I wanted that baby—George and I were still trying for the baby—and yet the sex was cold and joyless, because in my heart I no longer wanted *George*. A baby without a father . . . You should tell him . . . But then you won't get the baby . . . I am not going to think about this now. When I get the baby, *then* I'll think about it. The thoughts ran through my head endlessly. What a mess. It seemed that suddenly I had nothing, and Lizbet had *everything*.

And then, she didn't. Mummy called and told me, in a flat voice. I listened, in silence.

I said, "Is Lizbet okay? I mean, physically?"

"Mm," said Vivica. She gave a sort of moan and put the phone down. This from the woman who'd tried to cheer up my sister after Letty Jackson's Persian cat got into our garden and bit through the carotid artery of Lizbet's lop-eared rabbit, Miffy, by saying, in a comforting tone, "In a hundred years we'll all be dead and none of this will matter."

In a hundred years we'll all be dead and none of this will matter.

It didn't convince. I walked into my kitchen and opened a cupboard door. Inside was our gorgeous wedding crockery, our complete and valuable set of Royal Worcester bone china in Mountbatten Cobalt. It was my favorite possession. It spoke of another era. It said that life was elegant, and civilized, and genteel. Every piece was smooth and *beautiful*. Each dinner plate was thirty quid. The covered soup tureen cost two hundred and seventy-five pounds. I lifted each of the twelve plates out of the cupboard, carefully unwrapped them from their white tissue paper, and dropped them on the floor, one by one by one, until I was standing barefoot in a prettily glinting sea of smashed china.

"What are you doing?" screamed George.

"I didn't hear you come in," I said. I lifted the covered soup tureen out of its nest of tissue paper and held it lovingly at chest level.

"No!" shouted George. "I beg you! Not the covered soup tureen!"

We watched it break into hundreds of pieces.

"Are you *mad*?" screeched George. "Have you lost your mind?"

I shook my head, and reached for the sauce boat stand (twenty-four pounds). George gave me a sharp push away from the cupboard, and I lost my balance and fell.

"Oh, shit," said George, as the blood rushed from my hands and knees. "I didn't mean—Are you all right?"

I gasped for a bit, with the pain, even though it felt right. Everything was turning red. Then I said, in the smallest voice, "I can't believe it. My sister lost her baby."

CHAPTER 13

_____ *Lizbet*

The meanest thing Cassie ever did to me was on a family holiday in St. Moritz, in celebration of our parents' twentieth anniversary. (Our father never forgot a birthday or an anniversary—he remembered, he said, by *not* writing things down.) It was the prettiest place we'd ever seen, all snowy and sparkly, like a never-ending Christmas. I was wide-eyed for the entire week, as our usual holidays were a bit *scratchy*. This was because, unlike certain of his colleagues, our father refused to accept favors from his clients.

We could have stayed a month in a villa on the beach on the island of St. Barts, free of charge. We could have spent the New Year in Monaco, lazily cruising the bay on a white yacht. We never did. We'd rent an apartment in Crete with an ancient kitchen and blocked-up drains. (If you went to the beach and forgot to shut the bathroom door, the stench hit your throat as you entered the hall.)

Our mother sulked for the entirety of that particular vacation—her face darkened on day one, when a three-legged dog ran up and sniffed her you-know-where, and she didn't raise another smile until we saw the graffiti on the bridge as we left Heathrow. But our father said, "When I'm on holiday, I prefer to be my own person. I don't want an upgrade. I don't want to be known. I don't want to have to shave." I didn't like our father with a beard. The bristles emerged gray. I felt as if he was old and out of control.

Cassie adored the glamor of St. Moritz, and spent much of the time prancing around in a moth-eaten fur coat that she'd found in Aunt Edith's attic. I very much fear it was squirrel. Our father had booked a family suite, and Cassie and I were sitting on the sofa, talking. I didn't hear our parents come in, but Cassie did and said in a loud voice, "And stop talking about blow jobs!" then ran out of the room.

As talk of blow jobs didn't figure in their parental lexicon, our mother and father said nothing. It didn't figure in *my* lexicon either; I was mortified into silence. A few days later, I got a sore throat. Our father took a look, decided he could see an ulcer, and concluded that I had orally contracted VD. He took me to a doctor and said, *"Elle a eu de rapport orale."*

While it soon became evident that I didn't have VD, I never told our father the truth. I was so caught up in the lurid drama of his imagination that I actually wrote in my diary, "I don't have VD after all!" The trip to the doctor was humiliating. But at sixteen, I thought it was worse *not* to have ever given a blow job. I'm not sure that I ever forgave our father. I was hurt that he didn't trust me, but I was more hurt that he didn't *know* me. I forgave Cassie though. It struck me that I've always forgiven her.

After my baby died, Cassie was wonderful. Professional wonderful. Not many people were. They were full of consolation. But they were a little *brisk*. They seemed to have weighed it up and decided that this was worth just the *one* "I'm so sorry" conversation. They'd ask "How *are* you?" but the expression on their faces said, "Don't tell me." It was like in a nightmare, where you need someone's help to save yourself but you can't speak and they can't hear you.

So I never said that I woke every morning and for a blissful second forgot, and stroked my stomach. Sorrow was in my bones, set thick and gray in the jelly of the marrow. If the editor presented me with a problem at work, often I couldn't hear him because my whole head would be screaming, "Fuck off fuck off—can't you see I am half-dead with pain here?" The editor's PA said—with the confidence of the unbothered—"You'll have other babies." I didn't want other babies. I wanted *this* baby. I was knocked flat by the violence of my yearning for a person I never knew. "Oh, Baby," I'd whisper. "Poor little Baby'—and then, because I'd always spoken for her—"Ah, Mummy."

I kept winding back my life to survey the surreal horror of its disintegration—*Why? How?* At sixteen weeks and five days, we were fine. At sixteen weeks and *six* days, we were dead. Sixteen weeks and six days had destroyed me. Seventeen weeks ago, I'd been happy, with nothing. But for sixteen weeks and five days, I'd been lent the experience of having it all, and now nothing was no longer nothing. It was *minus everything*. It was beyond bearable.

The cramps were sudden and painful, and the blood was wet and slippery and everywhere in the bed. I made Tim look—I was too frightened to look myself. "It's coming out in *clots*," he said. Suddenly, I couldn't catch my breath, I couldn't take in the oxygen to scream. Grim-faced, Tim sped us to hospital, me in a dressing gown with a towel stuffed between my legs. He carried me into the ER—they wheeled me to a room by the maternity ward—and for a second, with the rush and the fuss and the pain of it, I could imagine that I was giving birth as normal.

I wasn't. I thought of it as giving death.

Each moment stood alone in its awfulness. My head telling me, "This is the end," and my heart refusing to believe it. Lying on a bed, hearing fetal heart monitors in the next room. The obstetrician telling me that I was "actively miscarrying." Feeling the contractions crushing, harder and harder, begging someone to stop them, keep the baby in, and the midwife saying, "The cervix is open, honey. There's no treatment, no drugs to stop the uterus contracting. I'm sorry." She told me I wouldn't need to push, and I felt sicker than I did already—a small mercy, in that I didn't have to *collude* with my stupid body.

The tiniest most perfect baby girl.

The obstetrician was kind, allowed that it was "traumatic," but made himself scarce. I formed the word "Why," and he said if I'd had a little bleeding at seven weeks . . . ten . . . recurrent episodes . . . could have opened up the cervix . . . bacteria . . . into the womb . . . blood clot . . . infected . . . labor . . ." The words floated here and there, and questions arose like bubbles. *Had* I had bleeding? Had I even known I was pregnant then? Was I such a bumbling idiot I'd assumed it was a *period*? But all I could hear was my own voice screaming, "Baby—dead." He tried to comfort me—the "sinister possibilities" of a late miscarriage, but mine being a "one-off complication"—but I was rendered half-deaf with grief.

I wanted nothing going in the incinerator, and so the hospital gave me a small cardboard box. A makeshift coffin for my first child. They were good. They really were. I could see it in their eyes. "You poor lady." I didn't want to be a poor lady. I wanted to be a mummy.

I buried our baby under the orange blossom, digging the soil with my bare hands. I recalled myself as a little girl burying my rabbit in a Clarks shoe box all those years ago, and I was glad that little girl hadn't seen ahead to *this*. My world shrank and everything reflected my grief. Staring glass-eyed into the garden, I saw a small white petal flutter to the ground—a mocking message from a sadistic god—and I collapsed on the floor, howling. I was as bad as Tim's mother (convinced the robin redbreast fluffing its feathers in the birdbath was Nan, Tim's grandmother, checking up on her).

My moron body still thought it was pregnant—it mocked me with two blue lines on the test I did, after. I felt empty—because I was. Like one of those cheap hollow chocolate eggs, what were they called, Kinder Surprise. Surprise, your kinder's dead.

Tim was useless—silent and grave. He'd been making me pot chicken. Now he stopped, as if I was no longer worth cooking for. A week after the operation, he caught me checking *The New Pregnancy and Birth Book* to see what stage we would have been at. His face paled, and he held out his hand for it, like a teacher confiscating sweets. Then he said, "Lizbet. Try to remember what the doctor told you. Carrying a viable pregnancy is similar to the predictability of throwing a dice. You can't guarantee a six every time. Sometimes you'll throw a two." I felt a lurch of hatred in my gut so fierce I thought I'd wrenched something.

But Cassie didn't put a foot wrong. She appeared on the doorstep, crushed me in a long hug, and whispered, "I am so, so sorry. How are you? This is a tragedy. It's horrific."

I waited for the "But." It didn't come.

She brought food with her. I stared at the glass casserole dish in disbelief. "Is this . . . *homemade?*"

Cassie nodded, blushed. "I followed the recipe," she said. "It's a bean thing."

"Great," I said. I was impressed. That girl could pillage Marks & Spencer like a Viking in a village. But while she owned a John

Pawson—designed kitchen, so white and minimalist that bliss could have set up a spa in there, I had never seen her touch her Gaggenau oven. In fact, as every knob, switch, and appliance was hidden behind white lacquered wood doors, I couldn't even be sure that she knew where it was.

A small, thin woman with a nervous posture and bouffant burgundy hair appeared behind her.

"Oh!" said Cassie. "This is Rumi. She's come to clean the house."

"But I—"

"Don't worry," said Cassie. "It's all taken care of."

"Thanks," I muttered. I managed a smile for Rumi. "Would you like a cof—"

"Rumi only drinks Coke," said Cassie. "Don't you, Rumi?"

Rumi grinned and affirmed. Her teeth needed work. "Where I start?" she said.

I stared at her, like she'd asked a maths question. Even the tiniest challenge drew a blank.

"Upstairs bathroom," said Cassie.

I knew that Cassie found the dirt levels in my house revolting. They probably were.

Because we were *us*—financial bozos, inept adults—even the one room we'd had redone wasn't right. Our new bathroom cost nine grand (Tim didn't realize that the sandstone was priced *per tile*) and was installed by idiots. I got an inkling on the first day when I trotted upstairs to see that James—charming, charming, *very* posh, total screwup—had sawn the top off a water pipe and was trying to stem the gushing water with his fist. By the time the bathroom was finished, they'd caused three leaks, and had to repaint the living room, twice. The first time I sat in our new bath, I seriously worried that it would drop through the floor and the paramedics would find me sat, dead and naked, in a giant enamel bath, in front of the French doors.

Within weeks, tiles cracked and wall paint bubbled. The button you pressed to flush the toilet bounced off its spring and into the bowl. The stainless steel switch on the power shower fell off the wall, clunked into the bath, and chipped it. The underfloor heating went nuclear, so every trip to the loo was like stepping across hot coals.

When the sink blocked, we discovered that the plug wasn't detachable, and that the unit had been installed in a way that made it impossible to unscrew the drainage pipe. I spent hours with tweezers prying gunk from beneath the plug, but it never made much difference, and every time you washed your hands, the sink would fill with water rank with regurgitated flotsam. It was quite, quite disgusting, even to me. But plumbers were expensive, and one day Tim really *would* get around to tipping a bottle of Drano down the plug hole. But he didn't, and eventually, I noticed that while Cassie might visit, she never used the facilities.

"There's a taxi waiting outside," she added. "I'm taking you to the Dorchester Spa for some pampering."

She did. The Dorchester Spa was sleek and superior, not like my local beauty salon where you'd go for a leg wax and try not to notice the unemptied bin of hair and lush carpet of assorted pubes. Cassie slid off for an Eve Lom facial, and a kind lady in a white coat laid me down under a warm towel and gave me a deep tissue massage. I remembered the books saying that you should avoid treatments and aromatherapy oils in the first trimester, and it occurred to me that she was literally rubbing it in that I wasn't pregnant.

Each week, there was a thoughtful gesture, some treat. One day Cassie turned up with a hamper from her local Italian deli. It contained Parma ham, soft oozing cheeses, chocolate espresso beans, and vintage red wine, all lying in a bed of pink tissue paper. I suppose the subtext was, there are advantages to not being pregnant. She meant it kindly, I know. But the truth was, her kindness came too late. She'd resented the existence of my baby, and now my baby was dead. I felt that her bad vibes had *willed* it to happen.

I hated her.

CHAPTER 14

Our mother had no idea of what was appropriate, and often, when she spoke, I dreamed of force-feeding her peanut butter until her tongue stuck to the roof of her mouth. Once, she and I attended a circumcision. Everyone, including the rabbi, was so busy yapping, they didn't notice that the poor baby was about to roll off his velvet cushion onto the floor. Tim yelled, "Look out!" And Vivica shouted, *"Jesus!"*

But to my surprise, she seemed to understand a little. She was sad and subdued when she visited, and then she blurted, "I never should have bought the baby clothes. I got carried away. I'd already imagined her as part of the family."

I had already imagined the baby as part of the family. I thought I was the only one. In my dreams, she lived an entire life. I was touched that Vivica blamed herself. Normally, any suggestion from our father that she might be responsible for anything bad—leaving a cigarette smoldering and burning his beloved Parker Knoll armchair to a blackened shell, say—and she turned cold and incredulous.

Actually, I was glad that Vivica had bought baby clothes. It showed me that she *believed* in the baby. It was important. Like believing in fairies. If you don't believe in something, then it dies. Cassie, for instance, hadn't believed in the baby. We, the faithful, had assigned the baby the room with pale blue walls, and every day I sat on its varnished floorboards, held the tiny trousers and tops to my face, and cried silently into their softness.

Tim's mother was all big bosom and soft voice, and I had expected her to be perfect—a one-woman crack emotional response team—but she wasn't. She came to see us and, beyond a brief "How are you," *didn't mention it*. In fact, she seemed almost sullen, as if I'd willfully done her out of a grandchild. Her parting words were "Next time, Elizabeth, dear, you must relax and let it happen."

I had known her for seven years, and suddenly I found that I didn't know her at all. She and Tim's father had always been polite, and respectful to our family, but then this politeness and respect was easy to maintain because they rarely *saw* our family. Also, it occurred to me that until now, I'd been the perfect girlfriend for their son. I'd never caused Tim's parents so much as an uncomfortable thought. I wasn't sexy, I had no desire to convince them of my political views, I didn't have any piercings, I was a good eater, and I adored their boy. Mrs. Higgins had been sweet to me all this time because I'd never given her reason to be otherwise.

Tim was full of excuses for her, and I wondered if he would have defended *me* as valiantly. "She's so sensitive that she finds it too painful to mention," he said. I smiled at him while, in my head, I let rip with a Tec-9 and splatted his brains up the living room walls, ruining the Mountain Mist matte finish (which was fine, as accidental damage was covered by our home insurance). I didn't care what mystery lay behind his mother's startling inability to acknowledge that anything bad had occurred—was I meant to *guess*? If I was, I might imagine that it just didn't seem important enough to her to express regret.

"No," I corrected. "She's so selfish that she finds it too painful to mention."

Tim couldn't have his mother less than perfect, and stalked out. I stamped after him, wanting the fight. Not long before, his parents had made the curious decision to attend a bullfight during their week-long holiday in Alicante, and Tim's mother had found it so traumatic, she felt compelled to share. She was like a tanker dumping toxic waste in a nature reserve.

"Then they cut its ear off. . . ." "The poor bull, he *wet himself*. . . ." On and on, the disturbing details gabbled out, and all the while I was begging, "Stop, stop, please! Don't tell me this!" but she *couldn't* stop; she talked over me. I'd made a "Can you believe this?" face at Tim, and he'd shrugged, half-laughing. Now I saw that Tim's mother was too weak to hold any pain inside her; she had to displace it.

I was stronger than her. *I* had no choice. So when I answered the phone and she cried, "Oh, *you* sound better!" I didn't bother to correct her. I just handed the receiver to Tim in silence, and held the pain inside me. I *moved* differently. (Tim: "Are you constipated? You're walking funny.") It was a delicate operation, like transporting a highly flammable liquid—I felt that if I jolted my hip on the table edge, the world would explode.

I think pain serves a function. It can be *something* when the alternative is nothing. To let go of the pain was to accept Fate—Fate, in the cruelest sense of that word—and there was no question: Acceptance would make me fickle. Still. The determination of others that I should "move on" was wearing. There is really no point in showing people something they have no interest in, so I filed the grief, inward.

It was best, I felt, to close a door on the subject, because everyone's reaction was annoying me. The consensus was, it was probably *my* fault. Now, I am happy to blame myself for almost every-thing. When it rained on Cassie's wedding day (in June), *I* felt re-sponsible. But I couldn't blame myself for this. I blamed my sister. I recalled seeing *Peter Pan* at the theater. Cassie was the only child in the audience who refused to clap to save Tinkerbell from dying. "I don't like her," she'd said, and folded her arms. I remembered the way she said it—like a gypsy curse.

Maybe they were right. I was overreacting. I wasn't, for instance, a mother screaming after a drunk driver, with her nine-year-old ly-ing dead in the street. There's no quibbling with a tragedy like *that*. You can tick all the boxes with a clear conscience. Bereavement? Yes. Grief? Yes. Sympathy? Yes. No one, not even the stupidest person, is going to tell a mother of a dead nine-year-old, "Maybe it was for the best." But a number of supposedly intelligent people had no problem saying those exact same words to *me*. It was confusing—I was used to being convinced by others, and now it felt strange to be resisting.

The only person who was any comfort whatsoever (Cassie em-pathized, but she was a fake) was Vivica. It was strange; it signified a total overhaul in our relationship. Before I fell pregnant, she'd never been overly bothered with me. If I called her on the phone, she wouldn't just sit and have a conversation. You'd hear her walk-ing around, lighting a cigarette, shuffling papers, *fidgeting,* to make the time go faster until I stopped talking about myself and she could put the phone down.

I always got the impression as a child that I was a disappoint-ment to her—not glamorous, not clever. I was quiet, squinty-eyed, with a gray tooth, I wasn't user-friendly. I was okay with that, be-cause she was a disappointment to *me*. But with the baby inside, I felt I had succeeded for her, for the first time. And when the baby left me, I felt the loss of status—as if the loss of life wasn't enough.

With Tim's mother, I went from VIP to invisible, so Vivica's response was a bonus. I appreciated her private devastation. There were signs. A Pampers ad came on the TV, and she screamed at our father, "Mute it! Mute it!" She didn't discuss her feelings because I don't think she liked having them. If ever she expressed an emotion, you suspected it had bolted when she wasn't looking—hence its wild, disheveled appearance. I'd had the same sense of her conscious and subconscious mind, not talking to each other, on leafing through early seventies copies of *Mother & Home*.

Under Vivica's editorship, the tone of *M&H* was cheery, upbeat, bursting with recipes (cake of the week: peach and coconut gateau), fun hobbies ("make your own dachshund cushion"), romantic fiction ("A Kind of Giving"), and decorating ideas ("A clever husband made this super pine dressing unit. . . ."). And yet the subtext was frightening. I saw our mother in every page, yelling, "I am propagating a nightmare!"

There were the endless advertisements encouraging readers to lose weight. ("There's nothing quite so ugly as great hulking thighs. . . ."). There were the advertisements that suggested that losing weight was a bit of a trial. (*How to Relieve Tense Nervous Headaches* . . . *All-Bran—The Natural Laxative Food* . . .)

There was the host of new convenience foods: Birds Eye Lamb Casserole, Shepherd's Pie . . . and the understanding that such shortcuts were simply unacceptable (the ad apologized for its implied slur on readers' culinary talents and was placed smack in the middle of ten cordon bleu cookery pages).

There was a wealth of products designed to make housekeeping a breeze—"Ajax Liquid: Twice the Ammonia, Half the Work!" There was a weary resignation, in features like *Beating the Blues*, that peace was impossible: "When things pile up, tell yourself firmly, Stop flapping around like a demented chicken."

There was a medical page, designed to restore the *M&H* audience to its peak mental and physical health. And the glaring fact that Doctor Frank found women both impertinent and disgusting. (His answers all began "Perhaps you are overweight" and ended "You should also think carefully about the way you are behaving." However, to the *Worried Reader*: "What you say your boyfriend is doing is part of normal sexual expression and no harm can come from it.")

I closed the final page of *Mother & Home* (an advert for Petito—the first ever calorie-reduced mashed potato) and imagined a woman shouting for help in a world that was stone deaf. After my miscarriage, I felt an affinity with our mother that I'd never felt before.

I did nothing about it. I couldn't be bothered to *relate*. She was probably hurt, and her visits dwindled. Meanwhile, Cassie was still turning up with fascist regularity, but I'd excuse myself and run a bath, and she'd talk to Tim instead. I'd fill the tub to the top with hot water and lie there like a hippo, submerged except for my nose. It was my little treat, like stepping off the planet for twenty minutes. The water muffled sound, and if I shut my eyes, I could imagine I was floating above the earth, serene, weightless—dead, actually.

Eventually, Cassie would leave, Tim would knock, and when I could, I'd reluctantly heave myself out, back to reality. Once, he actually splintered the door (he *said* he was scared I'd fallen asleep and drowned, but I think it was an excuse to be violent). It seemed he was always *calling* me, when really, all I wanted was to be left alone. "Lizbet, Lizbet"—he could never come to *me*, I always had to go to *him*. He could have got gangrene in both legs and his life would have barely changed.

I was in the baby's room one Sunday, when I heard him, shouting, "Lizbet, Lizbet."

I stormed out, screaming, "What the fuck is it now?" There was no answer, so I thumped downstairs—to see Tim, Tabitha, and Tomas standing in an awkward huddle by the front door. Tabitha had—I blinked—her new baby, Celestia, on her hip.

"Oh, ah, sorry!" I trilled. I lowered my palm in the vague direction of Tomas's head and added, "I'm in a bad mood with my husband!" I couldn't look at baby Celestia, but I could feel her presence, pulsing radioactive in the room.

"You said 'fuck,'" replied Tomas.

"No, no, no, I said, 'truck.'"

I smiled at Tabitha, when in fact I wanted to shout, "What's *he* doing here, get that kid away from me, and the baby, how could you, are you *insane*?" Presumably, if I were a recovering alcoholic, Tabitha would knock on the door and wave two bottles of vintage Krug in my face.

Tim turned to me with a stiff look. "Tabitha wondered if we could look after Tomas for an hour, she—"

"That doesn't make any sense!"

I glanced down at Tomas. "What doesn't?"

"'Truck' doesn't make any sense. You didn't say 'truck,' you said—"

"Tomas!" said Tabitha. "That's enough." She gave me a smile. "My sister's just gone into labor—it's her first—and I said I'd drive her to hospital, and I—"

My mouth fell open, I'm sure of it. Tabitha was beaming at me, and when she said *"it's her first,"* she gave me a "oh, you know, these novice mothers, aren't they a hoot" sort of look.

"What's wrong with a cab?"

The smile dropped off her face.

Tim coughed. "Lizbet means, wouldn't it be faster?"

"Actually, I—"

"And of course we'll look after Tomas," he added, putting a hand on my back and squeezing the skin between my shoulder blades.

Tabitha's smile bounced back. "Oh, you *stars*!" She sighed. "I wouldn't bother you, but the annoyance is, Nanny's ill, *says* she's run down—weak! Weak!—and Jeremy can't cope with Tomas *and* the baba. I left them for *five* minutes yesterday while I had a pedicure, and Jeremy *sat by* while Tomas emptied a great big box full of polystyrene chips from the new plasma, and *crumbled* them in *millions* of pieces all over the pine floor. Jeremy said he couldn't do anything 'because of the baby!'—although I saw he'd managed to read the *Guardian* from cover to cover. So I thought, aha, Tomas hasn't seen his godparents in a while." Pause. "I thought it would be nice for you too."

I choked. "You thought . . ."

"It *is* nice!" said Tim, briskly. "Tomas is my little mate, aren't you, Tomas? You're going to help me unblock the bathroom sink. We'll need drain fluid. I know! I'll show you how to get the cap off, and then you can pour it, how about that?"

"Tim"—Tabitha's voice was hesitant—"it's a lovely idea, but I'm not sure Tomas should be playing with—"

Baby Celestia started to cry, and Tabitha interrupted herself, "Oh, oh, come on, darling, hush now, it's okay." Her voice lost its habitual rasp, acquiring instead the softness of silk, and I felt my throat constrict. "Oh, she's bored of Mummy, aren't you, darling? Here, why don't *you* take her for a minute?" I realized with a jolt that she was addressing *me*.

I dug my nails into my palms, attempted to speak.

Tomas beat me to it: "Mummy, Mummy. *Her* said 'fuck.'"

"Tomas!" I said. "You're right. I said fuck! Okay? Fuck. Fuck. Fuck."

Tabitha was already backing away, opening the front door with her back to it, twisting Tomas in front of her with a steel grip on his shoulder, scurrying down our path at a brisk pace, baby Celestia clinging to her side like a small koala. "Not to worry!" she called, from beyond the hedge. "I can see it's not a good time!"

Tim shut the door, and ran his hand through his hair. He'd lost weight; it made him look tired. "Listen," he said. His voice was businesslike. "I know it's tough. *I know.* But, sweetheart, that's how it is. Sometimes, they don't stick. It's Nature's way. The baby probably would have been deformed. You heard what the doctor said. He said that if an embryo is genetically abnormal, often the fact is that—"

I screamed in an alien voice, "Don't talk to me about facts, you fucking moron—are you crazy? She wasn't deformed! You saw her! She came out of me! She was perfect! She had your face! What's wrong with you? I don't understand you! You're like a brick wall! Our baby is dead!"

If Tim was slightly surprised that the love of his life had just called him a fucking moron, he didn't show it. Maybe he had glue ear. He replied, in a calm tone, as if I was chiding him over a broken teacup, "Elizabeth. I am so sorry. But you have got to rein yourself in about this."

CHAPTER 15

Tim was right. I was making an exhibition of myself. And in our family, that was a bad thing. I refer you to Cousin Bernie. Cousin Bernie never married, and believe me, there was no mystery. He had a nervous habit of grabbing his hair—always greasy—and rubbing it between his fingers, again and again, and he had a compulsive, intermittent cough. He was a physics professor, good with equations, not so good with people. When Cousin Bernie turned forty, he decided, with great fanfare, to make aliyah. ("What's that?" said our mother, who disliked Cousin Bernie and took pleasure in baiting him. "Is it a cake?").

Making aliyah, as our mother knew full well, was to emigrate to Israel. In Judaism, this was a mitzvah, a good deed with spiritual overtones. And so the family was forced to make a great fuss of Cousin Bernie's midlife crisis, and the rabbi mentioned it in synagogue, and *The Jewish Chronicle* ran a story. (Really, *loads* of people made aliyah, but Uncle Bernie wanted his four pet ferrets to make aliyah also—"a great, attention-grabbing ploy," commented our mother sourly.)

Cousin Bernie, unused to being made a fuss of, reveled in the attention. There were three different leaving parties held in his honor. He offered to write a weekly column entitled *Jottings from Israel*, for a little known publication entitled the *Zionist Bugle* (the rather more prestigious *Jewish Chronicle* had passed on the invitation). He taught the ferrets to respond to "Dinnertime!" in Hebrew. He got a bigger send-off than the *Titanic*. Anyway, to cut a long story short, Cousin Bernie emigrated to Israel, couldn't hack it, and came back.

For a long time afterward, Cassie and I would hear our mother cackling aloud in the course of her day, for no apparent reason.

I did not want to be considered in the same league as Cousin Bernie, who now resided, alone and unfeted, in Dollis Hill. I didn't want to make an exhibition of myself. Trouble was, while I had truly intended to keep my devastation to myself, the consequence of doing so was that people like Tabitha assumed I was fine, and that the sight of children, babies, mothers, diapers, pacifiers, bottles, prams, didn't make me want to cut my wrists.

I apologized to Tabitha. I forced myself to walk into babyGap and buy a pair of faux suede fur-lined booties with little paw pads sewn on the soles, which I presented to her in person. Other people had it far worse than me, I told myself. I tried to imagine it worse—miscarrying at eight months, when the baby was all but cooked—and I tried to imagine it better—miscarrying before you even realized you were pregnant. Trouble was, I couldn't imagine worse than *this*, and it felt like an insult to anyone in this situation to use the word *better*.

Some women went through this three times, or more—I should get a grip. The only problem was, I wasn't sure *how*. The world was lousy with babies. I couldn't step out of the house without spotting a stroller parked under a porch. Even inside the house, I could hear Baby Celestia grizzling through the wall—*"mmmm-eh, mmm-eh."* They were everywhere! Everywhere except . . .

"Ladz Mag." Toby smiled at his assembled staff—perched on various hard surfaces around his office—and reclined on his sofa. He sniffed, and a faint crease appeared on his tanned forehead. He sniffed again, and leaned forward.

"Ah, *Ladz Mag*. It has been *my* pleasure, gentlemen—and ladies!—and I love you and leave you with regret. I know my sudden departure will come as a shock, so I'm glad to say that I personally— *not* the company—will be shelling out for a drop of booze to dull your pain—I trust you're all free tonight, and please, invite your other halves! *Ladz Mag* will always remain dear to my heart, and in my new capacity as editor in chief of *Elle Decoration*, please believe me when I say that I will think of you often. Now."

Toby paused, and we held our breath. "All that remains is for me to announce the identity of my successor."

I glanced at Fletch, but he looked as stunned as the rest of the staff. Toby whipped his Nokia out of the specially commissioned pocket in his Ozwald Boateng suit and dialed. "Kevin? Your subjects await!"

The office door flew open—it was a bit David Blaine—and in jumped a middle-aged man with spiky gelled hair and sunglasses on a cord round his neck. His trousers were three-quarter length, and his calves were very hairy.

"Kevin Docherty, I am sure, needs no introduction," cried Toby. "He is a lion of journalism, and you will all be familiar with the sterling work he did on *Weekly Chatter*, in particular, the Win a Child competition. Now, I have, ah, a little tête à tête scheduled with the legal department, so I'll see you at six in the Cock & Bull, but meanwhile, I'm going to leave you in the capable hands of Kevin, who is going to explain his groundbreaking vision for *Ladz Mag*—and its grand relaunch."

Toby slipped from the room.

We all watched in silence as Kevin sauntered in and flung himself at the sofa. He rested his camel-hoof sneakers on the desk (an impressive maneuver as it was two feet higher than the sofa). He picked up the latest issue of *Ladz Mag*, flicked through it with a dead look on his face, then held it up to his nose. "This magazine stinks—of old fish." He tosssed it over his shoulder. It bounced off the wall and glanced off the back of his head. No one laughed.

"*That,*" he said, "is a bunch of shite, yeah? It's bloody depressing. Ya gotta give the reader something to aim for. Facts they can use in the pub. How tall is a fucking giraffe? Social ammunition! I'm talking *aspirational*."

We'd heard this line often enough from Toby, but the magazine remained full of war wounds. Maybe Kevin would take us upmarket, and I'd get to write a spa column. I beamed at Kevin and nodded vigorously. Kevin's gaze flicked over me without interest.

"It's *Ladz Mag*'s job to sell blokes everything they already know they want, yeah? Like 'I want to be Wayne Rooney and have a Rolex and everything except sex with old ladies,' or 'I want to shag loads of women, not old ones,' *or* 'I want a woman—how much does she cost?' Or 'I want to *be* a woman, feel my own tits!' Got it?"

Everyone nodded, slowly.

"And here's a thing. *Birds'* magazines."

Kevin fell silent in contemplation. I wasn't sure of what. *Budgerigar Monthly?*

"*Vogue, Cosmo, Radio Times*. They've got real people in them! Not footballers like Wayne Fucking Rooney. Real people! Like, *we* gotta do that! Blokes will love it! So, my idea is, ordinary blokes doing what you really want to do—*I'm on a jet boat with my niece!'* Hang on. Not my niece. Shit. Why do I have to explain fucking everything? Think about it: *I'm young, I've got money, I'm breaking the law.* There is nothing more aspirational than breaking the law! Not sex laws! But screwing . . . hairdressers. It's every young man's dream. You!"

Kevin snapped his fingers at Ted, the chief sub. "Find me a bloke shagging hairdressers!"

Ted: "But I—"

Kevin: *"Now!"*

Ted sighed and left the room.

Kevin cleared his throat. "And I'll tell you something else. Gays. Not you lot. The reader. They're not gay, but they don't want to rule it out. Don't rule out a story because you think it's gay. I'm listening. We'll start with a yoga page and see how it tests."

"I could do that!" I said.

Kevin frowned. "You'd have to strip to a thong and titty tassles."

"Sorry?" I said. "I thought it was for gay men?"

Kevin shook his head. "Forget it. We'll get a professional model. We'll stick some bird in a thong, have her doing the lotus twist, with some serious copy next to her. Blokes can learn how to do the move, the bird just happens to be in a thong."

"Really?" I said. "Isn't that—"

But Kevin was on to his next point. "Going out," he said. "It's the new staying in. We're gonna have a regular slot on pubs, right. But one fucking word about how beer tastes, you're fired. Who cares? When I walk into that pub am I going to get my cock sucked? Is it a gay pub? Is it a carvery? What are the chances of me getting laid?"

"I see," said Fletch, making me jump. "So when you say 'aspirational,' what you in fact mean is—"

Kevin grinned and nodded. "Yeah," he said, proudly. "The tit count's gone nuclear!"

"Get off of me, get off of me, I don't want to go home, I want to *play!*"

"Is this man bothering you, miss?"

Tim let go of my arms as if I were on fire, and turned his back, his hands raised in a parody of surrender.

I tried to focus on Tim, to see if he *was* bothering me. There appeared to be two of him.

"Osifer . . . *Osifer*," I took a deep breath and attempted to say what I meant. "Mr. Policeman. This man"—I waved toward Tim—"this man has committed a bad offense."

The police officer glanced at his colleague, who was sitting in the van in a bulletproof vest, yawning. "And what might that be?" he said. Was it *me* or was his voice a touch less friendly?

Both Tims rolled their eyes and shoved their hands in their pockets.

"He . . . he's got *two heads*!" I pointed a finger and begged the police officer, "Look!" But as I did so, I felt an icy clutch at my heart: *The officer also had two heads.* Oh my God. I was the fat girl in the zombie movie who dies horribly.

I screamed loudly and tried to run, but stumbled against the second Tim and fell into his coat. The second Tim cupped a hand around the back of my head, so my face stayed pressed into the material.

"Ib suffogatig!" I shouted, but I don't think he heard.

"Good luck, mate," I heard the police officer say, and they roared off.

"It wasn't my fault," I said, when Tim released me.

It *wasn't.*

Toby's leaving drinks hadn't begun well. Everyone was in shock. Poor Fletch, he would have made a great editor. Instead, we had this *moron*, Kevin. I didn't like him. But, perversely, I wanted him to like *me*. Maybe this had something to do with not wanting to be fired. I'd rung Tim, told him the news, and asked him to meet me at the pub. And he'd refused! He'd said, "What about Friday Night? Your mother's expecting us!" Get him! He's not even Jewish! I said *he* could go, I didn't fancy food poisoning this week. I'd be in the pub, and if he wanted, he could join me later. And he went silent. "What?" I said.

"You *always* go to Friday Night," he said.

"Exactly," I said, and put the phone down.

So. Toby bought me a drink. And then Fletch bought me a drink. And I bought Toby, Fletch, and myself a drink. And then, because I felt sorry for Kevin, sitting all by himself in the corner, pretending to check messages on his phone, I bought Kevin a drink. Kevin was so pleased to be bought a drink by a budgerigar— "This is weirdly post-feministic!" he kept saying (he was odd)— that he bought me *three* drinks. And the more drinks he bought me, the nicer he got.

"You know," I said, patting his hand. "This new bosom—I mean, vision you've got for *Ladz Mag*?"

"Yeh?"

"I . . ." I drew my eyebrows together.

"What?" said Kevin, leaning closer, until our heads were inches apart.

"I don't think—"

"Spit it out! Ha! First time I've said that to a bird!"

"I don't think there's enough sex in it!" I clapped my hands and shrieked with laughter—only stopping when Kevin gripped my shoulders and stared into my eyes.

"Then," he said, breathing lager fumes straight up my nose, "*you*, Biscuit—"

"Lizbet," I corrected.

"*You*, Biscuit, like, that's going to be your new byline, yeah? *Biscuit*, because, because you're . . . sweet!"

"Ah! That's lovely."

"And men want to eat you!"

"Oh, that's grim!"

"Now. You, Biscuit, have gotta promise me one thing."

"What?"

"Promise first."

"Er . . . Promise!"

Kevin held out his arms and pressed me to his chest. "Congratulations, Biscuit!" he said. "I'm looking at *Ladz Mag*'s new sex columnist!"

"What!" I shouted, struggling out of his embrace. "Where is she?"

"You, Biscuit! *You* are the new sex columnist!"

"Me?"

"Yeah! Picture byline every month. Don't panic—we can work bloody miracles with an airbrush! We'll have you as a schoolgirl. You as a dominatrix. You as a porn teacher—"

"A *porn* teacher?"

"Yeah, like in a porno? The teacher's all buttoned up, raspberries straining at her white shirt, and square framed glasses, and hair in a bun, and tight skirt, all strict-looking—"

"You mean like a . . . porn librarian?"

"Yeah! *Yes*. Exactly! And then she—"

"But, wow. I mean, that's great. But you don't even know if I can write!"

"Write?" said Kevin, wrinkling his nose. He burst out laughing. "Biscuit," he said, wiping his eyes. "I love it! Buy that girl a pint!"

I grinned into my Guinness. I don't even *like* Guinness.

"So, when do I write my first column?" I said, dipping my finger into the froth.

"Like, *tomorrow*," said Kevin.

We hugged again. I think it was at this point that Tim arrived, tapped me on the shoulder, and suggested we leave. I didn't want to go, but he insisted. Hence our little struggle outside the pub, and the officer's intervention. I was subdued in the taxi home. So was Tim. So what. I was the new sex columnist for *Ladz Mag*.

"Dinner was fun," he said. "Cassie was there."

"Right."

"We missed you."

"That's nice."

Tim sighed, and took my hand. I sighed, and squeezed it.

"This probably isn't the right time," he murmured, "seeing as you are *exceptionally* drunk. But. I think we should try for another baby."

CHAPTER 16

A big personality is like an engagement ring. It tends to be an honor bestowed on you by a third party. The world's consensus is, *I* have a small personality—I realized this at an early age, and nothing has occurred since to change my mind.

Not so long ago, I was sitting alone in the packed weekend café in Kings Wood, and a woman asked if she could share my table. She bit into the biggest bean burrito you ever saw—she devoured it like a wolf. There was juice dribbling down her chin, mushrooms squishing out at the sides, strands of gooey cheese slipping down the inside of her shirtsleeves. Hello? I thought. Am I invisible? I knew that if I'd had more *presence*—like, say, *Cassie*—she'd have used a knife and fork.

Cassie said I didn't help myself. She said if ever I got a compliment I'd dodge it like anyone else might dodge a bullet. She also had words about my "refined sugar addiction." I liked my refined sugar addiction. It made me a nicer person. Hadn't she heard of self-medicating? What she was hinting at was that I'd let myself go. As if I didn't know that! Truth is, if you want to keep a big house in

London, and you don't earn what *she* earns, something has to go. And I really liked my house.

I wasn't quite resigned to my fate. I'd read an interview where a Siena or a Keira was asked to name her favorite designer, and I'd imagined the lifestyle where you were so inundated with designer goods that you might have a *favorite*. The other killer: favorite shop in New York. My great shame was that I was thirty-two and had *never been to the USA*. (A social no-no on a par with not knowing how to swim.) Also, the skin on my heels was so dry it flaked—if I touched it, it made me shiver. And my sneakers were so old that Cassie said they were almost vintage. All these things bothered me, but not *that* much, because I never did anything about them.

George once said I had "low self-esteem"—a lesson to all women never to let a man near an edition of *Cosmo*. I disagreed, but didn't want to offend him. I didn't have "low self-esteem," I had "high apathy." I went along with other people's preferences only because I didn't care enough to contradict them. Now that I did, it was like I'd smashed the glass to my real personality (only to be used in case of emergency). The core Lizbet was harder—focused and determined. I decided that people could bend to *my* wishes for a change. I'd help them adjust by adjusting myself.

I didn't throw out any of the drugs in my cupboards: four tubes of Smarties, two packets of M&M's, two Lindt Chocolate Suisse Au Lait, a pack of Droste Bittersweet Pastilles, and a 400g box of Belgian chocolates. Most of it had been bought *for* me by others happy to feed my habit. It could all stay there, reminding me of what I wasn't. Temptation didn't figure. It wasn't the taste of chocolate I craved, as Cassie was so fond of saying, it was the chemicals. I was no longer a woman who gorged on saturated fat every day. I was a woman who, if she were having her last meal on death row, would choose a salad, no dressing.

The editor could stuff his airbrush. They'd have to pad me *out* by the time I'd finished. (I'd quit bread, and potatoes too). Our flirtatious encounter at Toby's leaving do had made me despise Kevin *more*. I resented him for making me look cheap and foolish in front of Fletch and the rest of the staff. I hardly ever drink! (I said this to Tim when we realized the parlous state of our bank account: "It's not like we've frittered the money!" I said. "I hardly ever drink! I'm not a cokehead! You don't gamble, we don't own a fleet of Bentleys!" Tim nodded sadly. "I know," he said. "We've fucking wasted it.") Kevin was all out for himself, and I knew that he'd only made me the *Ladz Mag* sex columnist because I was free.

I was suddenly hyper aware of how other people saw me and I didn't like it. Aged ten, I was always picked second to last for rounders—only one in front of Veronica who had a National Health Service plastic foot. I still felt out of it. ("Tim," I said once, after friends begged off a dinner arrangement, "are we people other people cancel?") If Cassie came round, she and Tim would always end up quoting lines from films at each other. Stuff like "I am not an animal!" and "You can be my wingman!" I'd smile stiffly, wishing I could join in. I was the dullard who failed her movie education because she was too busy wasting time on her chemistry homework to watch TV. *Chemistry!* Who needs that in the real world?

Before, I could hardly see a fault in Tim. Now everything he did annoyed me. He'd sweep the kitchen floor, herd all the dust, crumbs, and general yuck into a neat pile by the garbage can—and then *leave it*. Why not go that extra yard with the dustpan and brush? That wasn't tidying! The mess was still there, it was just concentrated in one area! Another thing: "Lizbet? Have you seen my keys? Lizbet? Have you seen my phone? Lizbet? Have you seen my jacket?" Yes, yes, and yes, right there in front of you, why don't you *look*? I wasn't his girlfriend—I was his Seeing Eye dog. I felt my blood pressure rise just thinking about it.

However. We both wanted the same thing—*sex*—albeit for different reasons. He wanted a baby (like our goldfish had died and we should get a new one). I wanted material for my magazine column.

I had been introduced to *Ladz Mag*'s readers with a photo of me chewing suggestively on a fat ink pen, under the heading *Meet Our New Saucy Scribe!* The makeup artist had painted lips on me that took up half my face, and the wardrobe guy had forced me into a black rubber corset. My first column was a one-thousand-word tease about how men didn't want to have sex enough. (Or was it just me?) The harassment—sorry, feedback—from readers offering their services pleased Kevin, who decided to enlarge my picture byline for the following month and "style" me himself. ("I'm thinking red and black suspenders ... peephole bra ... It'll be pure class!") He also urged me to go forth and have sex adventures.

This caused some disagreement, as Tim wasn't keen on sitting blindfold, naked, cuffed to a chair for an hour as part of the trying-to-conceive process. He especially wasn't keen when Sphinx tried to make it a threesome by jumping up and clawing his bottom. Nor was he keen when I made notes. He didn't like that two hundred thousand young offenders and Aunt Edith would read about our horizontal exploits each month. Tough.

Whereas I—not wishing to replace my lost baby like you might replace a burst tire—could visit my doctor, obtain six months' supply of the contraceptive pill, keep the information to myself, and everyone was happy.

It didn't quite work like that. *I* was happy. It was a strange relief to feel like someone else—it was a nice break from the pain of being *me*. Maybe Tim was right and I was abnormal for being unable to recover even after the enormous period of five whole months— "Where's your Blitz spirit?" he asked me once—but the truth was, my life was stalled at the moment I saw my dead little girl, and in that sense, time had no meaning for me. The only way I could *be* was to be someone else—and so my personality had fractured, the practical half splintering off from Poor Elizabeth Montgomery Did You Hear What Happened To Her in order to survive.

I liked the reaction from readers—offers of marriage, requests for used knickers, etc.—even if I couldn't quite bring myself to read the column once it was in print. (The photos exposed a little *too* much cleavage, the subject matter was a little *too* coarse for me to stare it in the face.) If I didn't read it in the magazine, I could pretend it didn't exist, that it wasn't me, selling my private life for a bit of notoriety. But Tim wasn't happy. I wasn't pregnant. We'd remortgaged twice in six months. Meanwhile he was being nationally humiliated on a regular basis.

"I don't feel your heart's in this," he said, as I slung on a T-shirt and switched on my computer. He scraped a baked bean out of his belly button. "Shouldn't you be lying on the bed with your legs up the wall, giving the sperm a chance to *fertilize*?"

I sighed. "Sure," I said. I walked back to the bedroom and assumed the position. (It was a chance to file my nails, if nothing else.)

Tim watched me with narrowed eyes. "I feel this hostility coming off you, and I'm tired of it," he said. "It's been five months now. You're not making it comfortable for me to live in this house. I'm not your partner, I'm part of your job description."

"You're not, though, are you?" I said. "I protect your privacy. I change your name to Tom."

After this conversation, the sex waned, but that was okay. I did what all good journalists do. I made it up.

Tim retreated into work, thank goodness.

I was still angry with Cassie, but anger is like a log fire—it requires laborious effort to keep it burning. Secretly, I wanted us to be friends again. I missed her. I thought back to our childhood, and every recollection made me smile. Sometimes, to think kindly of a person, you have to scroll back a decade or two. We'd stay at Aunt Edith's every Saturday night, and it was a joy because Aunt Edith was so very different from our parents. Her desserts—my *God*! Once she made this thing called a gala ring. It was a cake with a hole in the middle, pineapple at the bottom, and glacé cherries on top. It was soaked in brandy.

Cassie didn't eat much at home, but at Aunt Edith's she ate masses, double quick. Then she'd lean over my plate and say in a tremulous voice, "Give a poor beggar something to eat!" (She always timed it when Aunt Edith was in the kitchen washing up.) I'd sigh and push my plate toward her; it was less hassle that way. Then Aunt Edith would sweep into the room—her dress sense was dramatic, a kaftan with red paisley print and silvery thread at the neckline, or a crocheted purple poncho with white trousers and Stetson—and boom, like a prophet: "Cassandra! Is that Elizabeth's food?"

Cassie would deny it, but after two large helpings of the gala ring, the brandy spoke for itself: She shook her head, and fell off her chair. That night, Aunt Edith fed us "plain food"—haddock poached in milk, string beans, and mashed potatoes. She sat with us, doing the *Times* crossword. Cassie nudged me, and I saw that she'd fashioned her mash into the shape of an enormous penis. I must have enjoyed being Cassie's stooge—maybe because at least I was her *focus*. I tried to recreate that meal the other week (no mash, or penis, as both were against my diet), but the fish was off, and the milk burned. I made Tim taste it and he gagged and said, "That is wrong in *so* many ways."

So when Cassie came to see me—calling ahead to ensure I wasn't planning a bath—I decided that I should give peace a chance. Cassie had decided the very same thing, because her first words were "Lizbet, I need to tell you something."

She seemed different. Sort of deflated. She didn't look like the woman who'd worked her builder so hard that he'd got sunstroke and had to go home early. She looked more like the little girl I'd bullied for the few years I had before she overtook me in wit. (There was a nice fairy, Bluebell, and and evil fairy, Primrose. I chose which fairy visited Cassie at bedtime. On Cassie's fourth birthday, Primrose held Bluebell hostage, and might have killed her had Cassie not given me all her new toys.)

I was full of saintly resolve, but Cassie hit a reflex. Because when she said, "George and I have been trying for a baby for eighteen months, but it isn't happening for us," I *wanted* to hug her. I wanted to say, "So that's why, now I understand!" But all the hurt rushed back, and I said, "We all have our crosses to bear."

CHAPTER 17

Cassie

When Lizbet and I were younger, we argued a lot. And then Lizbet would say, "Oh Cassie, we _mustn't_ argue. Let's have a word that draws the line!" We'd agree on the magic word that would command an immediate cease-fire, start to argue, and I would always forget the word. Now _she_ had forgotten the word. It was "decency."

I grabbed my coat, left her house. I wanted to cry. I wouldn't though, ever. I despise women who cry in public. A woman can't mouth off about equality, wear a power suit, then burst into tears when things don't go her way. It's socially irresponsible, like jumping a red light. If _one_ woman cries in the office, every man there thinks he's better than _all_ of us. I'm a barrister—crying at work is not an option and—like a buffer zone—I apply the identical rule at home.

Lizbet shocked me. I'd had no idea she was that bitter. It's common sense that if someone's furious with you, you confide your bad luck, and this makes them nicer to you. I'd never really cared about the psychological _why_, I just found it a useful tool with which to manipulate people. But I suppose resentment is born of jealousy, and if you provide information that shows you are *not* an untouchable golden girl, the jealousy crumbles into a harmless pink powder of smugness, pity, and guilt—with less attitude as a by-product.

Lizbet was breaking all the rules, and I'd had enough. I was sorry, I'd shown her I was sorry, I'd explained myself—what more could I do? I wanted us to be close again, but she seemed determined to kill our relationship with spite, turn it into a grudge match. I'm all for the motto "Feel my pain." (I regularly leave my spikiest shoes on the staircase when George has stayed too late at the pub; it's called "communication.") But that comment she made was too cruel. Also, it wasn't as if she was bearing *her* cross with any dignity or grace. She was using it as a battering ram, lashing out indiscriminately.

I would have liked to talk to her about how she felt, but I wasn't even sure she *knew*. Oh, the baby, sure, but to me her anger had an unfocused edge, and I suspected there was more to it than she realized. That said, I had my own problem to consider: George. I couldn't confide in my sister about disliking my own husband; it was embarrassing, it reflected badly on me. Especially as Lizbet had reinvented herself as Sex Expert to the Nation, and she and Tim were bonking for Britain.

After that food piece, I could barely look Tim in the eye; I kept thinking of him with a chocolate-coated penis, whipped cream on his nipples, and a baked bean accidentally stuck in his— Well, I don't want to put you off your lunch. I didn't want to picture my sister having imaginative sex, or pollute my mind with her sub *Sex and the City* style debates ("Chocolate-coated grasshopper, or chocolate-coated cock, which is more palatable? And I realized, it depends on the cock, because as a rule there's less variable in a grasshopper. . . .")

Every detail stuck in my head like a bad jingle. The writing was hair-raising—I didn't like to think about what else it might be raising, but with the *Ladz Mag* readership I had a fair idea—and the photos bordered on soft porn. I think Lizbet had stopped eating (the Nil by Mouth, All by Ego Diet), and she was determined to show off her new figure. There she was in a fussy corset astride a male model, tickling his chest with a pink boa—thank God, we were spared the sight of *his* pink boa. And there she was again, a foxy schoolgirl in black stockings (when I know for a fact that her uniform was frowsy: thick wool cardigan, skirt like a circus tent, and brown socks).

But plainly, she needed a distraction, and this was it. Don't think I was envious of her cheap fame. I got to do my showing off in court. Lizbet was at that stage of regression where she believed it was better to be desired than to be respected. I suppose being desired is more *fun*, moment for moment. But in terms of satisfaction, respect is what lasts you. Lizbet—who had effectively sashayed into two hundred thousand men's bedrooms and made a slut of herself—would realize that, eventually, when the tenth stranger shoved his hand down her top in a bar.

All of which didn't stop me wishing I could tell her about George. I was scared, an unfamiliar feeling. I didn't want to start again, put myself years behind all my friends. I knew more about ancient Egypt than about modern dating. Pubic hair, for instance—I have *no* idea what people are doing with it these days. What's the protocol? All off? Trimmed into a heart shape? I could just imagine getting naked with a new man for the first time, and him fainting with horror. *Clonk!*

If I thought about what I might do, it felt like a cold green hand squeezing my heart till I gasped. You only have the one life—can you spend it with the wrong person and still enjoy it? Money helps.

But not as much as you might think. George and I stayed at the Datai the year before last, on the Malaysian island of Langkawi. It's a gorgeous and exclusive hotel built on the edge of a rain forest—it also has a private beach. We stayed in a jungle villa, and fed bananas to the monkeys. It was perfect but for two details. First: One of the monkeys had a cough. Second: I was there with George.

I watched George, flapping like a goose in the Andaman Sea, and felt a lurch of irritation. I'd squashed it down, thinking that it's a rare man who looks his best in swimwear. Now it makes me think that the rot was there even before I found and lost Sarah Paula.

I'd waved to George, ordered him a cocktail to assuage my guilt. But I still thought of Lizbet and Tim, who were holed up in a B&B on the Isle of Wight. I know it's sacrilege, but I allowed myself to fantasize about Tim being with me, instead of George. (Nothing rude, you understand, just *there*.) Tim is *funny*. He's also cute, boyish. He's tall, tubby, with a freckled face, soppy grin, kind eyes, and this incredible hair. It's gingery blond, all over the place in unruly tufts, and it's quite beautiful. The color is so unusual—pale orange here, white blond there—that the first time we met I asked him who did it. Nicky, I was thinking. Maybe Frederick in New York, even.

"My parents," he replied. "Bastards."

George was very serious about himself, and it had started to bore me. Shoot me, but I thought his fussiness with food *unmanly*. What self-respecting straight male has ever said the words "I won't eat nonorganic raisins; they're pesticide pellets"? Also, he did yoga. Now that's all very well in, say, LA. In fact, it's probably law over there. But George is from Friern Barnet—it wasn't *right*. And it was impossible to watch TV sitting next to him, as every time a person appeared on screen for the first time, George would ex-claim, "He's porked up!" And if it was a newscaster, he e-mailed the TV company to complain. At the start of our relationship I'd found that habit funny.

It wasn't just the little things, although anyone in a long-term relationship knows that the little things are merely symbolic of the bigger things. (*God!* I think I just quoted Lizbet without realizing. Her next sentence was "Except for cocks. In a cock situation, I'm afraid that symbolism becomes meaningless." This is the woman who called a penis "a winkle" until she turned twenty-five.) The big-ger thing was that George did not put his energy *into* the relation-ship. He was fanatical about the house, but there is a point at which being house-proud is no longer a reflection of your relationship—and more a deflection *from* it.

When we first got together, I thought that George was popular. However, I didn't take into account what sort of people he was popular *with*. Now I saw that George fancied himself as a mentor to those of his friends who were bigger failures than he was. He spent four evenings in one week helping his idiot friend Kurt cre-ate a plausible CV. Kurt was his special project. (*I* thought Kurt would have been better off as Care in the Community's special pro-ject, but I accept that the social services are stretched.) Kurt lived in a ground-floor flat, in a neat suburban road, full of front gardens with red flowers in terra-cotta pots—streets away from Lizbet, in fact. *Kurt's* front garden was different.

Kurt did occasional work from home (doing what, I have no idea) and spent his endless leisure time buying up old books, toys, china, and other rubbish from charity shops. He'd arrange all of this junk in cardboard boxes on his garden wall, every day, unless it was pouring, with handwritten signs, "All books, 20p." If the neighbors said nothing, I'll bet it was only because they feared that any squeak of dissent might prompt Kurt to exchange all the twenty pences for a chainsaw and murder them in their beds.

There was no denying that George was a great, loyal friend—to everyone *else*. His other crony, Henry—a six-foot-four hulk of a man with a big moon face—was dating a petite paranoid psychotic drug addict who made his life miserable, and yet he refused to leave her. Instead he spent hours on the phone to George, whining and crying, and George never tired of having his ear bent and offering his wise and learned opinions on relationships. We all need someone to look down on, and I suppose that for my husband, Kurt and Henry fulfilled this role. I also suppose that George felt that *I* looked down on him. But if I did, I had good reason. He might give to others, but from me, he just *took*.

When I reached home after leaving Lizbet, George was at the David Lloyd health club (probably in the weight room trying to make the best of a bad situation). I was alone, and I allowed myself to think about Sarah Paula. If I wasn't cutting anyone a break just then, it was *her* fault. Thanks to her, I was a loser—in the truest sense. I had lost, when I was used to winning, when my overriding drive in life was to *win*. I had lost Mummy and Daddy, as real parents. I had lost Sarah Paula even before I'd found her. I'd lost Lizbet as a sister, also. And now I was considering losing George, and my substitute parents, the Hershlags.

Have you any idea how annoying it is *not* to take your parents for granted? Until recently, I'd treated them as a necessary inconvenience, like the dentist. I'd turn up to a Friday Night if I hadn't seen them in three months and fancied showing off my new coat, bag, whatever. (Vivica never said, but I know she was impressed with my salary and status. Money and power mattered deeply to her, more than being a nice person.) Now I found myself at their house every week. I didn't enjoy it; I was too chewed up with what might have been. Still, I needed to be there, sulk a little, be the focus of some clumsy second-rate parenting.

I surprised myself, because I was always a person who found it easy to cut off—even from those close to me. If you reject me, I reject you *more*, was how I operated and it wasn't even conscious. I would never have noticed, except that my ex–best friend, Natasha, moved to Madrid when I was twenty-four and—as she pointed out to me—I reacted like it was a personal betrayal. I didn't visit, I didn't write, I didn't phone. In fact, I lost her number. Natasha's opinion was—when I finally e-mailed to request it after she left me the answering machine message "It's my birthday! Call me, you cow!"—that this was no accident. I apologized, but even now our contact is intermittent, a friendship that skims the surface.

I sat in the living room, flicked through a ski brochure. Or maybe I should go to New York for a long weekend. Perhaps a diving holiday would be good—in the last four years I've become addicted. In Mauritius, I saw a small shark. What a buzz—identical, in fact to how I feel in court when I outwit opposing counsel. I took Lizbet, instead of George, but she didn't like it. Couldn't equalize. "I am just not a diving person," she said. "I think, even if I didn't get this horrific pain in my ears, I'd be twenty feet under water, think, Oh my God, I'm twenty feet under water, panic, speed to the surface, get air bubbles in my blood, and die."

I chucked the ski brochure to one side. I wasn't in a New York state of mind, and even the idea of diving was hard work. Instead I thought of my sister—she would always be my sister—sunning herself on the diving boat, smiling with her eyes half-closed, early R.E.M. on her headphones, as I toppled into the water. I felt restless and listless at the same time.

I don't really like it, loving people. It's not something I'm good at. Lizbet went through a phase of saying, "I love you" instead of "Good-bye" at the end of every phone call. "You too," I'd mutter. Once she said it, and I didn't hear, and so she said, in an indignant voice, "I *said*, 'I love you'!" "I love you too," I said, but I was *furious*. How dare she choke the words out of me. It should be against the law to say "I love you" in order to force a reflex response. She stopped saying it to me after that, but she joked about it once, when we were out with Tim and George. "Oh," she said, "Cassie can't even *spell* love." It was true. On the rare occasion that I typed the word in an e-mail, it always came out as "lvoe." I'd just leave it. People knew what I meant.

When the doorbell rang, I narrowed my eyes. I squinted through the peephole, and there stood my sister holding a bunch of daffodils.

"I'm so sorry," said Lizbet, as I yanked open the door. "I am *so* sorry. You know I didn't mean it. What a terrible thing to say. I was inexcusable."

"Ah, Christ, so was I," I said. "I'm sorry too. Casserole dish?"

"Pardon?"

"No, hang on. Er, continental quilt?"

"What?"

"Oh no, wait! *Ice pop.*"

"Ice pop!" said Lizbet.

This was formal command of an immediate cease-fire. We sealed the peace treaty with a tentative hug.

CHAPTER 18

Lizbet and I were collapsed on the sofa, eating roasted soy beans—her latest idea of fun. I was unsure of this new Lizbet, and perhaps she was still unsure of me, because in the absence of genuine warmth, we'd resorted to sniping about our mother. The time we'd visited for Christmas. (No tree—our parents had been shaken, a year before, when Evelyn Toberman's father died on *Christmas Eve*, and even as she opened the front door to the rabbi, her husband was trying to wrestle a six-foot fir, bedecked with red tinsel and twinkly lights, out the back.)

Vivica had remarked, "Ooh, Lizbet's had her hair cut!" Lizbet had stood there with a half smile on her face, but there was no further comment. There was also our mother's habit of marching into your home and announcing, "It smells *terrible* in here!" Once, Lizbet had grimly lit a Jo Malone scented candle—"actually burning money"—when Vivica was expected. Our mother had paused at the door, seen the candle, and exclaimed, "The heat in here is *stifling*!" We never told *her* that she kept *her* house like an icebox, and that when she hit the menopause, we feared that the temperature would drop further, and our father would suffer frostbite in his own living room.

"She's been a lot better lately," said Lizbet. "To me, anyway."

"Why do you think that is?" I said—before engaging brain. Lizbet had been destroyed by her baby's death, but she wouldn't talk about it, although everything about her appearance and behavior suggested to me that she needed to, even if she didn't know it. I wanted to say, "You're too thin," but I didn't, as I knew she was in a contrary state of mind and would decide it was a compliment. My only hope was that one day soon, natural greed would get the better of her. *I* was the thin one.

Lizbet rolled her eyes and said, "Because I've hardly seen her."

I smiled. So Lizbet had finally realized how to train our mother. The method was the same as a parent might use to train a small child. You rewarded all good behaviors with attention and positive reinforcement. Any bad behaviors (rudeness, cheek, showing off) and you ignored her. It was important to let our mother work out this basic correlation for herself. A direct reprimand would almost certainly spark an increase in the undesired behaviors.

"What about you?" said Lizbet. "I hear your attendance record has improved."

"Friday Nights are okay," I said. "I eat before I go. It's nice to see Tim. And Daddy. Especially if I've been in court, performing. It's a relief not to have to be *on*."

"Oh," said Lizbet. "She's always been in awe of you, anyway. She talks about your house. She's impressed by money. You can do what you like." She mimicked Mummy. " 'You went to *where*? I've not heard of that one.' Dot dot dot. 'Where is it?' "

I smiled. "Desperate to write down the name of the restaurant and get Daddy to make a reservation."

There was a short silence. We both knew that Mummy's attitude to me was different, but we never said. A meanness shared is invigorating, like a cold shower, but it was odd to hear Lizbet speak ill of our mother. I had always seen my sister as forgiving, honorable, *goodly*. You form an opinion of someone after a lifetime of close contact—it's a shock to discover they have a harsher side. I preferred how she was before.

She was funnier then. She had a sense of humor about herself, always telling self-deprecating stories—oh, she was in the supermarket, and her paper towel fell off the trolley, and a passerby shouted to her friend, "Wait! I'm just picking up THIS LADY'S TOILET PAPER!" And Lizbet gritted her teeth and thought, Not toilet paper—paper *towel*! Paper *towel*!

Or what about when the plumber came, and Lizbet knew he had a baby boy of about nine months, but she couldn't remember the child's name, so she said, "And how's your little man?" And the second she said it, she realized it sounded as if she was asking after his penis.

She would never tell tales like that now. She had permanently sucked-in cheeks.

At least the change in Lizbet made me realize that I had always been hard on Vivica. It was only now that I could acknowledge how much. It had been difficult for our mother. She'd lost her job at *Mother & Home* after twenty years of service. The company had offered her the editorship of *Fast Bikes*. (In other words, on your bike.) She'd chosen redundancy—she was fifty, and not about to jump on a Harley. They'd given her a gold bracelet, and when she'd had it valued for insurance purposes, she discovered it wasn't worth enough to *be* insured.

As a parent she was shoddy, but you couldn't fault her as an editor.

She'd enjoyed her work—despite the principles of the magazine being in direct conflict with her own—which made her a better person to be around. I do think that as long as you are happy somewhere in your life, you can convincingly hold the rest of it together.

Mother & Home ran pages of fancy recipes for your kids' breakfast—Cheese Pom-Poms I recall being one, as our mother regaled us with details of the stand-up fight she had with her chief sub as to whether there was a hyphen in Pom-Pom. Meanwhile, our breakfast was orange soda and biscuits, set in front of the TV the night before, with that sleep-saving invention, the Philips video cassette recorder, set to *play*. ("*Doctor Who* . . . chocolate digestives . . . shush . . . go," she'd mutter, when I bounced into her bedroom at 6:00 A.M. Lizbet would already be downstairs, watching Daleks on a sugar high.)

The redundancy sapped our mother's confidence, and she didn't find a new job. She did a little freelance work, but the *Daily Mail* tended to ring at the last minute when they wanted a middle-aged woman to write three hundred words on her preferred beachwear for a feature entitled *Swimsuit or Bikini?* Our mother would happily agree—"Oh, bikini, bikini!"—and the commissioning editor would add, "Great! There's just one tiny thing. We'd need you to pose *in* your bikini. We'll do a nice shoot, hair, makeup. . . ." She felt out of it, and our father wasn't that helpful.

It annoyed me that he was so straight he couldn't accept a free meal at what our mother called "A swish restaurant," just to make her smile. He *said* he didn't want to feel obliged. I thought this was an excuse. If I go to a good restaurant, I'll recommend it to people—out of the goodness of my heart! Whereas, it was our father's job to recommend good restaurants—he was paid to do what the rest of us did for nothing! In fact, we *all* deserve a free meal at a good restaurant. He'd only be getting what the rest of us were entitled to. But some people pride themselves on their principles—a posh word for "decisions"—to the extent that their principles take on more importance than people's happiness. I'm sure he thought he deserved respect for this.

Couldn't he see that his wife was unhappy? I felt that if he put half the effort into his marriage that he put into his job, Vivica would be a different person. She needed to feel special—not just to *him*—she wanted a special place in the world. Why couldn't he present her with complimentary tickets to the theater? Nothing flash, even the first night of *A Funny Thing Happened on the Way to the Forum* would have been gratefully received—anything so that she might read her *Daily Express* the following day, scan the theater review, and think *I* was there!—feel she was at the hub! But he didn't, so she wasn't. And when Vivica felt insecure, she was pure nasty. I mean, she'd hidden Sarah Paula's letters! I didn't blame her entirely.

Recently, I was seeing my whole family in a different light and I didn't like it. I wanted us all to *unite*. As I was a person who thrived on conflict—a person who *felt* love but felt equally gross showing it—this desire seemed a little crazy to me.

"We should go out, the four of us, somewhere gorgeous, blow some cash," I said. I blushed, remembering Lizbet's money situation. The previous week, George had taken Tim to the Lloyd—even though we all knew that Tim loathed the Lloyd. ("Those changing rooms are foul," he'd spluttered, on their return. "Hairy men, one foot up on a stool, drying their nuts with the *hair dryer*. That's going near my *head*!") According to George, Tim had said that, six months before, they'd remortgaged to pay his tax bill—"Seventy g's, gone!"—then found they needed to remortgage *again* for the next tax bill. Their mortgage broker had sent Tim an apologetic e-mail: "Afraid that Southern Rock are not being particularly friendly, talking about charging fees and requesting an accountant's certificate. . . ."

Knowing Lizbet, the idea of her mortgage company being *unfriendly* would have upset her more than the threat of penalties and charges. (An attitude that may have been partly responsible for her financial predicament.) As she hadn't brought any of this up with *me*, I didn't want to bring it up with her. This was how our family operated: everyone talking about everyone else behind his or her back; no one actually talking *to* the person about what they *should* be talking about, because everyone was scared of upsetting that person.

"Or," I added quickly, "you two could just come to us."

To my surprise, Lizbet shook her head. "Oh no," she said. "I like your first idea. Let's blow some cash."

"Are you sure?" I said, a touch sternly. I *hated* her being irresponsible like this. I suppose it was like other people seeing their parents decide to bet their house on a horse.

"Oh yeah," she said. "Tim's invented something. It's been picked up. He got an advance order and a check."

"That's *fantastic*!" I said. "What? When? How?"

Lizbet yawned. "I don't know all the details. I let him get on with it. He's been working on it for a year or so, I think. But recently—since the—he's shut himself away and really come up with something. He has a track record with the potty, which gets him an initial meeting. That's the crucial bit. Woolworths passed, but suggested he approach their Japanese counterpart—and they loved it, and—"

"What is it?"

"Oh, some kind of early warning system."

"What! Antiterrorism? I didn't know he was involved in—"

"He isn't. Well. He is, but on a different level. A while ago,

Tabitha brought Tomas round while he was being toilet trained. And he did two poos on our carpet. He was just in his pants when he did the second one, and *crouching*, and I could see it *in* there, leaking a bit of . . . poo juice onto our carpet, but, well, I didn't want to say anything to Tabitha, in case it seemed rude, as if I was keeping watch, I didn't want to offend her—"

"Are you crazy?" I shouted. "You should have just told her!"

"Yes. Well. *Now* I would. Anyway. After that particular incident, Tim had an idea. A tiny patch, like a plaster, which you stick on the child's bottom, but it has a sensor in it which sets off a bleeper—handheld by the parent, very discreet, so as not to give the child a complex—if there's the slightest change in humidity in the *area*."

"Tim is bottom obsessed, isn't he?"

"Yes, I do worry," said Lizbet. "Anyway, it has to be refined, but it enables the parent to suggest to the child that he might need to use the pot, *just* before the accident is due to occur."

"Genius," I said. "Brilliant in its simplicity."

"Mm," said Lizbet. "Apparently, some children are allergic to sticking plaster. So some varieties will be sensitized. And of course, he's thinking of blue plasters, and pink plasters, and possibly, some will be—"

"Pony shaped?"

"Yes, and—"

"Train shaped?"

"You guessed it."

"Well!" I said. "Big in Japan! He must be thrilled."

"Mm," said Lizbet again. "I suppose he is. I don't know—I'm just spending the advance! Still, if we go out, you can ask him yourself."

Our intentions were good, but actually the four of us didn't meet until five weeks later. I had a few heavy cases on and was doing prep till late most nights. Also, you had to book a month in advance for my favorite restaurant (Locanda Locatelli, there you go, a free tip!), so it made sense. When Lizbet walked in—not *flinch*-thin, but close—I fought to stop my jaw from dropping.

You have to know that Lizbet owns about four pairs of ancient panties, a pair of cords from M&S—which she rotates with The Black Trousers (French Connection circa 1998)—and about three tops—the stripey one, the gray one, and the One For Best—all baggy, all British weather shades, all from the Next catalog because she can't be bothered to get out there and *do* the shops. But if she sees me in anything, she'll say, "Where did you get that? *I* might get it."

She was wearing a strapless yellow dress—*"Givenchy!"* she said, with a beam, as she sat down.

"Bless you," I replied.

She was so pleased with herself, and my heart tweaked with love and pain. I was reminded of something my boss Sophie Hazel Hamilton had told me, the previous day.

Sophie had collected her third child from nursery in Chelsea on a recent day off. She'd walked into the playgaround and seen her boy wearing the furry winter hat with earflaps that she'd bought him a year earlier because it was cute. Now, however, it was a size too small and perched on top of his head. "He looked," she told me, shamefaced, *"silly."* She added, "He was the only child wearing a silly hat." What pained her, she said, was that he looked foolish and he didn't know it. It was his innocence that hurt. She'd whipped off the hat and stuffed it in her bag.

I felt the same about Lizbet and her Givenchy dress. Her first foray into haute couture was a disaster. The dress had bright yellow silk bra cups, yellow stripes to the waist in a bodice effect, and what looked like a layer of white tissue paper over the yellow pencil skirt. And two nasty yellow and white frilly flaps, one jutting over each hip. She looked like a slice of lemon meringue. Sadly, I couldn't whip it off her and stuff it in my bag.

"Darling," I said. "You're way too pretty for that dress. That *dress* is the feature, it's a dress for a woman with a face like an old boot. You need *simplicity*—Prada, Donna Karan—you need an easy design that lets your face and figure be the stars of the show."

"Oh," said Lizbet. "Do you think?"

She looked troubled and I wished she'd *listen* instead of filtering every comment via the insecurities of her childhood self. If ever you offered an opinion that challenged her or her behavior, she went into what I called On Receipt of an Official Document mode. She ignored the small print—the bit that *really* mattered—and absorbed its *generic* meaning. In other words, I'd criticized her appearance.

Tim kissed me hello. He was in normal clothes. I wondered if he had told his girlfriend that the dress didn't suit her. Probably not. He was so in love, he couldn't see a fault. However, the real world was not as forgiving, and I felt that Tim had a duty to protect Lizbet from public ridicule. Adoration made him sloppy. My irritation levels rose, and we hadn't even ordered drinks. There'd always be a point in the evening at which Tim would start to nuzzle my sister's neck. I don't like humans nuzzling. Horses nuzzle.

I tried not to watch too closely, but I did. Tim seemed preoccupied, and Lizbet's mouth was pinched—although, she could have been trying to perfect a Zellweger pout. She'd certainly perfected the Zellweger figure.

I'm usually happy to watch everyone fight. But that evening, I discovered that I *missed* the nuzzling. Trying to prompt it, I told

Lizbet and Tim about a bet I'd had with opposing counsel (Sophie, actually) that she couldn't get the word *knob* into her summary. She'd managed—I'd known she would and had bought the bottle of pink Taittinger in advance.

Tim and Lizbet ha-ha'd politely at arm's length from each other, and I gave up trying to amuse them into horseplay. Instead I poured their drinks faster.

Alcohol succeeded where I had failed. They loosened up, got a little smoochy. I sighed with relief, decided it was time for a cigarette. I presumed that Lizbet and Tim were trying again for a baby, so I waved my unlit fag and went outside. A man jolted hard into my shoulder as I stepped into the street.

"*Do* excuse me—Oh! Cassandra Montgomery. Hello!"

I looked up, faked a smile. Barnaby Alcock. (By name and by nature. What a *massive* dick. And just to be clear, I am not praising the actual appendage—I've never seen it. In layman's terms, the man is an *imbecile*.) There is so much I could tell you about Barnaby to make you hate him, so I'll pick and choose. He adores himself more than any woman ever could, because he's *not a conventional barrister—woo-hoo!*

He has this shaggy blond hair that according to legend he used to wear in dreadlocks (oh, save us). His main hobby is surfing, and he cycles to court (any excuse to wear tight shorts). He began his career in Exeter—Sophie once asked, "Why Exeter?" and he said, "Why *not* Exeter?" Jerk. I came up against him there once when I was starting out, and he was an absolute pig. He's only about four years older than me, but I suppose I looked very young, and he gave me this *smirk* when he first saw me at the bench, as if to say, "Is your mum in?"

He and his colleagues were falsely deferential to me. ("Counsel

from *London*!" they said, and their body language said, *"Oo-ooh!"*)
It was like stumbling into a provincial gentlemen's club. The rob-
ing room was full of smoke, and when it emerged that I'd written a
document for the judge (to save everyone from a long opening
speech), Barnaby said, "Oh, you've written a *document*." He might
as well have said, "Oh, you've drawn a *picture*." When I saw it, at
the bottom of a pile, on the judge's desk, I made sure I said, "Have
you had a chance to read my document?" The judge said, "Would
you *like* me to?" And so we adjourned for fifteen minutes. As we
trooped back into court, I shot a triumphant glance at Barnaby,
who murmured, "He'll be happy now he's read the sports page and
had a fag and a cup of tea."

However, the most damning evidence I have on Barnaby is that
he's written two really boring books (in between helping the homeless, and lecturing, and setting up an e-mentoring scheme for
lawyers to help prison inmates, and baking cakes for his local
bring-and-buy sale). Both are on family law, and available on Ama-
zon, each a steal at eighty-four quid.

His first reader review was a peach: "An undiscriminating cut-
and-paste job. . . . Prose style inelegant and tedious. . . . This is an
area of law that begs for an interesting and thoughtful guide. This
isn't it."

However. The second, third, and fourth reader reviews were violent in their praise. "Sexing up of the legal publishing world! . . ."
"As a family lawyer myself, I was delighted to stumble upon this
thoroughly enjoyable read. Written by the talented and wise Barnaby Alcock in a wholly accessible style while covering the legal
points in sufficient depth to be helpful to even the most expert in the
field. If only more law books could be so enjoyable and interesting!"
And—wait for it—"A new standard in legal writing has been set!"

How curious that these glowing testimonials *all* hailed from the mysterious "A reader, London."

God, he was annoying.

I wanted to have sex with him so much I felt sick thinking about it.

CHAPTER 19

"How are you doing?" said Barnaby. I always felt he was a whisker away from adding, "little lady."

"Great," I said, exhaling a cloud of smoke, watching him wince. "Although, I have to ask—*when* is your client going to get real? I must tell you, there's absolutely no point in negotiating, given your position. I assure you that your client will not want to be in the witness box when I ask her—"

"Cassie, Cassie!" Barnaby placed a hand on my shoulder. "Relax! Enjoy your evening! Threaten me when you're on the clock!" He grinned. "So what's going on?"

I bit my lip. The man had the effect of making me talk rubbish. I had a nasty feeling that I was going to have to face him in the High Court in the next few months, and I *so* didn't want to. Because I was going to lose. It was Hubert Fitzgerald's fault.

Hubert Fitzgerald had decided to formally end his marriage to his wife, Alissa, after twenty-eight years, just as his business began to make money. There had been some monkey business between my client and the au pair. Hubert didn't seem to think that Alissa deserved *anything*. Within a week of demanding a divorce, Hubert had moved three hundred grand out of his account, in bits. ("Oh, two of that was to pay back Dad for the money he lent me to buy the house twenty years ago.") He claimed his annual turnover was fifty g's, when their lifestyle—his 'n' hers four-wheel drives, kids at private school, holiday cottage in Cornwall—suggested it was four times that. I'd warned him the judge would find him an unreliable witness if he came up with that crap under oath, but he'd persisted. Hubert was a businessman who stretched the truth like underwear elastic, and he didn't understand that he couldn't do the same in court. I'd talked a lot to him about full and frank disclosure, but he just sat there with a blank face and I had the distinct feeling that I could have been talking to a dog.

Barnaby and I were obliged to encourage the Fitzgeralds to set-tle out of court, but it was like trying to force children to concen-trate on broccoli when there was ice cream for dessert. The trouble was, Hubert was angling for a fight.

"I want you to cross-examine her," he said, "about her holiday costs. Two grand, my arse! She and the kids go to Brittany with her parents every year. She only has to pay for the ferry."

I fought to hide a shudder. "We should go gently," I said. "There's no point laying into her, saying that's an outrageous bud-get, because it's not."

"I don't care," he said. "Do it. I'm *paying* you."

"Hubert, I'm expensive," I told him.

He said, "I'd rather give it to you than that cow."

What I saw in Hubert was a formidable reserve of black hatred toward a person he had once loved—the result of many years of un-spoken resentments, unfinished arguments, petty disagreements, fundamental differences, miscommunications, emotional inarticu-lateness, selfishness, immaturity, dissatisfaction, disappointments, envy, and disrespect. The law said he couldn't hit her. He hoped the law would hit her for him.

So Barnaby and I had exchanged fairy stories—sorry, financial statements—but a lot of issues had remained unresolved. We had met an hour before the first appointment hearing, and he'd presented me with a list of company interests that *I* didn't know Hubert had.

"Where did you get all this?" I squeaked.

"My client inadvertently opened your client's post," he replied.

"Did she inadvertently go through his garbage cans, as well?" I said.

Barnaby's eyes widened, and he said, "I couldn't possibly advise such a course of action. However, if she happened to *pass* the garbage cans, and . . ."

I bristled and spluttered, as I knew that Barnaby had me over a barrel (oh, I wished). Everyone, including me, had suspected Hubert of concealing assets. A decent judge would accept that Alissa had had no choice but to burgle documents.

"Awfully sorry," Barnaby had murmured. "Bit of a smoking gun, I'm afraid. But my client has only *just* provided me with the information."

Now, in the real world, I scrutinized his face. Was he *laughing* at me? I couldn't tell. "So," I said, summoning all the sarcasm I could into one syllable. "Baked any cakes recently?"

"Cakes?" said Barnaby. "I *did* bake a vanilla cheesecake for my mother's birthday last week. And a strudel. How did you know?"

"Guessed." I clenched my fist and pictured Barnaby whipping cream cheese naked—stop, save it for later. . . .

"And who's this then?"

Lizbet's booze-shiny face inserted itself between us.

"Oh, hi." They both stood there, waiting, so I added, reluctantly,

"Lizbet, my sister. Barnaby"—I *was* going to say, "fellow barrister, eminent author, rowing blue, philanthropist," but my brain stalled on "philanthropist" and what came out was—"pompous."

"A friend of Cassie," said Lizbet.

"Colleague!" I said.

She looked thoughtful, and my heart skipped. I couldn't have mentioned him. On occasion, Lizbet would hold up a copy of *Heat*, with a photo of, perhaps, Benicio Del Toro, and say, "Yes? Yes?"

She was happy to broadcast her *G-certificate* fantasies, even in front of Tim, and I'd reciprocate with, "Er, Harrison Ford was nice in, er, *Witness*." However, serious fantasies remained private.

"Your name sounds incredibly familiar," cried Lizbet. "I'm sure Cassie's mentioned you. Oh hang on, *you're* the one who she first met when you visited a friend at her college. You had a drunken neck, then you disappeared like Cinderella, reappeared in an Exeter court three years later, and she's hated you ever since!"

"Elizabeth," I said. "You need to get that brain virus checked out."

"Do you often talk about me?" said Barnaby.

"Never," I said. "I know what it is. She must have read your books. Ha-ha!"

"You're a writer too!" exclaimed Lizbet, lurching toward him. "Oh my God, so am I! What are you doing now? You *must* join us!"

Barnaby made a big show of checking his watch. It was a diving watch, because as everyone knows, there are lots of diving opportunities in London.

"What?" I said. "*The Apprentice* doesn't start till nine."

"Yes," he said. "But *Grey's Anatomy* is on at eight."

Was he joking? Why didn't he ever smile and give me a clue? I thundered ahead to our table. Barnaby and Lizbet showed off behind me. (Barnaby: "Love the dress. Givenchy, right?" Lizbet: "Oh my God, etc.")

George had never met Barnaby, yet in a display of uncharacteristic intuition, he greeted him as one might greet a decaying hyena carcass brought to one's dinner table.

Tim was his usual affable self. Unlike my own dear husband, Tim didn't bite until bitten. His relationship with Lizbet was so peachy that no man was perceived as a threat, not even Total Penis. Tim was very robust, like me. He bounced back.

I sighed. It was difficult, working with Barnaby. Previously, I'd avoided him. If ever I spotted him around the Inns of Court, I'd whip past him quick smart. I'd feared that if anyone saw us together for more than a second, my infatuation would be headline news. I felt that the lust emanated from my pores. Around chambers I was quick, sharp, and crisp, but when Barnaby showed, I turned into molten caramel. So as not to alert Barnaby to this fact, I was snappy with him, always. He must have thought—to quote my husband—I was permanently on the rag.

I sat, listening to Lizbet rattle on, wondering (no offense to George) what it would be like to pin Barnaby to the wall and tear off his clothes. I liked to look expensive in court, but Barnaby's suit was scruffy with a slight sheen, and almost certainly from a high street chain. This was unusual at the bar—at his level, anyway. Very few male barristers that I knew could resist having their suits a bit sharper when they started to make some money. When Mr. Hershlag came to see me at work he was *agog*. The linings are often quite bright—peacock blue, fuchsia, yellow. Barnaby was odd.

Tim picked at his food. Lizbet was downing champagne like it was about to be made illegal. Her nails were long and pink, with diamanté stars in the varnish—in her former life they were chewed raw. She laughed at something Barnaby had said (probably a joke about briefs) and clutched his sleeve, her talons digging into the material. Barnaby reached for his water glass, gently forcing her to remove her claws.

I'd noticed, around and about, that if another woman approached Barnaby, a growl started of its own accord in the back of my throat—but just then I felt sorry for Lizbet. She was a bad flirt—even though she was pretty, her belief in her own attraction didn't convince.

Tim hadn't said much. He looked as though he needed his face squashed in a big maternal bust.

George was staring at Lizbet as though she'd sprouted a second, very ugly, head.

I kicked him under the table. What—couldn't he tolerate the sight of a woman having fun? It wasn't as if she was flirting with *intent*. She only required validation. (Which is why I am not a flirt, whatever Lizbet might have told you. I get validation from myself. I don't need it from some idiot with a penis.)

My brain felt like congealed spaghetti. My sister had strayed so far from her normal self. Was it the baby? Could you *contain* a thing like that? Or had she let it tarnish everything? You had to fight it, and Lizbet's trouble was, she wasn't used to fighting. Don't tell me something was wrong with The Relationship. Impossible.

Meanwhile, I was annoyed with Barnaby for existing, furious with George for having the nerve to marry me—and I could have throttled myself for letting him.

Having been brushed off Barnaby's sleeve, Lizbet curled up like an earwig. She muttered, "I feel sick."

George snapped a breadstick in two and bit off one end. He must have been riled—he was off wheat. He pointed the shortened breadstick at Barnaby. "Your cuffs are fraying."

Barnaby grinned, and I nearly fainted in my seat. "I know," he said. "It's probably time for a visit to Marks."

"Marks & *Spencer*?" repeated George, incredulous. "You're standing up in the High Court! My wife"—he jabbed a breadstick stub in my direction—"spends a fortune on bespoke."

Barnaby shrugged. "It's for *work*." He pulled at his lapel. "You have to look smart, but ultimately, it's like a McDonald's uniform."

Lizbet giggled and covered her face. "I feel *ill*."

"I'll take you home," said George, standing up. "And you"—he nodded at Barnaby—"where do you live?"

"Thank you. I have transport."

Barnaby was one of those people who are so genteel that when they disagree with you, half the time you can't actually tell.

Tim stopped pushing his red onion ravioli around his plate. "I can call Lizbet a taxi," he said. "There's no need for us *all* to go. It took Cassie months to book this place."

George got an uncomfortable look on his face that meant he was annoyed. "It's no trouble for me to drive Lizbet home," he said. "Actually, some guys from work are meeting a few actor pals. Helena mentioned that she might pop in, and I *think* the pub's only down the road from your place. It might be wise to show my face."

"Unlikely," said Lizbet and sniggered. She linked arms with George, and said, "Joke. Come on then, Pudding. *Bye*, Barny, lovely to meet you, bye, Cass. Tim, here's two fifties."

I picked up the notes to give back to her, but she waved them away. "Tim invented The Poo Patch," she cried. "We're stinking rich!"

Tim said nothing as she wobbled into the night.

"Cassie," called George over his shoulder. "I won't be home till late, but I'll call at eleven to check you got back safely."

Barnaby gazed after Lizbet, and I *knew* he was going to elbow Tim and say, "She's a wild one!"

He said, "If you *did* invent The Poo Patch, and you *are* stinking rich, first, do you have a good lawyer, and second, why isn't Lizbet happy?"

Tim attacked his crème brûlée, and I thought if he was at drama school, and the improvisation was "Eat Cake Angrily," he'd have received an ovation. He placed his silver fork in the center of the bone china plate, leaned back on the plush leather banquette, and said, "She realized money isn't everything."

"True," said Barnaby, swirling his champagne in the glass. "But it is *something*."

"What!" I said. "*You* don't care about money. You're in this for the intellectual exercise and the camaraderie of the Bar."

"Am I?"

"According to your profile on the Bar Council Web site."

"Montgomery, you are *obsessed* with me!"

"No, I'm not! Your profile was passed round on e-mail to give everyone a laugh. All that stuff about 'unparalleled opportunities for advocacy' and 'helping with the day-to-day legal problems of ordinary people' . . ."

"They edited the bit about naked greed?"

"You—"

"Sorry to butt in," said Tim. "But I need some air. I'm going for a walk. I'll see you soon, Cassie. Thanks for this. I'm sorry. Barnaby, good to meet you."

"That was your fault," I said, as the door shut behind Tim.

"You know," said Barnaby. "After all this time—and incidentally, I *told* you I had a train to catch that night, it was my brother's wedding the following day, I suspect you were too inebriated and forgot—it's interesting to see you in a non-work situation. You're just as *combative*."

"No, I'm not, just the opposite."

God, I really was bad at arguing. You have to understand that in court, one doesn't just stand there making it up. A junior does a lot of the written work prior to the case, and constructs the skeleton argument. Obviously, *I* flesh it out, I do a lot of meticulous preparation the night before, but I know what the other side is going to *say*, more or less, before they say it, and all I have to work out is what I am going to say in response. So if Barnaby had faxed me a list of his proposed points before dinner, I'd have been wiping the floor with him. Mm, which if you think about it literally—

"What's going on with you and your husband?"

"I'm sorry?"

"What about?"

"Barnaby!"

"Yes?"

"Stop it."

"You invite me for dinner, and I walk into a war zone. I'm not going to pretend everything is fine when it isn't. That's ridiculous!"

"Yes, and all credit to you, but doesn't it occur to you that some things are private?"

"Montgomery, I'm a divorce lawyer. Tonight was practically a business meeting!"

"I'm glad that my life is a joke to you," I said, eventually. "Do you find your clients' failed relationships amusing also?"

Barnaby leaned closer, with a serious look on his face. His eyes were long-lashed and dark blue. If God had taken me aside, explained that Barnaby actually saw through his nostrils, the eyes were simply decoration, I'd have understood.

"I know," he said, "that you like me."

"No I don't!" I said.

Barnaby looked surprised and hurt.

I snorted. "Don't give me *that*. You're like a trained killer. You know exactly what you're doing and you don't care."

"Cassie," he said, quietly. "I'm sorry. I've confused you—"

"I'm not confused."

I stood up—and he grabbed my hand. "Listen," he said. "I didn't ask about you and George because your life is a joke to me. I asked because it *isn't* a joke."

I sat down.

"I like you," he said. "I think."

"You think! *Do* you think, though, Barnaby? Do you?"

"I—"

"You see that George and I are no longer . . . *honeymooners*, and you *think* it would be modern to come right out and just ask me if I fancy a bit on the side with you, in your spare time, in between all the good-doing!"

"No," said Barnaby. "No. That's not it. I'm not asking you to cheat on George."

"What *are* you asking?"

"I . . . I . . ."

I'd never seen him lost for words.

"What?" I barked.

"If . . . if you . . . if you did think that you were in a marriage that might not last forever . . . I, I . . ."

I blinked. "Are you . . . trying to *reserve* me? What am I? A table at the Ivy?"

"I should probably have done this after the case," he muttered. "Trouble is, I'm going to win and then you'll be in a huff with me."

"Barnaby," I said. "Don't deprive your fans on *my* account. George and I are trying for a baby."

CHAPTER 20

He put me on the defensive, or I wouldn't have said it. Babies and the Bar go together . . . not very well. My head of chambers, Sophie Hazel Hamilton, is the exception—she's had four kids—but she's made sacrifices. (Code for, she's seen them once.) She fell pregnant for the first time just as she was offered pupilage, and confided in a fellow trainee. *He* took it upon himself to seek advice on her behalf, from the Equality and Diversity Committee. To summarize his inquiry: "Has she messed up?"

I had. Barnaby would spread the news that I was planning to screw my career—sorry—husband, and rumor would become fact, regardless of reality. Everyone would forever be squinting at my stomach, waiting for me to swap my almond-croissant-and-espresso habit for coal, and if I ever chose Badoit over Beaujolais, colleagues would ask impudent questions. (In the first months of her second pregnancy, Sophie worked through severe morning sickness, and after retching in the toilet for fifteen minutes one day, was accosted by a pin-striped colleague.

"My dear, I have to ask," he drawled. "Are you *carrying*?"

"Carrying what?" she replied. "A gun? My dear, if I were, you'd be the first to know about it.")

My desire to put Barnaby in his place (under me, naked) had led me to stretch the truth, because my efforts to have a baby with George were not going well. We'd stopped having sex, so the odds of conceiving were reduced.

Barnaby stared. "That's clear enough," he said. "I apologize for disturbing you."

I was about to query his wording: Disturb me? I'd just rejected *him*. How did he always manage to make it seem as if *I* was the poor heartbroken soul with a ridiculous crush? I didn't *care* that he'd disappeared after our kiss, nor did I care for his excuses nearly ten years later. All I remembered was finding a jaunty note—"Call me!" next to an indecipherable phone number—scribbled on a ripped off flap of cigarette packet. Of course I didn't call him. He should have called *me*.

"I— Oh, never mind," I said.

"Are you all right?"

"Yes. Go away."

He fumbled in his pocket. "And don't leave any money," I added.

He sighed. "Cassie," he said. He paused. "I always felt you were the one who got away."

I laughed. "What," I said. "Like a prize salmon?"

"A prize, definitely. See you next week."

"Great!" I said. "It won't be at all awkward!"

He left then, and I gazed after him. Jerk. He was so . . . *Julio Iglesias*. Ah well. I took a gulp of champagne to take the edge off— but it tasted sour and flat. I paid the bill and went home. It was only nine forty-five. The house was pitch dark, which was unusual, as

George was meticulous about leaving random lights on if we were out, to trick burglars. (George was convinced of the general population's intent to commit crime, and once rang me bang in the middle of a business dinner to report that a "youth" was doing wheelies on his BMX up and down our road. This, to George, was delinquency. "Hello!" I said, when I rang him later. "I was expecting the phone to be answered by a young teenage boy!")

I glanced down the road, and noticed George's car parked badly on the corner—*why?* My Merc was in the garage, and we had a driveway. There was always a reason with George; I just couldn't be bothered to figure it out. I stepped inside, fumbled in the darkness. The lights snapped on before I located the switch.

"Caught y—Oh!" said George. He was aiming the houseplant water spritzer in a shoot-to-kill position.

I shook my head, and swept past him.

George lowered the spritzer. "I'm sorry! That Barnaby bloke. I thought—"

I turned on the top stair. I felt exhausted. "George," I said. "It doesn't matter."

I lay in bed, turning over and over like a cat.

I was a fool. I wanted a baby. I would never get my hands on my real mother. I *needed* to hold my baby in my arms. The yearning was a physical ache. And yet, in the past month, I hadn't slept with my husband. The last time we'd tried, he had been enthusiastic, *creative,* and I'd recoiled. He'd insisted we bathe together. Nuzzling had occurred. Grim. I felt sad, because I think to a lot of women, George would have been attractive. I may have misrepresented him. He was tall, only a little gangly, and his eyes were bluish green, pleasing contrast to his dark hair and pale skin. But I flinched when he kissed me.

We proceeded anyhow, but afterward he rolled away and said, "Thank you. Now I feel like a rapist."

We hadn't touched each other since.

I flipped the pillow, gave it a punch, considered my options. George wasn't working. He refused to be tested, but I suspected his sperm were inferior. Barnaby, however ... He claimed to "like" me. In other words, he'd sleep with me if I asked—the irresistible shag that would sour my reputation—the triumph of emotion over reason, what I'd always feared. But now my need was greater than the risk. It would be the horizontal equivalent of a snatch-and-grab.

George would assume the baby was his. The marriage would totter on. I would keep my parents-in-law in my life. A panic attack threatened every time I considered the reality of losing them. Ivan and Sheila Hershlag treated me like a princess. They did their food shop, bickering their way around the Tesco superstore, with a visit from *me* in mind. No mushrooms for the chicken goulash; Cassie won't eat mushrooms. Cow's milk mozzarella for the tomato salad; Cassie won't eat *bufala*. Mrs. Hershlag bought me hand cream. And new dishcloths. She wouldn't *sit* in my kitchen, she had to "do," and if she wasn't polishing the door handles, she was scrubbing behind the espresso machine. She and Ivan came to see me in chambers, dressed for synagogue.

No.

I couldn't trick that family, although when I saw a baby—even if it looked like Jackie Mason's impression of a mother-in-law—I felt a desire so great that I had to turn away. I couldn't trick the *baby. I* was aware, more than most, of the importance of knowing where you came from. My baby would know his real parents, *be* with them; I would not allow my child to enter the world bereft. In my experience, if you aren't known and loved by your biological parents, serenity eludes you. I denied the missing piece of my soul that was Sarah Paula, because my desire for her was raw and primal and it made me feel like an animal.

But if I stayed with George and was faithful to him, chances were there wouldn't *be* a baby. Unless, of course, we could conceive by clapping our hands in unison.

And if we did (fertile hand clapping is an area of research that needs further investigation), would the baby be at all bothered when he realized that Mummy and Daddy were united only in mutual loathing? I pictured George reading a small person a bedtime story. Would he assume a different voice for each character, and take the time to explain and discuss? Or would he be like my mother, who always read every tale in a flat, bored tone as fast as she could, only quitting the text to mutter sarcastic asides.

Thanks to our mother, Lizbet and I grew up thinking that "The Tiger Who Came to Tea" was about a housewife on sanity's edge, who couldn't face cooking one more meal or cleaning one more plate, and told her husband a ridiculous lie about a zoo animal in a feeding frenzy in their kitchen. The line about the tiger drinking "Daddy's beer" and leaving nothing for "Daddy's dinner" was like a red rag to a remarkably bad-tempered bull. "Of course," muttered Vivica. "Because frumpy *Mummy* exists on bloody water and fresh air!"

I flipped the pillow and thumped my head down on it. I was getting warm and woozy, then George clanged a saucepan in the kitchen, and my brain sprang awake. I jumped out of bed and screeched, "Stop banging ABOUT!"

" '*Koff!*" shouted George.

That was more or less the sum of our day's conversation. We really didn't like each other.

I would tell him it was over the next morning. But first, there was someone I had to speak to.

"Oh, Cass," said Lizbet, "I'm—*cak*! Sorry, the Paracetamol stuck in my throat—I'm so sorry. Hang on. Sphinx has a purr for you."

I sighed as my sister stuck the receiver in the cat's face and the feline impression of a starter motor tickled my eardrum. I had never felt needy in my life, and it was a new sick feeling. I wouldn't repeat it. Now I could see the sense of having a therapist—an employee paid to hear all your shit and bat it gently back to you, so you didn't alienate friends and relatives with your endless moaning. Lizbet was a good listener. Not that I ever burdened her with my problems—I didn't have any—but now . . .

"Hello!" I called, into the phone. "I'd like to converse with a human being now! Hello, Lizbet?"

"There!" said Lizbet. "She *knows* when someone's upset. She's so maternal. But, as much as I'm fond of George, if you think he is no longer right for you, you should leave him. It's only fair, for both of you. But you should do it now, while there are no children involved. Sorry, Cass. I know that probably wasn't the right thing to say, considering your . . . situation. But I think you have to accept that circumstances aren't ideal, and make a decision."

Was this why they called it the human race? Lizbet seeing her chance to get ahead. It was strange. I'd *thought* I wanted to confide in Lizbet, but the minute she started to talk with authority about my business, I wanted to shut her down.

"Has he any idea?" she added.

"Not yet." I paused. "I'm sure it will be fine. Not to worry."

"Oh, Cass," she said in the softest voice, and I realized that Lizbet would make the best mother. "Listen. It will be hard, but you *are* very strong, and I'll help you through it. You'll still have me. You'll always have me."

I sighed. "I know. Thanks." I stopped talking. Okay, let's wrap it up!

"There's something else, isn't there?" said Lizbet.

"No. Not that I can think of."

"I don't believe you. *I* think there's another man."

I didn't want to lie to her. Not . . . *outright*. Not when she and I were at such a promising point in our relationship.

"There may be. . . ."

"It's old Barnabypants!"

"*God!*" I shouted. How *incredibly* annoying. "No, it isn't! Please! Give me some credit!"

Well. It was only a small lie.

"Oh!" I could hear Lizbet seize the chance to steer this conversation happy. "Well. If not him . . . are we at liberty to say *who* this man might be?"

"Not yet."

"Do I know him?"

"Yes."

"Do I approve?"

"Yes."

"You don't sound too sure."

"Well. *You* approve of him. I'm not sure I do."

"Aha. A *moral* issue! How interesting. I—"

As she spoke I felt a lurch of nausea, and I wasn't surprised. Leaving George's parents was a scary move. I should have kept it to myself. The sickness rose.

"I've got to go, Lizbet."

"Okay, darling. Speak later."

I ran to the toilet and—"Why don't you FLUSH?" I screamed at George, and was sick into our Bette bath. He was persnickety about the house, yet did his bit for conservation. (His motto: "If it's brown, flush it down. If it's yellow, let it mellow." My motto: "That's disgusting.")

"Leave me ALONE!" roared George from the bedroom, as I retched. Plainly, he was still suspicious about Barnaby, because he didn't normally raise his voice. "Are you okay?" he said, from the doorway. He peered at what I'd done to the two-thousand-pound bath, and his mouth shrank. "I won't be eating chunky vegetable soup for a while," he said. "I'll get you the Flash Wipes."

"Tissue," I said, trying not to taste the vomit in my mouth.

George passed me a wad of toilet paper. Then he said, "Have you done a test?"

"A test?"

"A pregnancy test."

"G-ahh! No."

"Why not? We were shagging like rabbits until you went off it. Have you done a test since then?" He paused. "Or is it not *mine*?"

"Tell you what, George," I said. "If I *am* pregnant, we'll take a paternity test, how about that?"

He gazed at me. "I'm sorry, Cassie. You've been so . . . tetchy. And I saw how that bloke looked at you."

"*All* men look at me," I wanted to say. "Your attention is usually elsewhere."

George was ferreting in the bathroom cabinet. "Here you go," he said, handing me a Clearblue. "Piss on that!"

I sighed. "Please go out while I . . . *wee*," I finished primly.

Afterward, I balanced the stick on the edge of the limestone basin, washed my hands, glowered into the mirror. My cheeks were flushed, and my stomach ached. PMS, plain as that uncharacteristic spot on my face.

George opened the door—"Can I come in?" he said, halfway to the basin. He snatched up the stick, and I held my breath.

My husband turned to me with the bearing of a king, and said, "Wife, we are *expecting*."

CHAPTER 21

_____ *Lizbet*

George's parents were doing a Friday Night, and I agreed to go
along with Tim to please Cassie. She was the only family member I
was interested in seeing. For reasons she hadn't shared, she was
suddenly keen on playing the perfect wife, dutiful daughter. It was
strange, but I didn't question it—I hoped it might take the pressure
off *me*. Our parents were attending, and I felt the weight of their
expectation. They'd got the scent of a grandchild and were like a
pair of sharks who'd smelled blood.

It was simple for them. Dead baby, never mind, try again, hop
back on that horse, then share the good news! They had main-
tained a presentable sympathetic facade, but now their more selfish
needs were rising to the surface like scum in a pond. *Failure failure
failure.* My brain was starting to malfunction. I was also drinking a
lot for a girl who didn't drink, and had made what Vivica would
call "a spectacle" of myself with Barnaby, Cassie's lust object (it was
obvious, and George had a face like a halibut the whole way home).

"What size are you?" demanded Mr. Hershlag, peering with difficulty over the piles of food on the table.

"Me?" I said. I'd visited their house before, but I was always taken aback by the sheer quantity of framed family photographs, china ornaments, and silverware. It was like a bric-a-brac store. Everything was old (except the kitchen appliances, all of which had apparently conked out in recent years from overuse and been replaced on the advice of the fire brigade). Nothing matched. There were tins of chocolate wafers in every room. Cassie liked clean lines, and I was surprised that she could stand to be in the place.

"Leave it!" said Mrs. Hershlag.

"You got plans for a wedding?" said Mr. Hershlag, as if his wife hadn't spoken. "I've got a wedding dress for you. It's pink—"

"She don't want your wedding dress!" cried Mrs. Hershlag.

"Darling?" said Vivica, whose eye makeup was very blue that day. "Is there something you want to tell us?"

"Yes," said Tim. "We don't have plans for a wedding."

Everyone fell silent, and I squirmed in my seat. I'd been cool toward him lately, but I didn't like the compliment returned.

"You need a cushion?" demanded Mr. Hershlag, making me jump. "Take a cushion!"

"I'm fine," I said. "This chair is very comfortable."

"Nah, take it *home*! Take a cushion home! Take it! You'll be doing me a favor!"

"It's very kind of you," I said. "But we have more than enough cushions at home."

I glanced at Cassie, expecting to see a grin, but she was intent on her chicken goulash. (Lovely, but crying out for mushrooms.) Cassie hadn't spoken to me all evening. I didn't *get* her. I hoped it wasn't something *I'd* done. Actually, she was probably thinking about leaving George. She looked drawn. I'd hugged her at the door, and it was like two ironing boards collapsing on each other. I liked feeling thin, but I hated feeling hungry, and secretly I knew I should put on weight. Soon.

If I knew my sister, she was also regretting that she'd shared about George. She was so private it killed me. *I* was happy to talk about anything to anyone. Last month, before Tim's advance for his poo-ahoy system came through, I confided our money worries to a stranger on the subway. We were stuck in a tunnel between Euston and Camden Town. I told this man that I could be poor, but I refused to be fat and poor. He pretended to be engrossed in an advert for a toe fungus cure. Then it occurred to me that the man possibly thought I was strange, chatting away as if I knew him, so to prove my normality, I said, "Hey, don't you think it's weird that there are people who'll see a soap actor in the street and shout, 'You bastard!' "

The man looked scared. I sighed. Time to pull out the big guns. "Or what about people who have Christmas decorations up all year? They definitely have something missing in their lives."

The man jumped up, burst through the end door, and changed cars. Nut.

Cassie had similar problems communicating. If something was bothering her, she *wouldn't* talk about it. If you asked, she'd deny it, present you with a decoy problem.

I was beginning to suspect that there was more to it than the husband and the heir, but if she didn't want me to know, I wouldn't dig. I had some pride. If someone rejects you because they want to get their rejection in first, in case you're thinking of rejecting them at some vague future point, you *will* reject them.

I wanted to be close to Cassie, but there was a boundary that she was unwilling to let me cross. Sometimes I didn't even think she *needed* me, and that hurt. The warmest she'd been was when I decided I'd had enough lousy treatment from life, and withdrawn. The miscarriage had brought out my mean streak. Cassie had been shocked, and I was glad. It was good to have her fuss around *me*, for a change, worry about my moodiness, my rudeness and inconsistencies. The fact that she'd been prepared to play a subservient role had repaired a lot of the damage. We'd made some progress, but I was eager for more.

I didn't want this love-hate seesaw between us. I wanted consistent, unconditional love.

The problem was that she wasn't scared of me. No one was scared of me. Not even ... *mice*. In fact, a mouse would probably have stolen my cheese. That's how non-scary I was. And I suspected that Cassie only respected people who she was a little bit scared of.

Perhaps I just had to be grateful that she and I were back on track, as much as we ever would be. I supposed I would always be the big, ungainly sister to her, and I should accept that. Cassie would always want to be treated as the special, baby, bijou sister. I'd never had a problem with that; why should it be a problem now? She was being more supportive than she'd ever been. She'd read my sex columns, and said she liked them, although I knew she was revolted. I didn't tell her it was all made up. She was putting up a front, and it made me want to put up a front. I can only compare it to neighbors competing with extensions.

But, within those perimeters, our relationship was solid. Wait, isn't that word pronounced "perameters"? I don't get the English language. (Another thing, Cassie thinks I'm trivial. Although I'm not the one who owns three Hermès bags *and* has had her teeth whitened.) I do think Cassie had trouble with me changing. Cassie was sexy, whereas the boys always looked through me like I was plate glass. It was hard for her to adjust—I *knew* she'd criticize the

Givenchy dress—but she was trying. I hoped she saw that I was still the same in essence. I would still perform a shadow role to her shining star. Just not at cost to myself.

"*We* might need a cushion, Dad!" said George.

I saw Cassie shoot him a look of horror, and I couldn't see why. It was so rare that George was diplomatic. (He was, after all, the man who had said to our father, "You work in a hotel. Do you often get asked for threesomes?") Maybe she was merely surprised.

"You want cushions?" cried Mr. Hershlag, excitedly. "Take!"

George cleared his throat.

"This chicken is delicious, Sheila!" cried Cassie. "Tell me, how do you get it so tender? I've tried to make this at home, and I just *cannot* get comparable results."

I stared at her. Liar. I don't believe my sister had ever touched raw poultry. She must want something. But for the life of me, I couldn't think of anything the Hershlags might have that Cassie might want. They weren't wealthy people.

Sheila beamed in pleasure. She had a nice wide smile, and no malice. I caught myself. It was a sad day when you found yourself exhibiting mother-in-law envy. Tim's mother wasn't strictly an in-law, but she was behaving like one. The previous weekend, they'd forced us round to their house. Tim's mother had a face like a bloodhound the entire day. At lunch, she'd served me fewer roast potatoes than everyone else. (Which made me realize that I was bloody starving and wanted something *proper* to eat.) Then, afterward, we'd all sat in the living room with our hands in our laps, and she'd nodded toward her garden. "See that wood pigeon. A fox got its partner. It was injured, and this one was trying to distract the fox. Flapping round. Making a noise. But it was no use. It's lonely now. Just hangs around by itself."

A tragic tale, but I was no longer fooled. Tim's mother didn't have a bleeding heart—she didn't *have* a heart. I'd done away with her grandchild, and she thought I deserved to be miserable. We were in the living room, still staring at the bereaved wood pigeon, when there was an almighty crash from the kitchen. We ran in, and saw that three framed photographs, balanced precariously on a shelf above the oven, had fallen to the floor, and one had smashed. A portrait of Tim and me.

"I *told* him that shelf had slipped." Tim's mother sighed. And then, "Funny how a lot of pictures fell down but that was the only one that broke." Pause. "They say bad things happen in threes."

What did she mean? I was due another miscarriage?

To be honest, *I* thought I was doing fairly well with all that. There was the drink, but maybe I drank too little before. I was more lethargic than I had been. I scratched my ankle raw one night—itchy dry skin. Days later, I noticed that the scab wasn't forming properly, and saw that it was septic. Once, I'd have sped to the medicine cabinet and doused the wound in TCP liquid. Instead, I thought, Oh, let it sort itself out. Eventually it healed, but left a large brown and purple scar. I did wonder how far I would have let it go. Gangrene? Septicemia? Amputation of the foot?

"I'll write down a recipe for you," said Mrs. Hershlag.

"You never ask *me* for recipes, Cassie," said Vivica. She said it as if she was joking.

"That's because I know your recipes," said Cassie. "Or should I say, *recipe*."

I giggled. One fateful evening, our mother had watched a cooking program (I think the remote was out of batteries) and garnered from it that alcohol, cream, and butter added to the flavor of a dish. From that day forward, every meal she served was bitter with raw booze and drowning in grease. All that varied, some weeks, was the bacteria (lamb, beef, chicken, fish).

"Can I ask where you bought these beautiful Shabbat candlesticks?" inquired Cassie, who had obviously taken some mind-altering drug.

"They were a wedding present from my mother," said Mrs. Hershlag, proudly. "They belonged to my grandmother. They're at least sixty years old, but I polish them every week, and they look like new."

"Well," said Cassie. "It's amazing that as well as having sentimental and religious significance, they are so *stylish*. They make a superb centerpiece. They fit so well with the décor."

Décor? What décor?

My house was a design museum compared to this . . . abomination, and she hated it. ("Everything half works," she once told me. "You have to bang the microwave to get it open. You have to twist the handle of the bathroom door *right* down, spraining your wrist. The hot tap at the sink is actually the *cold* tap. You have to whack the boiler with a wrench to get the heating to come on. The kitchen garbage can lid is broken, and you have to *touch* the can to throw anything away. It's like an assault course.")

"Dad," continued Cassie, without a pause. "How's work? Any interesting stories?"

She *hated* our father going on about the hotel. We knew there were juicy tales of sex, drugs, and pilfered bathrobes, but we—"the children"—never got to hear them.

As Cassie once said, "*We* always get Aesop's Fables, and we'll be getting them when we're fucking forty."

"As it happens, yes," said our father.

Cassie beamed. Did anyone else realize my sister had been kidnapped by aliens and replaced by a robot?

"Today," said our father, "a gentleman checked in, a multi-millionaire. He's stayed with us for years. I took his Louis Vuitton luggage up from the valet. This gentleman always asks for four hundred Rothman cigarettes to be waiting in his room. I often organize him theater tickets. He has Parkinson's disease, and when I took his luggage up today, I said, 'How are you feeling, sir?' He said, 'I'm going to see a specialist in the U.S.' And then he said, 'You are much wealthier than I am. If I gave you one million pounds, would you sell me ten years of your life?' "

There was an awkward silence.

Cassie opened her mouth to fill it, but George got there first. ",Guess what, people. My wife is with child!"

CHAPTER 22

I stood up, and George's words ran riot in my head, making me stagger. I felt as if I was trying to keep balance during an earthquake. As I stumbled toward the door, our mother cried, "Darling, that's marvelous! Lizbet can give you her things!"

"Vivica!" said our father in a sharp voice.

She added, stuttering, "I mean, it's bad luck to have them in the house."

"Yes," I heard myself say. "Although I think that's *before* the miscarriage."

Mrs. Hershlag had jumped up to kiss Cassie—and she caught my arm as I squeezed past her. "My dear," she said. "Please God by you."

It was an old-fashioned expression, wishing the same good fortune on another person. (Every time I attended a Jewish wedding, I heard it a million times, as it was customarily spoken by women older than forty, to women older than fourteen.) I nodded, and tears filled my eyes. Why did she have to be *kind*? I could cope with Tim's mother's spite. It glanced off me, each little scar making me tougher. But compassion was a killer. It wormed its way into your heart, infecting it with sorrow, until you thought you might die of the agony.

The phrases appropriate to the occasion presented in my head—"Congratulations, Cassie and George, I am so pleased for you, what wonderful news"—but my brain refused to grant clearance.

So when I heard those same words spoken aloud—"Congratulations, Cassie and George, I am so pleased for you, what wonderful news!"—my head jerked in surprise and shock.

"Cheers, Tim! Cheers, mate!" said George.

Cassie managed a tight smile.

"Lizbet," said Tim. "Aren't you going to say something?"

Everyone's gaze focused on me. I stared back at everyone. Mr. Hershlag was wiping away tears with a handkerchief. Vivica looked like the class brain who knew the answer and was trying hard not to jump up and down and say, "Me!" Our father was polishing his glasses with a corner of the embroidered Shabbat tablecloth. George stared at me, proud and defiant. Tim's face was carefully blank. Cassie was cracking a piece of shiny challah crust into crumbs with her fingernail.

I said, "I'm going to celebrate with a drink!"

I bought a bottle of Stone's ginger wine—our father used to drink it and I liked the taste—and slumped in the car, taking dainty sips from the green bottle top. I noted that only Cassie and our father had tried to stop me from leaving. That *cow*. I slumped lower in my seat, spotted an empty Coke can on the floor, decanted the wine into it. Then I sat up, and drank in gulps. *Ah*, permission to relax! But I couldn't. My whole body trembled in rage, and my heart pounded.

Two-faced … crap about George … knew there was some-

thing . . . unless . . . other man's . . . brazen liar . . . unbelievable . . .
must have known . . . how dare she . . . not fair . . . always gets . . . me
never . . . so superior . . . disapproves . . . no one cares about me . . .
mortgage people . . . unfriendly . . . M&S . . . avocadoes . . . brown . . .
Sky . . . didn't record . . . olive oil . . . best trousers . . . cat sick . . . teak
table . . . discolored . . . so unfair . . . tired . . . home . . . seat belt . . .
slowly . . . careful . . . here we are . . . brilliant driver . . . booze . . .
helps concentration . . . mind . . . wall . . . pull into garage—
CRASH!

"Shit!" I said, just as the airbag punched me hard in the face.
"Jesus!"

I screamed, trying to shout away the pain. I thought airbags
were supposed to *protect* you from injury. I'd also wrenched my
neck. I sat there, dazed and trembling. I fumbled the car door open
and was sick out of it. I could feel my nose swelling. Then I
breathed deep, kicked the bottle under the seat, and scanned windows to see if any neighbors were looking.

Tabitha and Jeremy were peering from the front bedroom
window. Tabitha had Celestia curled over her shoulder in a pink
Babygro and looked annoyed. "What?" I wanted to shout. "You've
got your *baby*, warm and wriggly. You *haven't* smashed your
boyfriend's car into a wall." I could see Tabitha's mouth moving
really fast. Jeremy vanished from the window. Seconds later, there
he was.

"You all right, Elizabeth? You took that corner a bit fast."

Jeremy wasn't a favorite. No T-shirt was complete without a slo-
gan, and the previous week I'd heard him in the garden with
Tomas. "Tomas! Tomas! We're going out to lunch . . . to *Wagamama's*." Presumably, he thought the day would come when his
three-year-old would respond, "Wagamama's? But that's not *spe-*

cifically a child-friendly dining experience. Oh, Daddy, you're not like all the other conformist parents, you're so *rad*!" I couldn't for the life of me work out what he and Tabitha had in common.

"Migraine," I whispered. "I think I might have passed out for a second." I paused. "You don't think anyone will call the ... *authorities*?"

Jeremy saw himself as a rebel. "Authorities!" he said. "Yeah, right!"

"Well," I said. "When Evelyn Toberman put her foot on the accelerator instead of the brake and backed her car into a tree, Letty Jackson pressed the panic button in her bedroom and six squad cars turned up." (Usually, said our mother, Letty Jackson pressed the panic button if Mr. Jackson entered the bedroom.)

"Huh," said Jeremy. "The pigs! We don't *have* a panic button. I'm a brown belt in judo." He nodded toward Tim's slightly crumpled car. "So did you have a few jars then?"

"Pardon?" I said.

"A few bevvies! A few drinks!"

"No! Certainly not! I don't—"

"*I* was out on the lash with the boys last week, Christ almighty, we were in a state. Went out with some of the crew from the old job, just the professionals if you know what I mean, w-woooh, it was serious, had a beer at lunchtime, couple of white wines at five, back on the beers at seven, cor, I tell you, it was nasty, oof—"

"Jeremy."

"—coupla shorts, few cocktails—"

"Jeremy!"

"—a really big glass of Pimms, spat out the cucumber—"

"JEREMY!"

"Yes?"

"Can you help me get this car into the garage, please? I don't want Tim to see it . . . yet."

"Yeah, okay. What you going to tell him?"

"The truth, of course! I had—I have a migraine, yes?"

"*Right*. Or you could always say that Tomas ran out and you swerved to avoid him . . . into the garage door."

I stared at him. His own child! "I don't think I'd like to say *that*," I said, a little primly. "I might say . . . Sphinx ran out."

Jeremy shrugged. "What*ever*."

Jeremy heaved open the garage door—which now had a big dent in it—and drove the car in for me.

"There you goesy," he said. "Our secret, eh?"

He winked and tossed me the keys. I grabbed at air and they fell on the floor. I bent to retrieve them, and when I looked up, he was gone. Twit. I was glad that his wife made him eat the stale food in the fridge. I fell into bed, without looking at myself, and drifted into a prickly sleep.

The next day, I sat at the breakfast table, pale-faced except for two black eyes. I had a fat lip, bruising around my nose, and my entire body ached. The vertebrae in my neck had been replaced by a hot poker. My head hurt. I thought of Cassie, soon to be wafting around her walled garden in white chiffon with a baby in a bonnet, and I felt myself twist with envy. Apart from that, I was just *fabulous*.

Tim marched into the kitchen. His gaze flickered over me; he didn't comment. Ten minutes later, I heard our garage door open. It reminded me that when we first moved in, it came to our attention that our *other* neighbors were not only slobs (big urine-stained mattress in front garden instead of rosebushes), they were forever opening and closing their garage. We couldn't sit in our living room in the evening without hearing at least one squeak and thud from their garage door. Once, we heard the familiar squeak-thud, and Tim said in a sneering tone, "Getting something from your *garage?*"

Not quite Oscar Wilde, but I couldn't stop giggling.

Lately, there had been no giggling. It was so unlike us to be cold and silent, but though I wanted to, I couldn't break the cycle. Even if my intentions were good, the tiniest wrong move from Tim made me blow up. I couldn't stop myself. I'd lie in bed in the morning and think, Why don't you roll over and hug me? But there was no chance of that because I was nonstop horrible. He'd yawn too near to my face, and I'd snap "Your breath stinks!" I'd feel this heart-pounding rage, and I guessed it was because of the baby, but it seemed to have run like dye into everything.

I heard a squeal of tires, and Tim sped off in his damaged car. I wished he'd ring, tell me where he was going. Even if he'd screamed at me, it would have been *something*. I did try to goad him out of his silence with nasty remarks. He didn't return the whole weekend, although on Sunday, Tim's mother called and said, "I think you should know, Elizabeth, that Timothy is with *us*." She added, "I didn't want you to think that he was lying dead in a hospital morgue, God forbid, puh-puh-puh."

Tim's mother had been socializing with elderly Jews, or Madonna. "Puh-puh-puh" was a superstitious habit, the Kabbalistic equivalent of spitting at the Devil. If ever Aunt Edith made a smug observation, —e.g., "Elizabeth, such a beautiful young lady!"—she'd add, "Puh-puh-puh," in case God overheard, decided she was too cocky on my behalf, and had my fine features flattened by a truck the following day.

"Puh-puh-puh" could also be employed as insurance against an unpleasant occurrence—Tim lying dead in a hospital morgue, say—in case, having mentioned it, you'd put the idea in God's head.

I didn't step out of the house until Monday. Getting up seemed pointless, like wearing lipstick to the dentist. Cassie called my mobile, but I switched it off. She even came round, jamming her finger on the buzzer, but I didn't answer. I lay in bed, letting all sound wash over me. The phone rang, and I let the answering machine pick up. When I played it back, Tabitha's well-to-do voice rang through the empty house.

"Lizbet. Timmy. Hello! It's Next Door. Darlings, sorry to impose, I wondered if you might be able to do your godparental duty and take Tomas—for an hour, half an hour, half a minute—because if you don't, I might just wring his neck. Aha-ha-ha! Only joking!"

I played the message again. She didn't sound like she was joking. Her voice cracked on "wring." Also, at five thirty that morning, I'd heard Tomas crying, through the wall. "Please," he'd sobbed. "I want to sleep in Mummy's bed. *Please!*"

Seconds later, I heard a baby screeching, a series of thumping footsteps, and a bloodcurdling yell of "Get *back* in your bed *NNNNNNNNOOOOOWWW!*"

Since the birth of Celestia, I'd thought, rolling over and pulling the covers over my head, Tabitha seemed to be losing the will to retain her Best Mother in World title. I'd also heard her commanding Jeremy. ("*Multitask!* I never just stand there speaking on the phone!")

I felt a twinge of pity for Tomas, and Jeremy. No one wants to be spoken to like that by someone they love. No wonder Jeremy was doing a lot of advanced driving around North London in the black Volvo V50—I *bet* he had V70 envy—with his *Top Gun* shades on, and *Cigarettes and Alcohol* blaring out the windows.

Tomas—according to Tim, who'd heard it from Jeremy—was not coping well with the interloper. When Tabitha returned from hospital, Tomas had looked at the bundle in his mother's arms and said, "Are you *her* mummy too?" At the time, I'd only heard the word "mummy," and wondered if anyone would ever call *me* that. I still wondered. I decided against taking Tomas for an hour. I could feel his need, but *mine*—to be left alone by other people's children—was greater.

CHAPTER 23

"Biscuit, your *face* is totally unreal!" said Kevin, as he sucked up a long strand of spaghetti, spattering tomato sauce all over his Mango top. "Purple ... blue ... bit of green ... some yellow. Very David Lynch. Given me a storming idea for a shoot. Birds, all bruised up, but, like, *stylized,* yeah?"

I snappishly ate the fried cheese in my haloumi salad, feverishly buttered a white roll, and scraped the lettuce into a pile at the side of my plate. *No one* likes lettuce. I mean, *do* they? Really? "What," I said, "Sort of like *Wife Battering à la Mode?*"

"Yeah!" he said. "Yeah! I mean, we can't have the word *wife* in the mag, but apart from that—yeah! *Modish.*"

I was being sarcastic, but I don't think he was. For lack of contenders, I'd become his confidante, and I wasn't thrilled about it. It was great for my career—providing that my ultimate goal was the porn industry—but Kevin was quite the most stupid person I'd ever met. I disliked myself for humoring him, for, I suppose, money. Tim was doing well, but that had nothing to do with me, *I* was still hovering around the poverty line. I no longer had trust in us two as a *unit*.

"That makes you my muse, dunnit?" Kevin grinned across the

table and patted my hand. "Go easy on the cheese, love," he added. "Got yourself a nice little figure there. Don't want to let yourself go. Got to be careful at your age."

How old did he think I was? Fifty-five? *He* had a figure like a skittle. "Mm," I said, and laughed, which was the conversational sum that Kevin required of me before alighting on his next subject.

"We're going to have some girl-on-girl action, but get this—all the shots: *black and white*. Yeah? Yeah? So, like, it's not pornography, it's *art*. It's all about playing the market!"

"Mm. Ha-ha!" I said, adding, "Excellent!" for good measure. I wondered what Tim was doing.

The theme tune from *Miami Vice* exploded from Kevin's mobile, placed in front of him on the white linen tablecloth. Come *on*, I thought, as surrounding diners glared. Kevin popped a large chunk of walnut bread in his mouth and chewed casually, tapping his fingers to the music.

"Are you going to answer it?" I said.

"It's Fletch," said Kevin. He waggled his fingers, and put the phone to his ear. "Thought I told you not to disturb me during lunch. What? *Private Eye? What?* Ugandan *what?* Oh. Right. Riiiiight! Me and Biscuit, eh? Cool! Nah, like I give a toss! Nah, course it ain't, I like 'em blond, but, you know, walk the talk—lad's mag—ed's a bit of a boy. Sorry, *what?* Who's Elizabeth? Biscuit? Why should *she* care? She's up for a laugh! She's a frickin' sex columnist, goes with the territory!"

He snorted, then beeped off.

"What was that about?" I said. I felt shaky.

Kevin laughed like a seal. He reached for my hand and licked the top of my finger.

"Jesus!" I shrieked. "What's the matter with you!" I flapped about and sterilized my hand in his glass of vodka and lemon.

"Oy! That was my drink!"

"*Oy*. That was my *finger*."

"You asked, I was telling you. Showing you. This week's *Private Eye* says we're shagging."

"Oh my God. That's horrible." I burst into tears. Kevin stared at me. "What's *your* problem?" he said. "You should be pleased, being associated with a bit of class."

"A bit of *class*? What, *you*?" Suddenly, the tears dried and I was furious. "I've got a family and a boyfriend and a professional reputation to protect!" (A good third of that statement was correct.) "About what should I be pleased, exactly? Having vicious lies printed about me having sex with my—no offense, Kevin—moronic moron of a boss, I mean, look at you! Admit it—you're a bit of a worry! Wrong side of forty, those ridiculous bug-eye sunglasses, and *what* is that pendant, and your hideous, hideous tattoo, every time you bend over in those terrible cut-off denims, I have *nightmares* about that evil eye above your bum crack, not to mention the bum crack itself, get a *belt* why can't you, and everyone knows you wax your legs and use Boots fake tan and we *all* laugh about it, and your ideas for the mag—ideas! Hah!—they're shit! They're shit, okay? Whoever heard of making fashion *useful*? No one, not even a criminal, wants to look at a Tesco suit! They want Paul Smith and, and . . . other posh names, even if they can't afford them. That's what aspirational is, not a fanny on every page! You are a rubbish editor, because you have no original thought, no intelligence, and your writing is *painful* in its unfunniness, and I promise you that Fletch would have made a brilliant editor and the only reason *you* were hired is because you're a company lapdog and he isn't, because you're certainly not what I'd call a journalist, you're like a monkey with a typewriter, and we all are ashamed to work for you, and if we see the magazine on the newsstands, we *hide it*, and I hate the name Biscuit, it's not my name, and the whole staff is looking for other jobs—"

"I don't know about the whole staff, love," said Kevin. "But *you're* looking for another job. You are *so* fired."

"I resign anyway," I said. "And speak English. You can't be *so* fired. You're either fired, or you're not."

"Well, *you* are. Like a fucking cannonball."

Fletch brought my meager belongings to the door of the building, as I refused to step inside.

"You know it's not true, don't you, Fletch?" I said.

Fletch paused. "Babe, your sex life is up to you."

My eyebrows shot up. "You have got to be joking."

"Lizbet, I'm not judging you."

"Yes you are! When I didn't do it! I'm going to sue them. How could you even *think* I'd consider it? He's grotesque! Repellent. Vile. Disgusting. And he's my boss."

"Yeah. He is."

"Is that what you think of me?"

Fletch shrugged. "You have been pretty tight with him. What am I meant to think?"

"I forgot. You're a man. You're not meant to think. I've just been sacked because he was offended that I was offended at the allegation."

Fletch grinned suddenly. "I believe you. Though I did worry. Still, who cares what I think? What about what Tim thinks?"

My heart squirmed in fear. Tim! Tim wouldn't believe it. He'd *laugh* if he saw it, because it was so ridiculous. "He doesn't read *Private Eye*," I said. "I'd better get home."

Fletch ruffled my hair. "Give Tim a kiss from me. Or a firm handshake and a gruff, manly slap on the back."

I applied the same logic to the story in *Private Eye* as I did to my sex column—if I didn't *see* it, it didn't exist. Tim wouldn't see it either. Would someone tell him? *Who*, though? What sort of person does that? "Morning, Tim! Nice weather for ducks! Saw that piece in the paper about your girlfriend shagging her boss! Tut tut! I presume you're aware of the story? No? Shall I fax it over? Not at all! Glad to help ruin your life! Anytime!"

I had the key in the lock before I realized that Tim's car was in the drive. A pebble of fear lodged in my chest.

"Hello?" I shouted, as I let myself in. "Hello!"

There was no reply. But Tim's jacket was draped over the banister, and his car keys were flung on the hall table, next to his Prada wallet—a present from me when we thought we could afford such things. It was fat as a phone directory with receipts and credit cards and shopping lists, and it gave me a pang, just seeing it.

I ran upstairs. Tim was in the bedroom, digging through the wardrobe. There was a green suitcase on our bed, half-full of clothes.

"Hi! You're back! How were your parents? What are you doing?" I said, with fake cheer. I suspected that the last time we'd spoken, I'd been less cordial, but I was hoping that if I persisted friendly, Tim would overlook this.

"I'm packing," he replied. "What does it look like?"

"Packing," I said. "It looks just like packing."

I stared at him. He looked beautiful. Not to anyone else except maybe, his mother, but to me. The sunlight caught his hair and it glinted gold. He was wearing faded jeans and a dark blue Ralph Lauren Polo shirt. "Ralph," my mother had said. "Ralph does such nice things for babies." I swallowed. No more baby. And now . . . no more Tim?

"I suppose you saw *Private Eye* today?"

"Mum showed me."

Tim's mother reading *Private Eye*? What was wrong with *Weekly Chatter* and *Witches Today*? "Does she actually love you?" I said, before I could stop the words.

"Do *you*?" he said.

"I promise you. I am not having an affair with Kevin. Or anyone. I've never cheated on you."

"Yes, you have, Elizabeth."

He never called me Elizabeth. Only once, when I broke his MP3 player.

"Tim." There were tears in my eyes. I couldn't bear the waves of hostility coming off him. For a while now I'd thought I hated him, but I'd been fooling myself. He still had that power to make me crumple with one disdainful glance. "I probably have annoyed a lot of people by being friendly to Kevin. I don't feel good about it. Not very honorable. I know that Fletch was hurt. It wasn't loyal of me. But harmless friendliness—not even flirting—is all it's been, I—"

"Elizabeth."

"He's just sacked me, okay? He thinks being libeled is hilarious, so long as he comes out of it looking like a stud. So I told him what I thought, and got fired on the spot. See? Doesn't that prove to you that I—"

"Elizabeth!" shouted Tim. "I *know* you didn't cheat on me with that prick Kevin, so stop driveling on about it!"

"Oh!" I said, collapsing on the bed with a bounce. "Thank God!" My face was all smiles. "For a bad moment there, I—"

Tim was not smiling. "But you did cheat on me."

"Pardon?"

"YOU CHEATED ON ME!" he screamed at the top of his voice.

"NO, I DIDN'T!" I screamed back, incensed.

"YES, YOU DID!"

Tabitha and Jeremy would be ears aflap, glued to the wall.

Tim wrestled a small packet out of his jeans pocket and hurled it onto the bed. "WHAT'S *THAT* THEN, YOU LYING BITCH?"

My contraceptive pills.

I trembled from head to toe as I snatched them up.

"Where ... where did you find these?" I said, as if it was relevant. As if I could somehow claw back some moral standing if it emerged he'd been ferreting in my bedside drawer.

"What does it *matter* where I found them?" he said. "In your bedside drawer!"

"You went in my bedside drawer?"

He shot me a look of disgust. "Yes! You've got a bunch of my old design magazines stuffed in there. And a phone mike. And my cuff links. And in *my* bedside drawer, I've got your jewelry box. And a lace garter. And some mint green antique calfskin gloves. Don't try and make the issue our bedside drawers!"

In retrospect, I shouldn't have hidden my contraception in my bedside drawer.

"I thought we were trying for a *baby*," he hissed. "And all the time you were tricking me. I—"

I was too tired to have this conversation.

"Boohoo," I said. "Cut to the chase." I flicked my hand in the direction of the green suitcase. "You're leaving me."

Tim smiled stiffly. "No," he said. He folded his arms.

My gaze flickered to the contents of the suitcase. Hang on. *Pink* panties with lace edging? A black padded bra? Unless the relationship was faltering for shadier reasons than Tim was willing to let on, these were not his clothes.

Tim marched to my wardrobe and grabbed a jumbled mess of sweaters and T-shirts and jeans and dumped them into the suitcase. He pressed down the top and zipped it shut. "*I'm* not going anywhere," he said. Then he hauled the case off the bed and shoved it toward me with a haughty expression. "*You're* leaving me."

CHAPTER 24

_____ *Cassie*

I was having a baby.

George was the father, although I thought of him more as the donor. I had a sick feeling in my gut, but I had a very sick feeling in my gut every time I thought about Lizbet. George had trumpeted the proof of his virility—I'd told him not to—and she'd gone bananas. I'm not sure he didn't do it on purpose.

I'd attempted to contact her over the weekend, but she wasn't having any of it. I wasn't a masochist. After fifteen calls, I quit trying and feasted on the fact that soon enough, I'd be the proud owner of a pink, squally, wriggling pig. A wriggling roo. I meant, a baby. I just went all silly and goo-faced at the idea and my language changed to what a tabloid psychologist had called *"Mummy-ese."*

Sarah Paula was to be a grandmother. Ah, she would have been proud. I saw her, leaning over a fairy-tale cot—pale wood and gauze canopy—all sweet murmurings and smiles, her long, straight blond hair (because to me she was forever eighteen) gently brushing the baby's chest. Or maybe that baby was *me*. I killed the thought. It was what Aunt Edith would call "a flight of fancy." *Vivica* was to be a grandmother, a fully functioning grandmother with all the trimmings, a Ralph-buying, stroller-pushing, photo-demonstrative grandmother.

I was a bit previous. Lizbet had assumed along the same lines. George had gone off on one, ordaining that we Go Private. He had a million horror tales about the Health Service—curious, as not one of his friends had children. He'd booked me an appointment with The Top Man. "Isn't that a clothes shop?" I'd said, but I didn't object. I intended to hang on to this baby. George had prepared a meticulous case, should any liberal colleagues purse their lips: He wanted to ensure his baby received constant and efficient surveillance, the maximum face time with abundant and well-rested medical staff to promote the odds of safe passage, "and you can all fuck off!"

I should try that argument in court.

I sighed. Court. Give it a few months and I was going to have to suck in my stomach big-time. I felt a thrill of joy. Can you believe that? *Joy* at the idea of having to suck in my stomach? If that's not messed up, tell me what is. That's how much I wanted the baby. I'd gone right off coffee, God help me; I was twitching toward the concept of peppermint tea. It was a monstrous affront to all that I stood for. I felt like a helpless bystander, watching my brisk, brusque personality being washed away in a landslide. If I didn't keep a tight rein, I'd be regaling the judge with details of weak bladders and varicose veins. It struck me that all these little trials of pregnancy, Lizbet would have been grateful for.

I pressed 141, so she wouldn't know it was me, and rang her mobile.

"Don't hang up," I said, when she answered.

Silence.

"Where are you?" I added, taking this as a good sign. "Work or home?"

"Neither," she replied. "I don't have a work, and I don't have a home. I'm standing in the road with a suitcase."

Her voice was rock-hard with the effort of not crying.

"What?" I said. "*Your* road? I'll be there in a sec."

I jumped off the sofa, and found that I had zero strength and couldn't catch my breath. My head felt as if it was about to float off my neck, and it was an alarming sensation. My legs became rubber, and I fell back onto the sofa. "George!" I gasped, but he was in the power shower and incommunicado. I managed to grab a bottle of Badoit—agh!—that he had brought back from the gym and, after two minutes, felt better, although my hands still shook.

This time I got up slowly. Oh, how unpleasant. A preview of old age.

Lizbet sat in the passenger seat of the Merc, and if her high, pointy shoes scraped the beige leather as she fidgeted about, I wasn't going to mention it. I tried to prod her for information, but she turned to me and said, "I can't talk to you right now."

I shut up. Sophie Hazel Hamilton had a fat cousin who couldn't have children, and three months after Sophie gave birth to Justin, she saw the cousin at a wedding. The cousin greeted Sophie with the words "You've just had a baby and you're thin, you bitch." As far as I was concerned, my sister's conduct was impeccable.

"I don't want to stay here," said Lizbet, as she watched me haul her suitcase into the house.

"Drop the case!" roared George, thundering down the stairs, his hair wrapped in a towel. "You mustn't *lift*! She's pregnant, you know," he added, glaring at Lizbet.

I looked at my sister properly for the first time that evening. Her face was white. It was also yellow, green, and purple.

"Lizbet! Your face . . . ?"

"I had a small accident in the car on Friday," she replied.

That would be *my* fault then. I paused, then asked a question designed to show that I thought deeply about her. And botched it. "Will Tim look after Sphincter?"

"Sphinx!"

I sighed. That was Lizbet. She didn't see the big picture, even if it was the *Mona Lisa*; she saw the tiny, irrelevent flaw in the big picture, maybe *the frame wasn't nice*. I was a queasy mix of tottery and delirious. I sank onto the sofa again. "Drinks, George," I whispered, and he stamped off.

George returned with what appeared to be two identical glasses of water.

"Teensiest splash of vodka in yours," he said to Lizbet.

"I'm not an alcoholic, you know," she snapped. But she gulped it, and her body untensed with a *zing!*

"Difficult day," I said, eventually.

"Ya think?" she replied. Then she muttered, "Wanker."

"Who's a wanker?" said George, braced for battle.

"Who isn't," said my sister.

"Tim sent you packing, did he?" said George.

"He packed for me."

"You were a right cow," said George. "What did you expect?"

"I was expecting a baby, George," said Lizbet.

"So was Tim," said my husband, who didn't know when to can it.

Lizbet stared at him with bloodshot eyes. "You have no idea about *anything*, so why don't you shut your mouth. How dare you preach to me about—"

"I think," I said—the first words I'd spoken—"that George is trying to tell you, in his boorish way, that whatever's happened, it's plain to everyone that Tim has a deep love for you, that is very moving and incredibly special."

"What?" said Lizbet. "Did you swallow an American pill?"

"Lizbet," I said. "The man *adores* you. It's been extremely traumatic for you both is all I'm saying, and you're bound to take it out on each other. But don't be too hard on him, and don't let this end out of pride. It's too precious for that."

"He adores me?" she said, and was quiet.

"Yes!" I said, encouraged.

Lizbet sighed. "Whether this relationship ends is not up to me." She stood up, wobble-legged. "I'm going to bed."

In theory I was working from home the next day, but I couldn't concentrate. Lizbet was snoring in the guest bedroom, and I felt the intolerable frustration of someone who requires other people's domestic tiffs to be resolved. She wasn't budging. Which meant it was up to me to kick-start the reunion. Despite our reputation, divorce lawyers aren't just about scooping up the money in plows while their clients bawl into handkerchiefs. In family law, you have a duty to mediate. You try to negotiate a deal for your client before you issue court proceedings. Even a week before the final hearing, you're pressing for the two sides to see sense, before they throw away *all* their cash on a trial.

We're unofficial therapists.

("I don't want to see that bitch girlfriend of his. . . ."

"Well, why don't you do the handover at McDonald's in Neasden? We'll have a written agreement, and if he doesn't stick to it, we'll turn it into a court order!"

That sort of thing.)

If anyone could sort out the mess between Lizbet and Tim, it was *moi*.

I dragged a comb through my hair, slid into the Merc, and sped round.

Tim opened the door in his boxer shorts and a white T-shirt. He didn't look annoyed to see me, but he didn't look pleased either.

"Did *she* send you?" he said.

I hesitated, shook my head.

He shrugged. "Why are you here?"

I sighed. "Because—"

Tim held up a hand. "Doesn't matter. You can take away the rest of her stuff. Her makeup's still in the bathroom cabinet, even the Benefit Moon Shine I bought her. I think it's iridescent foundation; she paints it on. And her favorite boots, not that she can walk in them. And she'll need her pillow. It's very flat. She can't sleep on a fat pillow. She needs her neck to be in alignment with her spine." He paused. "Not that I give a toss."

"No," I said, puffing as I followed him upstairs. "No, I can see that you don't care at all." Then I shouted, *"Ti-im!"*

"Yes?" he said.

I breathed deeply for a second or two, trying to catch my breath. I felt weird. "Tim," I said, trying to bulldoze through the sick, floaty sensation in my head, "I came over because even though George and I are . . ."—I gestured at my stomach—"our relationship is at death's door. The truth is, while we are both decent people— well, *I* am—we don't like each other. We are not friends. I don't find him attractive. When he kisses me, the air in his nose smells funny. Everything he does irritates me. His jaw makes a cracking sound when he chews. He eats apples whole, leaving only the stalk. He never turns a tap quite off. He pronounces apricot '*ap*-ricot.' He pronounces ate '*at.*' He creeps into a room and stands right beh—"

Tim had paused from digging through Lizbet's shoe cupboard and was looking at me curiously. There was a tiny bit of pink willy poking out of the front of his boxers, but I didn't want to embarrass him by mentioning it. "Anyway," I said. "My point is, you and Lizbet are not like us. *You* have a viable relationship. You have a bloody fabulous relationship. You two are so cool together. There's passion, and respect; there's love, there's laughter, and admiration. It's very enviable. But I think it's got buried in the agony you two feel about losing your baby. It's become a grief competition. Have you talked about it? Because Lizbet comes from a long line of people who excel in not talking. We pride ourselves on it! There is no communication in our family. Bugger all! We don't communicate! No one says what they think! But I'm her sister, and I know when she's angry, and she is the angriest I've ever seen her. She says she's fine, but she's been rejecting *food*. She's been rejecting everything she loves the most! Don't some people do that when they've been hurt? Shoo away all love so there's no chance of feeling that pain again? But she won't be happy without you, and I don't think you'll be happy without her. So, maybe"—I gasped, I couldn't breathe, my heart was pounding, I felt as sick as a dog—"maybe"—my legs felt hot and weak—"I feel wrong, I—"

The world tipped sideways, and I fell onto the thin carpet on Tim and Lizbet's bedroom floor.

"Cassie!" Tim cried, and bounded over. "What is it? Oh *God*, it's the baby! I'll ring an ambulance!"

I shook my head. It took grim effort to say even one word.

"Don't. Not … serious. Just … tired. Dizzy. Need to lie flat. Water."

"I'll put you on the bed. Hang on."

Tim bent and gently scooped me into his arms.

Lizbet burst into the bedroom, stared at us gray-faced, let out a dramatic wail, and ran, slamming the front door behind her.

CHAPTER 25

The Top Man—Irish and softly spoken with a thousand pregnant women all in love with him—told me that I had low blood pressure and shouldn't run around so much.

"In Germany, they'd treat you for it, but in this country we don't see it as a problem."

He might not see it as a problem. I had to disagree. I'd called Lizbet on her mobile ten times, and so had Tim, but she always cut off. There was no sign of her anywhere, and I was worried. After a day of searching, her man and I conferred on the phone. He was in a harsher mood than I was.

"Stop looking," said Tim. "This is just another example of how she doesn't trust me."

"Yes," I said, from my prone position on the sofa. "But think how it looked. Anyone would have thought what she did."

"But this is *me*!" he cried. "She *knows* what I'm like! I'm a frickin' Labrador! And yet she'll believe I'm having it off with her own sister! It's so insulting! I'm so insulted! It's such an insult!"

I was a bit piqued that he was *so* insulted, but I didn't say anything. "You do realize," I said, "that she had come over to apologize."

"How do you know?"

"Tim," I said. I was continually amazed at men's capacity for selective vision. They saw *nothing*! A good half of them needed to be issued with white sticks. "Didn't you see what she was holding?"

"No."

"A box for an iPod dock connector."

There was silence.

"Tim?"

"I didn't even tell her I'd lost it," he said, in a small voice.

The phone rang again, straightaway, so I picked it up and said, in a crisp voice, "Hello?" (Another thing that annoyed me about George was that he liked to answer the phone as if the house was a cab firm: "Yellow!")

"Darling, you called. Is everything okay? Can I get Daddy to pick something up for you?"

"No, thanks. I'm fine. Have you spoken to Lizbet?"

"Not since Friday when she rushed off. I suppose she took offense at my comment about the baby clothes. I admit it was a silly thing to say, but I was only being practical. You have to move on. There comes a point when talking about an upset only makes it worse. I must say, though, she's looking well."

Our mother was the opposite of a normal Jewish mother in that *she* thought you looked well if you were stick-thin. And while there probably *was* a point where talking about an "upset" made things worse, the trouble was that for Vivica, this point came one minute after the "upset."

"Daddy says to remind you about Aunt Edith's," she added. "I'd forgotten. Why Cousin Denise sent out children's party invitations I'll never know. Edith's seventy-five! And it's in Bushey. What a schlep. And it's evening dress. You know it'll be wall-to-wall sequins. You didn't go to Ian's twenty-fifth. Denise wore a sequined longcoat. It was striped. Black, red, white. *All* sequins. She looked like a snake shedding its skin."

Vivica and I had scant regard for the rest of the family—excluding Aunt Edith. We thought they were narrow suburban bores. In return, they thought *we* were strange and eccentric, and felt sorry for us. I was happy to celebrate Aunt Edith's three-quarter century—less so with Denise, Ian, and a roomful of sequins.

"When is it again?"

"Six weeks from this Sunday. He says to put it in your diary. They asked Daddy to do the champagne. Of course. Not that *he* minds."

"What are you getting her?"

Vivica sighed. I could hear a cigarette being lit. "There'll be something in the John Lewis china department. I'm not going to drive myself crazy." I paused. I *had* forgotten Aunt Edith's seventy-fifth, and when I consulted my diary, I had actually arranged to go to the Dorchester Spa that day, with Peter-the-Hairdresser. I had a busy life, and my extended family did not occupy the head space that they'd presume to be entitled to. With respect, Ian and Denise could go hang, but I felt bad about Aunt Edith. She'd been such a strong, loving presence in my childhood, and I'd grown up and neglected her. I'd postpone the Dorch.

"Why don't I check out the Tiffany Web site and find her a nice vase?" I said.

"A *Tiffany* vase?" Vivica's tone indicated that this would be a waste of the brand name. "Darling," she added. "When you get to her age, John Lewis and Tiffany become interchangeable. In fact, John Lewis has more cachet."

I decided not to argue. "I'll have a look and get something from all of us." I had a thought. "Does Lizbet know about the party?"

"I left a message on her phone just now. Although she usually remembers these things."

Not only that, Lizbet usually corralled myself and Mummy into line, organizing the communal gift, the transport, ensuring we stuck to the dress code (give or take ten thousand sequins) and turned up. I wondered if *she* would turn up this time. Not even Lizbet could sulk for six weeks straight!

Actually, she could. The record sulk in our family was twenty-five years (Great Uncle Keith, shunning Cousin Malcolm Once Removed, because he disapproved of Malcolm's marriage to Korean Nelly. Mummy always claimed Keith was jealous, being stuck, as he was, with Scottish Miriam). I put my hand on my stomach, to soothe myself, but I still felt low. Things could have been perfect, but they never were.

Hubert Fitzgerald was as purple in the face as an eggplant. It was the morning of the middle negotiation hearing, and I was trying to persuade him that if we got as far as a final hearing we'd lose, but he didn't want to hear it. He'd reached a stage in life where people mostly agreed with him. He drummed his manicured nails on the table, and his eyes skimmed me with disdain. The room was airless; I felt lousy. I sipped water, hoping to ward off the dizziness. I was three months' pregnant—not a fact I wished to share with Hubert, although if I keeled over he'd demand some explanation—and I hadn't spoken to my sister for five weeks. It was affecting me more than I cared to admit.

"Look," I said, swallowing my nausea. "You'd be so much better off—in every sense—doing a deal. If you don't settle, you're making a bad bet. Go for a final hearing, and *she* is going to get a big cut. You don't know what the judge will award her, but my feeling is it will be significant. She has your children; she will need a house and an income. I don't think the judge will accept that she should move out of your Georgian mansion in the village into a small flat in Greater London, and work in a shop sixteen hours a week so that she can qualify for tax credits. Maybe you could enlarge on what you're offering Alissa?"

Hubert thought he was smart, but he hadn't been clever. He'd been too busy thinking with his dick. The *proper* way to do divorce is to plan ahead. You have to stick it out for a bit, while you squirrel away your funds. If you want to hide your money, you write checks for random amounts over a long period of time. Say, £212, or £447.50. The sum of, say, £5,000 on a bank statement is going to be queried. (Let alone Hubert's uncharacteristically charitable donation to his father of a fifth of a million quid.)

Unfortunately, only divorce lawyers, and people who've been divorced already, realize this.

While Hubert's most recent NatWest bank statements revealed a monkish, meager existence, reading through his less recent Barclaycard statements was similar to a jaunt through *Cosmopolitan*: sex shops, Internet sites, hotel rooms, restaurants, air tickets, weekends in Paris. Everything Hubert had claimed about everything? Alissa—who had emptied his entire filing cabinet into a black garbage bag with yellow ties—possessed the document to contradict it.

"I tell you this, love," said Hubert, who couldn't believe that I wasn't a secretary. "I'll enlarge my dick before I enlarge what I'm offering that cow! She's done *nothing*. She cooked a few meals."

Thinking ahead to my own divorce (a girl can dream), I thought that at least George wouldn't be able to say this of *me*. I had cooked no meals.

"So you can tell her and her fuckwit brief I'll see her in court, and she can stick that up her arse and smoke it!" he added. I could tell he liked that phrase, he'd said it ten times in the last hour. "I'm going for a fag!"

I stood up slowly and said, "I will indeed convey that message to Mr. Alcock. If deemed appropriate."

Barnaby and I were due to meet in three minutes, in a private room. Most times, if I knew my opponent—and I usually did—we'd spend the best part of an hour chatting about our weekends, and fifteen minutes discussing the case. Maybe ten. Nine at a pinch.

"You've put on weight!" said Barnaby, jumping up as I walked in. Only Barnaby could say that like it was a compliment. He pulled out a chair and kissed me on the cheek, as if the awkwardness of our last encounter was all forgotten. It wasn't. (In one of his fonder moments—a long time ago—George had issued me with one of those cutesy pet names that loving couples give each other. It was "The Sicilian Elephant." I bore grudges and I never forgot.)

I sat down and dumped my briefcase on the table. Barnaby beamed and leaned closer. He had nicked himself shaving and I wanted to kiss it better. "Are we soon to expect a little bundle of joy?"

I stared at him. No need to be so *jovial* about it. I thought his heart was broken! "I don't know where you get it from," I said. "Perhaps we could stop speculating on my personal life and attend to business. I feel that my client has, in the circumstances, been generous. Bearing in mind that Mrs. Fitzgerald has never worked—"

Barnaby laughed. "Cass. Cut the crap. She's bringing up his three kids by herself. He was never there. They couldn't afford day care. Or rather, he chose not to allow a budget for it. In fact, she had to account for every penny she spent with receipts. Hubert was a total stinge, and I really wouldn't say that Alissa has never worked." He nodded toward my stomach. "Not so long and you'll realize *exactly* how hard she's worked."

I opened my mouth to object and he rolled his eyes.

"So come on, Cass, give me something to work with. It's in *your* client's interest to settle. Alissa would love a hearing, she's keen as mustard. All he's done is lie to her, to the point where she's convinced herself she's going mad. She's desperate for him to be cross-examined; it's the only way she's going to find out the truth. And Hubert is not going to want to be trapped in the witness box when I get started—"

"Shush a minute," I said.

"*Shush?*" said Barnaby. "You can't tell me to 'shush'!"

I wanted to think. I thought of Alissa bringing up her babies, and I felt a twinge. She was middle-aged but had the air of a gauche teenager. She had dark, shiny hair, a shy smile, and didn't know what to do with her hands. I didn't think she'd tipped the contents of Hubert's filing cabinet into a black garbage bag without prompting. Poor woman. In my experience, women end a marriage because they are fed up. And men end it because they've found someone else. It's rare for me to represent a husband in divorce proceedings *without* a new partner. Which was no consolation to Alissa. I was glad she had Barnaby as her counsel—Jesus, what was wrong with me! Boo hiss, Alissa!

But the fact was, my client was a lying, cheating bully, and *morally*, if not legally (yet), he owed his faithful wife, the mother of his children, a decent living standard. In the crassest terms, Alissa and Hubert had made an equal contribution to the family unit— Hubert by earning the cash, Alissa by raising the children. His money wasn't his, it was theirs. I was certain that if it went to a final hearing, the judge would grant her at least half of his wealth, probably more. (I wondered what of mine George would think he was entitled to.) Whatever I thought, it was my duty, as Hubert's counsel, to prevent this.

I gazed at Barnaby, who—I couldn't be sure—looked a little ruffled. "So, Cass," he said. "Hubert's claiming he can only afford to pay Alissa the square root of bugger all, when last year, he burned plastic in smart restaurants to the tune of twenty-four grand. His accounts appear to be awash with money that hasn't got an obvious source or destination. I await his further disclosure with interest—"

"Barnaby," I said. "Hubert isn't going to budge."

Barnaby shrugged. "Glorious. We'll run it to final hearing. And he can pay all my costs! I'll be leaving the bike at home tomorrow, coming in by private jet!"

He was so smug. Barnaby had an arsehole quality that came from going home from work every day for ten years knowing he was right because the judge agreed with him, or knowing he was right and the judge was stupid and wrong.

"Not necessarily," I said. "Foraging in garbage cans? Alissa's not exactly coming to court with clean hands."

Barnaby gave a snort. His friendliness had all gone. "There was no foraging in cans; the documents had, er, spilled out. You wouldn't expect me to forgo the pleasure of carrying out the usual forensic exercise in relation to Hubert Fitzgerald's accounts. Given the circumstances, *you* and I know that the judge will treat Alissa like royalty. She's not put a foot wrong, whereas he thinks he can trick me with a *smoke screen* of worthless financial documents. He puts massive personal expenditure on his business card and thinks he'll get away with it—kindergarten stuff! I'm going to *demolish* him.

He's in for the shock of his life. I hope he'll enjoy shopping at Costco."

"You're very sure of yourself," I said, with my snootiest air. "But Alissa shouldn't count Hubert's millions just yet. That woman is too good to be true. Tell her to watch out. Because I am going to find *something*."

CHAPTER 26

I couldn't focus. I kept stopping mid-sentence with a blank head, and asking George what I'd been saying. As he never listened, just watched my mouth open and shut, he couldn't tell me. Perhaps pregnancy made me vague—not, I hoped, for any biological reason—I think it was mental. I couldn't stop wondering about Sarah Paula. How she'd felt at nearly four months. Still in denial. Not eating enough fruit.

And then I got a letter.

Dear Cassie,

I do hope you don't mind me writing. I do understand if you choose not to respond, although I would be so sorry if that were the case. I wanted to tell you that I thought you were so brave to try to trace your birth mother—it must have taken a lot of courage. I can only try to imagine your devastation at hearing the news of her death. We are all still in agony over it. It was so sudden, and she was so young, only forty-six. I can see that it must be a double loss for you, and am so very sorry.

I wanted you to know that while Sarah was very young when

she had you, and at the time, giving you up seemed to be her only option, she never forgot you. You were always in her heart.

Sarah wanted you to go to a nice, normal family, and to have a good education—I do so hope that her wishes came true. She used to say to me, "If people adopt, it's because they want a baby so, so much, isn't it, Luce?"—but please believe me when I say that giving you up was the most difficult decision she ever made. She did think of trying to find you many times—if ever we were out together, her eyes would always be searching, and she'd say, "Look, Luce! Could that be her? Could that be her?"—but she felt it would be unfair to intrude. She didn't know if you even knew you were adopted.

I am so sad that she will never know that you have made contact. I don't think I am being overdramatic in saying that is a tragedy for both of you.

I hope you don't mind that I am enclosing a photograph of Sarah. This is my little sister, around the time she had you. She never did have any other children.

I can imagine that you are in a state of shock right now, and I certainly don't wish to add to that. I just wanted you to know that you would receive such a warm welcome, if you were to decide that you did wish to meet the rest of the family. I would so love to meet my only niece (if I may be so bold!). I realize that nothing can make up for the loss of your mother—I suspect it must feel as if she abandoned you twice—but please know that you were very precious to her. I would love to tell you more about her, if you were not averse to it.

With best wishes,

Lucille Reeves (Sarah's big sister!)

I stared at the photograph of the woman who'd given birth to me, and found myself hyperventilating. I thought, You look like me. I crawled upstairs, stair by stair, and got into bed. I vaguely re-called a line from a fairy tale—at least, it was some story from childhood.

"But her heart was hard."

It had to be. What Lucille didn't understand, although she took care to portray herself as sensitive and loving, was that I couldn't let myself care now—*now*, when it was too late. Because I was only just able to cope, by pretending that none of it ever existed. If I re-sponded to Lucille, heard the kindness in her voice, saw the won-der in her eyes, if I so much as rested my head on her shoulder, I would be drawn into a web of unbearable regret, which would spin itself tighter and more chokingly around me until I was ready to die with the sadness of chance and missed opportunity.

I placed Lucille's letter, and the photograph of Sarah Paula, in my white filing cabinet, in a folder marked "BABY." That was my one nod toward sentimentality. Then I went downstairs and ate a bowl of basmati rice to stop myself throwing up.

I was brought back to the fabulousness of my actual life by George whining, "Do we *have* to go to this thing tomorrow?"

"It's Aunt Edith's seventy-fifth birthday party, George," I said. "She was like a mother to me."

"So *she's* responsible. Say you've got morning sickness. No one expects *you* to turn up. You never do. You've got a lifetime of tak-ing the piss to fall back on."

"Shut up. We're going. My sister's going to be there."

I hadn't seen Lizbet since I'd watched her run out of her own house, and I'd stopped calling her. I didn't want to force it, and to be honest, I didn't need the fuss of her. Some people create fuss around them. They can't *just* look at a millpond. They have to chuck in a rock. Lizbet had overreacted to the situation before she got the measure of it—as if she'd been looking for an excuse to blow up and had snatched at the first chance. I was pregnant, dog-tired, and my emotional life was as tangled as a thornbush. I could do without my sister screaming in my face.

I knew she'd spoken to Vivica. She was staying with Fletch, a guy she'd worked with on *Ladz Mag*. I think they were just friends. She'd told our mother that she'd quit her job and "needed a break." She hadn't said anything about me and Tim, so I presumed she'd realized that she'd been a fool. She was probably too embarrassed to see either of us, having made a twit of herself. Still, six weeks had to be long enough to get her over her mortification. We'd probably make eye contact at Aunt Edith's and burst out laughing. Or—more likely, knowing her—we'd act as if the episode never happened. It was all a dream!

The do was at Cousin Denise's house. The décor made you wonder if there was actually cognitive process behind each choice. Every surface—floor, wall, sofa, table—was wildly patterned. The eye couldn't rest. Also? Her idea of catering was to bulk-buy big and cheap, the sort of foods that were best bought small and expensive: tuna and pasta salad, fish balls. Go cheap on a fish ball at your peril. But there was Aunt Edith. I flinched at the sight of her swollen ankles, but it was good to see her clutching the mobile phone she never let go of. I guessed that she was expecting an important call—Uncle Pete, from heaven.

George slunk in behind me. We were barely speaking—for a change—despite the glue of our impending arrival. I'd mentioned the letter from my Aunt Lucille, and George had nodded dismissively, as if I were reminding him to change the lightbulb in the cellar.

"What's your problem, George?" I'd said. I actually wanted to know, as everything I said to him was now a test, and I liked to measure his reaction on a scale of "disappointing." It *was* disappointing. I'd really loved him, once.

He shrugged. "I don't know why this mother thing is such a big deal," he said. "It's not as if you knew her."

"Mm," I said, in a level voice. "My birth mother's dead. You can't see why I'm upset."

George paused, as if he really might have been about to say something intelligent. "I mean—if you weren't a success, then I could understand it!"

And there the conversation ceased, because if that was what he truly believed, then there was nothing more to say.

Aunt Edith smiled and said, "Ahhh! Hello!" when she saw me. Assorted relatives broke off from eating to stare. I knew of one adopted person whose "cousin" would preface every piece of news with "I know you're not family, but . . ." *That* wasn't the problem here. They treated Lizbet with exactly the same dumb curiosity. The last time I'd visited London Zoo, the spider monkey had decided that I was odd enough to merit closer inspection. He'd swung right up to the glass and gravely inspected my face, his little black hands painfully human. The encounter left me feeling troubled. This lot had the same effect.

"How are you?" I said, bending to kiss her.

"Ah, not so good," she said. "Full of aches and pains. It's the arthritis. I can barely walk. "

"I'm so sorry," I mumbled. I was not good with people aging. I would have preferred it if she'd lied.

"Never mind!" added Aunt Edith. "I've got wheels. Denise and Ian bought me the car last year. I said, 'That should see me out!' "

"Aunt Edith! Don't say that! You look lovely. Happy birthday!" I said. "This is from the family." I placed the Tiffany vase on the table next to her. She barely gave the parcel a glance, which shocked me.

"And how are *you* feeling, my dear?" said Aunt Edith. "What lovely news you have for us!"

Denise, Ian, and others crowded round. I tried to look as pregnant as possible. I'd been hoping that my state would grant me impunity from blank stares and loaded comments.

"You haven't put on any weight!" cried Denise, accusingly.

"*You* have, Denise," murmured George, behind me. And then, half to himself, "It's like Dorian Gray, fat-wise."

"Do you know what you're having?" demanded Denise.

"A baby, we hope," said George.

"Oh, shut up, George," said Denise, doing my job for me. Then, spying Vivica—who looked half Denise's age, despite being ten years older—"Oho, here comes the *granny*! Hello, *Grand*ma, got your bus pass?"

Vivica moved through the jibe like a ghost through a dagger. "Hello, Denise! Yes, I must say, it's a wonderful feeling, being made a grandmother. I expect you're wondering when Ian will make you a grandmother, Denise. What can I say? We're *all* wondering!"

Cousin Ian had once been seen shopping in Chelsea. Indeed, there had been several sightings. But plainly—impossible! Not in our family!

Denise reddened, just as Lizbet tiptoed into the room, and Cousin Ian tiptoed out. "My God, Elizabeth!" cried Denise. "You're skinny as hell! You should put on weight!"

At least thirty pairs of eyes swiveled on Lizbet. It was like *Robocop*: "You have twenty seconds to comply!"

"Where's Tim?" said Denise.

Lizbet pretended not to hear. I tried a sympathetic smile, but Lizbet wasn't looking at me. Her lips brushed Aunt Edith's dry cheek and she said, "Happy birthday!" She placed a soft parcel on Aunt Edith's lap and said, "Open it!" I bristled, without knowing why.

Aunt Edith took Lizbet's hand and said, over her spectacles, "You should have spent the money on food! You're wasting away."

She ripped open the paper—on which was a row of kittens in pink and blue collars, *honestly*—and pulled out an enormous, supersize red caftan. It would have clothed a house. Bloody hell, Elizabeth, I thought. She's not *that* fat. But to my surprise, Aunt Edith started to laugh, and so did Lizbet.

"What?" said Vivica, who couldn't stand not to be in on a joke. "What's so funny?"

Aunt Edith shook her head and giggled. "You've got a good memory, dear," she said. She turned her head to Vivica. "She was only five years old. Uncle Bruce, we hadn't seen him in a while, sent me a caftan for my birthday from Toronto. Your big girl and I could *both* fit inside it! Pete took a picture. Memories," she added. "When you get to my age, there's little more precious than memories."

She grabbed Lizbet's face with her puffy hands, her garnet and gold art deco rings like brass knuckles on both hands, and kissed her loudly on the forehead. I felt a twinge, and I knew why I was annoyed. What, so memories were more precious than a *baby*, were they? "All we have is now, Aunt Edith," I wanted to say. I kept quiet. Aunt Edith was a firm believer in fair play. But instinct had always told me that Lizbet was her favorite. It wasn't easy being our parents' favorite. But it wasn't easy *not* being Aunt Edith's favorite. I go to all that trouble and expense to buy a Tiffany vase and she doesn't even give it a glance. Meanwhile, Lizbet sends off for a cheap joke gift and is feted for it.

"You were asking where Tim was, Denise," I heard myself say. "Good question! Where *is* Tim, Lizbet?"

There was a silence, as an entire room of sequined nosey parkers held its breath for my sister's response.

"Cassie," she said, with a friendly smile. "I stopped caring after I caught you two in our bedroom together and realized that Tim was the father of your child. So you tell me!"

CHAPTER 27

Lizbet

Denise always was a bitch. When I turned five, she gave me a birthday present, and it was _The Passover Pop-up Book_. An event has to be hugely significant for you to remember it at that age, and this was, being the most miserable gift possible. And she knew it. Cousin Ian's room was full of _Mr. Men_ books. The family celebrating Passover in the drawings in my book gave me nightmares, because their eyes were completely green—also the father had a mustache—and the pop-up bits were not fun ("Open the secret doors and find the Hebrew and English names of the Ten Plagues. . . .").

It was nice to see her jaw hang when I revealed Cassie's secret. Although, it was better to see Cassie's jaw hang. My heart beat to a blur, and I couldn't believe I'd really said it—and in front of parents, friends, and the Gargoyles—sorry—_relatives_. Because, was I one hundred percent certain that it was _really_ true? Well. I'd said it now, so it had to be. And public shame was what she deserved. I _was_ sure it was true. Certain. If I hadn't caught them in _our_ bedroom—Tim with his dick halfway out of his underpants, _her_ all weak with postcoital abandon in his arms—I'd never have believed it of either one of them. Yeah. But I had. So I was certain. *One hundred percent.*

I had trouble holding on to good feelings these days, and the satisfaction of creating a fuss was brief. Actually, the satisfaction was brief to the point that it didn't exist. I hated the way the Gargoyles stared—with more pity than usual—at me, and Cassie, and George, and Vivica, and Geoffrey. I didn't care that Denise was barely hiding a fat smirk. But I did care that Aunt Edith shot me a sharp look. Not Cassie—*me*, the victim! It was gone in a blink, but I saw it and it made my insides heave. It was a look of disapproval. From the only person who ever thought I was special.

I ran out, and caught a cab back to Fletch, even though giving directions was purgatory—I didn't want the stress of interaction. Renting a room from Fletch wasn't the adventure in easy living that it was meant to be. Fletch resided in a surprisingly stylish three-story house in West London, and I was a lumbering elephant around his delicate furnishings. Within days, I'd pulled the chrome towel rail out of the wall, and flooded the walnut surface in his kitchen by yanking the swish tap the wrong way and being unable to turn it off for five seconds. I thought he'd wave away such incidents as part of my gauche charm, but he was put out.

Meanwhile, I didn't find *him* a bowl of rose petals either. I'd chosen him as a landlord rather than any of my girlfriends, because I'd wanted to be left alone, and Fletch acted like he didn't care about anything. But he did. He was curiously fussy. The books on his bookshelves were arranged in alphabetical order. And his taste in art was revolting. It was all modern and violent, with garish colors. He'd ordered all the paintings in a job lot over the Internet—you could commission artists in India to run you up a quick *Mona*

Lisa—but Fletch preferred *The Assassination of Pablo Escobar*, a fat man dying bloodily on a roof in a hail of bullets.

"I like it," Fletch told me, "because it's absurd. And because most people don't like it. *I* like things that are real. A lot of art is a bowl of flowers, but this is a moment of history."

It was bang in the middle of the living room wall, and I couldn't relax in front of the flat-screen television. (Even after five weeks, I was *still* always dumping a bag in front of its infrared signal then wondering why the picture was such bad quality).

I adored Fletch but he annoyed me, and his every quirk made me miss Tim. Fletch wasn't interested in food to the level *I* was. He was happy with Sainsbury's economy coleslaw; he didn't chew much, I noticed, he gulped his food, like a dog. (He grew up with five brothers.) But if I rebelled and bought M&S traditional coleslaw—the finest on the market and I'll brook no argument—he'd eat the lot, leaving me with the economy muck, *then* profess he "didn't realize, it's all the same, isn't it?" I thought it ungentlemanly. Had we shared a cave, ten thousand years ago, Fletch would have been in charge of catering, and *I* would have starved.

I thought of Tim's tradition of buying me a hamper every year. He liked to feed me up. He also understood my evil fascination with all things churchy and Christmassy, and he'd watch, grinning, as I opened the basket and happily sorted through fresh lemon marmalade, date and pecan biscuits, raspberries in liqueur, traditional butter fudge, and champagne truffles. And even when it wasn't Christmas, he knew what I was like about sharing food, and he didn't mind—hardly. He knew that I *always* ordered the wrong dish in restaurants, while he had an instinct for what was most delicious, and when I wrinkled my nose at the first bites, he'd sigh and swap plates. Even when he earned nothing, he was a provider.

Whereas the previous week, I'd made myself a Scooby Snack with avocado, cheese, and tuna and sweet-corn paste, and Fletch had walked into the kitchen and said, "*That's* a well-laden sandwich."

Then, thanks to him, I didn't enjoy eating it. I felt like a big greedy girl, who should have been pecking at a few seeds. *His* idea of a good lunch was hummus and Marmite on a bagel. Yuck.

Tim also understood that I wasn't stupid, even though I said things like "Jesus was born in the Middle East, wasn't he? So why's he got a Mexican name?"

Fletch called me "Blonde" even though I had brown hair. He had just started going out with a statuesque twenty-nine-year-old doctor, named Cornelia. They bonked all over the house, and I had to shut myself in the bedroom just to feel safe. Not only was she highly sexed, she was witty, clever, and, being a Catholic convent girl, spoke Latin. Worse, she was *lovely*. Kind, and sweet to me. I wondered if Fletch had told her about my baby. I didn't think so; he'd probably forgotten. But I came in from Denise's house, went straight to the kitchen, poured myself a large glass of vodka, and downed it. Then I turned around, and she was standing behind me.

"Oh!" I said, embarrassed. "Medicinal!" I added. I waved the glass, and started to burble.

Cornelia listened, without saying anything. When I'd finished, she said, "A lot of people believe that your grief should be measured by the size of your baby. You can only hope that some people have the compassion to try and understand."

I said, "I look in the rearview mirror, and I still imagine a car seat."

Cornelia held my hand.

The next morning, Fletch decided he didn't fancy her and dumped her by text.

* * *

On Monday, I looked at myself in the mirror.

"Pull yourself back," I said aloud. Drinking, crashing cars, and falling out with family was not what my favorite infant school-teacher had predicted for me. (Miss Marsh, a middle-aged Texan with dyed black hair blow-dried in the style of cotton candy. I'd removed a large black spider from the porcelain sink in the Art Corner for her, and she'd cried, "Elizabeth Montgomery, I see it now—the first woman on Mars!")

I would rein myself in. I allowed myself a minute of sentimental thought. That if my lost baby could see me now, she would be disappointed. No child wants a miserable, half-cut mother. I wouldn't want my baby to think that she had ruined my life. I would prefer to be a credit to her; I would want her to be proud of me. It was essential that her brief existence had meaning—that ultimately it led to something good. Was this sacrilege? Perhaps I was under the influence of the twenty-first century, where everyone has to be a winner, even those poor little ones too ill and frail to make the starting line. Did I *have* to conjure up a positive spin on my baby's death? Or maybe I was trying to find a path out of hell, so as not to waste *two* lives.

More than two lives. I'd whittled away at my relationship, when Tim and I were made for each other. Aunt Edith had said, and she didn't say that about just anyone. When Great Uncle Keith married Scottish Miriam, she'd said, "Saves spoiling another couple." Possibly, I had *driven* Tim into Cassie's arms. Jesus. There was no glossing over that one. It was inexcusable, on either side, whatever I'd done. I had treated him terribly, though. I'd needed *my* pain to be acknowledged as superior to his. When it was his baby too. As for Cassie . . . But I was still surprised. She was a cold bitch, but she was loyal.

I wasn't naïve enough to think that every one of us makes it to heaven with their principles intact. Cassie was wretched with George. And she was jealous of us. Once, I mentioned that Tim brought me a cup of tea in bed every morning and her mouth thinned. Then, another time—I must have had a drink or five— I'd said, giggling, that Tim insisted that I wear white panties, *no* other color allowed. She smiled, but her face twisted up. But for my sister to have intercourse (I was no longer a sex columnist; I never had to use the word *cock* again—it just wasn't *me*, darling.) with *my* boyfriend, betraying about ten people in one act . . . Now that I considered their treason in a less lunatic state, it seemed impossible.

But I had *seen* them.

As I burst into tears, again, I realized why the human mind does such a rip-roaring trade in denial. And yet. Creating mental diversions was hard work. I was pooped. Every now and then, a river in Britain bursts its banks and floods a town, and you'll see the poor people scooping water out of their homes, placing sandbags at the door—and you'll watch them and think, You *have* to know that the sandbags and the sloshing out with buckets is futile. The water's up to your roof! But it's easy for me to say, observing from a cool distance. When you're right there in the crisis, you'll do *anything* to make yourself feel better, distract yourself from the misery, deny reality, no matter how stupid.

I was drying my eyes, wondering what I was going to do for a living that would save me from penury and make our parents less ashamed. (Maybe I could become a tree surgeon? Then every time Evelyn Toberman served a conversational ace with mention of Nina Sara's job as adviser to the Chancellor of the Exchequer, Vivica could hit back with "my daughter, the doctor.")

The doorbell rang, and I peered out of the window and saw—speak of the Devil!—the tops of our parents' heads.

The full set!

I must be in trouble.

I opened the door, and Vivica said, "Darling, we bought you a Gucci key ring! *Daddy* saw one of a little London bus, but I thought you might prefer the Gooch! Can we come in?" She sniffed. "Why don't you open a window? It's not healthy to live in a sealed house!"

I stood aside, and they marched toward the living room, our father following his wife like a foot soldier. As Vivica headed to the sofa, Geoffrey veered off to the kitchen, murmuring, "Pot of Darjeeling."

I sat opposite my mother on a pouffe.

"I know everyone's talking about me," I burst out. "I know you all think I've disgraced myself, but *she's* the one who's a disgrace! No one is even capable of imagining how it is for *me*, the—"

"ELIZABETH!" shouted our father, holding a teapot perfectly centered on a floral tray.

I stopped. He never raised his voice, ever. "Elizabeth," he continued. "As you can imagine, your outburst at The Do caused a commotion. A shocking accusation such as yours presumably originates from somewhere, and we did ask Cassie to explain herself. She did, to our complete satisfaction. I understand that you haven't given her the chance to tell you the truth, and that was wrong of you."

I glowered.

"Darling," added Vivica. She paused to slide a small burgundy box with silver lettering across the coffee table. "She wouldn't do it to you. And nor would Tim. They both adore you. Cassie in particular."

She paused, and lit a cigarette without asking if this was allowed. I saw that her long, white fingers shook as she flicked the lighter. Her nails were blood red, perfect, not a single chip. I wasn't like her. She glanced at Geoffrey and he scooted out of the room.

Vivica inhaled and said, very quickly, "I *am* capable of imagining how it is for you, darling. I know how it is for you, in fact, because it happened to me."

"What?" I said. "You had a—"

"I had an ectopic pregnancy. Seven months after I had you. I had an emergency hysterectomy. The baby, and all baby-growing equipment—out, gone, good-bye."

I could feel my eyes bug. I was shocked out of my tiny mind. It did feel tiny, at that point. My pain was so great that no one else was ever allowed to have any. Yet here was my own mother, the finished article of *my* experience, thirty odd years later, and fine, quite matter-of-fact about it, able to function almost normally. It was amazing to me that she had gone through this, and survived. To cover the inadequacy of my response, I went into automatic sympathy overdrive. "Oh my *goodness*, Vivica, I'm so sorry, I had no idea, you poor thing, how—"

She waved away my sympathies. "I don't like talking about it. I was very upset at the time, and I don't like to recall it. I prefer to forget it."

She was so un-self-aware—it *killed* me.

"But, Vivica, just because you choose to ignore your pain, shut it out, it doesn't *go*. It's still there. It's just hidden."

"Hidden's fine. I like hidden. But," she said, her tone softening. "But I see you, and it all comes back, and I feel for you. I really do," she added. She almost sounded surprised.

You *do* feel for me, I thought, staring back at her with nearly equal surprise.

"Anyway," she said—brisker now—"the point of telling you this, darling, is to—"

"Sorry." My brain was like an abacus, slowly clacking beads. "You had a *hysterectomy*?"

"Yes."

I shook my head. "But Cassie . . . ?"

CHAPTER 28

Vivica leaned forward and crushed my warm hand in her cool one. Her wedding ring dug painfully into my skin. She closed her eyes and said—eyes still shut—"Cassie is adopted."

I stood up, even though my legs felt hot and weak. I heard those words and I couldn't *sit*.

"I don't believe this," I said, finally. "I don't believe this." I stared at Vivica, who was now squinting at me, like you might at a horror movie. "This is too big for my head."

She opened her eyes properly—they were full of fear. Geoffrey had padded back into the room, and now stood behind her, one hand on her shoulder and a sincere look on his face.

I wanted to scream. "Why did no one tell me?" I said. I could hear my voice, rising, high and hysterical. "Why didn't you tell me? Why didn't *she*? For all these years!"

I burst into tears. I had always felt like an outsider, never in on the joke. And now, I was proven right. Even though the beauteous better-than-us-all Cassie turned out to be the genetic outsider— good to know that *someone* didn't want her—they'd *still* managed to form a cozy little unit, with a scandalous secret, and keep me out of it.

"Darling, oh darling!" said Vivica, rising slightly from her seat but remaining in it. She stretched toward me, waggled her fingers, as if she was stroking my head—but she wasn't. "Please don't be upset. I know it's a ghastly shock. And you do have a right to be terribly cross. But I do hope you won't be. It was for the best. We didn't tell Cassie until she was thirteen—we didn't want anyone to be upset—and *she* forbade us to tell you. Not for any bad reason. She was—is—so proud to be your sister. She didn't want you to think of her differently. She didn't want your relationship to be any . . . *less*."

I swallowed. "Really?" I said.

"Yes," said Vivica. "She *adores* you. Adores!" (Again, the surprise.) She coughed. "She looks up to you, you know. She doesn't know we've told you. But I've kept quiet for long enough and I thought it best to make an executive decision. I am a businesswoman after all. And a mother," she added, as an afterthought.

Geoffrey then spoke for the first time. "We cannot stand by as parents and watch our daughters' relationships disintegrate to such an extent, and do nothing."

I nodded. He'd got his words muddled up, and they sounded awkward—but I *liked* that.

"This is a lot to take in," I said, slowly.

Cassie was adopted. *Did* it change things? My heart pounded. Maybe, yes. I had a sister. But she wasn't mine at all. I was amazed that Vivica and our father had managed to keep the secret for all these years. You'd have thought that *once*, after an anniversary dinner, when too many sherries had been drunk, too many glasses of pink champagne, a giggling confession would have tumbled out, the guilt and the pressure of Not Telling having booted it to the surface.

I would have blabbed it out. The fact would have simmered, always—at the front of my mind, on the tip of my tongue, and whatever I did, wherever I was, whoever I was with, I'd be thinking, *You* don't know, but *guess* what! I would have told. If only to dilute my guilt with reassurance, because you could squeeze a lot of sympathy out of your friends with a story like that . . . oh, first baby, so big and fat, irreparable damage to the pelvic floor . . . all whipped out . . . trauma . . . secret heartbreak . . . social duty . . . unwanted newborn . . . needed homing. Like a *cat.*

Vivica lit another cigarette, while I stared at Fletch's polished teak floor. I was her biological child, but Vivica wasn't like me. She was hard throughout, a peanut brittle of a person. She was more like Cassie, despite being no relation. Perhaps I shouldn't put it like that.

Now that I knew the facts, I both admired and despised Vivica for her steel ability to choose practicality over sentimentality. She'd been able to tuck away the less than perfect truth in a dark corner, banish it from her mind, and create a neat preferable reality, where she and our father were the accomplished parents of two perfect girls—even if the second was considerably more perfect than the first.

What annoyed me was that Vivica enjoyed the status of being mother to Cassandra Montgomery, a *barrister*—and I wasn't a total loss; even the sex column had a certain risqué cache. And yet, the job she'd done as a parent was shoddy. Once, Cassie and I caught a severe stomach bug, and the doctor said, "Only starches—dry toast and jacket potatoes—and perhaps soft-boiled eggs for protein. *No* dairy, *no* fruit, *nothing* fancy." Vivica led us from his office, cock-ahoop. "Marvelous!" she crowed to our father. "Pray they keep up-chucking, I won't have to cook for a week!"

If she were a builder, I would have reported her to the Trading Standards Authority, and they'd have fined her. Cassie's achievements were all Cassie, nothing to do with her. Cassie would have succeeded had she been raised by wolves. And *my* achievements—if you could call them that—were in spite of her. I decided that Vivica had lived a frivolous life. Her job was a selfish enterprise. She spent her salary on haircuts. There was little altruism. I didn't see her making sacrifices for The Children.

Maybe that was my problem—I expected every mother to be a martyr. Myself included.

Was I too harsh? After all, her parenting methods—or madness—had produced two fully functional adults. And now it emerged that Vivica had suffered herself—which, as everyone knows, is pretty much a free pass to inflict suffering on others. Was she excused?

I shook my head. Vivica and Geoffrey exchanged glances and shifted in their seats. They could sit and wait. *I'd* waited, for the day they might have enough respect for me to talk out the mess they'd made of *my childhood*, and here this day finally was, with the mystery finally revealed, and I was still disappointed.

True, that lately, Vivica was so sweet you could have stirred her in boiling milk and made toffee. And yet, as reparations went, it wasn't enough. I still felt an aching resentment. I was angry because of her bright, silly *breeziness*, that she was so blithely unaware that over the years she'd crushed my confidence into bits—like if you trod on a potato chip, again and again and again. She had no clue of the consequences of her behavior, no interest in finding out. As for Geoffrey! He was her dumb accomplice—Muttley to her Dastardly.

When I was seven, Vivica decided she liked the gamine hairstyle of Una Stubbs in *Summer Holiday*. So she tried it out on me first, cutting my hair so short that all that was required to complete the look was a bolt either side of my neck. (She then decided against.) She'd bought me an orange terry-cloth bikini for swimming in the local pool, and lost the top. She was useless with the washing, always shrinking stuff, inadvertently dying it pink, or dumping it in a scrumpled heap (folding and ironing were too much like housework) and not always in the right wardrobe.

"Just wear the bottoms, darling, it's not as if you've got anything *there*!" She would have said that or similar, I couldn't recall, but I did remember what a woman said, accusingly, as I crept out of the changing cubicle, bare-chested, hot with shame: "This is the ladies'."

At the time, I was too caught up in the mortification of being *me* to feel furious with *Vivica*, but now I looked back—with all the ammunition that their confession about Cassie had given me—and I was weak with rage. I tried, in fairness, to direct some of it toward our father, but I found he wasn't important enough, and that was *his* indictment.

I had to confront her. Now! It was the only way. I saw myself on *Jerry Springer*, immensely fat, my hair scraped back in a high ponytail, giving me an elastic band face-lift. Confronting Vivica! The orange swimming trunks! The key ring collection! The Hebrew classes! The boy's haircut! The bad cooking! The *Noel Edmond's Prank Phone Calls* cassette! Vivica would be sat in a chair, wearing red lipstick and tight jeans, and everyone would boo her as a terrible mother. The credits would roll with her sobbing, "I'm sorry, I'm so sorry, my darling daughter, please forgive me! I love you so much! I'll make it up to you, I'll . . ."

What *would* she do, exactly?

"I've always felt different to Cassie," I said, as a prompt.

"We can discuss it fully another time," said Vivica, stubbing out her third cigarette on an Arsenal ashtray. "We've had more than enough excitement for one day." She flapped the smoke out of her face, and the gesture brought to mind the action of brushing something undesirable under a carpet. "Now, what's all this I hear about you drinking? Jews don't drink, it's ridiculous!"

"Mother," I said.

I didn't know whether to laugh or cry. After a long pause, I decided that we *would* discuss it another time, and I would extract an apology whether or not I had to enforce it with a Chinese burn. But even now, she *was* trying to help me in her clumsy way—she really was. I had to remind myself that today's visit was all about helping Lizbet. I would do her the courtesy of answering her question.

"*That's* ridiculous," I said. "Jews don't drink! If you think that, you're no better than Cousin Denise, the only person in that room who refuses to see that darling Ian is gay squared!"

Vivica sniffed. "She's a fool. She's always complaining that her husband, Derek, won't see a musical."

A ray of sunshine fell across the wood floor, and I said, "I'll stop with the drinking."

Our father nodded, and Vivica smiled. He poured, and she took a sip of tea. "George has left Cassie, by the way," said our mother.

My mouth hung wide. It occurred to me that while some fat people have their jaw wired shut, I should have mine wired open.

"While he needs to know that she is innocent of any wrongdoing," added our father, "we think it is for the best."

"Yes," said Vivica. "It sounds sad, but it's not. Anyone can see that her marriage to George was disastrous, and it's much better for the baby that it ends now. Little ones need to see that their parents love each other, and if that's not the case, it's best that Mummy and Daddy live far enough away from each other that they can fake goodwill."

I nodded. And I thought, Cassie will *shower* that baby with love, and so will I. Stuff George. It won't want for affection. *Ever.* I blinked, shocked by the passion of my own thoughts. Of course, what I meant was, I'd do my duty. Was I even still the baby's aunt? Technically?

Then they stood up to go. Vivica kissed me lightly on one cheek, and our father kissed me on the other.

He turned as they left, and touched my arm. "We share your sadness about your baby, Lizbet. We look forward, but we haven't forgotten."

I shut the door and covered my eyes. Sometimes a few words are all that's needed.

CHAPTER 29

My mind was elsewhere, and the ring-around grovel did not go well. Cousin Denise had sniggered, and I was tempted to say, "Listen, pal—Ian was telling me about Great Cousin Tiffany In Australia's wedding to Sean From Perth, and he described the bridal gown as 'silk faille overlaid with beaded organza'—so stick that in your pipe and smoke it!"

However, Aunt Edith deserved an eye-to-eye apology, so I took a cab to her house. I hoped she'd see me arrive, as I'd recently heard her complain that a relative had invited *her* to pay a visit. "Why should *I* go? The car is at the garage, and she's not important enough to take a taxi for!"

I was surprised not to receive the great fuss of a welcome that I was used to. I thought I could detect a hint of sulkiness in Aunt Edith's voice, and it shocked me. Then again, I had sabotaged her birthday party, made The Do about *me*.

I suppose that Aunt Edith and I were locked in head-to-head battle. *I* was determined that Aunt Edith continue in the role she played in our childhood—nurturing, maternal. I wanted to act the child and be mothered. More so now than ever. She had other ideas.

She was old. Her beloved husband was dead. She lived alone. She wanted me to make a fuss of *her*.

I couldn't remember exactly when I realized that Aunt Edith no longer rang me, but expected me to ring her, regularly. And however frequently I visited, she would always say, "Don't leave it so long next time." As usual, Tim had been the voice of reason, saying, "She's at a selfish age. At her stage in life she's not interested in a two-way relationship. She's after a sympathetic ear." All the same, it was a jolt to discover that she'd canceled her subscription to *Ladz Mag*. "It's not really for my age group, is it, dear?"

"Aunt Edith, I am so sorry about making a scene at your party. Of *course* Cassie and Tim didn't have an affair. I was a bit overwrought. I got carried away. I've been a little upset lately."

Aunt Edith's face remained impassive, and I wondered if I'd have to go as far as pleading insanity.

I was almost certain that Aunt Edith knew about my miscarriage, and yet she'd never said a word. Now, she gave a hint of it. "Elizabeth. We all go through hardship in life. Where would we be if we buckled under the first time things didn't go our way? Young people today have no idea what it used to be like. They spend too much time feeling sorry for themselves. We just got on with it!"

I nodded. It might hurt not to receive a word of sympathy about the miscarriage, but at some point, as Tim would say, I had to "suck it up." Aunt Edith was all too busy with her sadness about Uncle Peter, and my acting up about a baby I never knew must have seemed laughable, insulting. I do think that people are territorial about grief—they don't like to share. She'd been with Uncle Peter for fifty-nine years. Now he was dead and *her* life could only get worse. I had hope and youth on my side.

"Aunt Edith," I said. "I am so sorry for what I did. It was inappropriate. I don't intend to buckle under."

I paused. Collected myself. She was so very different from the person she had once been. I wanted to tell her that I finally knew about Cassie's adoption—only because I wanted to hear good things about *me*—but this was Aunt Edith's time. I owed it to her.

"So what else happened at the party?" I said. "Was the food nice? Did Denise buy a nice cake? *Ian* made it. Good for him. Is he skilled in that department?"

Aunt Edith gave me a knowing look. Her response—"What do *you* think?"—told me that I was halfway back in her good books. And really, that was more important to me than everything else. She was seventy-five, what did I want from her? She didn't owe me, and if I was gracious toward her, that was enough.

Aunt Edith bustled around, making coffee, and I winced at her swollen ankles. They were purple and blotchy, and twice the size they should have been. She moved with difficulty, breathing heavily and leaning on the surfaces. She also had a "grabber"—a stick with a pincer on the end, that allowed her to retrieve an item from the floor without bending. She seemed to have aged since my last visit.

Maybe I *had* left it too long.

We talked for an hour—or rather, she talked and I listened. And then I kissed her good-bye and hugged her gently. "Ah," she said. "You're a good girl, Lizbet." And then, almost to herself: "You'd be silly to leave Timothy out in the cold for too long. Who knows what wonderful babies are waiting in the wings for the pair of you"—what a beautiful, beautiful sentiment, I thought—"to get a bloody move on!"

Even so. I was not ready to make that call. The truth? I was scared. Aunt Edith assumed that I'd snap my fingers and Tim would lollop to my side, doe-eyed with adoration. I wasn't so sure. And if he were to say No, that would be my life—gone! But I had an excuse for stalling. I had an equally important—and terrifying—appointment. With my sister.

The back of my neck prickled hot and cold with sweat as I approached her front door. It was imposing at the best of times—glossy black, with a brass knocker and two neatly pruned miniature trees in pots stationed like sentries, one on either side of the porch. I'd wondered what to bring her. Perhaps the most appropriate gift would have been booties—or a silver Gucci rattle—but I was wary. Also, much as I wanted to make the switch from bad fairy to good fairy, I wanted to *feel* the part before I acted it.

I took nothing. I wasn't going to offer bribes. (Not like Vivica—*she* thought a box of Godiva in the right direction would get you off a murder rap.) I was mortified at what I'd done to Cassie and George—more so now that I saw how much I meant to her. I believed what Vivica had said about Cassie's reasons for keeping the truth from me. Cassie has always wanted to protect me, and it was only now that I saw how much.

Our father had explained about Cassie's low blood pressure, and it made sense. I even allowed myself a smile at the thought that the Montgomery family suffers from *high*. I'd been fooling myself, wanting to believe her and Tim's betrayal, needing an excuse to keep myself riled up. I felt that in my ridiculous accusation I had shown my sour, childish soul for what it was. If I was a laughing-stock among the Gargoyles, I deserved to be. Apart from anything else, Tim *always* hung around the house with his willy tip poking through his boxers. It was practically a trademark.

I rang the doorbell, and waited.

I would keep focused on my apology. I wouldn't tell her that I knew about the adoption—yet. The more I thought about it, the more nervous I became. Cassie hadn't told me, because she feared our relationship would become *less*. If I told her that I knew, maybe it would.

Cassie opened the door after a second. I launched into my apology, trying to ignore the soft swell of her stomach, and the daggerlike needles of pain in mine. So much hurt, on so many levels. But she spoke over me. "I'm not bothered about the lie you told to the Gargoyles, but I will say, it's not been pleasant, Lizbet, having your bad feeling radiating over me in waves for the last few months."

She didn't add "while I've been pregnant" but I was sure that she thought it, and I felt ashamed. It was a rotten thing to do.

"I feel terrible, if it's any consolation," I said. "And I have retracted that statement to various . . . Gargs." I paused. "How are *you* feeling?"

"Fine," she said.

Cassie would face death before she admitted that pregnancy weakened her physically or mentally in any way. She was exactly the same about periods, even though when she was fourteen the pain made her black out.

"Good," I said. "Good." I added, in a rush, "You look very well." I tried to say the word "blooming," but I couldn't manage it. "I *was* going to bring you something but—" I stopped. Is there ever any point even beginning that sentence? I wished my voice didn't sound so strained, but I managed a genuine smile. Cassie expecting. I couldn't stretch to "lovely" but it was . . . nice. "And, er, how's George?"

"You did me a favor. George is gone!"

I was horrified, again, even though I already knew this. Is it possible to be re-horrified?

"Listen." I started to gabble. "I can fix that. I mean, Geoffrey did tell me but, well, I assumed he was being dramatic—George, I mean. I thought he'd be back in a day! He doesn't actually *believe* that you and Tim . . . er, does he?"

"You did."

For a moment, I couldn't speak, I was so sick of myself, of *being* me, a nasty person. I said, "I persuaded myself I did."

She paused. "Why do that?"

Her expression forbade tears. I replied, "The world felt so black." I offered her a weak smile.

I hesitated. Before it had all gone wrong, I'd read up on the nature of the baby, and one of the curious things babies did was to fling out their arms and legs in a start of horror if you plopped them into their cot too hastily. This was called the Startle Reflex. The newborn was used to being snug and tight inside the womb, and the world of open spaces gave it a fear of flying apart. I didn't want to say this to Cassie now, but after the miscarriage, my head had felt so full, my arms so empty, and my brain so mad and disjointed—I felt like *I* might fly apart, limbs shooting off in odd directions.

"You were a victim," she said. "But that's not what you want to be forever."

I nodded. The knowledge that she was adopted made her more vulnerable, and I wanted to make it right for her—make *something* right. I said, "I'd like to speak to George—and his parents. Explain myself. If that's all right with you."

"It's not necessary," she said. "*I'*ll do that. When the time is right." She added, "I hope you and Tim get back together."

She was really being very kind to me. I felt a rush of affection. Vivica hadn't lied. "Thanks, Cass."

I followed her inside—we'd been speaking on the doorstep. There were three cardboard boxes in the hallway. I jumped at the chance to be useful. "Do you want me to carry those somewhere for you?" I said.

She shook her head. "They're full of George's CDs. Kraftwerk, that kind of thing. I packed them up yesterday, and I'm going to ask him to come and collect them tomorrow."

I gulped. "Isn't this happening a bit fast?"

She laughed. "You're joking, aren't you? This marriage has been on the slide for a couple of years."

I sighed.

"What?"

"Cassie. Are you really going to be a single parent?"

Cassie made a face. "George's mother, Sheila, used to say that when George was tiny, she found it *worse* to have Ivan in the house, doing the wrong thing with the baby, than when he worked late and she had to do everything herself."

"I feel like this is my fault."

"No," said Cassie, sounding stern. "This is between George and me. The baby will still have *male influence* in its life. I'll do a Liz Hurley. Appoint ten godfathers. Peter-the-Hairdresser can be the Elton John figure. Greg from Hound Dog can be Hugh Grant. Rakish. Tim can—"

"Tim and I are not together," I said.

"He is *still* top of my list as a godfather," Cassie replied.

"Really," I said. "Then I won't mention the time he scared Tomas to death by letting him watch a Halloween episode of *The Simpsons*, then freaked him out for a week by saying, 'You mustn't be scared of skeletons, Tomas, you have a skeleton *inside you*!'"

"Nonetheless," she said.

"Fine"—I was scared of her, but I couldn't let it go—"but, anyway, there's a difference, isn't there, between an influence and a father. I worry that if George is feeling hostile toward you because of . . . misinformation . . . well, I would feel terrible if that had affected his relationship with his own child. He *has* to know that the baby *is* his. It's wrong to let him think otherwise." I could hear the pleading in my voice. "If he's a parent, you can't keep that from him. To *be* a parent, and to not have the joy of knowing it, of being it, it's—"

Now Cassie was shaking her head and holding up her hand for me to stop talking, but I just had to say one more thing. "And you can't keep it from the baby. Unless the parents are abusive, the best *influence* for a baby is the real parents. It's about *blood*, Cassie. No godfather is going to feel the same bond as—"

"Lizbet," said Cassie. "Do you seriously think that Mummy and Daddy are going to let the Hershlags continue believing that the baby isn't theirs, for more than five minutes?"

She stopped. And I realized what I'd said. I'd blithely confirmed that love was about nature, and nurture could go hang. When it just wasn't true, and she and I were the glorious proof of this (though recently . . . not so much). I had to tell her I knew, whatever the consequences. "Cassie," I began. My pulse started to race.

CHAPTER 30

_____ _Cassie_

They'd *told* her.

I flicked my hair while I decided who I was angry with.

No one.

I was pleased. Relieved. She deserved to know. And to hear it from them.

But I felt shaken.

"Lizbet," I said. "You do understand why I kept it from you?"

She nodded. "I think so." Her lips trembled. "I mean, I *still* am your sister, aren't I?"

My heart melted to a red sludge, and I got up—slowly so as not to faint and botch the gesture—and hugged her. "Lizbet," I said. "You are my sister, my *best* sister, and nothing could ever change that. Even if my birth mother had had ten other girls." I paused. "She didn't though. She had no other children at all."

Lizbet pulled away from the hug, her eyes red, and said, "Oh, Cass. You were her only one. You must have been so special. To have your baby and be forced to give it up—the opposite of how it's supposed to be! And now! And now she'll never know that . . . her baby came back!" She flopped her head onto the arm of the sofa and sobbed.

I stared, bewildered. I'd expected her to be upset. But I'd expected her to be upset for *her* loss. Not that I was going anywhere, yet there had to be a psychological loss, of knowing that our bond was nurture, but not nature.

And then, of course, I realized that she *was* upset for her loss. As a sister. But more as a mother.

Finally, she sat up. "Sorry," she said. "But I feel it. I feel it, so deeply, for both of you. The pain. And for *you*. To have been that close. To have so nearly made it . . ."

She flopped on the sofa again. Then sprang up. "I wish you would have told me. No wonder it was so hard when I was preg . . ."

"It's okay," I said.

"No, it isn't!" Lizbet was trying to sip from a glass of water, but she was trembling so hard, it kept slopping into her lap. "It's *not* okay; stop pretending it is!"

If I didn't take charge, Lizbet would spin around in chest-beating circles for the rest of the afternoon. "I realize," I said, carefully, "that this is a huge shock. It's bound to feel surreal. It's not going to be a set of facts to which you're going to be able to adjust—"

"Cassie," murmured Lizbet. "We grew up together. *Please* stop talking to me like I was opposite counsel."

"Opposing counsel. Am I? I don't mean to!" Maybe formality *was* a shield to hide behind. "It's just a way of speaking . . . efficiently." I tailed off, and we both giggled.

Then Lizbet frowned. "I think—there are too many thoughts— but now I know you're adopted, I think, I see our childhood, no—I *re-see* our childhood, er, no—"

Lizbet could dither for days over one word. She was a journalist, but it wasn't that. Each word had to create the correct image in her head, or it *felt* wrong. Her imagination ruled her, which—if you were an excitable person like Lizbet—bordered on dangerous.

"Review?" I said.

"Yes! I *re*-view our childhood. And—" She stopped.

I felt my heart curl like a dried leaf. "Yes?" I said.

"I hoped that knowing this would make sense of it. Make it *better*. But I don't think it does."

She was thinking of Mummy. Favoring *me*.

Her shoulders sank. I reached out, touched her hand. "Mummy was tough on you. They were *too* aware of the possibility of the adopted child feeling second best. They overcompensated. They're not sensitive people. Mummy is not a passionate woman. She's not maternal. Not in that slightly unhinged way that *core* maternal women are, throwing themselves in front of buses to save their babies. You get the sense that Mummy would . . . hesitate in the hope that some kind passerby would do it for her. But they both love you a lot, in their way, and I think, that after you had the miscarriage"—I looked her in the eye as I said it—"you might have seen that quite clearly with Mummy. And Daddy, even."

Lizbet was quiet, nodding. I saw that she'd tugged her sleeve over her thumb and was making her front teeth squeak on the material. It was a habit she'd formed aged three, according to Mummy, and the last time I'd seen its resurrection was when Great Uncle Keith had invited himself for dinner (without Scottish Miriam), whipped out the latest copy of *Ladz Mag*—in front of Tim's parents—and read out Lizbet's column on blow-jobs, with greasy relish, from beginning to end.

"We weren't a bad family," I added, quickly. "We rubbed along okay, the main unit, the four of us—I'm not talking about the Gargs, you mustn't be sad about the Gargoyles, darling. Yes, Mummy is away with the fairies, and Daddy never had a clue, but the *heart* was there."

Lizbet stopped the teeth-squeaking and pouted instead. "Well, that's a lie," she said, but there was a smile in her voice. Her eyes narrowed. "*How* old were you when they said you were adopted? I bet you were over the *moon*!"

I assumed an indignant expression, but she wasn't fooled. "Don't forget, Cass," she said, wagging her finger like I was five again. "I know you better than any of them. And I'll bet you *loved* finding out you were adopted. I bet you thought you were a princess!"

I blushed.

She shook her head, slowly. "So," she added. "What about the rest of the . . . your family?"

"My aunt wrote the other day. Wanting to meet me."

Lizbet gasped. "Oh my God! I'm so excited for you! What did she sound like?"

I shrugged. "Great. Nice."

"That's amazing! And what did you say? What did you say in your reply?" I shrugged, and she said, "Cassie! You haven't *written* a reply! Oh! How can you not? How can you not reply?" She paused, and said more quietly, "I'm sorry. I do realize that you need to mourn Sarah Paula. It's the most grievous loss. Just because you never knew her, people might think . . ."

"I know," I said. "I know."

She nodded, a quick, fast movement. Then she said, "But you have an aunt, a lovely aunt who is desperate to meet her dead sister's daughter. Who could, maybe, help you, in some small way, to heal. How can you not reply? I mean, presuming she's not a psychopath ... how can you reject a person who wants to love you?"

I raised an eyebrow and said, "How can *you*?"

That particular evening wiped me out—I was a wimp anyway, falling into bed at ten—so I was not delighted when I returned from work the following night to find George on my doorstep. (I'd had the locks changed, of course.)

"Your sister has clarified *everything*," he announced, with an air of petulance, as though—while I had been proven innocent, I remained guilty.

I sighed. So, despite what I'd said, she'd given Tim a miss and gone to see George.

He glared at me, adding, "Why aren't you wearing a jacket? It's freezing! There's a chill!"

George had a tiresome belief in "The Chill," and its insidious desire to infiltrate and overpower the madman fool enough to incite attack by leaving his coat on the hook.

"Have you had a break-in?" He barked the words like an Alsatian.

I looked him up and down. "Apparently not," I said, and smiled.

"Then why have you changed the locks?" he snapped, not getting it. "And why on *earth* didn't you tell me the truth? My parents were going nuts! And how did you think I felt? Hm? Hm? Torturing myself with the thought that I'd played *tennis* with the man who was stirring my porridge! I'd taken him to the *Lloyd*!"

"I am not your porridge," I said.

"I felt diminished as a man," added George. "I could actually sense the ego reducing. My core identity was fragmenting inside me. At one point I was lying on the floor in the fetal position—"

"Hey, is that the one traditionally assumed before doing a

roly-poly? Well, fun as this is, chatting in the cold, I suppose you'd like to come in and collect your things?"

George stamped his foot, and shouted, "Did you hear what I said? How dare you be flip with me! If a woman said that, and a man said what *you* said, you'd lynch him!"

"No, I wouldn't," I replied. "I'd tell the woman to butch up."

George glowered. "I don't know what you think you were playing at," he said.

I was losing patience. "George. I am not a woman who fucks around. You have been married to me for long enough for me to assume you know that. That you don't is a grave source of disappointment to me to say the least."

"Stop speaking in that pompous way!" yelled George. "It's like you're summing up!"

I was, sort of. "I gave you my best assurances that I'd been faithful. However, you persisted in your pernicious suspicions." (I couldn't resist.)

"Just speak English!"

"I was sick of it!" I shouted. "I wanted a bit of peace! And if you were dumb enough to think I'd shag Tim, you deserved every bit of crap that went with it!"

George looked mutinous. "Your sister's nuts," he said.

"So," I said. "Your core identity is fragmenting. But *she's* . . . nuts."

"Telling lies! Emasculating me in front of your entire family! This isn't her still banging on about the miscarriage, is it? That mishap was in the bloody Ice Age."

"George," I said, a great anger igniting. "You say that and I'm standing here with *your* child inside me? God knows what *you* feel like, but *I'm* a mother." I didn't realize I was till I said it—but it was true. I was shocked at the might of my emotion for this tiny scrap.

"It might be a blur on the screen to the rest of the world, but this is *my baby*. You think Lizbet is any different? Lizbet lost her child. She lost her hopes, her dreams, her future. The pain of it has felled her. It's dredged up every misery she ever suffered." I paused. I was no longer talking to George, really, more myself. "I was our parents' favorite. That was tough on her."

"Oh, so the miscarriage is an excuse to get attention from Mummy and Daddy."

"There's no point with you, is there, George? But if Lizbet wanted an excuse to get attention she'd wear a big hat."

"Right," he said.

"Every loss . . . rose to the surface."

"Fascinating. I'd like to get into my house now?"

"*Your* house?"

"Our. House."

I unlocked the door, and walked in, squeezing past the row of cardboard boxes to turn off the alarm.

"What's this?" said George. "Baby stuff?" He flipped open a flap. "That's my leather jacket! And my baseball cap! Why have you packed up all my clothes?"

"You wouldn't make a detective."

"I thought the back room was the baby's room. Babies are tiny! You think it needs the master bedroom and an en suite?"

I gazed at him to see if he was joking. But that I might have tired of him hadn't occurred. He thought his stuff was in boxes while our room was being adorned with bunny rabbit motifs. I doubted his ego had reduced. It appeared to be suffering from gigantism.

"George," I said. "How do you feel about becoming a father?"

He shrugged. "Great."

"How do you see your role?"

He sighed. "As you know"—I didn't, although perhaps he had told me—"I've just started work on a play that I plan to submit anonymously. That's going to eat up my time. Don't get me wrong—I'll help *out*. I can't wait to see what my kid looks like! They're supposed to look *exactly* like the dad, right after they're born, did you know? To prove to him that he is the father, encourage him to stick around." He grinned, and for a second I was tempted to smack him. "But," he added, "there's only so much I can do. You're the one with the tits."

"Indeed. How do you intend to support me?"

"Why? You get paid maternity leave. And when they accept the script, that'll be money in the bank."

"I don't mean financially."

"You're not still banging on about cups of coffee in the morning, are you?"

George was a sensitive, forgiving, emotionally perceptive guy, when it came to himself. Other people's feelings were dandelion fluff.

"Forget the coffee," I said. "Let's get divorced."

CHAPTER 31

It wasn't good timing. But it was *time*. Despite the Hershlags and—maybe—because of them. Because, in fact, of all the couples I knew who were happy together.

I thought of Lizbet boasting about Tim, in the guise of complaining. She'd tell Tim an important piece of information, and he wouldn't listen. So Lizbet would demand, "What did I say?" Tim would look up and parrot her last sentence. "But like a *robot*! He can say the words but they might as well be in *Latin*—it's *so* annoying!"

Boasting, plainly. Whereas George had an identical talent, and I found it annoying.

I thought of when George and I had spent a Saturday with Sophie Hazel Hamilton at the family home in Chelsea. Sophie's husband Mark was a wisp—compared to the mighty force that was Sophie. (I always though of Sophie as big, when she was actually tiny, five foot two—I confused her physique with her personality.) Their three elder children ran around the garden while Sophie fed baby Justin.

"Ma-ark!" called Sophie, as Justin drained his bottle. "Set up the trampoline!"

Mark was an artist—a *real* artist who painted *real*, recognizable paintings of objects and sold them to galleries, and banks, and collectors—unlike George, who merely used art as an excuse to feel himself up. I could see that George was in awe of Mark and wanted to be his friend. Mark, however, cared very little for anyone except his wife. I heard him say to George, "There should be a limit on how many two-syllable 'Ma-arks' she's allowed a day. Ten?"

Mark made the comment with a grin, and I saw that he didn't mind a bit.

George sidestepped a speeding child and replied, "Yeah. You know how you cue up a radio jingle? You should have a response cued up. She says 'Ma-ark!' and you press a button: 'Ff-fer-fuck off!'"

Mark laughed, but he shot George an odd look. Then, a second later, he looked at *me*. I looked away. It was embarrassing.

I'm not a dimwit. I do know that even happy couples have their lows. But whereas everyone else had dinky little dips, our married life was one big slough of despair.

Even Lizbet's and my parents laughed together. Even if the key to their harmony was to lead almost independent lives. Daddy wasn't *quite* the gentleman he thought he was; Mummy was shallow and wrapped up in what could have been. But, intermittently, he found her amusing, and she found him dependable. That doesn't sound like a great love story, or even a great compliment, and it isn't. But Mummy's way of coping with imperfection was to block it out, a Berlin Wall way of thinking, and with this defense in place, she coped very nicely. As for Daddy—a practical man—the luxury of dawdling over your sadness never occurred.

One time, I went food shopping with them. Without exchanging a word, Daddy got the cart and pushed it, while Mummy marched into the supermarket and beelined for Fruit. Daddy hadn't seen her take the left turn, but took it himself without hesitation. I watched the entire process—from Daddy paying for the parking ticket, to him packing the bags into the trunk, from Mummy selecting a Galia melon, to her folding the receipt into her purse. They didn't confer once. It was like a beautifully rehearsed ballet, and if the manager had run out at the end and presented Mummy with a bouquet, I wouldn't have been surprised.

There was comfort there, while George and I were itchy with each other. And now, bitterness with his career had turned him into a monster. He was unpleasant—it was the main thrust of his personality. It made me dislike the quirks that in a nicer person I would have found charming. For instance, George couldn't hoard enough Brillo pads—little wire pads infused with pink soap, popular with fifties housewives. George treated them with reverence, carefully ripping them in half, so as not to waste an entire pad on *one* saucepan. He refused to throw away a Brillo pad, but instead placed it under the sink, where it rusted red until *I* threw it out.

George couldn't win. He made me aware of *my* faults—the only good thing about him, yet of course I didn't thank him for it. I was incensed by his comments about Lizbet, because I was guilty of having similar thoughts myself. But when *he* made remarks that I *might* have made, I found myself leaping to her defense. I would have said any old thing for the satisfaction of a sharp argument with George, but in fact, it hit me that my explanations of Lizbet's behavior made sense.

"What! Don't be silly," said George. "You're hormonal. We're having a *baby* together."

I would say that the barrister in me picked a thousand holes in his words, but a monkey could have done it. "Don't be *silly*"—dismissal of my opinions as unintelligent. "You're *hormonal*"—the universal excuse used by men to discount women's emotions. "We're having a baby *together*"—au contraire: *I* was having it; he'd just hang around the hospital. (We'd attended one prenatal class. The midwife had emphasized the need for the partner to support the woman during the birth. "So," said George. "How do we distract them? Do we talk about the weather?")

There was no together with us. And George—who seemed to have studiously avoided any person under two feet for all of his life so far—bought into the Pampers version of a baby: clean as a whistle, big padded bottom, dimpled cheeks, no *bother*.

I had no doubt that when Junior finally arrived, with sound and fury, nocturnal tendencies, reeking and leaking from all orifices, George would be laid flat with the shock of it and no help at all. It would be like having newborn twins, and that was the least of it. George believed that when new parents moaned about sleep deprivation, *he* understood because he'd stayed out late at a few clubs. He presumed that babies' goo-goo glued falling-apart relationships together. He didn't get that if Mummy and Daddy were loose at the seams, a baby would tear them asunder. Like Mike Tyson ripping a tissue.

I didn't want to wait for that. I wanted the baby to be born into a calm environment. I wanted to get all the shit out of the way now. Without being overly poetic, my love for George was cold, and nothing he could do was going to reheat it. I've microwaved yesterday's mashed potato, forever with hope, but it *always* tastes old and wrong. I wasn't as naïve about my relationship. George was, though.

"Everything you just said is irrelevant," I said. "You are going to be a father. That doesn't change. And we are going to get a divorce."

George said nothing. I wondered if he might start shouting.

"You *had* to be expecting this," I said, prompting him.

He just looked at me, like you'd look at a princess who'd just turned into a frog.

"Expecting this?" he said. "How would I be *expecting* this? It's like my mother turning around and saying she's a *lesbian*."

"What? What are you talking about?"

"What are *you* talking about? You're talking shit! We're married! What do you want from me? Rose petals on the floor every time you get out of bed?"

"George," I said. "What I want from you is a divorce."

George turned and punched the wall with his fist. He gasped, doubling over in pain—"Dial 999! I've broken my hand!"

"I want a divorce, and I won't say it again. The next time I'll bike around the affidavit."

George shook his head, still wincing and squeezing his eyes shut, brave soldier that he was. "Listen, you mad cow, you don't know what you're saying—we're *fine*." He added, "I'm crashing at Mum's tonight though; you're really freaking me out."

He stormed past and slammed the door in my face. I felt a ripple of anger, or maybe the baby was making its first butterfly moves. George was the one person I knew who made me feel powerless.

Hubert Fitzgerald, however, came a close second. The judge had made her intentions clear in the middle negotiation hearing, describing Hubert's offer as "unrealistic and unreasonable," and telling him, "You will provide Mrs. Fitzgerald with a better house than you are proposing." A bunch of similar threats followed, that couldn't have been clearer had she grabbed Hubert's collar with both fists and heaved him off the floor by the scruff of his neck. But Hubert *wasn't taking her seriously*!

He'd instructed me to write to Alissa's mother ("She's eighty-six, doddery as fuck.") to ask if she was holding any funds for her daughter. Although I'd sworn to Barnaby that I'd find something on his client, I didn't want it to be *this*. I felt sorry for Alissa. The truth was, I wanted her to exit court shouting, *"Ka-ching!"* I was sure she hoped for this too, but I knew that for most women, no amount of money compensates for the emotional disappointment of a marriage not working out.

Alissa's future and prospects had been taken away from her, and it wasn't enough for Hubert to rob her of *that*—he wanted to take away her dignity too, send her to work in a shop! Hubert was like a lot of divorcing men in that he saw this process as a business trans-action. With some men, the desire to get out with as much money as possible was a defense mechanism—"If I'm rich, I'll feel better." I suspected that many were as distraught as the women, except their emotions were hidden from them. Not Hubert, though. He wanted a brutal quick cut—*him* doing all the cutting.

People are at their least attractive when getting divorced. Per-haps George would surprise me as the civilized exception.

I sighed as I stirred the pink straw in my glass of Badoit and stared out of the café window onto Fleet Street. I should have gone home, but I was too tired to move. I didn't want to see George; I didn't want to be shouted at. Last time I'd seen The Top Man, I'd asked him about the effect of stress on the baby. He'd smiled and said, "The baby is going to be born into the real world, not a bubble."

I thought of Hubert's twisted thinking. His anger had done away with his humanity—he'd upset his own children to spite his wife. He was actually proposing that his kids be removed from private school and sent to the local comprehensive, as, apparently, he would need a huge second mortgage to buy Alissa out of their home—a neat excuse that made *her* feel greedy and responsible. Meanwhile Barnaby uncovered my client's transfers to a bank account he couldn't trace.

I wondered if the judge would let Alissa stay in their home—from what she'd said in the middle hearing, I suspected she would. *Their home.* When you and your beloved move into your first house in joint name, it's very easy to think of it as "our home." You imagine it as your financial and emotional security, but few people really think of what this means in terms of *pounds*. When a couple is divorcing, the "our" becomes "my"—and the idea that your lover-turned-enemy can run a credible argument to steal a chunk of *your* home, force you out of it into alien and inferior ... accommodations, seems barbaric.

I really didn't think that George would be a Hubert—after all, it wasn't as if George had *earned* the money. He had to have enough pride to want to earn his own ... one day. And he knew I was bloody good at my job—it would be like David taking on Goliath! No. Bad example.

"I'll have a cappy, thank you very much, and charge me for extra cinnamon!" My neck jerked at the sound of Barnaby's voice. The server—tiny with a pixie nose and long blond corkscrew curls—giggled, and I wondered if she'd charge him at all.

"Montgomery!" he said, a moment later, and I turned around as if surprised. "How *are* you? How's little Boris?" He nodded at my stomach.

"*Boris?* I'm not calling it *Boris*! I don't even know if it's a boy!"

Barnaby grinned. "Sorry. Family tradition. We give the unborn baby a silly name—Dunstan, Errol, Ermentrude, Clyde. That way you give it an identity, but not its *real* identity, as that would be bad luck, so I'm told. The baby stays an undercover agent until it pops out, you see? Only then does it assume its real identity!"

I tried not to grin back. "And your real identity was.... *Barnaby*? What the hell was your undercover name?"

He laughed. "Barnaby."

Then I grinned.

"They *were* going to call me Philip. King of horses, or something. But, apparently, I'd assumed my undercover identity to such an extent that I popped out looking like a Barnaby! Exactly like him! Mother said it was uncanny! Also, I rather suspect she didn't want me to become a jockey. She doesn't like little men."

I was finding it hard to hate him. We'd part, spitting, and the next time he saw me, I was his best friend! Either he had the memory of a goldfish—not true, as he was brilliant at picking ancient detail from an opponent's argument and using it against them—or he was all bluster, a tomcat fluffing up his tail. Or—I didn't wish to consider it as a serious option—he still *liked* me.

I said, "I love this theory you have that the baby just 'pops out.' "

"Some babies do pop out. I was done and dusted in two hours!" He smiled. "How about you?"

"Me!" I found myself stammering. "I . . . I don't know. I . . . was adopted." I blushed. "I . . . should ask . . . someone."

Barnaby opened his mouth.

I said, "I don't want to talk about it."

"How are you preparing for the birth?"

"You have a chocolate mustache." I could lick it off.

"Are you?" He licked it off himself and I nearly fell from my chair.

"Well, Barnaby," I said, leaning forward. "If you *really* want to know, some women do special exercises, manually stretching the entrance to the womb."

"Surely there are better ways!"

I wondered if he'd make a cheeky comment about George helping me out, but he didn't.

"Not in my house." It was a joke, but it came out more serious than I meant.

"How is it with George?"

"I've told him I want a divorce." I searched Barnaby's face for a reaction, but his expression didn't change.

"I'm sorry," he said. "How did he take it?"

"Not great."

"You're expecting trouble."

I felt a lurch of fear. "I don't think so."

"What about the baby?"

"What about it?"

"Do you envisage coparenting? Does *he*?"

"Barnaby, I don't want to talk about it. I'm sure George will do whatever I want."

"Cassie, you've been in practice for seven years. Has there ever been a case where the respondent has done whatever the petitioner wanted?"

"It will be fine. I said I don't want to talk about it."

"Hey," he said. "You." And he touched my arm with his fingertips.

CHAPTER 32

_____ *Lizbet*

My life was like an apple core chewed by a rat. No man, no job, no home, no baby, there was no flesh to it—just teethmarks and a few pips. I didn't like it at all. I didn't react well to adversity.

"You are a serious person, Elizabeth," my head teacher said once (bent on persuading me into social work). That was the impression I gave—being a cautious person who preferred to refine my jokes in print rather than risk them in conversation. It wasn't true. I *wasn't* serious. I was deeply shallow. I wanted it to be Christmas every day—sorry, Mrs. Schuller. I loved Tim because he made me laugh. And when you laugh, for that brief moment, all of the shit, the misery—each one of the millions of unique tragedies in the world to be sad and sorry for—is blanked out.

It hadn't been Christmas in my head for a while. It had been December 27, the worst date in the calendar because Christmas Day and Boxing Day are the farthest away they will ever be. Tim and I were so intent on not being serious people, it was a rule in our house that we held a Boxing Day for every occasion. The day after my birthday, the day after Tim's birthday, the day after Sphinx's birthday, the day after Valentine's Day—every one was its own Boxing Day, with time off work and a relevant treat attached. Oh, and we also celebrated Birthday Eve.

And then I—we—had suffered one tragedy, and all the fun had been sucked out of me. I'd been forced to hold unhappiness in my head—the thing I was most afraid of. I'd become a serious, fun-free person, exactly what I didn't want to be. Every resentment I'd ever passed over because life was too short to be bitter—it was, it really was—had caught up with me. There was a whole unruly gaggle of them, and together we'd just about chased all the people I loved out of my life.

I thought of my godson Tomas—I hadn't seen him in so long. Tabitha said that when he was truly furious, he spoke in triple negatives—*triple*! "I don't want *nothing*—not—nothing!"

That was how I'd felt. Just—nothing!

I was slowly starting to feel something—but I was also scared to face up to the damage I'd caused. I couldn't bear the idea of Tim packing up his past with me, starting, fresh and new, with another woman. I feared it because I saw its appeal. The blessed simplicity of sex—when sex was pure lust and joy—instead of a complex tangle of emotions to be hacked through like a hundred years of thorns, before you could come together. I wanted Tim to start again—with *me*. I wanted a kiss to be a kiss, not a sorry, or an I forgive you. Was it possible? I found I only had the strength to wonder, not the courage to find out.

I'd never been a busybody, but now I discovered its appeal. If you concern yourself with other people's problems, you have no time to attend to your own. I'd rung George, confessed my error regarding

Cassie and Tim, and he'd shouted at me. I was grateful. It relieved some of the tension. Cassie had been super-understanding, excessively kind, which put me in a difficult position. If she left her accusations unsaid, I was stuck, right there. I couldn't shut the door on our fight and move on. I needed to be yelled at; it was the only way that my anger and guilt would rinse through.

And I was still brooding about our parents.

I accepted Cassie's reasons for keeping quiet about her adoption. But the more I thought about it, the more strongly I felt that Vivica and Geoffrey shouldn't have given her a choice. They *should* have told me—at the same time they told her. That they didn't was yet one more example of our unequal treatment. It was difficult. I was no longer furious with our parents, but nor was I delighted with them. And I wanted to be. I wanted Vivica to explain her inadequacies as a mother to my total satisfaction, so that I could rewrite the past, look back and think of myself as a beloved child. So that when we kissed hello, there was no rebel chatter in my head.

I had to admit, I *was* a beloved adult. I saw that now. Now that I was taller, with better table manners, our mother and father related to me with a lot more ease. They certainly weren't the parents of a child's fantasy, but they weren't as useless as I'd thought.

I actually felt proud when I thought of them marching round to tell me about the adoption—of course in an ideal world, they'd have told me sooner, but what's a couple of decades between friends? They had come to *me*, and that they had physically made the move toward me, without *me* having to budge—it felt significant. It suggested a gentle shift in the power balance of our relationship; it suggested that I was even seen as an important and respected family member.

It meant a lot to me, also, that Cassie hadn't abandoned *our* ship, jumped in the life raft, and rowed at top speed to her genetic family. I wanted her to know them, I really did. I felt that in some way it would complete her. But a small, selfish part of me was happy and defiant that she was playing it cool with the aunt—not even *playing* it—she actually *was* cool. See, I wanted to say to her blood relatives: "Me, Geoffrey, Vivica—we're not so bad. Cassie had the option to desert us for the newness and glamour of you— but she didn't take it."

And yet.

While the rational adult me was all for forgiveness and understanding, the stampy-footed five-year-old me remained in a sulk. I had a greater tolerance for my parents' mistakes, but I wanted a frank and full apology, complete with tears of regret and shame.

I thought of Tomas, who resisted being told off with all his might. The last time I'd seen him, his baby sister was wearing a sticker on her forehead that read, "Ripen me in the fruit bowl for 4–5 days."

"You do *not* stick stickers on your sister!" Tabitha had bellowed. "She is *not* a toy! Do you understand me?"

"Mummy!" Tomas had replied. "I'm sick and tired of this! If you say that again, I take your computer to the charity shop!"

"Stop threatening me! *You're* the naughty one! I'm the adult! I'm in charge!"

"Don't shout at me, you hurt my feelings!"

Tomas refused point-blank to admit any wrongdoing. However, he was the first—I noticed, and I hoped that Tabitha did—to extend the hand of friendship after a disagreement. The debate would descend into violence, Tomas scratching and biting. Tabitha would roughly haul him out of the room and shut the door. Tomas would scream and cry, then, after ten minutes, bounce back into the room with a cheery, "Mummy, I dress up as a fireman, okay?"—as if they were and always had been on the most courteous of terms. But he was the *tiniest* bit coy—showing, I felt, an awareness that he'd misbehaved and the desire to make up for it in a way that didn't require outright subservience.

Now, that behavior was acceptable, for a three-year-old. It was not quite so acceptable for two *sixty*-three-year olds. The desire to make up for old transgressions by acting in a pleasing way was a great start. But it didn't feel like enough. I wanted a full explanation and a detailed apology too. *Then*, perhaps I could let it go.

Tabitha would tersely remind Tomas of the screaming and biting, and he would say, "*I'm* sorry, Mummy."

And the tension in her shoulders would melt away, and she'd say, in the sweetest voice, "I'm sorry too, darling. I overreacted."

(Not that *I* had overreacted. Well, not much. But like Tomas, my parents were not going to volunteer a verbal apology unless directly informed of the misdemeanor.)

I rang Vivica.

"Darling! You don't know how to download music off a computer, do you? It's not letting me!"

"You haven't got the correct software, Vivica," I said.

"But it's all there, in the files. It just won't go onto the disc."

"Vivica. I—"

"Tim would know. Is he there?"

"*No*, he is *not* here. I'm calling from Fletch's house."

"I'll call him at *your* house, then. Or is he working?"

I made a rude face before answering. "I've no idea. We're not together."

"What! *Still?*"

This conversation was not taking the direction I'd hoped. "So,"

I said. "We were going to talk about me feeling different from Cassie, growing up."

Silence.

"I was . . . surprised not to have been told about the adoption, actually." My heart beat fast. Could this be construed as a reprimand? To rebuke Vivica with even a featherlight touch—it was the same to her as if you'd hit her over the head with a mallet.

"No one was told."

"What, not Cousin Denise? Not Aunt Edith?"

"They were older. Once, Denise made a comment, but your father spoke to her, and it didn't happen again. We didn't want *you* or Cassie growing up feeling awkward, or different, or unequal. You were sisters, our girls, full stop. Everyone understood that."

It was like she lived on a parallel plane and we'd experienced alternate realities.

I felt unequal. *I* felt unequal. I was trying to push the words out, but they wouldn't make the leap.

Vivica took a deep breath, and I bit my lip. Oh, God! She was going to confess. . . .

"Darling Lizbet, oh! I know I didn't treat you as well as I treated Cassie, but the truth is, it was only because she was so difficult, and you were such a good, easy, clever child, you were like a beautiful purring pedigree . . . car, never a rattle or a clank out of you, whereas your sister was more like a pedigree cat, always demanding attention and fuss, and we were scared witless that she would blame us for any problems she encountered later on, but Brownie's Honor, we loved you, our own flesh and blood, just as much, oh! We loved you to the stars and back! But we didn't want to be accused of favoritism, and nowadays, with the research done on adopted children, the potential they have to become lunatics due to the trauma of being ripped away from their natural mother and

parked with a bunch of strangers, we know we were right to pay close attention to Cassie as the child most likely to become a nutcase, but we do see that we neglected our most precious gift—you—all to your credit, of course, but we are so super-sorry about this, we cry about it every night, I'm in analysis and so is your father, three times a week, we're spending three grand a month on therapy, we've mortgaged the house to pay for it, but we feel it's worth it, in order to understand your pain, own it, and atone for it. . . ."

"So, what did you have for lunch today, darling? Marks do the most delicious tartlets—wild mushroom, leeks, or goat's cheese. Have you tried them? The pastry is simply divine. *I'm* addicted to the wild mushroom; it's doing my waistline no good at all."

Eh? *Lunch?* Where was her confession? Where was the emotional outpouring? I was owed some wailing and rending of cloth!

"I haven't eaten yet," I said. I felt itchy with panic. The subject was slipping away, we had to get back to it!

"So, you were saying," I said. "You didn't want Cassie or me growing up feeling awkward, or different, or unequal."

"No," agreed Vivica. "Darling. You must eat. I hate to say it, but Denise was right. You *are* looking a little thin. I'd hate you to look *fat*, but *scraggy* isn't nice either. You can't just survive on chocolate. Shall I bring over a couple of Marks tartlets? We can throw a bit of green over them, chop up some avocado, perfect! What a pity Tim isn't around; he does such a nice mustard vinaigrette."

"Vivica," I said. I shut my eyes. How to *say* this? How to prompt the big confrontation?

"I'm rummaging through the fridge. Baby spinach leaves, here we go. Folic acid. Ah, well, that's good. That's what we're after."

"Vivica," I said again.

"Yes?"

I paused.

"Darling, if I'm disturbing your work, don't worry. *Have* you found anything yet? Any interviews lined up?"

I smiled to myself then, because I finally got it. And I said to my mother, "You're not disturbing me at all. It all sounds lovely. Come over—we'll have lunch together."

CHAPTER 33

Vivica left at two for her manicure ("They've got a lovely new Korean girl at the club; they asked me what I thought, and I said, *'Beautiful.'*") and I waved her off, with a sense of peace. It is not always necessary to hold those who love you—however imperfectly—to account for every mistake. People do change, if only a little. And there are many ways to say sorry, without speaking the word.

Tim did make a good vinaigrette. I was full of folic acid. I was eating like a wolf again; it was just that my body had yet to catch up. Perhaps I would call him.

I called Tabitha instead.

"How—"

"Awful!"

"Oh, I'm sorry! What's wrong?"

Tabitha hissed one word, injecting into it the venom of a snake. *"Nanny!"*

I paused. How many had she been through? This was Nanny No. 666, surely. "Should I . . . come round?"

"You don't mind seeing the children?"

I knew it cost her to ask, and yet I heard the challenge in her tone. "I'd love to see the children."

She said, fast, "I said nothing. I'm sorry. I couldn't imagine your pain and I'm afraid I didn't want to."

"That's very . . . honest of you," I said.

"I suppose, Elizabeth, I was surprised that you were as upset as you were. Because it's terribly common, isn't it? Jeremy's cousin had five failed pregnancies, and she's now a mother of four—a case of be careful what you wish for! But I suppose people react in different ways. I know it's not my business, but *please* don't be scared to try again. Is that terribly crass of me to say?"

I sighed. "Only a bit."

"I was glad you kept away, actually. Dear Tomas is at the stage where he'd put anyone off children, but Celestia is an *angel*, such a pure and breathtaking little personality. I look at her, and she looks at me, and I think, What a gift, you truly are the light of my life; and I think so sadly of you, Lizbet. I think, poor Lizbet doesn't know the glorious, unsurpassable joy of a baby, and thank *God* she doesn't know what she's lost, because the pain would crush . . . Sorry. This is why I say nothing. Once I start, my mouth runs away with me. Jeremy often says, 'I'm going to go out of the room while you talk,' and I can see why. Lizbet, forgive me, I—"

"It's really fine, Tabitha," I said, in a stiff voice. "It would be worse for me if you *only* thought I'd made a fuss about nothing."

"Is it fine, Lizbet?"

"Tabitha," I said. "If it makes you feel better, then, yes. It will be."

I was hoping that when I arrived at Next Door, Tim would be lolling mournfully on our upstairs windowsill like Rapunzel. But he wasn't. I walked slowly and loudly up Tabitha's path—to give him the chance to spot me—and rang the doorbell. She answered after a minute. I was used to seeing her in crisp tailoring, black, white, with her hair in a sleek chignon, very *monochrome*. Today her hair was like fork lightning, and she wore purple mole-skin trousers and a red Adidas top—wardrobe desperation; I knew it well.

"*Color,* Tabitha?" I said.

She laughed, and said, "I feel self-conscious and irritable. I'll change in a minute."

Celestia was still on the hip, in a nappy. She'd doubled in size. She had pale skin and blue eyes. She stared right at me, unsmiling. I felt like a bird watcher sighting a golden eagle.

"Hello, Baby!" I said, thinking, *Oh, oh, oh.*

Celestia buried her head in her mother's chest and kicked her fat little legs like a jockey.

Tabitha kissed me on the cheek.

"I'll wash my hands," I said. Code for "Peace and goodwill to all babies."

But Tabitha didn't ask if I wanted to hold Celestia, and because she didn't, I found that I did. I didn't want to look at Celestia, be-cause I was afraid, but I couldn't take my eyes off her.

"Can I . . . have a cuddle?"

Tabitha looked at me. Then she handed me the baby. I held her, the solid, soft, warm weight of her, and sighed. I felt an itchy sensa-tion around my mouth, as if I might want to eat her up like a chocolate.

"Ah-*ma!*" said Celestia, and she bit me on the shoulder with both teeth, nearly to the bone.

"What a compliment!" said Tabitha, as I swallowed a scream. "She only bites *me*, and I say to Jeremy it's because she loves me so much!"

I stroked Celestia's hair; it was softer than goose down. I

touched my cheek to her head, and smelled the edible scent of her. And then I had to hand her back.

"Thank you," said Tabitha.

I shook my head. There was a dirty diaper on the living room floor. I didn't know whether to ignore it or stick it in the garbage. Tabitha followed my eyes.

"I've just changed her," she said, quickly.

I scooped up the diaper and said, "So, what's with . . . *Nanny?*"

Tabitha's eyes narrowed. "Tomas is *reeling* from all the change in his life: a new sister, a new nursery school. He's insecure, because his routine has been upset, so he's behaving like Saddam Hussein—no disrespect to Saddam Hussein. Tomas needs extra security and reassurance, and I'm doing my best, but I'm also getting the new business off the ground and Celestia isn't sleeping—it's hard."

She paused. "I don't always treat Tomas as I should."

I looked at her.

"I shout, and I sometimes wonder—were a stranger to listen in—if they would know I loved him."

She gazed at the floor.

I said, "Perhaps it's good for Tomas to know that he *does* make you angry if he does a bad thing."

"I think of when he was born, and I see myself treating that beautiful baby with . . . less respect and care than I should, and I feel evil." She added, "I expect you think I have some gall, saying this to *you*."

I paused. "No," I said.

"*Me,* complaining."

I considered. "You were honest. And you explained. This is you and me talking about normal life."

Tabitha put her hand to her throat. "I see! Everyday life is your rehab!"

I paused. "Sometimes," I said, "one bad thing happens—there's a death or you catch your sleeve on the door handle—and all your latent unhappiness falls in on you like a wet sandbank."

"Yes?" said Tabitha, as if I was telling her a bedtime story.

"So . . . if you want to climb out, it helps to identify all the separate grizzles that make up that one big gloop."

"Is that what you did, Elizabeth?"

"Maybe," I said. "Understanding a problem might not make it better. But it helps. So what happened with the nanny?"

Tabitha blinked. "Sorry? Oh! The nanny." She took a breath. "I advertised for a nanny. The agencies—useless—this girl, Sasha, replies. I tell her what I want—she yes, yes, yeses me."

Tabitha gazed at me, almost pleadingly. "I read her references. I didn't have time to *call* them. She has experience—no formal qualifications. She seemed *fun*. She turns up yesterday—yet another change for Tomas that fulfills his worst fear—separation from Mummy. So he tests her—tries to squirt her with the hose. A professional child carer would think, What's the *root* cause of the naughtiness?—might he feel threatened?—and work with him to change it. After two hours, this little madam tells me, 'I've never had trouble bonding with a child before!'

"Like it's *his fault*! He did a wee in our garden, and from the look on her face, you'd have thought he was Prince Charles. He's three! A nanny, with zero tolerance for the childishness of children! And then, she and Tomas sit in his room, and she must have had a face like a poker, because Tomas lashed out. Children only do that if they're frightened. She says he told her, 'You don't like me. I'm going downstairs to Mummy and Celestia, people who like me.' Sasha—stupid, stupid girl—says to me, 'I hadn't even told him off!'

"Tomas is a bright, sensitive child, she didn't *have* to tell him off;

he could sense her loathing! And she turned up for work today—arms folded—in a mint shawl, threaded with silver, and *wedge heels*! She doesn't even tie back her hair; it's like she's auditioning for a shampoo ad! And I asked her to give Celestia her lunch—chicken and mash puree—and Celestia has five bites and turns away. So Sasha puts the bowl to one side!"

I looked blank without meaning to.

Tabitha shrieked, "You don't give up on a baby's lunch after five bites! You sing 'The Wheels on the Bus!' You wave bread in her face, then sneak in the boring food when she opens her mouth!"

Tabitha shoved Celestia at me, collapsed onto the sofa, and burst into tears.

"Tabitha," I said. "She sounds awful, very ignorant—but you can get rid of her." I stopped. "What an unpleasant experience, but you've only had her for two days! I don't *quite* see why you're so upset."

Tabitha looked up. "*I* don't quite see why I'm so upset. Maybe it's witnessing a person actively disliking my child. I hate her. But I'm angry with myself—I *chose* her. I put Tomas through that experience. I see his bewilderment and his unhappiness, and I feel it's my fault." She looked at me—"It's the wet sandbank. It's the gloop!"

I said, "Forget the sandbank. You made a mistake. People do. Accept you made a mistake, and correct it. Sack the bitch."

Tabitha wiped her nose on her sleeve. The divine Celestia had humanized her mother. "You're right," she said. She stood, held out her arms for the baby. "When they get back from the park, I'll sack her. *I'll* be the nanny. I'll work . . . at night!"

I nodded. I supposed a good friend, or a nosy one, would have asked Tabitha to talk through her gloop. But I wasn't hard enough to play Obi-Wan Kenobi just yet. My arms felt empty. I knew I should offer to mind Celestia while Tabitha made up with Tomas. I couldn't. Even holding that baby for a brief minute created a dervish of emotions I fought to control. I'd return her after my allotted hours and be flat on the ground with the not-gots.

"Perhaps," I said, "I could take Tomas out for a morning. Tomorrow! Would that help you? If the baby slept, you might get some work done."

Tabitha was silent.

"I *would* offer to take the baby, but . . . I have no experience with babies."

Twang!

"That would be nice," said Tabitha. "That would be helpful."

"Right," I said. "Tomorrow. Say, ten?"

"Nine thirty?"

The following morning, there was still no sign of Tim, despite my noisiest trip-trapping up our neighbor's path. Tabitha—lurid in another panic outfit—attempted to alert her son to my presence, but Tomas was slumped in front of Nick Jr., mouth open, eyes a-goggle, and apparently incapable of turning his head. I felt a curl of fear.

"Ding dong, the witch is dead?" I said.

Tabitha nodded. "I wrote her a check. She came back from the park, with a sour face. 'We need to talk,' she said. Tomas had chucked sand over her. *God!* She judged his behavior as if he was her *boyfriend*—'My boyfriend chucked sand over me! My boyfriend urinated in the garden! My boyfriend tried to squirt me with the hose!' "

"But now she's gone," I said.

Tabitha took a deep breath. "Yes!" She smiled. There were two raspberry pips caught in her teeth. "Gone, gone, gone! Now. What will you do with Tomas? I've packed his juice beaker, his sunblock, his yellow fleece, his sun hat, his snack—raisins and oatcakes—a change of clothes, *just* in case, but he's very good, although do monitor any toilet session. You could take him to the playground, although he'll want to climb to the very top of everything so you *must* climb with him, and don't let him out of your sight for a second. If he's on a ride, and another mother comes along with a child and says, "Your turn in a moment, darling," smile and pretend you're deaf, *don't* make Tomas give up his place—no one gives a toss about other people's children around here, it's quite accepted! He'll want an ice cream, but say, "We'll see, maybe tomorrow," and here are the wipes, make sure his hands are clean before he has his snack, and he'll want to find a stick, you might have to play at knights and kill the baddies, and if he's——"

"Maybe I should write some of this down," I mumbled. "It's been a while since Tomas and I . . ."

Tabitha looked concerned. "I know!" she said. "I'll give Tim a call, ask him to join you, he's . . . fairly good with Tomas."

My heart pounded, because was this my plan all along?

"He's not *that* good," I heard myself say in a cross voice.

"Oh?" said Tabitha, and I thought of when Tomas last visited. He had a new Action Man and he and Tim were playing with it.

TOMAS: What's that line on his face?

TIM: A scar.

TOMAS: Why?

TIM: His friends were doing a makeover on him, and the mascara wand slipped.

"Tim," I'd said.

"Sorry," said Tim.

Minutes later, Tim was twirling Action Man around in a pirouette. "Da-deedee-da Deedeedee Da-Da-DAH! . . . I'm doing ballet!

I'm doing ball-*eh*! Oh! Here come my friends. What are you doing, Action Man? Humff, I'm doing aikido! Hi-ya!"

"What I mean is, I'd prefer to be with Tomas on my own."

Tabitha said, "When did you last see Tim?"

"Why?"

"When?"

"Why? Is something wrong? Is he working? Or is he . . . socializing?"

"Ask him."

I frowned. "Tabitha," I said. "Tim and I broke up."

Tabitha smiled. "Elizabeth. You made a mistake. People do. Accept you made a mistake, and correct it."

"Ho ho, Tabitha."

But she passed me the phone anyway, and left the room.

I sighed. Then I rolled my eyes, and dialed.

"Hi," I said. "It's me, Lizbet. Um. Look. I've borrowed a young man named Tomas for the morning, and I wondered if you might possibly be free to join us for a park visit? I was thinking that you could do with the practice? . . ."

CHAPTER 34

Cassie

Children distract people, like dogs. You could see why a bad marriage might have them, to fill the awkward silences. But, in fact, there was no undertone,—it was a sunlit pleasure of a morning, and I was crazily pleased that Lizbet had asked me. We took Tomas to the park, a world of a million mothers, buggies, and babies. I did wonder that it might be too much for Lizbet, but she fussed after Tomas with a gentleness that I hadn't seen in her for a while—he had her full attention; she wasn't thinking of herself.

At 12:30 sharp, we delivered a happy, sand-encrusted Tomas back to his mother.

"Will she mind?" I said. "He looks like a Scotch egg."

"No," replied Lizbet. "I believe that dirt is universally recognized as proof of a good time."

And then I drove her back to my house for lunch.

"Can you imagine?" she said, shaking her head.

"Not really." I grinned.

"That *mother*."

"My God! *What* was it?"

Lizbet rolled her eyes. "I said to her, 'Can Tomas borrow the spade to dig a hole?'"

"And she says, 'It's not up to me!' Your face as you had to ask permission from her three-year-old!"

"Honestly! Treat your kids with respect, but there has to be *some* understanding that the parent has the final say!"

I said, "I don't think I'm going to be a liberal mother. I think I'll be quite firm and strict. None of this patting and singing and rocking business, for instance—the baby is going to go *plop*! in the cot, and go to sleep on its own."

Lizbet smiled. "You wait. Pregnant women have a thousand ideals, and then the baby comes, and each ideal is knocked down like a skittle. Tabitha used to treat motherhood like an exact science, as if Tomas were a cake she was baking, and he'd only turn out right if she stuck to precise instructions. Now she's got about three ideals left! I think, when I have a—*if* I—I would like to be a happy mother. Then I'll decide on strategy!"

I liked to hear Lizbet talk like that. Seeing a future instead of one that was scribbled out.

I had more immediate concerns. What to give my sister for lunch. Three days after banishing George, I'd realized that the Fridge Fairy didn't exist. If I wanted to eat—which I did, it was the only thing that stopped the nausea—I actually had to *buy* the food. Happily, Sophie Hazel Hamilton had alerted me to the fact that certain supermarkets now delivered. You ordered your groceries online and, a few days later, they turned up in a van! Fantastic! Less fantastic was the apparent Parkinson's in my ordering finger—I'd managed to invoke eighteen bottles of bleach and eleven chickens.

"You've got all the ingredients for a coq au vin," said Lizbet, surveying the fridge with an expert eye. "These carrots are only slightly soft. Is this wine okay?"

I stifled a squeak. "That's too good for cooking!"

"Cassie, that's such a myth. Don't you remember the plonk Vivica used to throw into every dish, making it taste like vinegar? If you use nice wine, you get a nice taste."

"Fine. Use it! How long will it take?"

"Hours. But I'll make cheese on toast to keep us going. You do *have* bread, don't you?"

Proudly, I opened the freezer compartment, to reveal fifteen Seeded Batches.

We were clearing our plates, when the doorbell rang.

"George!" I said. "Hello! Come in!" (It *was* possible to keep this civil, and I half wished I could video the proceedings, to play to my warring clients, show how it *could* be done.)

"Thank you," said George. "Hope I'm not disturbing you?"

"Lizbet's here, actually," I said.

I wasn't used to courtesy from him. It made a pleasant change. *Now* he didn't take me for granted! Instead of his usual—as Aunt Edith would say—schlock-wear, he was smartly dressed, in a lilac open-neck shirt and pressed trousers. He'd recently shaved, his hair was freshly washed, and a delicious lemony scent of aftershave wafted after him. I'd always liked his aftershave—in fact after we were married I discovered I liked it more than his natural scent, which, later, led me to believe that my instincts had been tricked. Too late, I had realized that the wearing of cologne for romance purposes messed with evolution, it was a morally dubious exercise comparable to the creation of Jurassic Park.

"Ah," he said. "Fun. Well, I won't be long. This will only take a minute."

I smiled, not understanding. "What will?"

George gestured toward the living room. "Why don't we make ourselves comfortable? In *your* condition . . ."

"In my condition, what? I'm pregnant, not terminally ill."

"Sit," said George, marching into the living room and reclining on his favorite sofa. He nodded to Lizbet, who murmured, "I'll take the plates," and glided into the kitchen.

I sat down on a high-backed chair and folded my arms. "What?" I said.

"I've been thinking about our sitch, and—"

"Our what?"

"Our sit-yoo-ay-shun, Cassandra. I've taken advice, and I wanted to inform you of my intended course of action."

"Kind of you."

"Not at all. As you'll remember, when we bought this house— or rather, when *I* bought it—as *I* was the one with fifty thousand—"

"Which your grandmother left you. You didn't *earn* it. We bought this house in joint name. I've paid the mortgage ever since."

"Nonetheless, Cassie, I'm sure you understand that, considering the fact of my initial investment, I would expect at least half the equity of this house, if not more—"

"George, don't be ridiculous! I'm the one who earns the money, you earn nothing! I've put in about five hundred grand! I'm not selling this house; it's *my* house—the baby's room is already painted! What, are you going to turf your own baby out of its house?"

"*I* put it in joint name because we were getting married, but it was *my* inheritance, and taking uplift and inflation into consideration, and my contributions to this marriage in terms of emotion and time and toil, I am entitled to *more* than half of this house, and you know that. In addition, as you so rightly say, *I* can't earn the way *you* can earn, therefore I should have a great big slice of the p—a *larger* portion of the house."

Fuck. He'd done his research.

"I know no such thing; you're talking shit!"

"As a professional barrister," said George smoothly, "I *know* you know that isn't true. Now. Onto the matter of *raising* our child."

"You'll have access." I gripped the seat of my chair to stop my hands shaking.

"I'll have more than that, darling," said George—his placid expression dissolved into a snarl. He took a deep breath and smiled, a smile of hate. "We'll bring our child up together. We'll coparent. As you so rightly say, you're a clever girl, *you* earn the money, *I* earn nothing—therefore it makes perfect sense that *you* go back to work ASAP, and I'll bring up the baby. I'll hand in my notice, and you can support us all."

"Stop it, stop it," I shouted. "Shut up, you've gone mad, this is horrible!"

Lizbet appeared at the door, her face white. "What's wrong?"

George turned and waved her away. "Everything is under control. Please go away."

Lizbet glanced at me. I nodded my head. She pressed her lips together, glared at George, and went.

I stood up, breathing heavily, but my head spun and I could barely speak. "George," I gasped. "This is pure spite. Please, don't do it. You . . . have no interest in babies, no knowledge. It wouldn't be fair on the child. A baby needs its mother. A judge would recognize that."

"I believe the law says—and I quote, *do* correct me if I'm wrong—'A father is equally entitled.' " George leaned back and his eyes shone. "This is *my* baby," he said. "And in recognition of the fact that my child-care skills are a little. . . . rusty, I have enrolled in an accredited course. Shame—*you* don't really have time for that kind of commitment."

I tried to breathe slow and deep. I sipped my water, spilling a little down my front. I placed a hand on my stomach, as if shielding it. I knew what I would have advised a client in my place, and I felt sick at heart. I'd have urged her to wait—to wait until the child was one, or two, before she demanded a split, because this was one way of decreasing the risk of the enemy becoming the prime parent. Even if it meant unreasonable behavior—disappearing abroad until after the child was born, say—anything to ensure that there was no question of him being able to challenge her, make a case for *him* looking after the child for more than twenty-five percent of the time. I'd suggested it before, and more than one woman had acted on my advice, and I knew why: because there was little so frightening as a man threatening your sense of motherhood.

And because—if she didn't—he had the power to take it all away.

"Get out, you bastard!" I screamed. "Just, get out!"

George smiled again, and I threw the glass of water at him. He moved his head, and it flew past him, hit the wall, and smashed.

"Watch it, love," he said. "That's *my* wall." He winked at me, and left.

Lizbet rushed in. Plainly, she'd had her ear to the keyhole. "Cassie, Cassie! Are you okay? He's just bluffing, isn't he?"

I didn't want her to worry. "Yes," I said. "Just . . . bluffing."

"Phew!" she said. "Thank goodness for that! Anyway, he'll be no match for you—you're the expert! You could ask Barnaby to defend you! Or do it yourself! You'd decimate him in court, wouldn't you?"

I nodded, and looked away. I couldn't meet her gaze. Lizbet really was a child in her unshakeable belief that some magical power would step in to save us all. My unshakeable belief was fifty thousand costs, untold misery, and no resolution.

After Lizbet had departed in a cab, I fell asleep on my bed, and woke at mid-evening, groggy and confused. The blinds were drawn, and at first I wasn't sure if it was morning or night. I had a raging headache. The heating was on, yet I was freezing cold. The chill of fear. I lay and stared at the ceiling, both hands on my stomach, and the words ran through my head "I am so sorry, I am so sorry." George's threats from earlier jumped out at me like monsters from closets. I needed to sandblast them off the inside of my head or I wasn't going to be able to function.

I sat up, rubbed my eyes.

I was so scared.

I hadn't been scared for about twenty-three years, not since Lizbet had forced me to stare for four entire minutes at a drawing of a green witch with a wart-encrusted nose in her Walt Disney book. But George had scared me. Like every ruthless villain, he had gone for his opponent's weakest point—The *Kid*. Fuck it, until now, I hadn't *had* a weakest point. I'd always looked after myself—and what on earth is there to fear when you only have yourself to answer to? But now I had a tiny new person to protect, and now that this was fact, it scared the life out of me. I saw the potential for disaster. I needed backup.

I had Mummy, I had Daddy, I had Lizbet, but I needed *more*. I needed all my troops. Not to *do* anything. Just to . . . *be*. As if, by surrounding myself with love, I could beat George. I thought of Holly Golightly, saying of Tiffany & Co., "Nothing bad could ever happen in there." And I thought of the Hershlags' house, where I used to think the same thing. As long as I was under the Hershlags' protection, nothing bad could happen. I'd abandoned them. And now look.

(My *God*! If ever I'd cracked my head open and these thoughts had fallen out, I'd have been a laughingstock in chambers. Barnaby would have died laughing, as would Sophie Hazel Hamilton. I'd have been forced to resign from the bar and take a job more suited to my silly, sentimental, girly personality—say, arms dealing.)

On reflection, I found I didn't care. I stood by my convictions. Love is a battleship. Or something.

I heaved myself off the bed, waddled to my desk, and started to write. *"Dear Aunt Lucille ..."*

CHAPTER 35

Someone had removed my brain and stuffed my head with newspaper. This was not good for a barrister, on the morning of a final hearing in the High Court. Every time an intelligent thought occurred, I had to grab it with both hands and stare hard, or it would pop like a bubble. I no longer *looked* the part. I had the figure of Veruca Salt as she became a blueberry. Hubert had finally noticed that I was pregnant—I was seven months gone and my bump was visible from space. His disdain for my extracurricular activity showed, in that he ignored my advice more brazenly than he did already, if that were possible.

The previous week, I'd said, "This is your last chance to retain control over your private economy. Otherwise, you're allowing a stranger to carve up your financial life. Settle now, Hubert, or you'll be chewed up and spat out."

"I'll take a punt," he'd replied. "Anyway"—he grinned at me—"I was right about the silly cow, wasn't I? Sorting herself out a nice little nest egg. That's going to derail her case."

I felt a lurch of frustration. Or maybe it was heartburn. "It's *not* going to derail her case." I wished he'd stop parroting back phrases he'd overheard. "It's hardly the big dollar, Hubert. It's going to make us look petty. That's all."

I was gloomy with the knowledge that I was about to make a fool of myself in front of a barrister with a good reputation. Oh yes, and he was also a barrister I was obsessed with, and desperate to impress. But never mind *that*. After Barnaby had touched my arm in the coffee shop, I'd avoided him. I liked him too much. Despite his arrogance, he was kind, there was more to his personality than I'd supposed. *He* thought he was fond of me—but he was fond of an image I presented, and I didn't want to get hurt. Men like Barnaby had their fun, but they saw themselves ending up with a certain type: blond, ponies back in Hertfordshire, stick-thin, plum in mouth, a daddy on the bench. (And I'm not referring to a park bench.) Barnaby might present himself as sentimental, but there was no way that he would risk aligning himself—and his glorious reputation—with a woman expecting another man's child.

As for the other man. I was stalling—or maybe I was paralyzed with terror. George's solicitor was whining at me to complete the affidavit, a nightmare form, in which you have to detail every last penny, including the ninety quid in a building society from when you were seventeen, and the £1.13 in loose change in your bedside drawer. I didn't want to swear the affidavit because *then* George would put in his list of questions, and it would be like facing a firing squad. "What's your future earning capacity going to be, and can I have it all?" That sort of thing.

I'd mentioned to Mummy and Daddy that my husband and I were undergoing a "trial separation," hoping that if Vivica read her *People* magazine (which she did, religiously, it was where Lizbet got it from), she would understand. I didn't want to upset them—unusual for me, as there was a time when I'd thrived on upsetting them. I thought it best that they absorb the poison slowly, like slugs absorbing salt. That way there was more chance of acceptance. The last thing I needed on top of The Vengeance of George was parental kerfuffle. I didn't ask what he'd told the Hershlags, if anything—they were away for the summer; they had a flat in Lanzarote, overlooking a building site.

"We're shocked," Mummy had said on the phone, and it annoyed me that they couldn't have *two* responses, as they were, after all, two people. Apart from anything else, I didn't have time for their shock. It increased the burden of guilt.

"I'm sorry," I'd said. "But it will all work out."

If people want something badly enough, and you tell them what they want to hear, they often believe you. Also, I knew that Mummy liked to conjure up a terrible doom from the slightest mishap, so it was best to block off this road to ruin before it was embarked on. Once, in exasperation, Daddy had said—grabbing various objects off the kitchen table for emphasis—"*This* is a glass, and *this* is a plate, and *this* is a coffin!"

Mummy had stared at him and said, "No it's not. It's a salt cellar."

The judge had a cold, and it wasn't helping. Every time she sneezed, Barnaby said, "Bless you, Your Honor." I was back to thinking he was an arsehole. (Although, this might have been more because he'd been brusque with me before court. I suppose he *had* had two binders of financial documents to wade through the previous night; it was bound to put a grouch on anyone. As Barnaby charged four hundred quid an hour, Hubert would be looking at quite a bill—*he* would be paying, even if he didn't know it yet, and I felt a stab of satisfaction, despite myself.)

But then, in the case of *Montgomery v. Hershlag*—would the

judge regard me as an Alissa or a Hubert? Or both? The satisfaction dissolved, and was replaced by dread—like a lump of coal in my chest.

Normally, I'd feel a thrill as I walked into the High Court. Its austere Gothic beauty made you feel both powerful and insignificant: You were part of a historic tradition, but only a tiny dot. And there was a sexy edge to the crisp formality—so much repressed passion beneath the somber dress—not one person arrived in this building because they *didn't* care. But today, I reacted to none of it—I was too preoccupied with my own worries. For the first time, I saw what Lizbet had feared, as her finances dwindled to nothing before her eyes.

At the time, I'd had no patience for her predicament, I felt it was her and Tim's own doing. They'd whined about what they *hadn't* frittered their money on (silver Bentleys, islands in the Caribbean, black diamonds, etc.) and overlooked what they *had* . . . a house that was too big for them, too many posh meals, elaborate holidays, and endless tat. (Tim was king of the fad electronic, the novelty hat, the pointless accessory, and Lizbet was too weak to say, "Enough." I often thought that she was like an indulgent mother with Tim, and it would be the ruin of both of them.)

Now it looked likely that I'd end up living in a flat-pack apartment in a cookie cutter estate on the edge of a motorway, while my indolent ex-husband lolled around in *my* gorgeous pink and white townhouse, eating menopause cake (George was addicted to it—a revolting concoction of nuts, seeds, and dates, the weight and consistency of clay, purloined from an exclusive Hampstead patisserie for a prohibitive sum) and laughing his head off. Now I saw how *simple* it was to lose a fortune, and I blamed Lizbet a little less.

On the subject of losing a fortune, Hubert Fitzgerald was high on adrenaline and unaware of what was about to befall him. He'd dressed as if for a wedding—in a pink shirt, purple tie, and navy suit. He had half a tub of gel in his hair and he reeked of Paco Rabanne. A pressed lilac handkerchief poked out of his breast pocket, *very* dapper. All he was missing was a white carnation. I suppose the Royal Courts of Justice did have the look of a church—what with all the arches and stained glass windows, it was an easy mistake. I'd tried to warn him about Barnaby's cross-examination. "He won't ask you a thing he doesn't know the answer to," I said. "And he'll be ever so courteous, but he's a *rottweiler*. He's going to interrogate you about the transfers you made from this account which— Hubert! Are you listening? Do you understand?"

"Yeh, yeh. Whatever. Bring it on!"

Hubert had watched one too many teen movies starring Kirsten Dunst. Alissa, meanwhile, had the look of a nun. She wore a plain white shirt, a black skirt, and flat black shoes. She had a black velvet Alice band in her hair and wore no jewelry. I was surprised Barnaby hadn't encouraged her to show up in a wimple. Ah, Christ, this was going to be even worse than I'd thought. If only she didn't look *quite* so sweet and good. My toes curled as I thought of what a mean bully I'd seem if I asked her any question more challenging than "Mrs. Fitzgerald, is it right to say that, you are, in fact, a saint?"

Barnaby saw my gaze pass over his client. He glanced at Hubert, and smirked. The *shit*. I looked down, coughed, and shuffled some papers. "Good luck," I murmured, as Hubert was called to the witness box. The judge sneezed three times as Hubert passed and I guessed his cologne irritated her sinuses. I tried not to shrink in my seat as Barnaby fixed on his victim, and smiled. His voice was smooth and seductive, and Hubert fell into every trap, like a particularly stupid rat. Within minutes, the sweat was running down his forehead and into his piggy eyes, and his face was red with impotent rage. He started to stammer and contradict himself, mopping his forehead with his lilac handkerchief, which soon became a crumpled rag. Ditto Hubert. He'd swaggered to the witness box. He returned to his seat almost limping. He glared at me and hissed, "There was about fifty times there, you could have said 'Objection!' Why didn't you *say* it? What's wrong with you? Cat got your tongue?"

"Hubert. We don't say 'Objection!' in this country. That's in the States," I murmured. "And, there was nothing I could object *to*. Not legally. I'm afraid every single question was watertight. I would have jumped on him . . . mmm, at the first opportunity, but there wasn't one. Not a single one. Hubert, I did warn you."

Hubert said nothing; he shot me a look of absolute disgust and stared ahead, like a zombie. I felt my cheeks burn with embarrassment. Already, I looked a right chump.

Alissa walked softly, noiselessly, to the witness stand, her feet slightly turned in, her head bowed, like a geisha. I wondered if she was a member of Equity. I began with a few nonthreatening questions, to encourage her to relax. Then, I drew a sheaf of papers from my folder like a sword from a scabbard. I handed a photocopy to the judge, a photocopy to Barnaby, and—with a syrupy smile—a photocopy to Alissa. Assuming my prissiest voice, I said, "Mrs. Fitzgerald. Would you please read this letter to yourself."

Alissa scanned the letter and bit her lip.

"Mrs. Fitzgerald. Is it right to say that this letter is addressed to your mother?"

"Yes," she whispered.

"It was written to ensure we had full and frank disclosure of your every asset, do you agree?"

"Yes," said Alissa, in a baby bear voice.

"Mrs. Fitzgerald. Could you read out paragraph three?"

Alissa swallowed. "In the interests of full and frank disclosure, we would be grateful," she read breathily, with a girlish lisp, "if you could confirm what assets, if any, of your daughter, Alissa Bryony Fitzgerald, you are holding." Alissa's big brown eyes appealed to Barnaby, oh very *woodland*.

Barnaby, ever gallant, responded. "Your Honor! Madam! I have absolutely no notice of this . . . ambush! I would ask for an adjournment in order to consult with my client and take instruction."

The judge said, "Dough"—her nose was blocked. "This does appear to be relevant. Continue, Ms. Montgomery."

I smiled, and doled out another three photocopies. "Mrs. Fitzgerald. Is this your mother's handwriting?"

"Yes," squeaked Alissa.

"Have you seen this letter before?"

"No," squeaked Alissa.

I nodded. "Can you confirm that there is a bank account in *her* name holding premium bonds of yours that *you've* cashed, totaling four thousand three hundred and fifty-seven pounds? Can you confirm this, Mrs. Fitzgerald?"

Alissa nodded.

"Pardon?" I simpered.

"Yes," she whimpered.

"Thank you," I said, and waddled as primly as my great stomach would allow, back to my seat.

"Blinding!" said Hubert hoarsely. I shot *him* a look of disgust. I felt as low as a worm. And dizzy.

The judge gave me a disapproving stare over her spectacles. I could have sworn she had 20/20 vision and they were plain glass. "I quite see that you had to put this, Ms. Montgomery," she said in a stern voice. "But you did not give us advance notice, did you?"

"No, Your Honor."

"Have you any *other* such points, Ms. Montgomery?"

"No, Your Honor."

"Good."

How *dared* Hubert reduce me to this!

"It was his fault," I wanted to shout. "*I* know a piffling four grand isn't relevant! But you don't know what he's like! He wanted me to prove she was a lesbian!"

The shame roared loud in my ears, and I only woke to reality when the judge said, "I will give judgment on September the first at ten A.M.!"

"Eh?" whispered Hubert. "That's ages away! Law onto herself, bloody nutter!"

I didn't bother correcting him, just sighed inwardly and adjusted my diary.

I took a taxi home, digging in my bag for my lip salve. Get me out of here. Make it better. My fingers closed on an envelope and I pulled it out. It was addressed to Mrs. Lucille Reeves. I jammed it back in. Did *every* occurrence today have to remind me what a coward I was? I had indeed written a letter to my aunt. Maybe one day I'd have the guts to post it.

CHAPTER 36

_____ *Lizbet*

Becoming a journalist seemed an easy option when I was aged eighteen, as it involved no work. But fourteen years later, *un*-becoming a journalist was proving harder, as there was nothing else I was qualified to do, not even gardening—although I did own a hoe. Meanwhile, Fletch had a friend who worked on *Ford Week*. The magazine had a column that involved interviewing celebrities (any person mentioned in the *Daily Mirror* more than twice) about their favorite Ford. No one wanted to do it, as barely any celebrities owned Fords, so they gave it to me. Fletch also knew the editor of *Pussies Galore!*

"Fletch," I'd said sharply when he mentioned it. "I'm not working for a porn mag!"

"On my mother's life, this is a magazine about cats. They're in uproar. A week ago their chief sub defected to *Doggy Style*."

"Oh, stop," I said. But it was true.

I called the editor, and she was distraught. "I know that leaving to go to another cat magazine would be worse from a business angle. But to go to a publication that celebrates *mutts*—"

"Celebrates *what*?"

"Dogs! How could she? It's so *hurtful*!" She sniffed. "Fletch says you're pedantic and you know everything there is to know about cats. Okay. So, what did Cardinal Richelieu, Charles Dickens, and Florence Nightingale have in common?"

"Mm . . . They all owned cats?"

"Well done!"

"In ancient Egypt, the terms 'maau,' 'mau-mai,' 'maon,' or 'mau' all meant what?"

"Er . . . cat?"

"Excellent!"

"A lilac-cream is a what?"

"A chocolate!"

"No, Elizabeth. It's a cat. It's a diluted form of tortoiseshell. But you did very well. Would you be able to do Wednesday, Thursday, and Friday for the next two weeks, and we'll see how we go?"

It went fine. The office was cozy and informal—the features editor brought her white Persian in every day in a basket—and the junior sub was a compulsive tea maker. The editor was incensed one day, because *Your Cat* was persuading best-selling authors to write short stories (involving cats), *and* "We have no one! Elizabeth! Can *you* write a fictional tale—or tail! That's what we'll call it, *Fictional Tails*! Elizabeth, I'm sure you can do it—I mean, fiction—pah!— you make it up! Anyone can do it! We'll introduce you on the cover as 'Best-selling Author Elizabeth Montgomery'—which *is* true— you write for us, and we're the third best-selling cat magazine in the UK!"

"How many cat magazines *are* there in the UK?"

"Three. Now. Of course, there *is* one proviso. The story has to involve a—"

"Dog?"

"Gosh, no, that would be disastrous! A—"

"Cat?"

"Elizabeth, you're psychic!"

Pussies Galore! couldn't be described as the high life, but it amused me, and *Ford Week* was a surreal contrast. So while my career wasn't exactly on the up-and-up (more the across-and-down), I no longer dreaded going to work in the mornings.

I dreaded coming home.

I'd made my peace with Vivica and our father (not that they'd noticed), and Cassie too, just about. But it wasn't enough. Ever since I'd held Celestia, the fact had bounced around my head like a Ping-Pong ball: "I want one of those." I was ready to try for another baby.

Tim's.

Which meant, if I were to approach Tim, and he were to refuse me, I'd have to wave off my hopes and dreams forever. I thought of Cassie, receiving the box of documents from Vivica and our father, and keeping it, unopened, in a dark corner for all those years. When you feared the truth that much, it was better not to know. Although, had she acted sooner, the outcome might have been different. As it was, she'd left it too late, and missed her chance of knowing the woman who'd given birth to her. Were my fears of rejection going to make it too late for *me*—would Tim's and my wonderful babies wait in the wings for all eternity?

I couldn't think about it. I preferred to put my energies into fussing after Cassie—the guilt hangover was a hard one to cure. Not that she *let* me fuss. (I found a Perfect Pregnancy Kit, containing prenatal massage oil "with nourishing sweet almond oil blended with pure essential oils of lavender, ginger, and eucalyptus" and anti-stretch oil, "a rich softening blend of avocado and rosehip . . . with lavender, neroli, frankincense, and mandarin." I couldn't *tell* Cassie what I felt for her, but I hoped that if she read each label, it would be as good as a love letter.)

I handed over the goods on a Friday Night—the only time we ever got to meet. Friday Nights these days were a reduced affair, just Cassie, me, and our parents. It wasn't easy, and I longed for a jolly cousin to visit from Acapulco or Hawaii and inject some *fun* into the proceedings. Alas, I was hard pressed to think of a cousin of ours who could in all fairness be described as "jolly"—and they all lived in unfun places, like Dollis Hill, where they were welcome to stay.

Cassie and I would arrive at eight, and Cassie would say, "Mummy. Are these fishballs fresh?"

And Vivica would say, "Yes! Of course they are, don't be ridiculous!"

And our father would say, "Are those the fishballs that have been in the fridge since Tuesday, Vivica?"

And Vivica would say, "Well, *you're* the one always telling me to waste not, want not!"

Our father would then eat twelve stale fishballs to allow both parties to save face (and presumably to ensure the health of his unborn grandchild). I would ring the next day—bad Jew alert—to thank them for "a nice evening" (I felt more comfortable in a moral sense if I avoided the word "dinner"), and our father would answer in a weak rasp, throat hoarse from vomiting, saying, "Of course it's not food poisoning, it's a stomach bug!"

There was one Friday Night—Cassie was about seven months'

pregnant—where she looked as if she *had* eaten one of Vivica's fishballs.

"Are you all right?" I said. "You look pale."

She nodded, unconvincingly. "Fine. I was hoping to get shot of Hubert Fitzgerald yesterday, but the judge decided to string it out for another two weeks."

"That's annoying." But it didn't account for a complexion straight out of a flour barrel. "And how is it going with George?"

She tensed. "He only wants to take me for every penny, the house, car, everything. *And* he's planning to fight me for custody of Cleetus."

"*Cleetus?*"

"Cleetus the Fetus."

"Cassie! Are you ... I mean ... er, it's an interesting name ... ah, I ... do you know it's a boy, er ..."

She smiled then, a real smile, not a grimace. "It's a *holding* name. A working title. I don't know the sex."

My brain was pedalling hard to catch up. "Wait. George wants the house? He wants to bring up baby while you see it at weekends? I wouldn't trust him with a houseplant! He really *meant* that?"

She nodded, and the skin around her eyes turned pink.

"What do his parents think of this?" I said.

She shrugged. "I haven't heard from them. Either they're furious with me, or they're still on holiday. But George is their golden boy. Whatever he wants, *they* want." Then she smiled—a fake, this time. "Oh well. I'm sure it'll all work out."

"Of *course* it will," I said.

But I didn't believe it.

I wanted to discuss it with her, but I was scared to. The critic in my head crossed her arms and curled her lip. *Oh, Elizabeth. The horse that always backs off at the final fence. You just can't face the fight, you're forever avoiding confrontation, because you're* weak.

"I'm *not* weak," I replied, feebly. "I do *not* avoid confrontation. I took those black avocadoes back to Marks & Spencer—"

The Return of the Black Avocado! Change the record! The pinnacle of all your achievements, we'll put it on your gravestone! How I faced down the junior manager and his teenage acne in the local branch of Marks & Spencer. Man, it was tough—guns, knives, few survivors— then he forgot to call me "Madam. . . ."

I shut my eyes, shook my head. Then I grabbed my coat and caught a cab.

Mrs. Hershlag was too much of a lady to sit opposite a guest with her mouth hanging open, so after three seconds she shut it. Mr. Hershlag stared at his wife and shook his head. His grip tightened on the armrests of his chair, and I noticed that his hands were gnarled with arthritis. Then he turned his gaze on me, his face so full of rage, I nearly whimpered. I placed my china teacup on its saucer with a clatter and braced myself to be shouted at.

"I'm *ashamed*!" cried Mr. Hershlag. "Ashamed!"

"Of me?" I was about to squeak. "But you're not even my parents!"

"Ashamed of my own son!" he added. "That a son of mine would even think of doing such a thing! To his own wife! To his own child! Over my dead body!" He lurched toward the cake knife and snatched it up. "Wait till I see George! I tell him, 'You do this, it's like you take this knife and kill me!' "

"Ivan," said Mrs. Hershlag. "Put down the knife. Elizabeth isn't used to it."

Mr. Hershlag put down the knife (after cutting me an enormous square of lemon cake with quaking fingers).

Mrs. Hershlag dabbed at the corner of her eyes with the back of her hand. "George has told us none of this. He said that Cassie and he were going through a difficult patch, and we were happy to have someone living in the house for the summer. He said she had a lot on at work, and that we were to leave her alone. I don't like to call the house anyway; I don't like to intrude, you see. And Cassie is usually so good at keeping us up-to-date. Better than George. We only got back to London last week. We had no *idea* they were thinking of *divorce*! This is devastating! Devastating! At such a time! The baby's due any minute! How will she manage? Would you like stewed apple and cinnamon with that, dear? I'll—"

The front door slammed, and a voice shouted, "I'm ho-ome!"

"George!" roared Mrs. Hershlag in a voice that made me jump about a foot in the air. "Get in here!"

There was a rustle, and George appeared at the door in cords and a navy kagoul. His face paled when he saw me.

Mr. Hershlag heaved himself up and hobbled bowlegged toward his son. Then he grabbed his earlobe, and George screamed, "Ow!"

"What is the meaning of this?" shouted Mr. Hershlag. "Elizabeth says you bullying Cassandra, telling her you'll take away her home and all her stuff! You tell her she can't even see her own baby? It's rubbish! Rubbish! For crying out loud, what's the matter with you? You don't even tell us you're divorcing?"

"Dad," said George through gritted teeth. "You're hurting my ear."

Mr. Hershlag gave George's ear a yank.

"Argh!"

Mrs. Hershlag stood up and jabbed a finger at George. "You think you're getting money off her? I'll tell you this! You're not taking a penny, do you hear me? Not a penny! What's wrong with you? Haven't you any decency, any pride? You want money, you earn it, you don't take hers, you don't take it off your wife and child! What kind of a man are you? And what's this nonsense you're talking about the baby living with *you*! You don't know one end of a baby from the other! I won't let it happen, George, do you hear me? I put my foot down! This is my grandchild we're talking about! I'll have no bad feeling between you and Cassandra, and I tell you why—because she's a wonderful girl and we love her, and because *you* and your *spite* are not going to come between me and my first grandchild! As long as I live and breathe"—Mrs. Hershlag puffed hard in George's face—"I'm surprised she put up with you for as long as she did!"

Mr. Hershlag tugged at George's ear, "You hear?"

"No," muttered George. "You've probably damaged the entire ear apparatus permanently."

Mr. Hershlag tugged harder. "I said, you HEAR?"

"Yes!" roared George. "All right! I hear!"

Mrs. Hershlag pointed at a hard chair. "Sit," she said. George sat. "Now, you listen to me. Whatever Cassie wants, *you* agree. Do you understand?"

"But—"

"Or by my life"—Mr. Hershlag piped up—"we leave this house to a cats' home!"

"There's no need to threaten me," said George in a sulky voice.

"So," continued his mother. "I suggest you ring Cassie *right* now, in front of us all, and tell her what you've decided. Then you pass the phone to me because *I'd* like to apologize on your behalf, because God knows, I went wrong somewhere. Then you ring the lawyer, tell him of the change of plan. You get him to write a legal letter, saying that you will contest nothing, and you give one copy to us and one to Cassie." She turned to me. "Elizabeth. Is that satisfactory?"

I grinned at George, who slumped in his hard chair. Then I nodded and said, "Very!"

CHAPTER 37

I caught the bus home with a silly grin on my face, which meant that I got a double seat to myself. George had a nerve. Tim would never behave like that to me, no matter how bad things got.

And how bad *had* they got? I'd made them get bad, because I was in such a fury at my life that I'd wanted to destroy it. Thing was, when my laptop malfunctioned, I wanted to hurl it through the window, yet I had the common sense to hold back. Why couldn't I apply the same principle to my relationship, which was a lot more precious than my laptop?

Tim knew everything about me. He knew I liked to sleep with one ankle on top of the duvet (otherwise I got too hot) and my ears covered (otherwise I got too cold). He knew I liked to keep each component of a meal separate on my plate (Vivica would dump the gravy on top of the peas on top of the potato on top of the meat until the food resembled a rubbish heap). He knew that I hated sitting in a car poring over a map—I liked to devise a route in the comfort of my own kitchen. The only thing Tim didn't know was how to prevent a miscarriage.

I needed to see him—I needed to see him so much, I didn't even stop off at Fletch's on the way to scrub up nice. Although, I did wipe the grease off my nose with the back of my hand. (In a longterm relationship this is what counts for grooming.) As I walked fast toward our house—or his house—I thought about what I knew about *him*.

I knew that if he lost his keys, mobile, or wallet, they were either in the car, a pocket, or his backpack. (After over thirty years of living in his own head, Tim still didn't know his own hiding places.) I knew that Tim often talked with his mates about how much he'd enjoy shooting dead various animals (rabbits, pheasants, deer), but the one time he'd got it together to go fishing, he'd released all the live bait into the garden because he felt sorry for it. I knew that if Tim were sat in a café eating chips and five lads made a run for it without paying, Tim would chase after them and encourage them to extract money from an ATM to pay the nice lady owner. (Who would then treat him to a full English breakfast, which he'd eat grinning.)

That was the man I'd quit on.

It had been intensely annoying to me that everyone—Vivica, Cassie, Aunt Edith, the Man in the Moon—had been pressing me to get back with Tim. After all, no matter how well matched we appeared in public, none of them *actually* knew what our relationship was like when we were alone. For all they knew he was beating me to a pulp, and I was slowly poisoning him with salt. It was sheer coincidence that our relationship was wonderful and that, in fact, they were all right.

Tim opened the door with a towel round his waist and his stomach sucked in.

"Hello," I said. "Do you mind?"

He looked surprised—shocked, even—to see me. But not unhappy. He stood aside for me to walk in. "I'll get a T-shirt," he said.

He galloped up the stairs, and reappeared ten seconds later in a blue T-shirt and beige shorts.

"Have you got underpants on under those?" I said, before realizing that it was a question I was only entitled to ask as the longterm girlfriend, *not* the longterm girlfriend whose services had been dispensed with a while back.

"*Yes,*" said Tim, rolling his eyes—which I took as a good sign.

I smiled. The house was a pit. I spotted two apple cores on the side in the front hall and there were so many odd shoes and discarded clothes and backpacks and newspapers and other debris on the floor, it was hard to find space to put my feet.

"After you left, I got a cleaner," said Tim.

"Crikey," I said. "She's awful."

Tim sighed. "She resigned, after one week. She said, 'I'm a cleaner, not a tidy-upper.'"

I looked at him and wanted to throw myself into his arms, but I knew I couldn't. Wasn't "sorry" the hardest word to say? Ridiculous, it was only two syllables.

"I'm sorry," I said.

"I'm sorry too," he said.

I stepped toward him and gave him the biggest hug. After one second he squeezed me back, so hard I squeaked.

"I love you," I said. "Please have me back."

"I love you," he said. "I'm so glad you're back."

"I'm so much better," I said. "I'm good to go!"

"Me too." He held me away from him and said, "Let's look at you."

I pouted.

"You're beautiful," he said. "My beautiful girl."

We fell into a kiss, and Tim groaned and said into my hair, "Let's go upstairs."

"Okay," I said, giggling, and we ran upstairs holding hands.

I was pulling him toward the bedroom, when I realized he was pulling me *away* from it.

"Wait," he said. "I want you to see this."

He was standing outside the baby's room. My heart thumped. It was a test! He wanted to see if I *was* better, or just faking. I took a deep breath as he gripped the door handle. I was ready for it—the pale blue walls, the polished floorboards, the lamp shade in the shape of a dolphin, the tiny clothes, still folded neatly on the changing table, waiting for a tiny person to wear them. I'd let that tiny person go, because I had no choice. I would never forget her, but I was ready to welcome the *next* arrival if—please God—there was one. Tim opened the door, and I actually flinched.

"What have you done?" I shouted. "Where is everything? What have you done with her clothes?"

All of it. *Gone.* The lovingly polished floorboards—vanished, buried under wall-to-wall brown sisal matting. The walls were claret red, as if to hide blood spatter. No dolphin, instead a gloomy white cotton lamp shade that fell in uneven drapes like a shroud; a vase of dead—sorry—dried flowers (who *bought* those anymore?); a framed sketch on the wall of a naked woman (by Tim's mother, who'd taken life drawing classes—she'd scrawled the face in later; it reminded me of *The Scream*); a desk; a chair; and a bookcase, full of my best girl books—Elizabeth Berg, Adriana Trigiani.

I looked at Tim and he was chewing the skin around his thumbnail. He saw me look at him and he said, "This is your new study!"

I yanked open desk drawers to see if they might contain a tiny yellow undershirt with a red embroidered butterfly. I found Tipp-Ex and an eraser. "It's not my new study!" I panted. "It's a room of death!"

"A room of death! What the hell are you talking about? Room of death! I thought—"

"Where have you put her clothes?" I shouted. "Where are they?"

"I threw them in the trash!"

"You—"

"They're in my bedside drawer, you nutcase!"

"Oh my God!" I tried to run past him, but he caught my wrist and pulled me to him until his face was an inch from mine.

Then he yelled, "I thought you *wanted* this! Because you didn't want another baby! I thought you said you were better! You're not! You're the same! You're going to let it ruin your whole life, when this happens to millions of people again and again, and they just get on with it and try again until they get a family—"

"You don't *know* that. Some people end up childless, and you don't know what damage it's done inside!"

"What do you want from me, Elizabeth? Shall I put the room back the way it was and get you a black veil and you can sit in there for the next fifty years?"

"Tim—"

He let go of my wrist and sat in a ball, hugging his knees, and crying. "I can't win, can I? I can't win! It was my baby too! It was my baby too! And you never acknowledged that, you blamed *me*, like I killed it, like you were the only one in pain, and you never apologized—you *never* apologize! This is all your shit! You say sorry, but you don't *know* the meaning of the word!"

"Tim," I said, and crouched beside him. "Tim," I said. "Please forgive me. I've been a monster. You're so right. You're so right. Forgive me. I don't blame you. It was your baby too." I stroked his hair, and he let me. His eyes were red. I crawled closer, and hugged his head to my chest, and stroked his back.

Eventually, he pulled away, and sniffed. "I even laid the carpet," he said. "It was a bugger. I had to stick it with superglue in the end. I bent all the tacks."

"It's a very good study," I said. "It was a shock. That's all. I wasn't expecting it. I saw it and it was like a cover-up, like you were pretending the baby never happened."

"Lizbet," said Tim. "Not every action has ten hidden meanings."

"I know."

"And how could I pretend it never happened when it's all I've thought about for the last five months? I'm not the enemy. I'm the *father*."

I bowed my head.

"But I don't want to go *on* and *on* about this. I want us to have a *life*. That's not disrespectful, or callous, because I will always think about that baby. It was my *baby*."

"I know," I whispered.

"Do you?"

"I do now."

"At some point, you have to start seeing the good, not the bad."

"But," I said—because I felt I didn't deserve to be *totally* the bad guy—"you didn't *say* you were thinking about the baby. As far as I could see, you were just doing a lot of work."

"Elizabeth," said Tim, with a note of irritation in his voice. "That's the clever thing about thoughts. They occur inside a person's head."

I laughed, but I wasn't amused. "I take your—"

"So *you* mourn the baby in an all-singing, all-dancing manner— enough for both of us—while *I* chop on with the selfish business of pursuing my career. That's how you saw it."

"Tim! Of course not! I mean, of course, I see what you're saying. I also threw myself into work." I paused. "I *didn't* mourn the baby in an all-singing, all-dancing manner. That's a really nasty thing to say. Like I was putting it on."

"Right, so there was no drama-queen, poor-me element to your behavior? Not eating till I could have hooked a clothes hanger off your collarbone! This false *gaiety*, making everyone uncomfortable? Pouring yourself drinks all the time like JR! Locking yourself in the bathroom, running a never-ending bath and not answering when I shouted "Are you all right?" so I had to kick the door down?"

"I had my ears submerged! And you *wanted* to kick the door down."

Tim sighed and ran his hands through his hair. "And if I did, doesn't that tell you something?"

I nodded. "Yes," I whispered. "I'm sorry."

"Forget it."

This was not going to plan. "Tim. I came here to make up with you, not make things worse."

"You're not ready to make up with me."

"I am!"

"No, you're *not*!" He flung an arm out. "You say you are, but then I show you the study and you freak."

"I wasn't *expecting* it. That was all." I took a deep breath. "I actually came here because I'm ready to try for another baby. So, ideally, I suppose I'd have liked the room to be . . . *altered*, so this baby has its own style, so, say, an elephant lamp shade, instead of a dolphin lamp shade, and maybe the floorboards could be painted another pale color, maybe mint green, and—"

"Stop," said Tim.

"Oh!" I said. "Why? But . . . But I thought *you* were ready. I thought *you* were ready to have another baby months ago."

"I was," said Tim. "I am. But now"—he hesitated. "I'm not so sure I want it to be with *you*."

CHAPTER 38

_____ *Cassie*

I don't go overboard on smiling. It gives people the wrong impression. But then George rang to apologize for his malicious behavior, to assure me that he wouldn't contest so much as a teaspoon, and was there anything he could do to help, buy some maternity pads, perhaps, or an electric breast pump? And while I knew that Mrs. Hershlag was most certainly holding her son at gunpoint (with Mr. Hershlag in the background, posing the tip of the bread knife at his be-cardiganed chest), I felt so light and happy and relieved that our baby would be born into a house of peace, the smile refused to budge.

I rang Lizbet to tell her that George had retracted all threats—I knew she'd want to know—I'd been surprised and touched at just how indignant she'd been on my behalf, actually. Perhaps she didn't think I was a spoiled brat. She didn't pick up, so I left a message. I was secretly thankful; the following morning was the grand finale of the Fitzgerald case, and I didn't need a ninety-minute squeal-filled phone call jangling every nerve just before bed—I knew how

Lizbet would react to the good news (vehement joy and loud enthusiasm), and sweet as it was, she'd have the same effect as a triple espresso.

"Hello there!" I said to Barnaby, who was in front of me in the coffee shop queue.

He spun around, and raised an eyebrow. "Cassie, hell-*o*!" he said. "You look cheerful, for someone who's about to crash and burn." He grinned. "Ah, you see, your mind's on motherhood now. You're not *really* bothered that I'm going to *slaughter* you this morning, that your client is going to have to pay every single cost ever invented, including my bus ticket and my graduate loan; you're way too busy thinking, Ooh, should I buy the choo-choo train mobile for baby Clyde, or should I buy the one with little sailing boats? You don't give two hoots that *my* client is going to make out like a bandit, and—ah! Mr. Fitzgerald! Good morning to you! Didn't see you come in there! And what a nice day for it!"

Hubert glared. "You're supposed to be at each other's throats! You look as thick as thieves."

Barnaby coughed. "I applaud your simile. Most apt."

Hubert shot him a scornful look.

"It's all right, Hubert," I said—a blatant lie as far as *he* was concerned. "Mr. Alcock is feeling the heat, and resorting to childish taunts, and outlandish threats, all of which I may sue him for at a later date." I stuck my nose in the air, pointed a finger at Barnaby, and hissed, "Enjoy your cappuccino, *sonny*. We'll see *you* in court!" Then I scurried out of the coffee shop, as I knew if I looked Barnaby in the eye, we'd both fall about laughing.

"Right!" I said to Hubert, all mirth evaporating as I met his cold gaze. When I was a kid, there was a craze at school for a product called Slime. It came in a can and was bright green and slippery. Hubert had the aura of Slime. He also had jug ears and hair that stuck up like a toilet brush. What had Alissa seen in him? It is true that nice people get together, but it is equally true that nice people get together with utterly *awful* people. No idea why.

"Right!" I said again. "Are we ready?"

"No," said Hubert, sulkily. "I went in there for a cuppa. Bernice has me a brew, piping hot, waiting on my desk, without fail, every morning, rain or shine."

Bernice is probably hoping you'll scald your mouth, I thought.

"Oh, poor you!" I said briskly. "Never mind! Chop, chop, we don't want to be late, do we?"

Man wrangling. Certain men, of a certain age, reacted well to it. They did as they were told, as if they were twelve again and I was matron.

In court I glanced at Alissa—her shiny brown hair was tied back in a modest ponytail at the nape of the neck (none of your brazen-hussy ponytail, jutting out high and insolent from the crown). She wore black kitten heels, a somber gray suit, and a slick of pale red lipstick, which made her skin seem whiter and darkened the shadows around her eyes. She caught my gaze and looked right through me, and I thought, Oh I know, absolutely. (I wasn't bothered. If she liked me, I'd have been insulted.)

Poor Hubert. And I mean that in *every* sense. When the end came, it was swift. The judge fired a few questions at Hubert. Then she zipped straight into her judgment.

"This is a case where Mr. Hubert Fitzgerald decided to divorce his wife Mrs. Alissa Fitzgerald, after twenty-eight years of marriage. He wishes to set up home with a new partner. He offered to provide Mrs. Fitzgerald with monthly maintenance payments of a thousand pounds, on the basis that his business has a modest turnover and he can't afford more, and that her contribution to the marriage did not entitle her to more. He is suggesting that Mrs.

Fitzgerald find herself a menial part-time job to supplement his contribution. Mrs. Fitzgerald has said that this budget is inadequate, and that she requires more to live on and to provide for their two teenage children. She includes adequate housing in this. Having examined Mr. Fitzgerald's assets, liabilities, income, and outgoings, I find Mr. Fitzgerald has *greatly* underestimated the financial performance of his business. I prefer the evidence of Mrs. Fitzgerald. She will need a proper house, and it is unreasonable to expect her to go back to work when she has young children. As for the four thousand pounds held in her mother's name"—the judge gave me a reproving look over her spectacles that, I estimated, would cost Hubert fifty thou—"Ms. Montgomery, I found that a particularly unattractive part of your cross-examination."

I pursed my lips and hung my head. I felt mortified. There was a downside to losing quite so robustly: I looked like a crap brief. I avoided Barnaby's gaze. I couldn't have borne it if his expression had been smug. Or worse: sympathetic. Pity—ugh.

The judge then made a few fairly obvious points about the law, during which Hubert failed to stifle a wide yawn—another fifty thou—before awarding Alissa the two-million-pound Georgian house and all its contents, monthly maintenance payments of ten thousand pounds not including the children's school fees, a lump sum of two million pounds, and forty percent of all Hubert's future earnings. *Plus*, the Humvee that Hubert was having shipped in from the U.S. (he hadn't told me about that, either) and Barnaby's costs.

Hubert, who had been slumping in his seat—another fifty thou—jumped to sit upright, and he was in such a panic, like a drowning man, his leg shot out from under him and he kicked me hard on the ankle. He glared at *me*, and didn't say sorry. He was as red as a beetroot, and his eyes bulged. He took a gulp of water, and choked on it. I made an "Ah, well" face at him, and he bared his teeth.

Alissa, meanwhile, was crying and hugging Barnaby. I sipped my water and shook my hair back, trying to look unbothered. I *was* unbothered at the verdict—served him right—but I hated to lose, *whatever*—plus, Alissa was hanging off Barnaby's neck, and I thought, Not too close, old girl. Still, she *was* looking at a cool five million. Any excuse. I'd have hung off his neck for a fiver.

Hubert recovered his composure pretty fast. He stood on the steps of the High Court, flipped open his mobile, and said, "The bitch is dispatched. I'll pick you up as agreed." Then he hailed a cab and jumped in, with a curt nod in my direction. I stared after him, shaking my head. Admittedly, Hubert had been stripped of everything except his underwear, but I had *tried* to limit the damage. I'd warned him and warned him, and *he* hadn't listened, so he only had himself to blame. He might acknowledge that!

I shrugged inwardly (outwardly, there was no movement). What I really wanted was a cigarette and a glass of wine. I swish-swashed to the coffee shop and ordered a bottle of Badoit, a peach smoothie, and the biggest chocolate brownie they had. ("I'll have that one, three across, second row from the back; it's a lot bigger than the others," I said, so there could be no mistake.) Then I sat in the window, like a particularly gloomy prostitute in Amsterdam.

I *was* happy, but the morning had momentarily derailed my happiness. I thought of Barnaby and me, flirting—there was no other word for it—in this same coffee shop only a few hours before. We were equals then. *Now* I was a lowly jerk, who'd had her bottom smacked in front of the whole class. Inches away, a large face pressed itself against the other side of the glass, nose and lips squashed flat and white, eyes crossed—I reared back in fright, before I realized it was Barnaby. He grinned and trotted in.

"You're vain, so here's a tip—don't do that," I said, with only the lightest touch of sulkiness.

His grin increased in wattage. "I love a bad loser," he said. "I always think a good loser is just a loser. Can I buy you a drink? Bitter lemon?"

"Barnaby," I said. "I am *not* in the mood."

"It wasn't your fault. You did everything you could for that silly fuck."

"Barnaby!" It was the first time I'd ever heard him swear. I must say he swore beautifully. "*Please* don't try and make me feel better about losing. It's not possible."

"I'm not trying to make you feel better. I'm stating a fact. The pleasure of winning was muted. It wasn't a fair fight. It was about as hard as robbing a baby of his cookie."

"I agree," I said. "You're not trying to make me feel better."

"You were pretty chipper this morning, Montgomery. What happened? The verdict was a given. It can't be a shock."

"It's like someone dying after a long illness," I said. "You think because you know what's going to happen, it won't affect you. Then it does and you're knocked flat." I glared at him. "You better not put this in one of your books. I tell you, if I'm flipping through *The Totally Fabulous Guide to Financial Dispute Resolution* this time next year, and I see a reference to the Rupert Fitzherbert Case, *you* are for it!"

He giggled. It was very attractive. "What are you doing now?"

I glanced down at the bump. "I thought I'd finish this brownie, then go on to a club." I smiled. "On the whole, I'm extraordinarily demanding, but right now, all I want is a jacket potato with lots of butter, a hot bath—not *too* hot, and just three inches of water—and then, I want to fall into a bed with clean sheets, and sleep for twelve hours, without being kicked."

"*I* don't kick in bed," said Barnaby. I looked at him, and he blushed, and said, "But of course! You were referring to bébé Clyde! The little scamp! I knew that!" He paused. "Any update on George?"

I kept looking at him, and I said, "George backed off. His parents heard and went loopy. Now he's offering to buy me breast pads and such. So, I think it might turn out okay with him. A *good* divorce."

Barnaby said, "That's terrific news. Terrific. I'm delighted. Not that we wouldn't have crushed him to a fine chalk in the witness box, but we can always do without getting our knickers in a twist—terrific!"

I smiled. I liked the way he talked, as if *he* was a part of my divorce. "Thank you. So what are *you* doing now?"

I found I couldn't wait to hear his answer. I was intrigued to hear how the great Barnaby Alcock celebrated victory. Did he fire off a few cannonballs in his extensive backyard?

Barnaby opened his backpack and got out his ankle clips. "*Ideally,*" he said. "I'd like to run you a bath, bake you a potato, wash your sheets, and tuck you under them. What do you say?"

I said, "You want to *what* me under the sheets?"

"*Tuck* you," said Barnaby. Then he blushed. Again.

"Oh," I said. "You wouldn't like to have sex with me?"

"Cassie," said Barnaby. "I *dream* of having sex with you. In fact, I think about it so often that I've probably ruined it for myself. If, theoretically, of course, it were to happen. Ever. Or tomorrow morning, after you've had the twelve-hour sleep."

I tried to keep my face stern. "Barnaby. Look at me."

Barnaby looked. "I think you're God's earth beautiful."

"No," I said. "Look at my situation."

"I know," he said. "I should find a woman with a less . . . *complex* situation. But, she wouldn't be you. And I do like babies. They're like little animals. I might make a hash of it at first, giving it a water bowl instead of a bottle, but I—"

"Barnaby," I said. "For the love of God, will you stop talking for a minute, and kiss me."

CHAPTER 39

Lizbet

I've always been bad at arguing. Cassie was always good. I preferred it that way. She was always convincing me to do things I didn't want to do. I convinced her that she was right. I didn't mind—I didn't want the responsibility. I knew—from my experience of being convinced—that while it is possible to win people over to your opinion, this is only a good outcome *superficially*. Because after a while, some tiny thing will go wrong, at which point they will revert to their original viewpoint, and resent you for bullying them out of it (and for exposing their weak will)—so you won't have won after all.

If Tim didn't want my children, then I wasn't going to argue. I just wouldn't have children.

I informed him that I'd return the following day to collect my thesaurus, my thermal vest, and other essentials. It occurred to me that I now had the rest of my life to correct the nation's grammar. I should feel grateful that—at least, within my head and possibly a notebook, in which I'd detail each mistake and my amendments—the world would now be orderly, regulated, and error-free. I also had to think about keeping myself warm, as there was no one else to do it. The next afternoon, I found my belongings in a plastic bag on the doorstep.

I was walking away from the house with a face like a barracuda, when Tabitha emerged from next door. She was dragging an enormous black garbage bag along the ground, and muttering.

"*Not* a woman's job, but no, I have to do bloody everything—Lizbet! Darling! Come in for a coffee." She heaved the bag into the wheelie bin like Atlas dropping off the planet. "We've got a new coffeemaker—it grinds the beans from scratch—I said to John Lewis" (Tabitha often spoke of John Lewis as if the store were a personal friend) " 'I need a machine that wrings the beans for every last drop of caffeine' and the woman recommended this beast! It cost over a thousand pounds—which Jeremy wasn't too happy about—but it's worth it. I see it as a serious investment in staying awake. Darling, you seem quiet."

"I'm fine," I said. I was about to say, "Except Tim doesn't want to have a baby with me—so no babies for me—a bit of a spoke in the wheel of my life," when I decided against. I was thirty-three, not three. In fact, I was about to be thirty-four. I had to make the choice to live my life as it was, not as it might have been.

"It's my birthday on Sunday week," I said, instead.

Tabitha washed her hands at her porcelain sink, dried them on paper towel, and stared at a thick instruction manual. After a minute, she looked up. "Your birthday!" she cried. "Ooh, I love birthdays! What have you got planned?"

Tabitha set a lot of store by birthdays (her own in particular). Jeremy was always required to lay out the red carpet—dinner reservations, bunting, fireworks over the Thames—or else. Whereas I felt she was at the age where you started scaling *down* the celebrations.

I said, "Last year we went to the seaside."

It was one of our rules. You don't work on your birthday. Ever! I'd taken the day off, and Tim had driven us to Botany Bay, near Margate. It was a lovely sandy beach, not crowded, everyone eating hot dogs behind windbreaks. All the men had tattoos, and most of the women. Everyone was brown, except me, and I wondered if I was the only person who spent most of every summer indoors. Tim asked if I wanted a coffee—there was a little blue hut in the corner selling food and drink—and I said, "Only if it's filter." Tim laughed and said, "Lizbet. Look around you."

I'd looked, and felt my middle class primness like a boil on my neck. That was the thing about Tim—he teased but there was no malice. That was my trouble. I *appeared* easygoing, but I took a lot of patience.

"The seaside!" cried Tabitha, tossing the instruction manual and reaching for the *cafetière*. "What a super idea! We'll all go! A family day out! I'll make a cake—well"—she sighed, and didn't quite meet my eye—"I'll probably buy it, if the truth be known. I don't have a minute these days. Well. That's not strictly true. I have *a* minute, at least four times a day. But I need *more*. I need, say, four lots of *twenty minutes*."

I felt that Tabitha wasn't content. Or maybe it wasn't that. Maybe she just required backup. I saw that she loved her children, more than anything, but that she couldn't always cope. It made me think of Vivica, and reevaluate. As a little girl, I was renowned for my compliments, mainly to our mother.

"Mummy, I like your dress."

"Mummy, I love you."

"Mummy, I like your shoes."

"Mummy, I really like you, Mummy."

And Vivica would reply—tersely, and with a tense look on her face—"Thank you, darling. I like you too."

If I didn't initiate the conversation, I never got a compliment from my mother. When I did, I could eke one out of her, but the jagged look on her face was never absent for long. Maybe she just wanted everything to be perfect for us, and was forever disappointed that we, as children, made perfection impossible.

Tabitha seemed to need a day at the beach—her relationship with Jeremy functioned better in a group—so I didn't resist. I had nothing else planned, and I had no wish to be alone on my birthday with the Morrissey album of my own mind for company. I decided to invite Cassie. She'd left an ecstatic message on my phone the day before, announcing that Ivan and Sheila had forced George to call off the dogs. I was piqued that his parents had omitted to mention *my* part in his downfall, but tried not to be. I wasn't naturally selfless—I thrived on being told what a delightful person I was.

I took after our mother in so many ways it was embarrassing.

I decided to invite Vivica and our father too. They could be incorporated into Tabitha's Could You Hold the Baby for a Sec roster. (Leaving Tabitha free to scour *Homes & Gardens*, Foxtons' brochure of "Unique & Exclusive Properties," and a thousand overpriced catalogs peddling childrens' clothes, toys, and various unnecessary handmade wooden accessories.) Some people invite parents and siblings to their birthday events without even thinking, but for me it was a bold move, as my natural assumption was they all had better things to do.

"Darling, we'd *love* to come! Will I, as the matriarch, be required to bake a cake? Thank God! I'll send your father to Tesco. What's that, Geoffrey? He says we'll have to set off at nine sharp to avoid the traffic. He's looking it up on the computer now. He says it shouldn't take longer than an hour and a half."

As I recalled, the journey took *two* and a half hours, but I didn't comment. Our father was a mild-mannered and peaceable man, but he drove like a devil with his bum on fire. Tim and I followed him once to a wedding out of town and, in our efforts to keep up, found ourselves airborne for most of the journey. "I doubt," Tim had said, "if there was any wear and tear on his tires at all."

Cassie's response also surprised me.

"Of course I'll come."

"Really?"

"No. I'd prefer to sit at home and listen to the roof contractors across the road cutting metal."

I smiled. "It wouldn't be a strain on Baby Cleetus?"

"Baby Cleetus would like it known that he'd be much amused by a day at the beach."

"The toilets are a bit third world. I'll bring packs of tissues and antiseptic wipes."

"Oh, God, Lizbet," said Cassie, suddenly. "You're far more suited to this mother thing than I am."

"What!" I said, my voice shrill. "Don't be silly. What are you talking about?" All of a sudden, my ugly inner thoughts came pouring out—a great writhing brainlike mass of black worms— *thunk!*—landing on the carpet. "Please, Cassie, I know you mean it in the kindest way, but the fact is, I'm *never* going to be a mother, so don't say it again. It's too painful, and I can't think about it. I saw Tim on Friday, and he . . . ended everything. He said he doesn't want children with *me*. So that's final. Because *I* don't want children with anyone else."

Cassie was silent. Then she said, "If that is really true and you're not exaggerating—"

"I'm not," I said sharply.

"Then," said my sister—a woman of absolutes—"you strike him off, and begin again. You want children more than anything. Don't make a decision that goes against your heart's desire" (What! Pregnancy was turning her soft.) "because you're afraid to hope. You can still hope. You can still wish. There's no point in living if you don't wish for anything. You might meet Someone Else."

I was touched, not convinced. What spurned woman wants *Someone Else*? Someone Else was a man who folded his socks, had a select cache of racist jokes (A man's home is his castle—say what you like there!), disliked badgers, couldn't spell anagram—or tell you what one was. I wanted a Tim! Someone Else wouldn't *get* me. I was too weird, too special interest for Someone Else.

I'd been going out with Tim for three months when I walked into the living room with an open pack of pancetta.

"Tim," I said. "Is pancetta mainly fat?"

"Yes. Why?"

"Oh, okay, then, I'll put it back."

"Why? What have you done with it?"

"I ate a strip, just the red bit."

"Babe, it's *raw*. It's raw bacon."

"Oh! Is it? I thought it was like Parma ham."

I studied the pack, accusingly—smoked, blah, unique flavor, blah, and in tiny (capital) letters, MUST BE COOKED. Tim was smiling up at me from the sofa, but I was feeling like a woman (never mind a *Jew*) who'd eaten raw bacon. You are what you eat. I was a pig. I'd literally spelled it out for him! He'd called me *Babe*. That was the name of a pig, right?

"Lizbet," Tim had said. "It's . . . *similar*."

I dragged myself back to the unappetizing present, and said to

Cassie, "I don't want kids with someone else. So . . . it looks like I won't be having them."

"You are so like Vivica I could scream. Plate, bowl, coffin, remember? See things for what they *are*. Know the difference between a challenging situation and a tragedy."

"Yes," I said.

"And yet," she added, her voice gentle. "There are so many differences between you and Mummy. You always consider how everyone *else* might feel, or what they might need. I'm going to be a crap mother. I'm only good at thinking of myself."

"That's not true," I told her. "And how can anyone know how they'll be as a mother, until the baby's right there?" I paused, relieved of a chance to change the subject. "Are you worried about doing this without George?"

"No. And—George will be around. I realize I want him to have a part in this. Despite everything. It wouldn't be right otherwise. But he'll have to fit in with *my* plans. Do you remember Barnaby?"

"The blond six-foot super-barrister with the beauteous face, fabulous physique, and charming conversation? No, I don't recall."

"He seems to think he'll be sticking around."

"Cassie!"

She was trying not to sound too happy, I could tell.

"We'll see."

"My God!" It was good to feel another person's joy—it made me feel human. I realized also that it didn't matter if she was unaware that I'd helped tame George. All that mattered was, I'd helped to make my sister happy. I was like a celebrity backing a worthy cause without boasting about it. I *liked* myself.

"That's wonderful! So what happened?"

"Oh, the usual. So may I drag him along on Sunday?"

Oh, the usual! Was she even female? "You may. I don't think he'll spoil the view. Lovely. Okay then."

I was edging toward good-bye, but Cassie interrupted. She never had cared for hints. "So when you spoke to Tim, what did he say exactly?"

I considered saying, "Oh, the usual," but told her the whole saga.

"Hello?" I said, when I finally stopped talking and there was no response.

"Elizabeth," said my sister. "You have high expectations of the people who love you. You think they should *know* everything about you—and when they don't, because no one's that smart—you take it to mean that they don't love you. Well, you're a big girl now, and it's time to apply some rational thought. Tim made you a study because he thought that was what you wanted. You flipped out because the sight of it scared you to death. It was a shock. The nursery, gone! There was your fear of never having kids, in 3-D, right in front of you.

"Listen, girl." Her voice softened. "He wants you. He wants your children. But I am instructing you to do something proper—write to him and explain the scariness of yesterday, for God's sake. Then give him time to get over it, and it will all be fine—on one condition. There is one crucial *error* that you could make, and you have to *promise* me that you will avoid it at all costs. So I am telling you,"

She paused. I held my breath and pressed my ear to the phone, eager to catch this bright jewel of wisdom as it fell.

"Just don't wig out."

"Sorry? What? Is that a legal term?"

"Yeah, it's what I tell the judge."

"All right," I said, and I felt the beginnings of a smile. "I promise, I won't wig out."

CHAPTER 40

_____ *Cassie*

Barnaby was sitting on the floor, a vision in boxer shorts, trying to put the cot together.

Quick, somebody, make a poster!

"So, do your parents know that you're shacked up with a . . . *me*?"

I found I couldn't say it.

At Cambridge University, my friends were—apparently—some of the most intelligent people in the country. Their confidence was inbred; they'd been packed off in short trousers, from their Queen Anne houses to the finest public schools in the land, and their ascent to Oxbridge was not an amazing achievement—as it was for the likes of *me*—it was an expectation, a tradition. Generations of their families were, for instance, Magdalene men. And yet, despite this wealth of education, once or twice, they showed their ignorance.

"Did you get a taxi from the station, Matthew?"

"No, I walked. I'm a bit of a Jew."

It wasn't malicious. Matthew, Mark, Luke, John, whatever—

they *liked* me, I was cute. But they'd never met anyone Jewish before—or so they thought—and so I was always the little Jew to them; it was how they defined me. Here, I was *exotic*—a shock to me, having grown up in the city, gone to a good state school with white kids, black kids, middle class, working class, Jewish, Protestant, Catholic, Buddhist, Muslim, Japanese kids, Romanian kids, Pakistani kids ... blond, ginger, curly haired, and oh, I don't know! No one *cared*—perhaps because if you did, you'd have *no* friends—as there was no uniformity, we were *all* different.

I'd never been self-conscious about my religion before. But at Cambridge, I was. And while there were other differentiating factors between me and the Lukes and Johns—after all, the entire point of private school education is to leave its distinguishing mark on the forehead of each subject—for the first time in my life, I felt like an outsider.

I just wondered what Barnaby's parents would think.

"They do!"

"How do they . . . feel?"

"Mother loves babies. I believe she's very much looking forward to biting Baby Clyde's bottom. At the risk of sounding too familiar. I have no doubt she'll want to shake his hand and exchange pleasantries first. Father says he's never changed a diaper in his life and he isn't going to start now. Which is a lie. Mother says he's changed approximately ten thousand diapers. He's merely hoping to get away with it."

"Barnaby! I'm serious! Really. What do they think? Come on! I can hardly be what they expected for you. What they"—I injected a little steel into my voice as, to my horror, I realized it was in danger of cracking—"hoped for you."

Barnaby placed the screwdriver on the floor and smiled at me.

"Cass," he said. "What my parents hoped for me is that I'd find a woman who'd make me happy."

I rolled my eyes. "Barnaby. You've been reeled in by parent propaganda. They *all* say that. But they want for you what makes *them* happy."

"Is that what *your* parents want for *you*? They seemed jolly friendly when I met them. Were they secretly disappointed that I was a gentile?"

"Oh!" I wanted to give him an honest answer. "I think," I said, "that there will be a few cousins who will mutter and disapprove. But the people who matter—Mummy and Daddy—I think they can see how much you . . ."

"See how much I adore you?" said Barnaby.

I blushed. Nodded. "And that's enough for them."

Barnaby beamed. "And so, why should my parents be any different?"

"Because what with the horses, the nannies, the estate, the boarding school, they've been gearing you up, your entire life, for a grand society wedding to the daughter of an earl!"

Barnaby curled over toward the floor and shook and—I would have jumped but—I got up slowly in a panic. "What's wrong? Barnaby! Are you okay?"

He uncurled, and I saw to my relief—and surprise—that he was laughing.

"Cassie," he said. "You always get a few bad apples, but you can't write off the whole cart! That would be ridiculous! Not to mention, offensive to a lot of decent people."

"You're right. I'm sorry. My persecution complex. Down, boy!"

"I think it's time you met my parents."

My heart thumped. "Are you sure? But I have nothing to wear!

I've only got these ghastly maternity trousers, and this top is stretched so tight it's see-through. And I have nothing to take! They'll expect jam from Harrods, a pashmina for the dog basket, won't they?"

Barnaby helped me stand up, and then he kissed me, long, slow, and sweet.

"That didn't help my giddiness at all," I said.

"Come on," he murmured. "Let's go."

"Let's go . . . after a *bit*."

"For the record," said Barnaby, as he drove us along the North Circ, a while later, "I approve of your delaying tactics."

"So how long is the journey?" I said, as the car chugged through West Ealing—a neat suburban district of North London, green as well as gray, served by the usual suspects: Blockbuster, Woolworths, Sainsbury's.

"I forgot to bring food and water. We might need to stop for supplies. If I don't eat for a few hours, my blood sugar drops and I get light-headed. So, where is the family, er, seat, again? Cheshire? Hertfordshire? I can't remember what you said."

"I didn't," said Barnaby, pulling into a crazy-paved driveway. "Here we are! The family seat!"

I sat in mine, and didn't budge. We were looking at a sprawling semidetached house, with whitewashed bricks and a green roof, a varnished wooden door, and the largest burglar alarm I'd ever seen. Barnaby's car was squeezed in between a blue Ford Fiesta, parked at a rakish angle, and a gray Mercedes.

All I could say was, "Is this a joke?"

I was certain that we were trespassing on a stranger's property and in three seconds a madman was going to storm out of the house and bash in our windshield with a cucumber.

As I spoke, the front door opened, and out scurried a tall, slim woman with a honey-blond bob. She wore black jeans, sling-backs, and a white open-necked blouse. She was followed by a man, slightly shorter than her, with a shock of gray hair and a shy smile. He was wearing hospital scrubs (not the mask though).

"It's not a joke," I said breathily. And then, "Your dad's a surgeon!"

"No," Barnaby said. "He was in shoe shops. Now he repairs saxophones."

"Oh! But the scrubs . . . ?"

"He says they're jolly comfortable. He gets a friend in LA to send them over—they sell them in Costco for next to nothing."

"Hello, precious!" said the woman to Barnaby, tapping gently on the glass with French manicured fingernails. She smiled at me. "Look at you, my dear! Well, it *must* be a boy—they say that girls take away your beauty!"

"Hello, son!" said the man. He peered into the car, and grinned at me. "And this must be Cassie, who we've heard so much about! Get the door, son! Where are your manners!"

"Dad, Cassie; Cassie, Dad; Mother, Cassie; Cassie, Mother!" said Barnaby. "Mother!" he added. "You look lovely!"

"Thank you, presh, and so do you!" She darted a mischievous look at me. "Honestly, Cassie. He wasn't like this when he left for Oxford. He was dropping his h's then!"

The next morning, I lay in bed eating buttered toast, thinking, "This maternity leave's a riot!" When the phone rang, I picked up, sure it was Barnaby.

"Hello?" said a quiet voice. "May I speak to Cassandra, please?"

"This is she," I said, trying to swallow the toast—suddenly a dry lump in my mouth. I struggled to sit upright.

"Cassandra! You sound . . . so grown-up! It's Lucille. I'm Sarah

Blatt's elder sister. Thank you! Thank you so much for writing back to me. It meant so much to receive your letter—you have no idea. And such beautiful handwriting!" There was a pause, and a small sniffle. "Excuse me. It sounds as if you have become a ... most accomplished young woman. I'm so glad. I ... can't believe this moment is here at last. It's incredible to be speaking to you. Did you like the photo of Sarah?" She hesitated. "Or was it ... too much?"

I cradled the phone to my ear with both hands, and smiled into it. "It's incredible to be speaking to you too," I said. I hauled myself out of bed, lumbered into my study, and pulled out the file marked "BABY." I riffled through the papers, and out fell a small black-and-white photo of a young woman with a clip in her curly hair. She had a cheeky grin, and naughtiness in her eyes.

"The photo of Sarah is lovely," I said. Now I looked at it properly, I decided that we had the same nose. *Genes.* Crazy.

"I have so many more. I could send them, if you like."

"You could," I said. "Or, you could always bring them over."

I wasn't a tactile person—not like Lizbet, who would hug a cat, a tree, anyone, anything—but Lucille was so very huggable. She was short, and tubby, with hair like straw and a ruddy face. I, being the shape of a beach ball, was less huggable—so she hugged me from the side. When she finally released me, her face was streaked with tears. The white roses she'd bought me were also a little squashed.

I *could* have cried, but I kept it bubbling under. There was great joy, and great sadness. I squeezed her hand, and let it go.

"Look at you," she said. "Just look at you." She shook her head. I was dizzy suddenly. "I have to sit down," I gasped.

"Of course! I'm sorry! If you tell me where the kitchen is, I'll get you some water. It was so good of you to invite me! I won't stay long—well! I'd *love* to stay for a week—I'd sit in a corner and look at you and admire; I wouldn't say a word! But that would be odd, wouldn't it! I don't want to overwhelm you! You must have so much to do! How long is it before Baby arrives?"

I giggled. "My due date is in two weeks," I said, and she clapped her hands like a small child. I liked Lucille—she seemed nicely nutty—and the relief swept over me like a cool breeze. The last thing I needed was another dull relative.

Lucille fetched me a glass of water—I had to persuade her to get one for herself, as she didn't want to "make work for a pregnant woman."

"I can stretch to putting two glasses in the dishwasher," I said.

"Top or bottom stack?"

"Top," I said, and she relented. Then we sat on two hard chairs (unless I remained ramrod straight, I couldn't breathe—I had to sit there like a ruler) and Lucille pulled a wad of photographs out of a tapestry bag.

"This is another one of your mother, around the time she had you," said my aunt, and the words resounded in my ears, as I stared at the young woman in the photo. *She* had *me*. *I* came out of *her*.

Her hair was wavy, and mine was straight. Her eyes were brown, and mine were blue. But there was something in the shape of her face, especially her cheekbones, that was familiar. I held the photo, and I wanted to leap into it, and hug her. It was hard. It was hard to bear.

"She's so pretty," I said. It was all I could manage.

Lucille was still, beside me. She didn't move, but I could feel the warmth radiate from her. "Sarah would have loved this," she said.

Lucille kept her promise and stayed for exactly one hour. I was glad. I was so happy to meet her, but her scrutiny was so intense—I could sense her desire to inspect me, pick up strands of my hair in her fingertips, like an ape. I needed time, space, to breathe, and adjust. We had the rest of our lives to become close—and I felt we would.

We hugged again on the doorstep, and with both hands raised, she traced the line of my jaw without touching my skin. "My baby sister's baby," she said. "Thank you, for coming back to us."

She ran to her car, her head bowed, so she didn't notice Vivica, who marched past, one arm raised to remote lock the tornado red Beetle. *Click-click!*

My heart constricted as I saw Vivica's face. "Who *was* that?" she said, and I knew she knew.

It was strange, how life worked. All those years ago, when she and Geoffrey had announced I was adopted, I'd been coldly satisfied, planning my escape, my reinvention. And now, when I had the freedom to go, I found that I couldn't leave. Lucille was wrong. I hadn't come back—I hadn't gone anywhere—both sides had come to *me*. There was a part of me that wished I could split in two, like an amoeba. Lucille, adoring as she was, hadn't asked one question about my adoptive family. And I looked at Vivica and saw a blank lack of comprehension, that strangers would seek me out, after all this time.

"What does she want from you?"

Vivica wasn't interested in the semantics of emotion. She felt what she felt, and if she didn't like it, it showed. She was like a feral cat, guarding her young. There was no tolerance or understanding of someone *else's* claim.

I smiled at Vivica. "A relationship," I said. "Oh! And my firstborn."

Vivica didn't smile back. She seemed to deflate. She handed me a bag from babyGap, in silence.

"Mummy," I said, and I touched her shoulder. "You know. This isn't instead of. It's as well as."

I wanted to tell her of my recent discovery. That while the heart is a small, ugly, misshapen organ, prone to spill with jealousy or rage, like any muscle it expands with use, and its capacity for love is curious and infinite. I didn't, though. I knew it, and she knew I loved her. And that was enough.

CHAPTER 41

_____ *Lizbet*

The white truck rumbled past, "CHILD DISTRIBUTION" emblazoned on its side in black. I blinked, looked again, my heartbeat frantic. This was a new thing. *Chilled* distribution. Oh. It was refrigerated. Bloody hell. Who was I fooling? Cassie was right. I wanted to be a mother more than anything. Desire was blinding me—at the very least, it was making me hallucinate. I'd climb mountains, eat a bucketful of slugs, sell my soul—ask me!—I'd do anything to have a baby to hug.

Cassie was also right in her assessment of Tim. He loved me. I loved him. I was just being a brat about it.

The second I reached the office, I sat down and wrote to him—I told the editor I was composing the short story. Often, she'd skulk behind my computer—she was anxious, control-freaky, quite frankly a person who needed to be around cats, to maybe learn something about poise—but she left me alone that day. There was a crisis. We'd had three irate phone calls before ten-thirty, which—let me translate this into mainstream journalism—was like ten thousand readers ringing the *Times* to complain.

Lily, our features editor, wasn't paid much, and was bent on becoming an entrepreneur. (Or entre*purr*neur, as she called it. I'd been at the mag for two months, and the purr/miaow/tail gags showed no sign of wear.) Her Bengal—Miss Aphrodite Leopardtail—had given Lily the idea of purr therapy. This was similar to music or dance therapy. Patients would come to Lily's house, lie down in a big fancy cat basket, right up against the beautiful spotted belly of Miss Aphrodite—a gentle, maternal feline—and she would purr away their stress and troubles.

Like any cat lover, I could vouch for the soothing properties of a deep, crackling purr. What I *couldn't* vouch for was the reaction of a cat to a succession of strange humans sticking their great heavy heads into her delicate stomach area. Despite the glorious puff piece we'd run the previous week, Miss Leopardtail had emerged as an unwilling—dare I say, unprofessional—therapist. Every single patient's head had been furiously clawed with all four paws (Miss L's back legs kicking and pummeling the scalp), as if it were a large ball of catnip, or an oversized mouse.

Tim's letter was a lot harder than I'd imagined. I tried to think of it like a maths problem. Tim didn't think that I loved him. I had to convince him that I did. He was a confident man—I must have done an awful lot of unraveling to make him doubt me. This letter would have to be the length of the Bible. I'd have to explain my behavior over the miscarriage—how, when he said "I love you," I couldn't say "I love you" back, because to love requires joy and every scrap of joy was gone out of me.

I'd have to make him understand that I knew that my love for him was forever, so I thought it could be put on hold, while I devoted myself to being miserable. And that now I realized how wrong I was. I needed him to know that my love for him was not conditional on having babies, but that I would like us to have a pop at conjuring up a few.

I wasn't sure if that last bit was love letter language. In fact, I wasn't sure about love letter language at all. It was hard to stop it from sounding like an overblown open letter in *Chatter Weekly*, where they got some poor woman to confess her dreadful life story—bankruptcy, murders, fraudsters masquerading as wealthy husbands, etc.—and the subs frillied-up the language until it was rancid with emotion and sure to squeeze a few sobs out of their readers—who only felt a tea break was worthwhile if they'd shed tears into their PG Tips, alongside the Digestive crumbs.

The exercise would have been easier had Tim had zero emotional radar, like Cassie's and my mother. The other day, out of nowhere, my sister had said to me, "Lizbet. Do you think Mummy knows that I love her?"

"Cass," I'd said. "It would never occur to Vivica that you wouldn't."

I labored over the keyboard for five hours. I waffled on about seeing Tim lying on the bed, eyes wide and blank, Sphinx purring in the crook of his arm—how it made me feel lousy. How *I* should have been the one to comfort Tim, but I'd left it to an animal. How I knew that feeling of being so lost and broken that words of comfort are too much, all you can bear is to curl up with a creature that won't judge you, doesn't need anything from you. It was one up from a good book.

I wanted to tell Tim that I knew all this. But I thought he would *cringe*. In the end, I deleted all of it (one thousand, three hundred and seventy-nine words). Except for one or two paragraphs.

Tim, this is a love letter. I'd like to spell that out.

I love you as I breathe the air. You have no idea how much I love you—and that is my fault. It isn't easy, being in love, or showing it, or telling it, giving it, or receiving it.

I'm so sorry that I made it worse for you.

I think of you, and I wonder if you still lie on the bed and let the cat purr you to sleep. But this time, I want it to be me who makes it better. Please let me,

Love,

"Elizabeth!"

I quickly pressed *close* and the file shrank to a small rectangle on my screen, entitled "timstail.doc." (The "tail" bit was me covering my tracks. I didn't need to be fired from both *Ladz Mag* and *Pussies Galore!* That might look bad to prospective employers.)

The editor peered over my shoulder. "What's that you're working on?"

"The short story."

"How's it coming along? Can I take a look?"

"Gah! No. No. It's going well. It's just going to be . . . short."

"A Manx tail!"

"What? Yes!"

"Fine. We'll pad it out with a huge shot of . . . hm . . . I wonder . . ."

"A cat?"

"Great idea! It's only going to be a page—the other page is"—she sighed—"an apology and full retraction about the benefits of purr therapy to each of the twenty-seven named victims."

I made the appropriate noises, then bashed out a truly toe-curling short story: lonely woman has cat, cat keeps disappearing, turns out it's playing away at a lonely man's house (he eats a lot of fish), except it's spraying his furniture, he rings up the number on its collar to complain, she comes round to collect cat and pay for the carpets to be cleaned, *obviously* they fall in love—despite the fact that his house stinks of fish and cat wee (Subtext: love conquers all, even ammonia, so romantic!)—they sell the cat, buy a Shih tzu. (The ending needed work.)

But it took me fifty minutes. Money for nothing!

The rest of the week was a little less frenetic. I dithered about sending Tim the love note—the thought of him receiving it flustered me. I tried to distract myself, but it was hard. Every decision I made reminded me of him. My birthday was on a Sunday, so I decided to take a day off in lieu. *Tim* would approve, I thought, before I could stop myself. I already worked from home on Mondays and Tuesdays, so I decided to have Wednesday off too, make it a five-day weekend.

"But that's *press day*!" said the editor. "We put the magazine to *bed* that day! You *have* to be here!"

"Kat." Her name was Kathryn, but she preferred Kat (for some reason). "I'm sorry to bore you with my personal problems," I said, and her ears twanged. "I split up with my partner, Tim, after a personal ... *upset*. I'm hoping for a reconciliation. But if not"—I paused—"I *may* have to fight him for custody of our cat, Sphinx. I need Wednesday off to assess my position."

"Gosh! How stressful! Poor you! I didn't realize there was a child involved! That changes everything! You should have said! Oh my! Have Thursday off too! And Friday! Compassionate leave!"

"There isn't a— Oh. I see. Thank you! Okay, I will!"

My pre-birthday holiday passed without incident—except that on

Friday I posted the note to Tim. Which meant I spent Saturday—my Birthday Eve—feeling sick. At least I didn't have to make an effort to look less than hideous and ill. Fletch was engrossed in an affair with a new woman—she was eighteen and wore braces on her teeth—and he was spending every spare moment at her university digs. Apart from the obvious, I think he got a kick out of being back at college.

Cassie rang, and Tabitha rang, *and* Vivica—all questions and fuss about the seaside trip. I liked it that such a simple idea was so exciting to everyone. Every person has particular childhood memories of the seaside—and yet it probably means almost exactly the same thing to all of us. Cassie and Barnaby were going in his mimosa yellow Triumph Spitfire GT6 (a real baby car—*not*). Tabitha and Jeremy had a Volvoful of children, and "the only way to stop Celestia from crying is for me and Jeremy to sing 'The Lion Sleeps Tonight' (awimba-weh!) for an hour solid," and so Vivica and Geoffrey were giving me a lift.

"We'll pick you up at nine sharp, Daddy says," Vivica told me.

I was glad that there would be a limited amount of time between waking up on my birthday (alone, giftless, in a bed that didn't belong to me) and having company. Of course, Geoffrey being Geoffrey, there was a sharp rap on the door at *eight*. God's sake! I had one point of a triangle of peanut buttered toast jammed in my mouth, my hair was flat at the back where I'd slept on it, and I was still in my pajamas. (In my defense, I can go from nasty to nice in fifteen minutes—hairwash included.)

I opened the door without bothering to remove the triangle of toast—probably to make a point. Also *they* were the ones who had to cry, "Happy birthday!"

"Happy birthday," said Tim. He was holding the latest issue of *Pussies Galore!* in one hand, and was wearing a massive pink ribbon in his hair—the bow on top of his head, which looked like a fluffy Easter egg.

My mouth fell open slightly—enough for the triangle of toast to drop onto the floor at his feet. "Sorry," I mumbled. "Thank you! Hello! Hello! Er, what *is* this?"

"*I'm* your birthday present." He blushed. "I didn't have time to get to the shops."

I wiped toast crumbs from the sides of my mouth, and smiled. "You're the only birthday present I want." I paused. "Apart from the one from a shop."

"I love you," he said.

"I love you," I said.

"I know." He beamed at me, and held up *Pussies Galore!*

"You read that, do you?" I said.

"Your editor biked it to the house."

"Now, why would she do that?"

Tim flapped the front cover at me. There, in bold: *WORLD EXCLUSIVE TO PUSSIES GALORE!—A short prelude to A LOVE STORY, BY THE INTERNATIONALLY ACCLAIMED BESTSELLING AUTHOR (AND FELINE FAN) ELIZABETH MONTGOMERY.*

"Jesus, God," I muttered. "I forgot to change the ending."

"The ending hasn't happened yet," said Tim.

"Well, it's an open ending. It's the modern way. They sell the cat, and buy a dog. But you have to guess the rest. They might buy it back."

"I'm not selling Sphinx!" said Tim. "Ah, here we go." He cleared his throat, tweaked the pink ribbon, and began to read. " *'Tim, this is a love letter. I'd like to spell that out. . . .'* "

CHAPTER 42

Before the baby was born, I overbought on big quilted bodysuits, the sort that transform newborns into yetis. I had a fluffy white one, with hood and bear-cub ears. I had a blue fleecy one with silk lining and tiny toggles. I had a yellow one with detachable mittens and booties. I had a soft, beige, duvetlike wrap, and a rainbow of cashmere blankets—and still, I kept buying. Lizbet also went crazy, presenting me with a sheepskin rug for the baby carriage, a moo-cow snowsuit lined with polar fleece, and a tiny faux fur Russian winter hat with earflaps.

I saw that we thought alike. There wasn't enough padding in the world for my baby.

There still isn't.

That's a shock to women like me, spoiled by everything being *do*able. Being a parent forces you to consider the imperfections of the planet. But it also forces you to note your own lapses as a human being—a pastime I never bothered with before. I was always around grown-ups, and my feeling was, if I displeased them, they'd bear their disappointment. It's not the same with kids. You upset them, *your* head's on the block—with your arm wielding the axe. And if you please them, it's usually by some underhand means—television.

Your fears and faults meet you head-on—before, it was easy to avoid them, look at other people. Like the sociologist across the road who always parked his car in front of my house. I didn't care what anyone thought of me—*I* thought I was near perfect. But when your temper makes a small child cry, you ache to wind that moment back and do it again, right—because for your children to think bad of you is torture.

I thought George was going to cause no end of trouble with Barnaby, but he didn't, and that was why.

He said at the hospital, "I don't want my daughter to grow up thinking her father is a louse. I want her to be proud of me."

The birth of my first child was an unusual day.

I was about to call my sister, when she rang me. "Cass! I can't make it to the seaside. I'm really sorry. But something came up." She paused. "It has to be dealt with immediately." Then she started to laugh.

Tim was there with her; I knew it. He has the same effect on her as the sun on the sky.

I think he always will. Tim's love makes Lizbet carefree, quite a feat when you're the parents of month-old twin boys. But I'm impressed with Lizbet—she's a lot more relaxed than I was. She rang me twenty minutes after the boys were born to say that they were both beautiful but she was concerned that James had a weak chin. I said, "All babies have receding chins, darling; it's to make breast-feeding easier."

Then I giggled to myself.

I arrived at the hospital an hour later—Barnaby and George were looking after Sarah (three years, and makes me shine a flashlight at her feet while she pirouettes) and Joseph (twelve months and an angel from heaven, though his godliness will be tested when he realizes his middle name is Clyde). My ex-husband is now quite the child psychologist, having quit the BBC and created an evil empire—Tootle Pips—a music and drama group for babies and toddlers. All the mothers think he's fabulous (it's amazing, how little men need to do to impress women—*who* did these girls marry?).

And Barnaby is shaping up to be a fine dad. He adores Sarah and talks to her as a contemporary—"Ah! My dear! Would that chocolate lollipops for breakfast were the order of the day!" And he dotes on Joseph, who he is already preparing to be the next star of Tootle Pips. (He'll take the porky little hand, rap it on the kitchen side, and bleat, "A pint of milk!"—*Rap! Rap! Rap!*—"And make it snappy!").

Sometimes, I look at Barnaby, making "Moo-OOOSE!" faces at our son, or playing Grandmother's Footsteps with Sarah, alongside various dolls, and I think that I saved him from a terrible destiny.

Lizbet was propped up in bed, a beatific look on her face. I knew that look. *We are a mother.* It was the look of the Virgin Mary, as depicted by Michelangelo, only more tired. She looked stunned, pale, and in a state of grace. Two tiny red bundles were asleep at the bottom of her bed. Tim was asleep on the floor. I gazed at the twins—each with a shock of orangey blond hair—and I couldn't stop crying.

Ah, babies, you made us wait.

"They're perfect," I said to Lizbet. "They are gorgeous and divine. Look at them."

She beamed and said, "I've just got off the phone to Tabitha. She laughed when I said I'd had boys. She says she feels that people with all girls don't really *have* children. I think she meant that girls are easier."

"Possibly, but then they make up for it as teenagers, I'm told. She's still a nutcase. So when's everyone getting here?"

"I fear they're en route."

She rolled her eyes, but I knew she wouldn't have it any different. That was the point of families. They pestered you when you felt battered half to death and desperate for peace; they burst in with soppy grins, arms of flowers and gifts and silly balloons, creating noise and fuss, passing around the baby like a rugby ball, saying nothing that hasn't been said a thousand times before in every maternity ward in the world—and, everything said, showing you how much they love you, and how rarely they get the chance to reveal the depth of that love.

My Sarah's birth day, I was torn between wanting Lizbet to be in the hospital (not in the room—she hadn't gone through childbirth yet—who was I to ruin the surprise?) and wanting her to spend the entire day making up with Tim. My waters had broken at six that morning, suggesting that a seaside trip was unwise. Also, I'd squeezed into Barnaby's GT6 the previous afternoon, and become wedged. I'd pried myself out just as he came to my rescue—he said it was like watching a sardine get out of a can.

I confessed to Lizbet, *and* the parents (though I was tempted to casually update them when the baby was a week old)—and they all went bananas. Amid the excitement, we forgot to tell Tabitha, who ended up spending a day at the beach alone with her husband and children. Lizbet said that when Tabitha rang her mobile that evening, she didn't dare answer. When she got up the courage to listen to her message, she found that her neighbor had discovered that without the supporting yet dissipating force of nannies, friends, and relatives, diluting the family unit, she, Jeremy and the children managed together okay.

That day, Lizbet and Tim, and Mummy and Daddy would have got to the labor ward before *I* did. I had to reassure them that there was no urgency—they should proceed as normal. My contractions were intermittent. I was going to wash my hair, and *then* Barnaby and I would call a cab, get to the hospital for lunchtime. Barnaby would call in the evening, to let them know if the baby was on schedule or dragging its heels.

Twenty minutes later, Barnaby and I were speeding through Central London in the GT6—him, with his hand on the horn, me with soaking wet hair, my head out of the window like a dog, screaming, "Help meeeeeeeeeee!" Four remarkably medieval hours later, baby Sarah arrived. She was purple, covered in blood and a whitish wax, and her black hair was matted to her round head. Her eyes were puffy and screwed up tight, and her mouth was open in a mighty bellow of rage. I'd delivered a Halloween pumpkin—I was slightly shocked.

The doctor put her on my chest, and I whispered, "Hello, Baby," and held her to me.

She looked right at me, deep into my eyes; it was like an exchange of information, direct from soul to soul, and it took my breath away. I felt a click in my chest, a physical shift, as if something had broken—or maybe was whole again.

Before George took her to be weighed, he was trembling.

"You should have been a doctor," I said to him, nodding at his green scrubs, and he smiled, weakly.

"You did so well, Cass," he said. "I'm proud of you." He hesitated. "I didn't know it would feel like this." He shook his head and glanced at Barnaby, who was standing in the corner, also in scrubs, grinning. I saw he felt overwhelmed, and awkward. "You can come, if you want," George said, gruffly. "You might as well."

Barnaby stood up, and sat down again. "You go," he said. "You're the father."

George swept out, and there was a new dignity and poise to his bearing (although it could have been the scrubs). I lay back on the pillow and gazed at the ceiling in a daze, while I was stitched up like a burst seam. I have a *daughter*, I have a *daughter*! I thought.

I smiled at Barnaby, and he squeezed my hand. "You're brave," he said. "I've never been so frightened. I don't think I could have done that."

"*Don't* make me laugh," I said.

"How does it feel?"

He might have been referring to the tears and bruises. But I knew he wasn't. "Just . . . right."

George returned with Sarah, perfection in a white baby suit, and peacefully asleep. He gently placed her in my arms and ran to call his parents.

"I've been relegated," said Barnaby, stroking Sarah's head with the tip of a finger. "And rightly so."

Baby Sarah took it upon herself to give Barnaby a crash course in advanced parenting, saving every leak from every orifice until the second *he* held her. She also woke four times a night until she turned one. He took it very well. Alcock wasn't perfect, however—I suppose it was inevitable. More than once I swayed downstairs at dawn to find my daughter bolt awake, zipping to and fro in her musical swing chair, while Barnaby, lulled to sleep by "Frère Jacques," lay motionless on the couch.

The first baby is always revered, but I do think that Sarah was blessed. She had two besotted fathers, three and a half sets of doting grandparents (Mummy, Daddy, Sheila, Ivan, Mr. and Mrs. Alcock, *and* Sarah Paula's elderly mother, Valerie, who—the first time Lucille introduced us—fell on me like a bald eagle on a sparrow). Great Aunt Lucille vied with great Aunt Edith to crochet personalized patchwork blankets. I was touched, and made sure to fold them all neatly in a high cupboard. Vivica knew me better, and bulk-bought steadily from Ralph.

A first baby throws all your relationships into relief with the clarity of a cut diamond. Your parents suddenly loom large—for better or worse—while friends disappear, and who knows if it's you or them doing the vanishing. There was a great lake of hitherto untapped love sloshing about. I did have my anxieties about Aunt Lizbet. She treated her niece like a Ming vase. And then, she had the second miscarriage, at seven weeks.

I thought Lizbet might not want to see Sarah. For a while, she didn't want to see anyone. But three weeks on, Lizbet told me to stop visiting her "barren!" Sarah was eleven months then—an age at which they make you smile, and make you weep. That child had six teeth and the bite of a wolf. Her screams could pierce an eardrum same as a knitting needle. She slept like she was in training for the SAS. And yet, when Lizbet was as close to hell as a regular person can get, Sarah put her little chubby arms tight round my sister's neck and patted her, with soft little baby pats, on the back.

"You know," said Lizbet, drawing a deep breath, her eyes shut tight, "that just puts the life right back into you."

And then—as if she could see into the future—my sister smiled a glimmer of a smile.

ACKNOWLEDGMENTS

I would like to thank my U.S. editor Trena Keating, Cathy Gleason, Emily Haynes, and the rest of the talented team at Dutton. Deborah Schneider—a wonderful agent, and an equally wonderful friend. Jonny Geller—the same goes for you, and I can't thank you enough. Douglas Kean—this man has the patience of at least three saints. Thank you twice to Mr. Karl Murphy—for the book info, and for the boys; to Ruth Bender Atik, the book is in the post, I swear; Sasha Slater, for being a good friend and for sisterly stuff; Michael De Cozar at the Ritz, it was an honor to meet you, Geoffrey labors in your shadow. Lovely Shelley Silas—thank you for talking to me about your work, and shamefully belated mazel tov (it got to the point where I was embarrassed to write). Liz Webb, and Claire Grove at the BBC, and the playwright and comedian Chris Green—all so talented! Oy! And the fantastic Antony Bond—you were helpful beyond the call of duty. Chris Manby, thank you for bringing the fabulous Sophie Hazel Hamilton to my attention. Maybe in sixteen years' time she'll read and (I hope) approve. Thank you to my dearest Leonie (sorry I made you look at that witch ...). Thank you to the brilliant Kirsty Fowkes, what would I do without you and your knowledge of Ruskin? and I *love* the name Barnaby. John Nathan—no book is complete without your input! And superwoman herself, Louise Potter—I love ya! Nicola Fox—you are a star! Cassie owes you both (as do I, mainly for making me laugh so much . . .). The very handsome Greg— sorry, Paul Hawkes—all my love and thanks to you and Martin for *everything*. The lovely Caren Gestetner, for putting me in touch with the fabulous Sam Leek. Thank you to the lovely Suzanne Pye—especially for the Clive-isms! Ella Colley—you helped, I know it! Phil Robinson—I love you. Grub Smith—my darling! My wonderful Uncle Ben—George's father owes his generosity to you . . . and still can't compare. . . . Now please forgive me anyone I've missed, as it's been quite a year. . . .